BY NATASHA LESTER

The Mademoiselle Alliance

The Disappearance of Astrid Bricard

The Three Lives of Alix St. Pierre

The Riviera House

The Paris Secret

The Paris Orphan
(also called *The French Photographer*)

The Paris Seamstress

Her Mother's Secret

A Kiss from Mr. Fitzgerald

THE CHATEAU ON SUNSET

BALLANTINE BOOKS

NEW YORK

The CHATEAU ON SUNSET

A NOVEL

NATASHA LESTER

The Chateau Marmont is a real hotel in West Hollywood, California. However, the characters, events, and situations in this novel are entirely fictional and any resemblance to actual persons, living or dead, or to actual events is purely coincidental. This book is not affiliated with or endorsed by the Chateau Marmont.

Ballantine Books
An imprint of Random House
A division of Penguin Random House LLC
1745 Broadway, New York, NY 10019
randomhousebooks.com
randomhousebookclub.com
penguinrandomhouse.com

A Ballantine Books Trade Paperback Original

Originally published in Australia by Hachette Australia, Sydney.

The content of the Book Club Guide was adapted from materials created by Hachette Australia.

ISBN 9780593726556
Ebook ISBN 9780593726563

Printed in the United States of America

1st Printing

Book Team: production editor: *Annette Szlachta* •
managing editor: *Pamela Alders* •
production manager: *Jane Sankner* • copy editor: *Shasta Clinch* •
proofreaders: *Emily Zebrowski, Kimberly Broderick, Hope Clarke*

Book design by Barbara M. Bachman
Title page art by AdobeStock/MSPhotographic

The authorized representative in the EU for product safety and compliance is Penguin Random House Ireland, Morrison Chambers, 32 Nassau Street, Dublin D02 YH68, Ireland. https://eu-contact.penguin.ie

To my readers everywhere.
Thank you for making it possible
for me to keep doing
the thing I love best in the world.

I see at intervals the glance of a curious sort of bird through the close-set bars of a cage: a vivid, restless, resolute captive is there; were it but free, it would soar cloud-high.

—CHARLOTTE BRONTË, *Jane Eyre*

THE CHATEAU ON SUNSET

PROLOGUE

...

CHATEAU MARMONT, LOS ANGELES, 1957

AT 8221 SUNSET BOULEVARD STANDS A FRENCH CHATEAU, AS incongruous as an escargot in a burger shack. It watches from its limestone haunches as its rooms fill with unknowns who become well-knowns, with stars who implode as well as those who shine—at least until the next twinkly young thing arrives. Oh, the things it sees! The Chateau Marmont could write the definitive Hollywood novel—except that it keeps secrets the way Alcatraz keeps prisoners. Nothing escapes.

As studio boss Harry Cohn once said, *If you must get into trouble, do it at the Marmont.*

And perhaps everything would have stayed a secret, but for a brown-haired, green-eyed, almost fourteen-year-old girl who arrives in a cab in September 1957 carrying a blue suitcase that's thumped purple bruises over her shins. She steps onto the sidewalk and glares so ferociously at the castle turret—as if she knows what's hiding there—that the Marmont shrinks back and everyone thinks it's another earthquake when the ground moves sideways beneath their feet.

Then the hotel reminds itself that it's in charge and it does what it always has to new arrivals—it looks into this girl's heart to see what has brought her to 8221 Sunset Boulevard and what will take her away in the years to come. And despite having witnessed the arrival of many women over the years, each carrying more tragedies than the complete works of Shakespeare, what it sees this time makes a drop of water splash out of the swimming pool and roll like a tear over the redbrick paving.

Never has it seen one so young as this. Never one who's here so emphatically against her will.

Just two weeks ago, she was standing beside a window in a Manhattan apartment, chanting with her parents, *Star light, star bright, first star I see tonight, I wish I may, I wish I might, have this wish I wish tonight.*

Mrs. Jones's wish had been that her family would always stand hand in hand and make wishes. Mr. Jones's was that his fledgling photography studio would capture enough smiles that they could afford to vacation out of state once a year. Their daughter Aria's was . . .

Nothing. Aria couldn't imagine being happier than she was right then.

And Aria's childhood would have continued to be so idyllic that wishes were unnecessary except that her parents stopped for gas on their way home from the Copacabana. At the same time, an elderly gentleman backed his Cadillac into a gas pump. Fuel spilled over the ground.

If only the elderly gentleman hadn't been smoking.

From the depths of sleep, Aria heard night break apart like a bone. She crept down to the living room and saw Tina the babysitter sobbing on the sofa. The book they'd been reading, Mary Norton's *The Borrowers,* about teeny people who lived beneath the floor and could never be seen by humans or else they vanished, lay open beside her.

A man dressed in a policeman's uniform was saying, "Calm down, miss."

Tina pulled Aria into her arms. "You poor orphan girl," Tina wept. "You poor orphan girl."

While the poor orphan girl—who's flown by herself from New York to Los Angeles—stands at the foot of this place she's been delivered to like a piece of junk mail, the Chateau Marmont looks beyond her past to her future. Then it exhales so far down into its ground-floor rooms that the curtains fly out the windows like voile birds. For it sees a life in which every woman Aria meets is either mad or mean or poor or dead. The mad and mean ones are the bad guys, of course. The poor and dead ones are the angels.

But what kind of story is that?

So the Marmont does what it's never done before. It reassigns the roles.

It nudges a young woman called Flitter and one called Calliope (yes, their names are ridiculous, but they're actresses, so what do you expect?) into the lobby. It makes Aria wear the kind of vulnerable expression on her face that both Flitter and Calliope once vowed they'd never again wear on theirs. It creates that connection so they can all come together in a story where there *are* women who are mad and mean and poor and dead—but it's not quite that simple.

The madwoman deserves more than an attic. The mean ones deserve more than forgiveness. The poor ones deserve more than to say they're a bird and then to let the net ensnare them anyway. And the dead ones . . .

You'll see.

PART I

.....

THE POOR ORPHAN GIRL

CHAPTER I

...

1957

IT TAKES AN HOUR OF WAITING FOR SOMEONE TO CLAIM HER before Aria starts to believe. If you didn't believe in wishing stars, then your wishes wouldn't come true. If she didn't believe that her parents were dead, then they couldn't have been burned up by fire. She'd step off the airplane and there they'd be and she'd hold them and hold them and hold them—and she'd know to never let them visit a gas station.

But in the small dark cave of the lobby, as disregarded as the fringed gold lamp beside her, Aria finally understands that nobody will kiss her good night again. That to be motherless—parentless—is like being dropped into a void and no matter how much she scrabbles at the air, she'll never stop falling.

What should I do? she wants to cry out. *Just tell me what to do.*

But she has nobody to advise her, not anymore. She tries to stop the snotty little sobs that soak her handkerchief and both her sleeves. But she can't. In the end, she has to wipe her nose on her skirt and for the first time in two weeks she's glad of something: that her mother can't see how disgusting she is.

"Holy cow. A kid."

A young woman, or perhaps an old girl, appears suddenly in front of Aria. She's chasing beautiful, hasn't quite caught it yet. Then another girl-woman glides over. She isn't beautiful either—but this time it's because that word is wholly inadequate.

"What are you doing here, honeybee?" she says to Aria.

The endearment makes more tears leak from Aria's eyes. She points to the luggage tag on her suitcase: *c/o Miss Devine Rey.*

"You're here for The-Legendary-Miss-Devine-Rey?" The not-quite-beautiful woman runs the words together. "Holy cow," she repeats.

"You'd better come with us," her excessively beautiful friend says, leading the way out of the lobby, which contains one witchy-looking chandelier, a baby grand piano, and a scattering of ancient chairs, as if only spells, musicians, and ghosts ordinarily occupy it. "I'm Calliope Burns," she says. "And this is Flitter Reeve."

Aria's tears pause. Maybe, for the first time ever, her name will help rather than hinder her.

I wanted to add some sparkle to your surname, her mother used to say. *Imagine if you were plain old Jane Jones.*

Aria loved her mother so much she never said that, in a classroom full of Bettys and Marys, she'd much rather have been plain Jane.

Now, desperate to keep talking to anyone kind, but especially to these two, she whispers the name that finally fits in. "People think my name is weird. But yours . . ."

"They're our stage names." Calliope smiles, and Aria has the most peculiar urge to become one of her insignificant possessions, like a pocket perhaps, so she could travel always in the circle of her radiance.

Calliope is blue-eyed and blonde-haired, and her skin looks like soft apricot clouds. She somehow occupies both the space of her body and the space outside herself. Flitter also has a vibration of some kind, juvenile perhaps, but discernible if you pay attention. But she's too precisely put together—her hair is more white than blonde, her brows are arrowheads, and her nails the startlingly red color of danger signs. Whereas Calliope—her nose is crooked or off-center, and it's that imperfection that makes Aria keep staring, trying to figure out how nine-tenths extraordinary plus one-tenth flaw equals lightning plus auroras to the power of heaven.

"If I can't have a face like hers," Flitter says, indicating Calliope, "then I can at least have a beautiful name."

"Is my aunt beautiful?" Aria blurts. They've stepped outside and into such a parade of gorgeousness that Aria needs to know if her aunt is lovely enough to pay what seems to be the entry price around here for short, brown-haired Aria too.

Calliope says, "Aria, next to your aunt, you are Marian Monti."

Aria beams. Her father thought Marian Monti was a real looker; he took Aria and her mother downtown to the Rialto Theater last year to watch *The Girl Who Married a Millionaire,* and Aria's mother had joked, *Perhaps I'll get a few tips.*

Aria's father replied, *There's more than a million bucks of love for you in my heart,* and her mother had kissed him like he was a river and she the desert.

Her tears are back. She's afraid that Flitter and Calliope will flee, but instead they take her hands. "We'll give you a tour," Calliope says. "You can't disturb your aunt between one and five."

"Why?"

"You'll find out soon enough," Flitter says, words Aria doesn't pay attention to because the gardens are full of trees with white star-shaped flowers and, lower down, there are star-shaped jasmine flowers too, like she's surrounded by so many potential wishes.

"Here's the pool," Calliope says and *look*!

Sunshine pours down with abandon, spotlighting cabana chairs. Bikinis color triangles onto the bodies of platinum blondes who look so much like Marian Monti from the back that Aria's whole body starts to quiver with excitement. But then they turn and their charisma is dull, like silver tarnish. Still, that over there is definitely Judith Crown!

It's like nothing Aria has ever seen—famous actresses worshipped by everyone in America are now standing right in front of her.

In the center of it all sits a blond man. He's talking on a telephone whose long cord stretches like gum over the brick paving. His skin is slick and tan and he's smiling graciously at all the people trying to catch his eye. He beckons them over, shakes hands if they're a man, drops a charming kiss onto the knuckles if they're a woman. He juggles the telephone, the hands, his own finger crooking to catch the attention of a delivery boy with an armful of drinks, as well as the conversation he's having on the phone and the drinks orders he's eliciting from the people pulling their cabana chairs around him. In between all that, he makes jokes that have the crowd laughing and raising their glasses, chinking them against his.

He's part cowboy, part gladiator, part man in a suit riding a Vespa through Rome.

"Welcome to Hollywood." Flitter grins.

The man hangs up the phone, shakes hands with everyone again, blows a kiss or two, then strolls over to the path. "Hello, ladies," he says to the three of them in a movie-star voice, low and articulated, and Aria feels her posture correct itself like it does when she's in the presence of a teacher or doctor or other higher being.

Flitter and Calliope chorus, "Hi, Bob."

The woman at his side smirks and says to Calliope and Flitter, "Sorry I stole the part, girls. You need more practice."

"There'll be other parts, ladies. I know it," Bob tells them.

Then he and the woman walk toward a narrow path leading uphill, leaving the scent of riches and Coppertone in their wake.

"Did you hear what he said!" Calliope whispers to Flitter. "Maybe he thought our auditions weren't half bad." To Aria, she says, "That's Bob Ashenhurst. King of Hollywood."

The king of this castle. It's the first thing anyone has said that makes sense to Aria. Bob walks as if there's an invisible crown, heavy with gold and rubies, on his head, and he alone has the strength to hold it aloft.

"That's Lacey Magee with him," Flitter goes on, not bothering to whisper. "Who hides daggers in her beehive just so she can actually stab you in the back. We went to a casting call yesterday for a part in one of Bob's movies. She got it."

"There'll be other parts for us," Calliope reiterates with conviction. "But now," she looks at her watch and says to Aria, "it's time to meet your aunt."

CHAPTER 2

...

SEVEN YEARS LATER

1964

I'M FLYING DOWN THE STAIRS FROM MY TURRET TO THE FIFTH floor to babysit Judith Crown's latest kid when I round a corner and *wham*!

I crash into him like an accident, strewing bruises and curses over the wooden treads. They've been worn to such a high shine by the housemaids' feet that no matter how much this man wheels his arms and recombines the words *damn, god, sons,* and *bitches,* he topples backward. Thankfully a landing is only a few steps behind, but the fall is enough to make his ankle turn at an awkward angle.

The Chateau Marmont echoes the man's curses back at him. He catches me smiling at the reverberating blasphemies and God is damned again.

"Are you going to laugh or help?" he snaps.

A golden-haired dog bounds over, a grin on his face too. I rub his head. "Hello, boy. What's your name?"

"His name is Pilot. His ankles are intact. Whereas mine . . ." The man tries to step forward and winces. "Dammit."

In the lamplight of the stairwell, I can't see much, just that the stranger is exceptionally tall and has black hair, which is a little long and a lot scruffy. His lips are extravagantly pouty, the kind the starlets would kill to have adorning their own faces, or else to have paving the road to hell down their necks. Dark sunglasses cover his eyes, like he's the wayward friend of the blond lead in the big summer movie—the guy who isn't handsome exactly, but who you can't stop looking at all the same.

Yes, after seven years in Hollywood, even I've started describing people using movie tropes. Which means it's definitely time to leave.

"Lean on me. I'm an expert at helping people who are unsteady on their feet," I say to my injured acquaintance, assuming the sunglasses hide the start of tomorrow's hangover or this afternoon's high.

"I'm not under the influence of anything except being used by you as a human skittle," he says curtly.

So I put him in the latter of the two categories of people at the Marmont: those who swallow liquor like water, and those who are drying out. It's usually only a few days before they're soaking wet and wilder than ever.

I offer him my shoulder as a crutch. "It's ten steps up, then the elevator is close by."

"You're half my size."

He looks around for a better option than an almost twenty-one-year-old Aria Jones, who can only say she's five foot three if she's standing on her tiptoes. He must realize that unless he thinks he can ride his dog up the stairs, I'll have to do. He puts an arm around my shoulders, leaning more of his weight on the wall than on me. The dog patters up behind.

"I'd rather not have the whole hotel see me like this," he mutters.

"As well as being an excellent crutch, I'm an expert at being invisible."

I crack open the door to the corridor and spy Chester Meringue, who's clinging to vaudeville with the same fervor as the Hollywood censors and their rules about three-second screen kisses. He's juggling two kitchen knives, a pair of panties, and a banana, an uncomfortable combination at the best of times. I shut the door, wince for the fate of Chester's toes when I hear a *thunk,* and reopen the door when his groan sounds resigned rather than bloodied.

Chester moves away. But now we're interrupted by gunshots. My companion jumps, jars his ankle, and his curses flow as freely as the Chateau Marmont oddities.

"It was just two shots, so it's okay," I tell him.

His eyebrows soar to exhilarating heights. "What exactly is the number of gunshots that would concern you?"

I check my watch. It's six o'clock. I'm going to be late.

"Too busy to deal with a massacre?" he says acidly. "Ankle-maiming enough for today?"

I make myself smile politely and explain. "The author Paul Rydell is in residence. He has a love-hate relationship with the forty-foot neon showgirl on Sunset Boulevard. Sometimes he shoots her—just with an air rifle—in the ass. Two buttocks equals two shots. Now the coast is clear. So let's go."

I've finally silenced him. We hop along to the elevator, and I pray that it doesn't break down until we're out of it. Part of the Marmont's charm is its careless antique shabbiness, like an aging French courtesan whose couture gown is frayed—but it's Chanel, so who cares?

"Miss Aria!" Isaiah cries when the doors open. He kisses my cheeks. "You always take the stairs." Then he sees the man. "Ah, you have cargo."

My injured companion says, "Seventh floor," and the elevator lurches upward like an incompetent cat.

"Need a hand?" Isaiah asks when the doors open.

The man shakes his head and I hope it's because he really is eager to have as few people as possible see him like this rather than because he's the kind to search for another elevator when they see the color of Isaiah's skin. If I find it's the latter, I'll tell Maisie the housekeeper to short-sheet his bed.

Pilot leads the way, stopping outside the large penthouse, which means my acquaintance is someone important.

"I'll send the doctor up," I tell him as he slips his key into the lock.

He nods and closes the door behind him. A second later it cracks open and a gruff, "Thank you," issues from within.

Then he's gone, taking his shades and his lips with him, leaving behind the sensation of gentle pressure on my arm as well as a hint of musk and devil-may-care.

I shake my head. Who was that? He isn't a wannabe actor—dreamers can't afford penthouses. Perhaps he's one of the studio-contracted actors who's done something bad and been put here to hide away until the fuss dies down. But they're usually the most conspicuous of all, enjoying their notoriety and their free accommodation.

The infamous don't hide in stairwells. Only the invisibles do, like me.

I check my watch again. It's that time between martinis and valium that's the most dangerous of all. I can't go to Miss Devine Rey's room to call the doctor. So I hurry down to the lobby where a guest is banging out an impassioned version of "Les Toreadors" on the baby grand, an apt metaphor: the Marmont is full of posturing bulls and overconfident matadors. As for me, I'm the red flag, the one who gets out of the way just in time.

Not today. No, today I'm rounding another corner, and there beneath the gothic chandelier stands a girl with a suitcase sitting like a forlorn puppy at her feet and I'm flung so violently backward seven years that a sound flies out of my mouth. But she isn't the ghost of Aria-past. This girl is pretty, for a start. She's around fifteen, I'd guess, but she's trying to look older with false lashes and hands-on-hips attitude.

"Can I help you?" I ask. Even though I have a doctor to call, an air rifle to confiscate, and a baby to sit, I can't leave her standing there looking so vulnerable, so lost.

She glares. "My dad just bought this place, so I don't need help."

Another gasp escapes me. It's like this girl is the murder scene in *Psycho,* put here to scare me silly. "Bought? The Marmont? Your dad?"

I make myself stop bombarding her. I need to tuck her away where she's safe—and quickly. "Owning probably isn't the same as knowing. What room do you need?"

"The only thing I know is that I have a headache."

"Les Toreadors" becomes a chord-heavy version of "The End of the World" and even *my* temples start to pound. All we need is for the air rifle to go off again.

Thankfully the desk clerk appears. I hand the girl over, then shut myself behind the carved wooden door of the phone booth. "It's Aria," I say when Doctor Foster answers.

"What do you have for me today? Judith Crown's stomach needs pumping? Augusta Hepworth has another black eye?"

"Just a sprained ankle. In the penthouse."

"I yearn for the days of sprained ankles, Aria. Thank you."

I laugh and hang up.

Then I frown, remembering what the girl said.

Someone's bought the Chateau Marmont.

Which could ruin all of my plans.

I RUN BACK UP the stairs, knock on Paul Rydell's door, and hold out my hand.

He sighs and passes me the air rifle. "Can't live with her, can't live without her."

Over his shoulder, I can see her—the forty-foot giantess in silver boots and a scanty blue leotard who twirls on the edge of a silver dollar, advertising the Hotel Sahara in Vegas. She arrived the same year I did and casts flashing green and red light into Rydell's room, as well as a smile every five seconds, before presenting him with her rear end. The lights would give me nightmares, but Rydell keeps writing her into his books and only shoots her when the words won't flow.

"Ask for a different room," I tell him.

"Then the words might never come," he says mournfully.

Like everyone here, his need for fame outweighs the pain of earning it.

I take the rifle up to my turret, where there are so many books stacked in piles around the room that it looks like the walls are made of stories. I hide the rifle among the eclectic mix of objects—a lamp whose base is a foot in a high-heeled shoe, a black Art Deco cat that I call F. Scott. Then I barrel down to Judith Crown's room only fifteen minutes late. Thankfully she must have drunk exactly the right amount of gin and hot water because she just kisses my cheeks and dashes out while I collapse onto the sofa.

"What a day," I say to the baby, who giggles through pink lips so like her momma's. Maybe those lips will just smile and sing, like her momma does. Maybe they'll never taste gin, nor fear; maybe she'll use them to ask for what she wants rather than to swallow down what she doesn't.

God, *I'm* the one who needs a gin and hot water.

"Let's take a walk." I carry the baby downstairs in search of Mr. Mason, the manager, who'll be able to tell me about the Marmont's new owner. But Mr. Mason's office is locked.

It's never been locked before.

I take out the skeleton key I was gifted by the housekeeper on my fourteenth birthday, push open the door and see immediately what's missing: the photograph that used to sit on Mr. Mason's desk of himself, his long-dead fiancée Toni—Bob Ashenhurst's sister—and Miss Devine Rey.

If the photo's gone, it means Mr. Mason is too.

No.

The baby grizzles, oblivious to my shock, so I take her upstairs, feed her, bathe her, read her a story, and tuck her into bed. Then I stare out the window at the endless lights of LA.

Fourteen years ago, something happened. I don't know what. Just that Toni Ashenhurst died and my aunt locked herself in her suite and hasn't left it since. Yet we somehow keep renting a two-bedroom suite at the Chateau Marmont, when surely the money from my aunt's career ran out long ago. I've always assumed that because of their past friendship, Mr. Mason has been very inventive in the way he accounts for our suite. And I try not to cost my aunt anything: I wear the clothes the stars leave behind—whatever they lose at the Marmont, they never want to see again. My aunt wears the clothes she's had since she cloistered herself in her suite. But we order everything else from Schwab's, the pharmacy and diner across the road, which can't be cheap.

And now the Marmont has a new owner. Which means I have a problem.

When Judith returns, I tuck her into bed too, remind her that she has to get up when the baby cries rather than roll over and go back to sleep. Then I go to my aunt's suite, where everything is the same as it was seven years ago: chinchilla stoles hang on the coatrack by the door; ambergris incense sticks burn on stands, hiding the stench of decay; and monogrammed luggage sits beside the dressing table as if Miss Devine is always dashing off.

I fetch her a glass of water, hoist her into a sitting position, and try not to let it ache too much when she cries.

"Someone's bought the Marmont," I say, and that's enough to rouse her.

"Who?" she whispers.

"I don't know. I'm trying to find out. But I need to know if you can pay for this room."

"I can't," she weeps before she falls back into the Quaalude sea.

I exhale. Check my watch. It's two in the morning. But I haul myself back up to my turret and pull *War and Peace* from the stacks of books. Inside, I've cut a rectangle through the pages to hold all the money I've earned from babysitting.

$4,552. I'm four hundred and forty-eight dollars and three months short of my goal.

For almost seven years I've lived here under the guardianship of a woman I hardly know. But on December the first, three months away, I'll be twenty-one. An adult—no longer the ward of an aunt. My plan has always been to walk out of here with five thousand dollars in one hand and my life in the other, thus fulfilling the promise I made to myself seven years ago—to escape the Marmont and leave poor orphan Aria behind. And I'm so close. I just need three more months and less than five hundred dollars. But now I have to somehow earn enough money to both pay the rent until then and to add to my escape fund too.

Or I need to make miracles happen and convince the new owner to let my aunt and me continue to stay here for free.

I'm living in Hollywood, the land of miracles. Surely there's one—*just one, please God*—out there for Aria Jones?

A sharp breeze bullies its way in through the window, demanding, *Who'll look after your aunt after you've gone? She kept you when you had no one. You owe her.*

I slam the window against wind and guilt. I have enough problems to solve right now and, besides—don't I owe myself something too?

CHAPTER 3

…

1957

A SICK FEELING CURDLES IN ARIA'S BELLY AS SHE FOLLOWS Calliope and Flitter to the elevator. She tries to make it go away by reminding herself that she just made two friends and has met the King of Hollywood. Perhaps that's a sign that she isn't falling through an endless void, but has landed on the solid ground of a place where goodnight kisses are given out by loving aunts. She refuses to acknowledge the *rat-a-tat* memory of her father's eyes on the few occasions he spoke of his sister, an expression like the one everyone has directed at Aria over the past fortnight. Not sadness. Something that hurts more than ordinary tears. Like people thought that all Aria had ahead of her was the graveyard of buried hopes that Anne of Green Gables talked of, an idea Aria had struggled to grasp when she'd read the book a few months ago.

The elevator attendant pulls the metal grille shut behind them, jolting Aria back to the present. Flitter and Calliope kiss his cheeks.

"You girls," he says, his smile so hearty you could warm your hands on it. He bends down to Aria's level, gloves starkly white in comparison to the dark brown of his cheeks, like his hands don't really belong to him. "What's your name, sweetie?"

"Aria Jones."

"A beautiful name," he says. "Means 'air' in Italian."

The sick feeling vanishes as Aria marvels at the potency of a name she's never thought belonged to an ordinary girl like her.

"I'm Isaiah," the attendant continues. "How old are you, Miss Aria?"

"Thirteen and three-quarters."

Those extra months are important. She needs Calliope and Flitter to know that she's bigger than she looks.

"The right age for candy." Isaiah pulls a bag of Tootsie Rolls from his pocket at the same time as Calliope says, "On the cusp," and her eyes have a conversation with Flitter that Aria doesn't understand.

"Cusp of what?" she asks.

"Of when the fairies die," Flitter says grimly, but Aria's more interested in what Isaiah's telling her—that he has a son around her age and will introduce her, meaning that maybe now Aria has four new friends in her life.

"How old are you?" she asks the girls.

"I'm eighteen," Calliope says. "Flitter's nineteen. We've been best friends forever."

"We came to LA last year," Flitter adds.

"We work nights here and we persuaded the manager to rent us a tiny room nobody ever stays in." Calliope picks up the story. "It fits a bed—"

"Just!" Flitter grins. "You can't open the door the whole way."

The elevator pings. The doors open on the fifth floor. Nobody steps out.

Flitter points along a dim corridor with red-and-black carpet patterned with snakes. "Room 53."

"ROOM 53," ARIA REPEATS to herself as she drags her suitcase behind her. She taps on the door.

No response.

The snake carpet writhes beneath her feet. The void opens around her again.

What if Miss Devine Rey doesn't really exist?

Then a sonorous voice calls, "Enter," and the intensity of Aria's relief has her bursting through the door, not knowing that all her hopes are shining like tears in her eyes.

The room is so dark. She slows, puts out a hand to feel her way.

A woman stands on the other side of the room. She's full-figured, wearing a fitted black dress whose scooped neckline shows off her skin all the way to her breastbone. Her blonde hair is chin length and her bearing is as majestic as Bob's, the man from the pool.

Aria inches forward, her suitcase banging against her legs too loudly in this whisper-quiet room.

Miss Devine Rey's eyes travel from Aria's brown hair to her green eyes to her hastily purchased black dress to her skinny, bruised calves.

"Plain," her aunt pronounces. "If your hair was lighter, you might at a pinch have been able to play the role of an orphan in a Dickens adaptation. Have your monthlies begun?"

Aria gapes. The monthly visitor is like a disgraced cousin—something only ever spoken of in whispers.

"Perhaps then you'll at least grow a bosom."

Aria's arms fly up to cover her chest, tears scalding her eyes.

Why, when she's just one small, unimportant child in the vast scope of the world, is God trying so hard to break Aria Jones's heart?

So that she doesn't cry, not in front of this woman, Aria explodes.

"I hate you!" she screams. "I hope that one day you're standing in a room wishing for one bit of kindness and all your clothes fall off and everyone laughs at you. I curse you right now," Aria shouts like she's a sorceress and, by god, she feels like one, like her rage could fire out of her fingers, straight into this woman's heart. "I curse you with that future!"

"Go to your room!" her aunt shouts, pointing in the direction of a door.

Aria runs to it, lets it crash shut, trapping her in a salmon-colored bedroom where the vomity feeling returns because the walls make her think of the food she used to put out for her cat, Rosie. But now Rosie lives with Aria's five-year-old neighbor back in Manhattan.

She flings the window open, searches for a drainpipe, imagines climbing down five stories, and never coming back. But in her pockets are only three used tissues and the melted candy Isaiah gave her. She won't get far with that.

But one day she will. Because for the first time in her life, she has a wish: to escape from this life she's been put into.

This is not her story.

CHAPTER 4

...

1964

THE FOLLOWING AFTERNOON, STILL SHORT OF ANSWERS TO MY money problems, I go out into the September sunshine. It's that glorious time of year when the heat gentles, the wildfires relent, the grapes taste like candy, and you think life will always be this sweet and free from fires. I want to swim before cocktail hour begins, but last night's parties must have been Prohibition era–themed because instead of napping, everyone's by the pool.

Wearing a bikini and holding a book she isn't reading is the girl I saw in the lobby yesterday. Bob Ashenhurst is in the cabana beside hers.

Damn.

"Pete!" he calls to Peter Oldham, a leading man who makes box-office gold.

Peter lopes over and the men shake hands.

"Martini?" Bob asks, holding up a bottle of vermouth.

Peter pulls up a cabana. More cabanas slide over to join them because how can anyone resist the King of Hollywood in conversation with a prince? Bob starts to tell the story of how he found this kid working in the prop shed at the studio and had him do a screen test and, that day, purely by accident and circumstance, Peter Oldham, silver-screen heartthrob, was born.

Everyone's heard it before. But they all listen because Bob tells it so well, drawing out the moment when he waited with all his fingers crossed to see if the kid looked as good on-screen as he did running skulls back and forth to the set of a horror movie.

Suddenly, everyone's eyes move left, following the movement of a woman along the path—Calliope Burns in green velvet hot pants.

I fling myself into her arms and beneath the perfume, the hairspray, and the cigarettes, I catch the memory of morning breath and pajama parties.

"You're ungluing my eyelashes," Calliope says, dabbing her eyes, then slipping her arm through mine.

We don't have to say where we're going—our bodies lead us to that little room in the Marmont's rear end, uninhabited now, but lived in by the ghosts of three girls who once lay in a bed together, dreaming. The bed is still there, so we wriggle onto it.

"I'll order mint juleps from Schwab's," Calliope says. "For old time's sake."

She picks up the phone and puts on her husky actress voice. "This is Miss Calliope Burns. I'd like two mint juleps and two burgers with fries and extra ketchup brought up to my old room, please."

Order placed, she turns to me. "I'm dying to know if you've seen Theo Winchester."

"I thought he stayed at the Beverly Hilton?"

Calliope grins. "He bought the Chateau Marmont."

Holy Mary, Mother of Jesus, I've lamed the person whose charity my aunt and I are relying on.

Theo Winchester—or Win, as everyone calls him—is a rock star, that new breed of man whose music makes you feel as if he's reached into your chest, wrung out your heartache, and set it to music. A man who doesn't just stand on a stage and sing; he tosses guitar chords into the crowd like they're filthy invitations.

He has dark hair. Pouty lips. *He's* the man from the stairwell. And I doubt he's the kind of guy who'll let a penniless former star who hasn't paid rent for years, and her niece as well, stay at his hotel for free.

"I need a job." I flop despairingly onto my back. "Babysitting isn't enough."

"Do you want me to get you an audition?"

"God no! For what part anyway? The duckling with no hope of ever being a swan?"

"That's not true," Calliope scolds. Then she frowns. "Besides acting, what other jobs are there for an LA girl? Or any girl, for that matter." She ticks them off, doesn't even need a whole hand of fingers. "Secretary. Maid. Waitress. Salesclerk. You're too smart for those. And you need to go to college to be a nurse or teacher. What else?"

We sit there, unable to come up with anything.

"Well," I say, trying to smile, "at least now they've passed the Equal Pay Act, I'd get paid the same as a man if I *could* come up with something."

"But men aren't maids at the Marmont or salesclerks at Bullock's. So equal pay is just another lie. As if anyone would ever pay me as much as Peter Oldham when we're in a movie together." Calliope flops onto her back too. "It's like what that book said—the Betty Friedan one you made me read. The women are trapped in their husbands' homes, mopping floors. Which is why they need movies. You know, I thought maybe—and in some ways I hate thinking it—that after Marian died, the era when all you could be was a wife who believed that if she got her Sunday roast and her hair just right, her husband wouldn't cheat on her is over. Marian *was* the poodle-skirted, tiny-waisted, cleavage-powered fifties. But I hoped that with Win's music and The Monolith's music, with tights and no garters, with equal pay and the pill, a new era's arrived. But"—she sighs—"here we are. Poor Marian."

The overdose death of screen queen Marian Monti last year hit everyone, but especially the women of Hollywood, who believed it was deliberate rather than accidental. That she didn't want to be the figurehead of vapid blondes. No, Marian wanted a quiet place where she could paint the sky. "It's always different," she told me when I asked her why all her watercolors were of the sky.

Now she lives up there, destined to be forgotten in a few years' time.

Calliope opens her purse, takes two pills out of it, pops them in her mouth, and swallows. "I have a headache," she assures me when I frown.

Headache. I remember the girl in the lobby. "Does Theo Winchester have a daughter?"

"Well." Calliope leans in. "Whether she's really his daughter isn't certain, but a woman he dated as a teenager died in a car accident a few months back and she left him a fourteen-year-old in her will, claiming she was his."

"Another orphan."

"Who the gossip columnists say has been kicked out of Hollywood High for bad behavior. Meaning she most likely *is* Win's daughter. Have you seen him yet? I can't tell whether he's devastatingly sexy or quite ugly. He has one of those faces. Like an eagle—all gothic and stern, but your eye just wants to stare anyway. Stormy thoughts and brooding brows. Don't you think?"

A knock interrupts my laughter. The boy from Schwab's gapes at Calliope like he's just seen his first *Playboy* centerfold. After he deposits the food and drinks on the dresser, she signs a napkin for him and he runs off looking like he's going to need a moment to himself in the phone booth before he can return to work.

Calliope and I only stop giggling to stuff the burgers in our mouths. We chew contentedly, then I ask what she's been up to.

"Debating how many fractions of an inch of areola should be permitted on-screen in a millisecond most people will miss." Calliope flicks her cigarette lighter with irritation. "When I sat up in bed after my fake lovemaking, an unscripted rim of pink could apparently be seen. It delighted the director, but the producer is scared of the censors, the pearl-clutchers, and the husbands of the pearl-clutchers, who'll question my morals in mixed company but jerk off to the memory in the shower. I told him that if he was so concerned about nipples, he should have given me something to cover them under the sheet. If you're going to play the game, at least own up to the fact that you're playing it."

She swallows half her mint julep. "It's so hard to see that it couldn't possibly contravene the Production Code. But nobody's sure if barely visible areolas will pull in the crowds or deter them. For a town where sex will get you more than a thousand-dollar bill, there's a hell of a lot of pretending nobody gets screwed. The thing that irks me is that it's a damn good film. And I'm damn good in it. But my areola will forevermore be the subject of attention."

The Production Code, otherwise known as the Hays Code, is a set of rules drawn up thirty years ago by a priest, of all people—a priest in Hollywood, an idea that stretches the imagination more than a movie about male virgins. The Code sets out what is and isn't allowed on-screen, its goal to ensure that movies don't corrupt anyone.

But on the first floor of the Chateau Marmont, there's a library that could tell you a different story.

"Do you ever get tired of it?" I ask, putting my burger down and studying her face, which is even more hyper-beautiful than it was seven years ago.

"I'm so tired I could sleep for one hundred years."

It's the reference to a fairy tale that does it. Makes me remember the other trope we spoke about a few minutes ago: the orphan.

I jump up, collect my fries and Calliope's, which I know she won't eat. "I have an idea that might earn me some money."

I lead the way to the small penthouse on the sixth floor, which people have started calling "Calliope's Room"—having your moniker attached to a Chateau Marmont room is a surer sign of celebrity than a star on the Walk of Fame. Once there, Calliope reaches into the nightstand and takes out three more pills.

"I'll call the doctor," I tell her.

"I'm fine." She shines her famous smile. "I'll stay in bed and read scripts. I need something to change my bio from Academy Award nominee to Academy Award winner."

"You know that everyone loves you."

"They love to look at me. But do they love *me*?"

I can't believe that Calliope Burns could ever lose faith in herself. Before I can remind her what she said to me on our first sleepover, she says, "Enough about me. Tell me what you're up to."

I fill her in, then point to her wardrobe. "To pull this off, I need to borrow a shirt. Everything I have is too plain or too bright. Nobody ever leaves in-between colors behind."

"Go to a shop. You don't have to wear everyone's leavings."

"Those *leavings* cost more than I can afford. I'm happy to shop in the Marmont's checked-out rooms." I pull out a deep blue, short-sleeve knit top.

Calliope won't let the conversation go. "Have you still not gone further than Schwab's?"

Last time she was here, I promised her I'd jump on a bus and go at least as far as Hollywood and Vine, dip a toe into the city I look out at from the turret, familiar to my eyes, foreign to my feet.

"Aria," she presses. "There's a whole world beyond this."

"That's what I'm saving up for."

"Experience some of it now. Otherwise I'm worried that . . ." She inhales cigarette smoke, breathes out sparkling diamonds. "This has been your home for seven years. A home is as necessary to a person who's found herself homeless as air is to a lung. If you try to leave it behind in small pieces, it might be easier."

I tamp down the memory of the first time I stood at a bus stop on Sunset Boulevard, the day of the nineteenth-birthday party we didn't have for Calliope. I'd realized that if something happened to me, nobody would come looking for me. The sheer aloneness of thirteen-year-old Aria has caged me here ever since. But on December 1, the adulthood I'll step into will give me the courage to walk out of this place I've lived in for seven years, but that hasn't been my home.

I haven't found home yet.

I hold the blue top up against my black capri pants, which I found last year in Augusta Hepworth's room. *You keep them, Aria,* she'd cooed when I'd called to let her know she'd forgotten them. *It's my thank-you.*

She didn't say what she was thanking me for. But I knew.

"Look how green your eyes are with that top," Calliope says. "You've always suited that hairstyle better than anyone."

Years ago, after what I did to Bob Ashenhurst, I'd paid Judith Crown's hairdresser most of my babysitting money to chop my hair off into a pixie cut. I'd wanted to be invisible and had no idea it was fashionable. Back then, the cut did nothing for me. But now I see that I've grown into it—and I'm momentarily disconcerted.

"You look demure and wise," Calliope says. "Don't be afraid to show him that you're funny and bright and kind too."

I kiss her cheeks, leave the room, melt into the walls, emerge on the ground floor, and knock on the door of Theo Winchester's office.

No answer.

I push open the door, go inside, sit down and wait.

"CHRIST!"

I don't hear him come in, even though I hear everything at the Marmont. He's either stealthier than I am or I've let my guard down for the first time since 1957.

"Mr. Winchester." I offer my hand. "I hope your ankle is better. I'm Aria Jones."

"Aria Jones, who makes a habit of wiping out people in stairwells and lurking in offices. Do you have a vendetta against me or has someone paid you to kill me?"

It seems that Theo Winchester will fit right into the Marmont with that tendency to create a drama out of everything. In five seconds I've gone from causing a tumble to being an assassin.

He opens a drawer, pulls out a pack of Lucky Strikes and a gold lighter in the shape of a guitar. He's sans sunglasses today, so I can see his eyes, which are as dark as his hair. He's wearing a collared gray sweater, dark jeans, and a square-cut black onyx ring on his left pinkie finger. His hair is unkempt, his face just as Calliope described—Win is obviously a man who celebrates midnights and loathes middays.

Now *I'm* being melodramatic. I smile.

"Is my face amusing?" he asks.

"Not at all," I reply truthfully and he barks out a laugh.

"Why are you here, Aria Jones? I can't find the fifty-thousand-dollar guitar that was supposed to be brought to my room. And I haven't had breakfast yet."

"Your guitar is most likely in bungalow three. The guys from The Windows are staying there and they pick up every instrument that comes in the doors. But the reason I'm here," I press on, ignoring the eyebrows quirked up at me, "is because I'm offering you the chance to employ me as your daughter's tutor. Like a governess, but without the nineteenth-century dress." I attempt a joke to get his eyebrows to relax.

It doesn't work.

"You're offering me the chance to employ you," he repeats incredulously. "How old are you? And who says I need a governess, if they even exist, for Adele?"

"I'll tackle those in order," I say, trying to sound like the governesses the Brontës and Thackeray served up in their novels. "I'm almost twenty-one. I'm the most intelligent person in this building and possibly in the city. If Adele was expelled, she's rebelling against something. Sending her to another school means she'll rebel all over again. Then she'll be left to wander around the Marmont unsupervised. You can't—"

I cut myself off, my fists tightening into hard balls of memory.

I try another approach. "What do you know about teenage girls?" I ask, thinking to prove my expertise. After all, until recently, I was one. Then my mouth says, "Scratch that. You're a rock star. I don't want to know what you know about teenage girls."

God, this is a horror movie only Hitchcock would be proud of. Indeed, Win's face is a riot of expressions, like I promised him a symphony but howled like a wolf instead.

I try to fix it with a more concise summary. "That came out wrong. What I mean is that you bought a hotel in a city of earthquakes and wildfires. So you need to be careful."

He stabs his cigarette into the ashtray and walks over to the window, limping a little. From here, the Marmont looks glorious—the bird-of-paradise flowers ornament Eden with licks of shimmering flame. He rests his hips against the windowsill and says, a challenge in his voice, "All right. You said you're the most intelligent person here. Prove it. Tell me something I don't know."

This is almost too easy. Someone schooled by encyclopedias knows more obscure facts than anyone. The key is choosing one that interests him, and quickly, because he's tapping the window frame like he's either taken too many dexies, has discovered the bass line of his next hit song—or is dying to kick me out.

"Most people think that only male birds sing. But Margaret Morse Nice wrote a chapter about female birdsong in her book *Studies in the Life History of the Song Sparrow.* She thinks female birds have evolved to be the quietest for survival reasons. So while you might think they never sing, it's just that most people don't listen." I can't resist adding, "I wonder if there's a parallel between that finding and the reason her research is mostly unknown?"

A surprised laugh escapes him and it's like watching an eagle stretch out its wings and your breath catches because you weren't expecting such grace from something so fierce.

Then he says, like he just can't help but turn back into a regular man, "Is that true? You could make anything up."

"That would mean assuming you're stupid, which I guess you're not if you've made enough money to buy the Marmont." I should stop there, but the fact that he hasn't made a pass and I'm enjoying the conversation makes me say, "Do you think a thing is only true if you've heard it before?"

"You're feistier than you look." Win returns to the desk and takes out another cigarette, looking amused, like he's just found a new toy to play with, or break.

But Theo Winchester isn't the first and nor will he be the last man who looks at me and sees something plain and ordinary. To everyone, I'm a wisp of black, like smoke or midnight. A dull piece of background you just don't see. Which is how I like it.

So I don't know why I retaliate. "Are beautiful people always kind? Ugly people always mean? Small people always worth overlooking?"

"It would seem not." He rubs a hand over his forehead as if he has a headache, which are an epidemic at the Marmont. "Do you always ask so many questions?"

I'm guessing he doesn't want to hear that the answer to that is a solid *yes.*

But I need this job. Need to make rent and add to my *War and Peace* savings account so I can finally make my wish come true.

I need to save his daughter in a way that I didn't save Calliope.

I shove that thought away with both hands.

"Please let me help your daughter."

Silence.

Then, "What are your terms?" he asks.

"Fifty dollars a week. I don't need vacations. I'm happy to work day and night."

Unfortunately, he proves himself as un-stupid as I'd suspected by saying, "And? You must want something else if you're asking for so little."

I come out with it. "There's a tiny room on the first floor. A closet really, beside the restrooms. It's been unoccupied for years. You'd never get any money for it. I want that room for myself, rent-free. And my aunt, Miss Devine Rey, lives in a suite on the fifth floor. She needs to stay there. But she can't afford to pay for it."

"So she sent you here to charm me?" He says it with satisfaction, as if cynically amused that the young, plain girl could be so trite.

"If she'd wanted to charm you, she'd have sent someone else. Charming people isn't my style, as I'm sure you've noticed."

"Then tell me why I'd forgo bookings on a suite to do your aunt a favor."

Because being thrown out of here would kill her. I can't be a murderess, even to Miss Devine Rey.

That's a truth I don't want to tell him.

But his hands are pressed to the desk and he's leaning forward, waiting for me to convince him. This is my last shot.

I reach for euphemism or metaphor, but out it all comes, each word a sledgehammer. "You don't understand this place. I do. I know that all anyone here cares about is fame—getting it, keeping it. I know it's the place where you order hot water, not for your teakettle, but to put in your gin—the tea bags are to hide your stash. It's the place where a girl might start the day with one man in her bed and end it with a different one beside her and she'll walk away trying to convince herself that the only thing she regrets is diluting the gin with hot water."

I press my teeth into my tongue to make myself stop, can't fight the urgent need to bite my fingernails despite the fact that Win is watching me and will see that all of my nails are bitten right down to the quick.

"How long have you been here for?" he asks, voice softer now.

"Seven years."

He crosses to the empty sideboard, fist clenching around air when it doesn't find a bottle or a decanter. Then he strides back to the window and the glorious sun falls over his face, and for a moment I can see that his eyes are brown and there are lines around them as if he's flung himself at life and told it to give him everything it has.

"Can you start today?" he asks.

"I'll start now." I slip away.

I'M BEAMING WHEN I reach the lobby. And as if the Marmont has set this up just for me, a note sounds from the piano. Judith Crown is seated there in all her glory, long black gloves making us focus on her hands, which are as elegant and lovely as when she was sixteen and starring in her first movie. It's only her eyes and her skin that show the stain of reds downed with vodka, but false lashes, low lights, and foundation do a good enough job of hiding that. She's wearing her rings over her gloves and the diamonds glisten beneath the chandelier.

Then she starts to sing and everyone who hadn't already been staring stops.

Her voice is like sunshine on the back of your neck after a cold, dark winter. The desk clerks, the other guests, all of us unfurl into that light, and it's not just Judith's jewels glistening now but our eyes too.

This place is so damn beautiful sometimes.

CHAPTER 5

...

1957

ARIA WAKES THE NEXT DAY TO THE AWARENESS THAT SOMEONE is watching her.

"Get up and get dressed and we'll discuss how to make this arrangement work." Her aunt's voice isn't cruel, but impatient.

Aria scrambles out of bed, washes her puffy face, puts on her black dress, and brushes her knotted hair. Then she steps into the main room where the windows are covered in gauzy drapes that permit only filtered light, and the walls are hung with movie posters. In each of them, Miss Devine Rey is caged in the arms of a man.

"Flitter said you were the Legendary Miss Devine Rey," Aria says, curiosity and a good night's sleep overcoming her anger.

Her aunt smiles and she's transformed into the woman who glows like the moon in every poster. "Of course. Why else would I be here?" Miss Devine spreads her arms wide, indicating the hotel. "They do let painters, singers, and poets through the doors, but that always ends in tears. Too many women want to be the subject of a sonnet or immortalized like Madame X. Fights ensue. Most of the guests at the Chateau Marmont are actors and actresses, producers and directors."

"What should I call you? And where will I go to school?" Aria asks, desperate for a sensible, practical soul in the form of a teacher to enter this scene rather than someone like Calliope, Flitter, or Miss Devine, people whose very names indicate their fleeting acquaintance with solid ground.

"This, Aria"—Miss Devine waves an actressy hand around her

again—"is your school. You'll never learn more about the world than you will at the Marmont. You will call me Miss Devine Rey like everyone else. And you will be discreet at all times. The minute you cross the threshold of the Chateau Marmont, you sign the contract—kiss and never tell. These"—she walks into Aria's room and pulls out of the opened suitcase two cameras that belonged to her father—"have to go. No photography allowed."

One by one, the cameras tumble into the trash can, dropped from such a height that the lenses let out little screams as they shatter.

"No! They're mine!" Aria rushes forward but her aunt grabs her wrists, stopping her, and in her eyes Aria can see things that remind her of something her mother always told her: *There are no mean people in the world, just hurt people.*

"One warning stands between us and the prospect of having to find a new home, Aria. Those cameras of yours will earn us a warning. Trouble is, I used up my one warning years ago. Like I said, the Marmont is your school. It's time to learn your lesson."

Aria opens her mouth to protest that she's only thirteen. She doesn't know anything about contracts or who Madame X is. But the straight, unembraceable line of her aunt's back tells Aria that her age is her own problem. While her friends Hilary and Katie are probably sitting on the floor of Katie's room sticking eyes into Mr. and Mrs. Potato Head, the fire at the gas station has incinerated Aria's childhood.

"I *have* learned my lesson," Aria says fiercely. "There's nothing you can't lose."

"Well done," Miss Devine says, her praise as sincere as Aria's teacher's when she gave Aria a gold sticker for a story she wrote. Her aunt picks up the telephone. "We'll have breakfast. Then I have a surprise for you. One that I think you'll like."

Aria isn't so sure about that.

A HOT DOG AND Coke arrive for Aria's breakfast. "Call Schwab's to get food sent over," Miss Devine Rey explains as Aria tears off a bite. "The garage boys can get anything else you need. And absent yourself from the suite between one and five each day so that your presence doesn't crush me the way it's crushing my evening dresses, which I've had to rehouse in my wardrobe now you've taken over the spare bedroom."

Then her aunt smiles, whiplashing Aria with the speed at which her moods change. Now it's like being caught in what you thought was a shower of rain only to find sunbeams falling down on you instead.

"Come, Aria," Miss Devine says. "Your surprise awaits."

Aria scoops up her Coke, shoves the hot dog into her mouth, and follows her aunt to the elevator. Inside is Judith Crown—the second biggest star in the world after Marian Monti. Miss Devine and Judith embrace, then Judith bends down to pat Aria's cheek before waltzing out on the third floor with so many sparkling rings on her fingers she could be an entire galaxy. Aria's not quite recovered from that when her aunt exits the elevator on the first floor, opens a door, and Aria finds the magic promised by the castle's facade.

A library. Shelves full of books. A red sofa any actress would love to recline on. A leather chair. A stuffed giraffe, a cardboard replica of Venice, a lamp whose base is a foot in a high-heeled shoe, a wax hand with red-painted nails, a black cat statue, a camera. And not just any camera—an RCA Sound Camera, something her father had always wanted to own.

The air is stale, the curtains drawn, the dust ought to be accruing a bill for its domicile, but Aria doesn't care. This room is hers.

"Your schoolroom," Miss Devine says. "Educate yourself."

"Thank you," Aria says fervently.

Her aunt tilts Aria's smiling face up to hers. "Never let them see your soul in your eyes. Keep it hidden unless you want to have it taken from you."

CHAPTER 6

...

1964

ADELE WINCHESTER IS STANDING ON THE BALCONY OF THE penthouse, staring at the pool.

"Adele?" I say and she whirls around. "I'm Aria. Your tutor or governess." *Your guardian,* is what I mean.

"Governess?" Her shocked laugh is the same as her father's. But that's where the similarity ends. Adele is like Flitter a few years ago, on the brink of beautiful. Whereas Win is on the brink of unhandsomeness, but not quite there either.

"I don't need a governess." She scowls.

"Tell me what the current interest rate is and how much you'd earn over two years with compound interest on one thousand dollars—if you were able to find a bank who'd let you open an account in your name."

Her glare intensifies. *Now* I can see the resemblance to her father. "Who cares if I can't open a bank account?"

"Don't you want to be able to do things on your own without having other people decide everything for you?"

She has no comeback. It's the fierce desire tucked into the heart of every orphan—or almost-orphan, in her case.

"Look, my childhood wasn't ideal, neither is yours," I tell her. "But you know what? Most girls are sitting in a BO-scented classroom wishing they were someplace else. We *are* someplace else. A place where, so long as you use your mind, I won't tell you off. If you get a math problem wrong, I'll only care whether you tried. If you tell me you hate Shakespeare, that's fine too, so long as you read him first. Go ahead and sing out of tune—but just make sure that you sing."

Her glare has faded, but her arms are still folded across her chest.

"Let's take a tour," I say. I need her to accept me—not necessarily to like me, although that'd be nice—by the time her father returns tonight.

Adele leads the way out of the penthouse, wanting to show me that she can find her own way, thank you very much. I slip into one of the hidden doors in the walls with Pilot, press my finger to my lips, and he wags his tail like I've won over one Winchester already.

Five seconds later, Adele's footsteps stop. "Aria?"

I pop my head out. "Do you want the behind-the-scenes tour or the regular one?"

"Where does it go?" she asks, peering into the stairwell.

"Everywhere."

Her mouth lifts up just a little at the corners.

I take her through the Marmont's intestines, show her which panels are doors and which aren't, introduce her to Maisie the housekeeper, and to Isaiah. In the lobby I point out Phillip, the young poet with a quarterback's build and a lovesick heart who comes to stay whenever Calliope's in residence. He waits there all day, his sole purpose to speak to her. Nobody has any idea how he affords such an existence, but I'd bet on a trust fund.

The only room I don't show her is the library. Others believe the turret is haunted by Bob's sister, but I know for sure that the library is the only haunted room here.

Our last stop is with Jupiter, Isaiah's son, who's one of the garage boys. He's two years older than me and he never stops smiling, not even when guests wipe the car seats with their handkerchiefs and curse the Marmont for letting a "colored boy" handle their cars. From him I've learned that there's power in not letting others hurt you, although I haven't yet learned how not to hurt.

"When did Phillip turn up?" I ask after I've introduced Adele.

"Today. I warned Miss Calliope so she knows to come and go via the garage."

"Do you think he'd leave if she just spoke to him a couple of times?" I muse.

Jupiter shakes his head. "Why should she have to speak to him just to make him leave her alone?"

He's right. And I'm ashamed that I thought for even a moment that Calliope needed to take responsibility for another man deaf to the cues that are shouting, *No*!

"Wanna try this one?" Jupiter points to a navy car, a panther outstretched. It's a Lamborghini, so of course I nod.

I slide into the passenger seat with Pilot. "I like to sit in a car I can never afford, close my eyes and imagine I'm driving away, seeing all the things I've never seen," I tell Adele.

"Like what?" she asks, putting her hands on the wheel.

"The ocean. The desert."

"You've never seen a desert? LA's surrounded by desert." The skepticism in her voice is so great it's like I said I'd never been to the bathroom.

"Close your eyes. Go on," I tell her when she rolls them instead.

I reach over and turn the keys so the radio comes on. With impeccable timing, "California Girls" plays and Adele's face swings into a smile.

For three minutes, we're just California girls in a Lamborghini in the basement garage of the Chateau Marmont, like we actually belong here in Hollywood.

OUR LAST STOP IS the gardens. I introduce Adele to the one-legged woodpecker that lives in the dead tree trunk hidden behind the palm trees. It has red feathers atop its head and around its neck and the day I first saw it, I thought someone had slit its throat.

I take out the suet that I begged from Maisie and feed it to the bird. Adele seems to like this even more than the Lamborghini.

"Do you think Maisie will give me suet if I ask her for it?" she says, and that's when I know this girl is absolutely worth saving.

Suet gone, we emerge opposite the path that leads to bungalow four: Bob's bungalow, the farthest from everything, the one with its own gate to the street. Nobody's stayed there besides Bob the whole time I've lived at the Marmont. He pays for it even when he's overseas or in New York.

Today there's tape barricading access to it. A sign reads: *Construction zone. Keep Out!* Other signs around the path warn: *Do Not Enter.*

Pilot barks, then lunges for the tape. Adele grabs him just before he slips under.

"Wow," I say. "Bob must be . . ." My voice trails off.

"Bob. That's the guy who came to our suite this morning," Adele says. "Win told him it needs renovating or something."

"So Bob's left the Marmont?"

"He's been moved to a suite. I don't know. Pilot, *shhh,*" she scolds the agitated dog.

I look across to the pool. Bob is there, gifting kingly smiles to those who wave at him, encouraging them into his circle; the only studio boss who doesn't hide behind secretaries and vice presidents, who sits down with the ordinary folk and makes them his friends.

My hand jumps out to guide Adele away. Pilot slows our progress, still barking at the *Keep Out* signs like there's something in Bob's bungalow we ought to have paid more attention to.

I TAKE PILOT AND Adele up to the safety of the turret—our schoolroom. She walks over to the window and looks out at the view of movie studios and the San Gabriel Mountains. One whispered "Cool" escapes her determination to be unimpressed, then she does a circuit, taking in the stuffed giraffe and the piles of books that once lived in the library downstairs until that room was ruined forever.

She halts beside the mattress in the corner. "Do you sleep here?"

I shake my head. "It's for anyone who needs a safe place to sleep."

"Why would anyone sleep here when they have a whole hotel room to stay in?" Adele asks incredulously.

Instead of answering her question, I gesture to the walls made from stories, the reading chair draped with a blanket that Isaiah's wife crocheted for my sixteenth birthday. The view some people would pay a million bucks for. "This is one of the nicest rooms in the Chateau Marmont."

Pilot wags his tail at F. Scott, the black cat statue, then curls up on the mattress and closes his eyes. Adele sits in the chair, pulls the blanket over her lap, and lets me quiz her as I try to figure out what she knows and the best way to educate her in math, science, English, and art, as well as Marmont Life. Despite the depressing conversation I had with Calliope this morning, I'd like to believe that teaching a woman to be curious and giving her an education could lead to something other than mopping her husband's floors and using the silver screen to escape her life.

By nightfall I've discovered that she's better at math than she thinks, that she's read very little, that she could name any song or musical instrument, but doesn't care to play. We agree that she'll read Sylvia Plath's *The Bell Jar,* that she can play records while she works, and that I'll teach her knowledge rather than subjects.

"I don't know what that means," she says, stretching out her legs, which are long like her father's. "But it sounds better than school. Now I'm starving."

My stomach is complaining too. "Are you having dinner with your dad?"

"No idea."

In the penthouse, we're greeted by darkness.

"I guess I'm not having dinner with him." She gives an I-don't-care shrug that only serves to show how much she cares. "I don't even know when dinnertime is. I've only lived with him for a couple of months and that was at the Beverly Hilton. I'd come home from school and he'd shout, *Not now!* like he thought I was the maid. Then he'd apologize and pretend like he hadn't forgotten he owned me."

I snap on the lights. "Not having a daughter and then suddenly having one probably isn't easy. But not having a father and then suddenly having one wouldn't be simple either."

She shrugs again, on the brink of descending into teenage angst, so I point to the faces stacked in the hallway, to the wall stained with white rectangles where the paintings once hung. "Baroque portraiture doesn't suit the rock star aesthetic?"

Adele shudders. "Those men were old and creepy. Why is everything so weird?"

She gestures to the oak chiffonier carved with open-mouthed lions, to the stuffed owl that looks to have its eye on everything, as if it's the Marmont's henchman.

"They got the furniture from fire sales after Wall Street crashed in the 1920s, bought out entire households of once-rich Californians. So no two rooms are the same and, depending on your perspective, they've been designed by an antiquarian with a sense of mischief or are good examples of haunted-attic chic."

Adele actually laughs. We're in the kitchen now, which is more ordinary than the hallway and living room—besides the Black Forest executioner's clock on the wall where a woman gets her head cut off every hour.

"Do you want grilled cheese?" I open the fridge. "*French Cooking in Thirty Minutes* says you need three cheeses, bread, and butter. Hopefully grilled cheese won't take thirty minutes. And you've got French Brie, cheddar, and mozzarella. I'm sure that'll work."

When I emerge from the fridge, Adele is staring at me. "Haven't you ever made grilled cheese before?"

"Nope. Schwab's won't let me into their kitchen." I wink, then explain. "My aunt doesn't have a single pot or pan in her suite. The fridge is rusted shut. This"—I look around the kitchen contentedly—"is the first time I've ever cooked anything. So you're either very lucky or very unlucky, depending on how it turns out."

She's so completely gobsmacked that she flops onto a stool and watches as I spread butter on the bread, cover it with cheddar, thin slices of mozzarella, and thick ones of Brie. I pull the skillet out of the drawer, toss in a spoonful of butter.

"How do you know where everything is?" she asks.

"The second year I was here, I neglected my turret school in favor of a year of Marmont school. I spent a couple of months with Jupiter, who showed me how to change a tire and fix a motor. I studied on Lambos and Ferraris, so don't ask me how to change a tire on a Chevrolet. Then I spent a month with Jilly on the switchboard and now I can plug a wire into a socket faster than Jupiter can park a Ferrari. Another month with the gardener and I can graft a scion to a rootstock three different ways. A few weeks with the handyman and I can tune the piano to either encourage or discourage early morning serenades, as well as crack your safe when you've drunk too many margaritas to remember the code. A couple of months with Maisie, who gave me a tour of every room, means I can show you where you shouldn't hide the things you don't want anyone to find."

"I bet that will come in handy."

Adele lets out a little scream and I jump, neither of us having heard Win come in. I turn my attention to the grilled cheese, hoping he didn't hear everything. Not that it was bad—but it was revealing. And my aunt's words still hold true: you don't let anyone see your soul unless you're prepared to lose it.

I scoop the sandwiches onto plates, pass Adele hers, take a bite of mine in spite of how hot it is, and can't hold back the grin. "I really am a genius," I say through a mouthful of melted Brie, waving a hand in front of my mouth in a useless attempt to stop my tongue burning. Then I start making another, figuring I'll eat it if Win doesn't.

"How was your day?" he asks Adele in the interrogatory tone of a school principal.

"Better than any I've had lately," she says tartly.

I throw more butter into the pan so the sizzle fills the subsequent silence, then ask, searching for safe ground for all of us, "Did you find your guitar?"

He nods, takes out sodas, passes one to Adele—who refuses—one to me, one for himself: the first rock star I've met who isn't clutching whiskey the way a baby clutches a bottle.

I offer him the last grilled cheese. "Further proof of my genius."

"I think that after tonight's summary of your abilities, the evidence I really need is that you're not teaching Adele how to be Bonnie or Clyde."

"I'd never teach her to be the woman who dies at the end," I tell him.

Both Adele and her father laugh and the mood finally relaxes. Thank god. If it's going to be like this every night, Adele and I might have to eat dinner in the turret.

From the pool comes the sound of screaming, but I've heard enough screams to know it's just an attention-seeking yelp. Still, Win moves toward the balcony and Adele follows, her eyes never leaving his face, like she's trying to make him see her rather than hold her at arm's length like a sweater he thinks doesn't suit him.

I wash my plate and the fry pan, put everything away, and turn from the sink to find Win standing on the other side of the counter.

"You didn't come outside," he says.

"I thought I'd leave you to it."

"Neither Adele nor I like being left to it."

I contemplate not saying the next words. It's not my place. But I don't know where my place is, only know that I haven't found it yet. "Don't treat her like a puzzle you're trying to solve.

And don't be . . ." I pause, certain he'll bite my head off. "Don't be scared of her."

His expression turns to anger and I brace. He notices the way I rear back and shock crosses his face.

"The balcony," he says, pointing the way with his soda bottle.

The view from there is impressive. It's hard to see much of the grounds; the gardens are lit by only the smallest embers of light. The pool is a mere ripple of blue, and it's not until you look beyond the boundaries of the Marmont and across to the city that you see the lights. Hollywood glows so brightly you can't see that there's a universe of light above us.

"Hollywood," Adele breathes. "If you can't be happy in Hollywood, where can you be happy?"

Happy, I think when I leave. I just cooked my first meal. I didn't take a bus somewhere like Calliope wants me to, but it's still a step toward my house by the sea. I have money. A job. The rent is taken care of. Adele is safe. And maybe this time I know enough to avoid what lies in wait for those who think they're happy.

Then why does the dream come again at midnight, of the voice from the past saying, *I will never forgive you.*

CHAPTER 7

...

1957

ARIA SHUTS THE DOOR ON MISS DEVINE'S MAXIMS AND THE knowledge that on any previous Thursday at nine in the morning, she'd be walking into her classroom at Joan of Arc Junior High giggling over Hilary's or Katie's attempts to sew herself into her flannel skirt, attempts that usually ended with gaping holes or oxygen deprivation. She strokes the giraffe—could it actually be real?—pokes the waxy hand with a suspicious finger in case it suddenly comes to life, then pulls books from the shelves: *The Miracle of the Movies,* issues of *U.S. Camera Magazine,* and issues of *Photoplay* magazine. Her goal for this week is to understand both how to use the RCA Sound Camera and her new world. Otherwise she'll suffer a similar fate to Eggletina Clock in *The Borrowers,* who was eaten up by the cat.

Hours pass. Hours of looking at her aunt's smiling face on cover after cover of *Photoplay,* of reading interviews that detail her aunt's beauty tricks, her worst fault—daydreaming, apparently, although Aria can't imagine Miss Devine Rey doing anything so childish; that's Aria's domain—and, bizarrely, her thoughts on bats.

There are also photographs of a beaming Miss Devine Rey embracing Bob Ashenhurst, the man from the pool—the King of Hollywood. There are questions about weddings and babies.

But in the space of one issue to the next—as if a decade had passed rather than a month—Miss Devine Rey is no longer kind, beautiful, or glamorous. She's a lush. Immoral. She fooled the people of America into believing she was an angel.

Aria searches for clues about how this transformation happened, but there are none. She selects two magazines, one from before and one from after. Then she creeps through the hallways of the Marmont searching for Flitter and Calliope, who are out by the pool.

Calliope's wearing a red-and-white polka-dot bikini, and is surrounded by men. Flitter, in a blush pink one-piece, stands outside the circle.

Aria lifts her hand into a half wave, something she can pretend not to have done if the women ignore her. But Calliope waves back in a rainbow arc and says to the people around her, "It's been a pleasure, gentlemen." Her voice is husky, and for the five seconds it takes to say those words, Calliope is someone else entirely.

"Later," Flitter says.

Nobody replies. Aria wonders how Flitter feels every time she walks into a room with her friend. Maybe like Aria felt when Katie and Hilary forgot to invite her to a sleepover.

But Flitter is smiling at Aria now. "We were worried The-Legendary-Miss-Devine-Rey had eaten you."

Aria giggles and holds up her magazines. "Nope. But I have questions."

Flitter shakes her head. "Sorry, kid. We've got a party to go to."

Aria's about to beg, not caring if she lets these two see her soul in her eyes, when Calliope says, "Maybe we both need a real night off. We have the night off work here. But what if we take a night off from being Flitter and Calliope too?"

Flitter studies her friend. Now Aria would recognize the single fine line of fatigue that isn't quite hidden by the pan stick foundation on Calliope's face as a warning sign. Back then, Aria has no idea what she's looking at. Perhaps Flitter does; perhaps

Flitter doesn't—it's a question Aria will turn over in the years to come.

Flitter nods. "We'll start on the roof."

"Can we go up to the turret?" Aria asks as they cross over the driveway, enter a secret staircase on the ground floor, and ascend.

Flitter demurs. "Never go up to the turret."

"Why?"

"It's haunted," Calliope says thrillingly.

"By who?"

"Bob Ashenhurst's sister."

Aria is shocked into silence. The man who made time to smile at everyone by the pool had a sister whose ghost haunts the fairy-tale turret above them?

Calliope pulls open a door and they're blinded by sunshine. When her eyes adjust, Aria sees they're at the top of a small tower next to and lower than the turret. Below them, Los Angeles sprawls without inhibition, so different from Manhattan, which is all sharp skyscrapers you can't see past. Here, a giantess in a blue leotard spins on a silver dollar beside them, and for a moment, Aria thinks she can hear the hum of the hotel breathing. She strokes her hand along the balustrade of this marvelous creature she's standing atop, a bareback rider poised on a golden Palomino horse.

"Over there is Millennium Wolf, to the left is Bronte Bros., down there aways is Supreme Pictures." Flitter points to buildings in the center of it all. "Just past that is ACE Studios, and in the middle of it all is Golden Mare. The big five Hollywood studios. They own this town and every actor and actress in it—if you're lucky enough to be under contract to one of them. Me and Calliope would give just about everything we have to sign a contract with one."

"It's the first step to becoming a star." Calliope throws her arms into the air and stands, legs akimbo, mimicking the points of that celestial body. "Bob Ashenhurst is the boss of Golden Mare, the biggest of the big five. That's why he's the king."

"And because he remembers everyone's name, and he isn't just a dreamboat—he's like a fantasy ocean liner." Flitter grins.

"Oh my." Calliope fans herself.

Aria holds up Miss Devine Rey and Bob Ashenhurst on the cover of *Photoplay.* "Is she famous?"

"Your aunt was a once-in-a-lifetime star," Calliope says with such longing it's like you could wring out her words and find the sweet nectar that dreams are made of. "I saw my first Miss Devine Rey movie when I was five—far too young, but my parents' attitude to children was about as careless as your aunt's. I wanted to be her so bad."

"After Calliope saw that movie," Flitter picks up the story, "it was like she'd found the meaning of life. She snuck me into the movie theater—her parents owned the place—and I fell just as much in love."

"Why haven't I heard of her?" Aria asks, enchanted by the idea of her aunt wielding that kind of magic—that just by watching her, you'd want to be her.

"She hasn't been in a movie since 1950," Calliope says.

"Why?"

"Nobody really knows." Flitter shrugs.

Calliope's French-manicured fingernail traces over the photo of Miss Devine Rey and Bob Ashenhurst smooching. "They were engaged. Imagine being the Queen of Hollywood."

"I'd give just about anything for that," Flitter says and her tone is yearning too.

Which makes as much sense to Aria as the reasons why her cameras are now shards of glass. "I don't understand!" she protests.

In the September sunshine, her neck is sticky with sweat; she's tired and hungry, and the only thing she wants is the one thing she can't have: to go to Jan's ice cream parlor with her mother and sit at the counter and order banana splits while her mom explains the world to her.

Calliope puts her hand on Aria's cheek. Aria wants so much to nuzzle into it like a kitten casting around for just one scratch under her chin. But she can't afford to frighten away these two women, can't be childish or needy or forlorn. Can't be thirteen. Can't show her soul in her eyes. Can't get a warning. Can't understand—but needs to.

"Back in the day when your aunt was famous, Bob owned a smaller studio," Calliope tells her. "He broke off his engagement to Miss Devine around the same time he bought out Golden Mare. I don't know why. But you look cold. Come on, we'll show you our room."

Yes. Seeing where these two live, what posters they hang on their walls, whether their dressing table holds barrettes or bandanas, sounds like something Aria can comprehend.

They descend to the first floor and in they all go, squeezing around the door that, yes, you can't open all the way without hitting the bed. Lipstick-stained glasses, balled-up Kleenex, still-wet bikinis, hair curlers, negligees, stockings, and a paperback novel called *Lolita* cover the floor. Through the middle is a path that leads to the bathroom, with one branch shooting off to the bed and another to a brown dresser that looms like a bear in the corner.

"Home sweet home," Flitter says.

She and Calliope start tugging off their swimsuits. Aria whirls away, cheeks crimson.

"Look at her—face like a Russian flag." Flitter grins.

"Doesn't she remind you of us, once upon a time?" Calliope says wistfully.

"Us before the fairies died, you mean." Flitter's laugh is sharp, humorless.

"What does that mean?" Aria peeps over her shoulder.

Calliope's smile is a quarter-strength. "Just that we'd like to make sure you still blush when you see a naked person in a year's time."

"Aria reminds you of me," Flitter interjects. "Not you. Nobody's ever had your glitter, Cally-o-pee."

"Have you always looked like that?" Aria asks, happy to shift the conversation to something less foreign than fairies and nudity.

"Calliope's always been a traffic-stopper, jaw-dropper, gobsmacker, eye-popper," Flitter replies.

Aria giggles, but Calliope says glumly, "'Miss Most Likely to Succeed,' my school yearbook says. This week, you wouldn't know it."

She slumps on the bed. Flitter sits on one side, Aria the other, and their arms wind around Calliope.

"Another failed audition," Flitter explains.

Aria tries to hold in her next question, but she hasn't spoken to anybody since breakfast and a whole day is a long time to stay silent. "If Calliope was Miss Most Likely to Succeed, what were you?"

"The girl whose hopes were the only things higher than her skirt," Flitter wisecracks, pulling up her miniskirt, making Aria and Calliope laugh.

Calliope leaps up. "Let's have a pajama party."

"Well, if we can't go out and get screwed, blued, and tattooed, then let's have ourselves a pajama party," Flitter says.

When Aria replies, "I don't know what that means, but I think a pajama party is safer," Calliope says, "See, you're getting the hang of Hollywood already." She picks up the phone and orders three burgers with fries, one mint julep, and two lemonades from Schwab's. Before she hangs up, she says, "Screw it. Make it four mint juleps and one lemonade."

Flitter raises an eyebrow. "We'd better answer your questions now, Aria. Because soon Calliope will either be snoring or dancing. Two mint juleps for someone who doesn't drink is going to be either a pick-me-upper or put-me-downer."

"Should I tell my aunt where I am?" Aria asks.

"I don't think she'll remember that you're not there." Calliope squeezes Aria's hand.

Aria stares. Her mother *always* knew where she was. But Aria's mother will never again know where she is, a thought she shoves down beside everything else that makes the vomity feeling come back. "Tell me about the ghost," she blurts.

"I don't know—" Calliope starts.

Flitter interrupts. "She'll find out soon enough. You know the way stories travel like herpes through here." Flitter whacks a hand over her mouth. "Shit." Then she claps the other hand on top and breaks into giggles.

And over the top of that incongruous melody, Calliope says, "Bob Ashenhurst's sister jumped from the turret seven years ago."

CHAPTER 8

...

1964

WAKING MY AUNT IS LIKE WAKING A CORPSE OR A LION. IT'S impossible, or could result in me being short of a limb. Thankfully her stupor this morning is too heavy for violence. I move the pills out of reach and kneel on the ground where her half-open eyes can see mine.

"I'm moving to the first floor," I tell her. "I'll come and check on you every day."

She laughs. "The orphan is leaving *me*? Ungrateful orphan."

Yes, family always knows exactly what will hurt the most.

I know I should stay with her. But while I could describe the difference between a heroin overdose and a barbiturate overdose, I couldn't tell you what it's like to sit on Santa Monica Beach. Last night I made grilled cheese; today my baby step toward the future is to move into my own room. There's always the fear that the world out there is where people catch fire, but that's something I'll just have to conquer.

"I'll see you just as much as I do now," I say.

But she's already lost in the tranquilized world where she can escape from whatever happened fourteen years ago that's erased her piece by piece, taking away her career, her confidence, her Friday parties, her self-worth, her spirit, and her future. I don't know why she hasn't been able to, like Calliope, carry on in spite of whatever she did. Don't know if it's because she's a weaker person, or because she did something worse than Calliope had to.

Don't know if I want to know.

But unlike my aunt, I have a future. I can't stay in this mausoleum of the past in case I end up buried alive too.

OVER THE FOLLOWING FORTNIGHT, I finish with Adele around nine o'clock at night, which is when her dad returns to the penthouse from wherever he goes all day. He doesn't use the office at the Marmont. He doesn't spend his days at the penthouse. I arrive at eight in the morning and he walks out the door with his sunglasses on and isn't heard from again for thirteen hours. I guess being mysterious goes hand in hand with being a rock star.

Each night when I return to my room, I make it feel more like mine. Tonight, I'm sewing a set of curtains when I hear a moan, deep and low, like an animal in pain.

I hurry through the lobby and out into the gardens, never quite sure how these sounds echo in my room when the laws of vibrational energy tell me it should be impossible for me to hear them. It's like the Chateau Marmont is a spirit, sighing into my ears, its ghostly arms guiding me on.

I find her by the tree where my one-legged bird lives. He's on a branch keeping watch, eyes two droplets glistening in the night.

I turn her face toward me. It's Nathalie, a starlet who's been here for a few months and had very little work. She raises her hand to cover her face, elbow bent like the wing of a wounded bird.

There's too much blood.

"It's Aria," I whisper.

"I . . . I . . ."

"Shhh," I tell her. "We need to get to the turret."

A second later, footsteps sound. Nathalie curls into a ball. I peer around the tree and see Win, his expression dark as night, ducking under the barrier that reads *Keep Out!,* then striding down the path to Bob's former bungalow. More mysterious errands.

"It was just someone going the other way," I tell Nathalie.

She's so pale I don't know if she'll make it to the turret. I wrap her arms around my neck and we limp to the garage where Jupiter scoops her up and Isaiah gets us straight to the seventh floor. Jupiter lays her on the mattress and I thank him, knowing his dad will have called the doctor and I just have to keep Nathalie alive until then.

I sit with her head in my lap, biting the nails on my left hand, smoothing her hair off her forehead while blood soaks the sheets. I wish I had hot cocoa and a warm bath because, looking at her face, I'm almost sure that a bit of comfort and kindness is all it would take to lure her back home to Pennsylvania.

Doctor Foster arrives soon after and I help him stem the flow of blood from the womb she's paid to have scraped clean, but which has been ruined instead.

Nathalie whispers, "He gave me a phone number and a hundred bucks to fix it."

"Who?" I ask.

She turns her head away.

Suddenly it's like there's a madwoman battering the walls of my mind, wanting to scream at Nathalie, *Say something!* Wanting to scream at the night, *Is everyone blind or stupid?*

A whisper scratches at the window: *No, Aria. They're smart.*

So all I can do is make sure the starlets know where to find a mattress to lie down on until they're ready to walk to the pool and start all over again. But that isn't enough to quiet the madwoman, and she screams at me again for being so afraid of consequence that my focus is on aftermath, rather than stopping these things from happening at all.

DOCTOR FOSTER SENDS ME down to bed a couple of hours later. Each time I make the journey from turret mattress to my own bed, my feet feel heavier and I wonder if one day I won't be able to move at all, will find myself stuck inside this staircase, part of the Marmont's walls.

I shiver, decide to go outside. I need fresh air.

Out on the driveway, I inhale, head tilted toward the sky. When I straighten up, I lock eyes with someone who shouldn't be walking down the driveway from the street at two in the morning.

Adele.

I wrap my hands around her wrists, pull her in close by my side where she'll be invisible too, but she's too tall. "What are you doing?" I demand, trying not to squeeze her wrists too tightly even though I want to slap her.

"I suppose you'll tell Win," she snaps. "Then he'll have to find someplace else to lock me up."

We stand there, both of us breathing hard, me from anger and fright, her from I don't know what. *He* should *lock you up,* are words I only just bite back.

I let go. Step away. What am I trying to do? Make Adele into me, the ghost of the Marmont? Nobody should be locked up anywhere, especially not a fourteen-year-old.

I examine her face. Her eyes are red. Booze? Junk?

"Were you doing anything illegal?"

"No." She crosses her arms, throwing down the gauntlet. It's up to me what happens now.

There's noise at the end of the driveway. Paparazzi, stationing themselves on the curb, the closest they're allowed to the Chateau Marmont.

"Come inside," I tell her, knowing the last thing we need is her face in the newspaper.

In the small foyer in front of the ground-floor elevators, I make a decision. I hope it's the right one. But I don't want to ruin any chance of Adele and her father ever having a relationship. At least one person around here deserves a parent.

"Go to bed," I say. "Don't ever sneak out again. Promise me that, and I won't tell your dad."

Surprise flashes over her face. "Fine."

Unspeaking, I accompany her to the seventh floor and watch her slip into the room she sleeps in, which is next door to the penthouse—whether because Win figured out that she'd need some space or because he wanted privacy while he conducted the nocturnal life of a rock star, I don't know.

I'm exhausted. But I never did get my fresh air.

Back outside, I sit on the edge of the pool, dip my toes in the water, close my eyes, and pretend it's the sea that I'll live beside when I leave here in December. I can almost smell the salty air, hear the waves rolling in and out. But then I hear footsteps.

My eyes fly open.

A shadow slips out from behind the *Do Not Enter* tape barricading access to the path to Bob's former bungalow. One of the lights from the garden illuminates, just briefly, a face.

Theo Winchester again.

What is it with all the Winchesters sneaking around tonight?

A moment later he's on the main path back to the hotel. Maybe rock stars need some kind of kink in the form of construction sites to excite them. Hopefully his daughter's escapades had nothing to do with either kink or excitement. Hopefully Win never finds out. Hopefully she keeps her promise, or else I'm screwed.

None of this is relaxing.

When I return to my room, I'm still too edgy to sleep. I finish the curtains I started hours ago, then survey my room.

I've sanded back and painted white the dresser Flitter and Calliope once shared, as well as the walls. On the dresser is a photo of me, Flitter, and Calliope, taken last year after Calliope was nominated for an Academy Award. There's a shelf with my favorite books from the turret: *The Secret Garden, Rebecca,* and *We Have Always Lived in the Castle.* In the corner is a hanging rail holding my borrowed clothes.

A knock sounds, preceded by the jingle of a large ring of keys clipped to somebody's waist, meaning it's Maisie, who's in her mid-seventies but whose energy is boundless. "For your new digs." Maisie passes me a bundle of blue that opens into a quilt the color of the sea.

I throw my arms around her and she pushes me away.

"'Bout time you did this." She sweeps her arm around the room. "Just like it was about time Mr. Mason left. Time for all of you to move on."

I sit down on my bed, quilt cradled in my arms. "Move on from what?" I ask. "All I can come up with is that my aunt cheated on Bob and he found out and told the press, and that's why she fell from grace and locked herself in her room." I remember the abrupt shift in those magazines I'd found in the library, how my aunt had been a goddess one month and immoral the next. As a theory it makes partial sense. "Except why did Bob's sister jump off the roof? Unless . . ." My mind scrambles around in the mud of a new possibility. "Did my aunt cheat on Bob with Mr. Mason?"

Maisie frowns at me. "No, your aunt did not sleep with her best friend's fiancé. You've been in Hollywood too long, Miss Aria, if you're making up stories like that."

I grimace, chastened.

Maisie heaves herself onto the bed, kicks off her scuffed shoes, and takes my hand, my fingernails ragged compared to her bright red polish. "Bob's sister Toni and your aunt were like your two pals, the ones with the crazy names. Miss Devine was like the famous one and Toni was like the other one."

"Like Flitter?"

She nods. "Miss Devine had all the roles. Miss Toni tried so hard, but had no luck. For a time it was quite the foursome—Mr. Mason and Toni; Bob and Miss Devine. Then only Mr. Mason and your aunt were left, and he tried to do what he could for her, but there are some things you can't fix. All I know is that I spoke to your aunt that night when she was on her way out with Toni. She'd always stop and chat, ask how my grandkids were."

"Miss Devine Rey asked about your grandkids? Wow." I can't imagine my aunt caring about anything besides herself.

"People become what the world makes them, Miss Aria,"

Maisie says and I'm reminded of my mother's words: *There are no mean people. Just hurt people.* How hurt do you have to be to transform from a woman who asks the housekeeper about her grandkids to the woman in my aunt's suite right now? But what hurt her? Bob breaking off their engagement?

"I remember that night because it was the first time I saw Miss Devine not smiling," Maisie goes on. "I asked how she was doing and she told me she was going to break off her engagement. The power was going to Bob's head and she wanted someone who loved her more than power."

"Miss Devine broke it off? I thought Bob did? Holy cow."

The shocks keep coming. My aunt broke off her engagement to the man who was about to become the biggest of the studio bosses, which is about the bravest thing a woman in 1940s Hollywood could do. How did the woman upstairs, addicted to stardom, left prone by its implosion, have the guts to even contemplate it?

And it's not enough of a reason for her to have gone from goddess to goose egg overnight.

Maisie's on her feet. "Two bright young women went out that night. When they got back, they never left again. Well, I guess one of them did—in a coffin. Seems to me like your aunt could do with someone to save her before she ends up in a coffin too. Someone who's already so busy trying to save everyone else around here. Know anyone like that?" She puts her hands on her hips and stares pointedly at me. "Seems like family should be who you save first. Talk to your aunt, Miss Aria."

Then Maisie lumbers out my door and I'm left sitting on my bed, gobsmacked. Chastened too.

Talk to your aunt. She won't tell me anything.

Besides, I have a brand-new quilt and a room of my own. Why not just enjoy those tiny victories?

I brush my teeth and slip into a pair of silk pajamas that Flitter gave me for Christmas. Calliope's gift had been a box of silk underwear, presented with a kiss and the words, *You absolutely cannot wear Schwab's cotton panties for the rest of your life.*

So in my silk underwear and silk pajamas and with a blue cotton quilt lapping over the bed, a regular job and a future beckoning, I write in my journal—a proper notebook now, rather than the notepaper Doctor Foster purloined from Marian Monti—then fall asleep.

I WAKE WITH A start not long after midnight. I can hear music; someone is playing the piano in the lobby, the keys jangling and sliding into the melody for "Great Balls of Fire." It isn't a ghost—people play the Marmont's piano at all times of day and night. But why is it playing that song? *Who* is playing that song?

It's the same one that spun on the turntable in the library that day. Only two other people in the world know that.

I slip out of bed, don't realize that my hand is shaking until it fumbles with the key to my door. I glide along the corridor to the lobby, silent, stealthy.

There are the arched windows, the wooden ceiling, the red velvet armchairs, the fringed lampshades, and crystal tumblers. There is the piano.

Nobody is sitting on the stool.

I stretch out my fingers. Make my hand relax. I must have dreamed it. It's a popular song. Anyone might play it for any reason. It means nothing at all.

IT'S OCTOBER NOW. THE Santa Ana winds have been pouring down from the Sierra Nevada all week, bringing dust and hot tempers and the smell of wildfires. It's the month of overdoses and tainted dreams, of ambition getting into bed with hope.

It was October when I sat in the library and a camera recorded something I didn't understand.

In the turret I push memory and *The Bell Jar* to one side. What was I thinking, asking Adele to read that? That she'd learn something about a woman's struggle for freedom? Don't we suck in the knowledge of that struggle along with our very first breath?

Plath will stay confined today. But we won't.

"Let's swim," I say. "It's too early for anyone else; we'll have the pool to ourselves."

"Meaning I'll be safe from corruption?" Adele says archly.

"Meaning you'll be safe from corrupters," I tell her in a faux teacher's voice. "It's up to you whether or not you're corrupted."

She groans and I laugh. "Put on your swimsuit. I'll meet you outside the penthouse."

"Because I'm absolutely not allowed to wander around the hotel alone in my bikini," she says in a terrible mimicry of me.

I wish she *could* parade around in her bikini. But that freedom isn't for her, not here.

It takes me hardly any time to retrieve my bikini from my sparse wardrobe, a black-and-white polka-dot number that Flitter liberated from the costume department of ACE Studios. I pair it with cat-eye tortoiseshell sunglasses that had lounged unclaimed by the pool for a week last summer until I, knowing what it's like to be orphaned, adopted them.

I'm at the penthouse five minutes later. I turn when the door opens, expecting Adele.

It's Win.

He jumps, not expecting anyone to be lurking outside. Predictably, he curses.

"Do you want Adele to grow up with the filthiest mouth in Hollywood?" I ask.

"Do you want to give me a heart attack so Adele can inherit the Marmont and gift you a penthouse instead of a closet?" he counters, tone gruff, eyebrows relaxed.

I laugh. "I think Adele would choose any of about a thousand actors to put in the penthouse ahead of me."

He leans against the doorframe, which decreases the height difference between us a little. "In a month, you've made her talk about actors a hell of a lot less than she did for the first few weeks I had her," he says. "She even said something about wanting to be a writer. I don't know if I should ask what you've got her reading to make her think of that."

I wince. "Sylvia Plath."

"Jesus." I'm not sure if the subdued imprecation is disdain for my literary choices or if he's trying not to laugh.

"Why are you here anyway?" I ask.

"I live here."

"But you're never here during the day." *Nor at nighttime when creeping into bungalows seems to be your fetish.* I keep that thought to myself lest it sound like I've been spying on him.

"I'm having a party tonight. I'm sick of everyone asking when I'm having one, so I decided to get it over with." He says it like it's tuberculosis. "I need you to chaperone Adele. Ideally," he says as Adele exits the penthouse, "you won't be in bikinis."

I turn to Adele. "Let's go get some exercise before the poolside resembles the French Riviera, otherwise I might forget myself under the influence of all those nipples and come to the party dressed like an extra in a brothel scene."

Adele just about falls over laughing. Win does not.

We make our escape, Adele whispering, "Nobody talks to him like you do. They're all 'yes, Win; no, Win.' You make me remember he's not just famous Win; he's a human being."

"There's a way to break through everyone's reserve," I tell her. "Keep trying and you'll find a way that works with him."

"But shouldn't he be trying too?" she asks.

Gone are the folded arms and the eye rolls. She looks fourteen and vulnerable and as if she isn't sure whether there's a person alive who loves her. God, I remember that feeling. I'd hoped Win was doing more to show her that she has arms rather than a void around her. I still don't know what he does all day—he never takes his guitars anywhere, so he can't be making a new album. What else do mysterious rock stars do during the day? Sleep like vampires? Maybe I've made it too easy for him to get out of being a father; he knows someone is taking care of Adele's basic needs and to hell with the rest.

Well, party or no party, I'm going to have words with him tonight.

Outside, one cabana is occupied by the sleeping form of a man I don't know—a leftover from last night's bungalow parties, the wildest in the hotel. There's a woman curled up beside him and, while she's missing her bikini top, at least the lady garden is under shade and the little birdie beside her is asleep.

There's someone at the far end of the pool too. Matt, a screenwriter in his mid-forties who started calling himself Matty a few years ago, as if adding a *y* to the end of his name was the elixir of youth.

"Aria, hey," he calls.

"Any progress?" I ask, indicating the typewriter. He's signed on as writer-director for a much-publicized and highly anticipated project green-lit by Bob's studio to adapt *Jane Eyre*—the novel about the orphan girl.

He shakes his head. "It's not like it doesn't happen around here. Young girl falls for older, richer man. But why does he fall for her when she's so plain and dull?"

"Because she's his second chance," I say without thinking. "We always think we'll eventually live our lives right if only we get enough practice."

"Fuck, that's good." Matty starts a percussive clacking on the typewriter. "I'll give you a screenwriting credit."

I laugh. "I'm content to remain anonymous."

Adele and I move to the top step of the pool at the same time as Calliope steps out of Matty's bungalow. She's blurry and half asleep, dressed in tiny shorts and a bikini top. The bungalow has lately been visited by an increasing number of stars and starlets all wanting a part in the movie Matty hasn't even finished writing. He's won a Best Director Oscar and probably has the credentials to get Calliope the Academy Award that she wants.

I just wish she didn't have to do an overnight audition to get it.

Calliope rubs her eyes and reaches for the cigarettes on Matty's cabana. Beside me, Adele's eyes are in danger of becoming permanently crossed with the speed at which they're changing direction. "Calliope Burns?" she says. "Oh my god, Calliope Burns!"

"Hey," Calliope says. Then she sees me and her face breaks into a smile. "Well, if it isn't my favorite person."

"Last night you said that was me," Matty grouses.

"Calliope, this is Adele Winchester." I do the introductions, but I'm distracted by the sight of two men hauling a leopard-print sofa up the long hill to bungalow four. The renovations must be going well if they're replacing the furniture already.

"Is your bungalow getting a facelift too?" I ask Matty.

"Nope. I told Win I can't move until I've made this damn movie and he told me it's just Bob's that's getting its wrinkles smoothed."

The crash of glass breaking makes us all turn.

The man on the other cabana has woken, stretched, and a highball has lost its inevitably short life in the process. Calliope grimaces when she sees him, then walks away in the direction of the main building. Not before the highball killer sees her and tries to push the half-naked girl off him.

"Another day in paradise," I say to Adele, who follows me deeper into the water, asking, "Are you friends with Calliope Burns? Really?"

"You say that like it's the equivalent of me being friends with God."

"Well, you're not exactly anyone. Although everyone here seems to know you."

"I've been around a while, that's all." I dive underwater to stop the stupid sting in my eyes. Even after all these years, I'm still just plain, nobody Aria.

When I resurface, the cabana-boy is stumbling after Calliope, the semi-naked girl falls back to sleep, and Matty keeps writing words for a story where orphans are second chances, rather than a first chance truncated.

A HOUSEMAID DELIVERS A note from Win to the pool to say that the penthouse is a chaos of staff and Adele should get ready in my room. He's sent something for her to wear.

She looks horrified. "Do you think he bought me a kid's dress?"

I refrain from telling her that she *is* a kid. "If it's hideous, you can borrow something of mine. Hopefully it won't be too short."

Like most people, Adele has at least three inches on me. But when we get to my room, there's a yellow-and-white-striped box from Giorgio Beverly Hills and inside it is a mini dress in a perfect golden-yellow color. It isn't too young nor too old, but just right.

She beams. "Maybe having a dad isn't so bad after all."

I wince. And I hope Win doesn't think that he'll break through his daughter's facade of grumpy indifference by buying her things. I really do need to talk to him tonight.

Half an hour later, Adele emerges from my bathroom in a halo of steam, eyebrows decidedly more arched than when she went in, dress on, hair pushed back off her face with a black headband. "Can I use your makeup?"

I consider. "I have some Tangee Natural and Maybelline in the top drawer. You can wear that. I need to chat to your dad about the rules."

"If you don't know, then you can't get in trouble," she wheedles.

"I told your dad I was a genius. Letting you go to a Hollywood party with a face full of makeup would prove otherwise. Besides, you're beautiful. You don't need more than lipstick and mascara."

She pouts, but sits down at the dresser. I take my turn in the bathroom, hoping that shower steam can work some kind of zoetrope miracle and make me at least average by the time I step out. If Adele or Win overhear anyone make one of those *Beauty and the Beast* comments while I'm talking to Calliope tonight, I'll lose the tentative respect Adele's granted me, and maybe my job too.

With no transformation achieved, I rummage through my clothes rack, searching for magic. I find a deep green dress with a square neckline and belted waist that Judith Crown gave me one time in lieu of babysitting money. It's very fitted, but some kind of strange evolutionary effect of the environment means I now have copybook Hollywood curves.

When I look in the mirror, my eyes are traffic-light green. Because maybe there's a part of me that wants more than I've let myself have since the night six years ago when I took my vow of hiding away as much as possible. A part of me that looks at fourteen-year-old Adele and says, *Fourteen-year-olds are meant to go to parties dressed in mini dresses and anticipation, not be investigating things that go bump in the night, then calling Doctor Foster for help.*

But wanting more is terrifying. Wanting more is why starlets are found comatose beside swimming pools.

I shut my eyes. Blink my lids open.

My eyes are still green and exhilarated.

"Let's go to a party," I say.

CHAPTER 9

...

1957

SISTER. JUMPED. ROOF. THE WORDS THAT REVEAL WHY NOBODY goes up to the turret are like quarters in a gumball machine—much too big.

"Why—" Aria starts.

A knock and the appearance of a young man carrying brown paper bags in one arm and five paper cups in the other cuts her off. Her tummy lets out a growl and she unwraps her burger only slightly faster than her friends unwrap theirs. Her eyes close as she bites into melted cheese and sweet ketchup and the delicious honesty of ground beef. When she opens her eyes, she sees that Flitter and Calliope have theirs closed too, three girls in reverent contemplation of a burger. It's the first truly golden silence Aria has ever experienced—she had too many treasures before to need to find riches in the things she took for granted.

Maybe Flitter feels it too because she says, "How about tonight we stick to the funny stories? The sad ones can wait. I'll tell you about the time someone drove a motorcycle through the lobby."

When she's done, Calliope recounts what happened when Marian Monti fell asleep with a cigarette in her hand, setting fire to her room. "She walked out saying, 'that was a little too hot to handle' and went for a swim in the pool!"

Aria giggles nervously. Fire isn't to be trusted and Marian must have the luck of all the wishing stars in the sky. Unlike Aria's parents.

Flitter puts "Heartbreak Hotel" on the turntable. "I'll teach you the bunny hop, kid," she says and soon Aria's jumping around the room next to Flitter and Calliope, and Calliope's ordering more mint juleps until she stumbles into the bathroom and Aria can hear the sound of someone being sick.

She peeps in. Calliope is on her knees in front of the toilet. Flitter is holding her hair, saying, "Let it all out, Cally-o-pee. Let it all out."

Calliope leans an elbow on the toilet seat and groans. But Calliope doesn't belong on a dirty toilet floor. So Aria finds a glass among the debris, fills it from the tap, and offers it to Calliope.

Which makes Calliope cry.

"I'm sorry!" Aria drops to her knees beside her friend.

"It's not you, kid," Flitter says. "It's just that sometimes you forget what kindness is. Here." She presses the glass into Calliope's hand. "Have one on the city."

Calliope manages a few sips of water, then crawls into bed. Less than a minute passes before Aria hears a gentle, elegant snore.

"Looks like you get both Calliope's dancing and her snoring tonight." Flitter rummages in a pile and pulls out a T-shirt. "Sleep in this. It's Calliope's. She won't mind."

The T-shirt envelops Aria in a haze of vanilla ice cream and the sachets her mother put in their bureau drawers. She presses a fistful of cotton to her nose and breathes in safety, knowing she'll hug that shirt like a teddy bear tonight and hope that, with two friends, a library, and lavender-scented cotton, she'll be okay.

She scrambles into bed beside Flitter and asks, "Is she all right?"

"Yep. She'll survive anything. She pretty much brought herself up, you know."

Flitter speaks to the ceiling, telling the kind of story Aria thought applied only to fairy-tale girls with stepmothers. "Her dad was a drunk who left her mom to manage the movie theater, so she was never home to look after Calliope. Calliope fed herself on movies and clothed herself with money she made from beauty pageants. She doesn't usually drink because of her dad and she could walk into any gangster's club on the Strip and get herself a gig as a mistress with one snap of her fingers, but she'll never do that because she wants just one dream untarnished. And you know what? She deserves to get exactly that."

Aria is silent for so long that Flitter says, a smile in her voice, "What? No questions?"

"What about you?" Aria says.

"Me? I probably grew up in a family just like yours." Flitter rolls away and the heaviness of her breath suggests she too is asleep and doesn't hear Aria whisper, "If your story's like mine, then it's a sad one too."

ARIA ISN'T SURE WHAT time Calliope wakes, just that, even though it's deep dark, she can hear people laughing as they pass through the lobby, and that the footfalls along the corridor are unsteady, accompanied by murmurs and, once, a whimper.

Aria refills the water glass for Calliope, who says, "Thank you. Sorry about before."

"You've been the nicest person of anyone to me. I don't care if you vomit all night." She tucks her head onto Calliope's shoulder and asks, unwilling to let go of the opportunity to understand the woman beside her who is, she sees now, part-unicorn, part-tragedy, "Why do you want to be an actress?"

Calliope smiles. "Come with me."

Aria pulls on a too-long pair of pajama pants, then follows Calliope to the elevator.

"Would you mind setting up the screening room for us?" Calliope asks Isaiah.

"Not a bit, Miss Calliope," he says.

So Aria finds herself in a room at the end of the first-floor corridor where there's a movie screen. Isaiah hefts a spool of film onto a projector. "How about *Fresh Faced*?"

"Perfect." Calliope sits in one of the chairs, as does Aria, while a girl in a bookshop appears on-screen.

As the girl walks across the wooden floor of the bookshop, Calliope says, "Hear her footsteps? That sound is made at a Foley studio. They have things called Foley pits, which are all different floor types—marble, gravel, concrete—and a sound artist walks on them in time to a sequence of film. What you hear in a movie is the sound of someone fake-walking on a fake floor. The real sounds recorded when they're filming are too dull. Everything in a movie needs to be bigger, more magnificent. Look, now she's pulling a book off the shelf. I bet they made that sound by sliding cellophane out of an envelope right next to the microphone. Walnuts are ice cubes clattering in a glass, frozen lettuce snaps like a broken bone; frying bacon is the rain. It's magic."

The room they're in is lit only by the screen and Calliope's words. It's dark but not scary, like a winter's night in front of a wood fire whose flames transform into fantastical shapes before your eyes.

"What else?" Aria asks.

"The movie studios have jungles on their lots, Aria, and lakes. There's one soundstage they can fill with two million gallons of water to make oceans swell. Can you imagine? And see—they're in Paris, aren't they?"

Aria nods because an airplane has just flown over the Eiffel Tower and a man and the girl with the big round eyes are walking over lamplit cobblestones with delicate lace buildings behind them.

"What if I told you they were just down the road? On another soundstage. That the buildings are made of cardboard. None of it's real. But we all believe that it is. Watch this." Calliope jumps up and selects, from all the movie paraphernalia on the shelves lining the room, a circular object on a base, like a lamp. Inside is a series of pictures of a horse, its head and legs in all the various stages of a gallop. Calliope sets the object spinning and at first there's nothing to see except the separate pictures of the horse going around and around. But as the cylinder hits a certain speed, it transforms. Now Aria is watching a horse flying along, its neck stretching out, its legs extending then regrouping, extending and regrouping.

She gasps and says delightedly, "Look!"

"It's called a zoetrope. More magic. Don't you see," Calliope says as the cylinder slows and the horse stops galloping and the wizardry ends, "if I'm an actress, I'm making magic every day. Who else in the world gets to do that?"

When the movie ends, Aria feels bereft. Wants to stay in that room where the magic lives. But she's yawning and sleepy, so she follows Calliope back out into the corridor, where they pass two men. One is Bob, who nods and says, "Calliope. Aria," and Aria is so surprised that he knows her name that she almost misses the hiss of his companion's voice.

"Jeez, talk about beauty and the beast. Are they letting anyone in the doors now?"

She freezes.

Her hands, the only things she has to hide behind, creep up to her face. She bites down hard on her fingernails, tears off a piece. Why did she leave the screening room? Why didn't she stay in the place where stilled horses could gallop and where Paris wasn't across an ocean, but a mile or so down the road? Where, if she surrounded herself with enough magic, it might transform her into something better too?

Before she can flee, Bob says, "That's Miss Devine Rey's orphaned niece. Be kind."

The men continue on. Aria still can't move. Did the King of Hollywood just defend plain, beastly Aria?

Calliope squeezes her hand. "That's why we'd all give anything to work for Bob. And don't listen to idiots who know nothing. You *are* beautiful, Aria. One day you'll see it."

Aria shakes her head vehemently. No magic can achieve a transformation that big.

"Let me tell you something," Calliope says once they're behind the closed door of her room. "I don't just want to be an actress." Her face transforms under the light of the lamp, her eyes ferocious—frightening even—her jaw a sharp line of bone. "I want to be famous. And I want you to want something big too, no matter who tries to convince you that you can't. Because why live if you die unremembered? Why get up in the morning if you make no difference at all to the world? Your parents, Aria, when you're gone, who'll know their names? Nobody. Just like if I die right now, this room will be given to some other girl who'll put her own sheets on the bed and her own perfume in the air. She'll go to auditions and she'll either get the part or most likely not, and to think of how meaningless it might be, this one life I've been given, makes me want to throw myself from the turret too—get it done right now so I don't have to watch myself vanish into nothing. Name one famous woman, Aria. Someone who isn't just a name. Someone who has a face you can picture—a whole woman with a name and a face and a body and a legacy and a legend."

Aria discards Jane Austen because she can't picture her beyond a cameo silhouette; discards Florence Nightingale for similar reasons—she's even less than a silhouette. Cleopatra is just a head with black hair, bodiless. "I can't."

"Exactly." Calliope sits on the bed, pulls her knees in to her chest and hugs them tightly, the way Aria's mother used to hold on to her. "A handful of women get to be a name. But almost no woman gets to be an entire remembered *person*."

Aria suddenly feels the injustice of this, how cruel the future is likely to be to the three girls in this room just because they're girls. She shakes an imaginary fist at the world.

"You know what else?" Calliope says, still ferocious. "Onscreen, I get to have a different story from the one I was born with. Being famous is how I'll show all the other small girls with drunk fathers and careless mothers that you *can* be something else entirely—and be loved by everyone as well."

It's like watching Scarlett O'Hara declare, *As God is my witness, I'll never be hungry again*. A moment Aria will remember forever.

Calliope's dreams are enormous, like a double-bed sheet Aria's arm span isn't long enough to grasp. But these dreams are also necessary. Otherwise all Aria and Calliope have is a bed that isn't big enough for three in a room where you can't even open the door properly, deep inside a castle where people jump from the turrets.

Calliope lets go of her knees and smiles at last. "That word we use for Hollywood's leading ladies is the metaphor for what I want to be. A star, hung forever sparkling for all the world to see."

BESIDE THEM, FLITTER STIRS. "Why is everyone awake at . . ." She peers at the clock. "Three in the morning."

"We're talking about dreams," Aria says. Then she tries out a joke. "It's always better to do that at night."

Calliope and Flitter laugh and some of the sting of being called a beast dissipates.

"So, what's yours?" Flitter asks, sitting up now too.

How she wishes she could want something enormous, something that would please Calliope. But the only thing Aria really wants is tiny—yet also impossible. She wants to walk in the door of the apartment on West End Avenue in New York City, drop her schoolbag on the floor, and have her mother pop her head out from the kitchen and say, *Aria! I made peanut butter cookies. Want one?* Her dad would be in the kitchen too and they'd drink milk and eat cookies and Aria's heart would fill up from all the love she hadn't known hung in the air of their home. She wants to go back there and grab great big fistfuls, stuff them into all the empty places inside her.

"I want to live in a house by the sea," she says fiercely so that she won't cry. "My parents always said they'd take me to see a proper beach, like in Hawaii, but . . ."

They died.

All Aria has left of that promise is a photo of her parents on their honeymoon in Honolulu, a wave curving up behind them like the water that came too late to save them from fire.

"I want to keep their promise for them," she says despairingly. "So they're not quite gone, not yet. Most of all"—she brushes away the tears she's powerless to stop from falling—"I want to never feel like I do right now with no money and no home and no . . . no . . ."

"No power," Flitter says, and Aria nods because that's it exactly.

"That's *my* dream," Flitter goes on. "I want power. Then nobody can ever hurt you."

Perhaps that's true. But thirteen-year-old orphans can hardly aspire to power. "I need to earn some money," Aria says. "I can't leave here without money."

"And I need a part in a movie," Calliope says. "I can't be famous if I've never had a starring role."

"No amount of fame or money matters without power," Flitter insists.

Maybe that idea depresses Calliope as much as it depresses Aria because Calliope just says, "God, I think I'm still breathing bourbon. Hope I'm not suffocating you both."

She exhales like a dragon all over them, making Aria squeal. Then she lies on her back, legs draped over Aria's and Flitter's laps like they're a new kind of geometric shape, and Aria uses every ounce of her courage to say, because she wants to formalize this arrangement in the way a family is fixed and permanent, "We need a name. Like The Three Stooges. But better."

Flitter wrinkles her nose. "That stuff's for kids."

"Haven't you always wanted to be part of a gang?" Calliope wheedles. "Not the Three Little Pigs though."

"The Three-Ring Circus," Flitter snorts.

Suddenly Aria knows exactly what they are. "The Three Sisters," she declares.

Sisters are forevermore. They're Jo March pulling Amy from the ice; they're Elizabeth Bennett soothing Jane's broken heart.

"The Three Sisters," Flitter whispers.

The subsequent silence holds within it the flutter of eyelids closed to keep the tears from falling out. Aria can feel it, their history being written, Chapter One of the stories all sisters have so they can say, *remember when,* and the phrase is like the magic word that opens caves and hearts and entire worlds.

Then Calliope asks Aria, "Won't you get lonely, living at the beach all by yourself?"

"If I'm by myself, no one can ever hurt me again."

Calliope touches her cheek. "But no one can ever love you either."

Not long after, they fall asleep. And none of the three girls crammed onto the bed knows that the wishes they've chosen are probably the things that will hurt them the most, in the end.

CHAPTER 10

...

1964

WE ARRIVE AT THE PENTHOUSE, WHERE ADELE AND I SQUEEZE past the unknowns, then proceed along the hallway where those with either more balls or sharper elbows have reached. Lacey Magee, the woman I met on my first day at the Marmont, is among them. While she definitely has the balls, she doesn't have the face—the camera doesn't adore her the way it does Calliope. Her beehive is more of an ant nest now—small, crumbling—but she's still here, a resilience that's either admirable or sad. I turn my attention away from her before I start applying that same thinking to myself.

Besides, there are so many other things to look at.

The living room holds more stars than a night at the Oscars. As Flitter explained to me a few days after I arrived at the Marmont, the Beverly Wilshire is for people who *think* they matter, but the Chateau Marmont is where the scripts are written and the deals are done—it's where the people who really *do* matter live. There's Judith Crown in red sequins, Augusta Hepworth in white silk and pearls. Peter Oldham elegant in a tux.

Adele's head spins like a zoetrope and I smile because—wow. I forget sometimes that these people are beloved, that for so many Americans, what I have right now is an experience they would die for. Judith waves at me, Augusta too, and Adele gapes like she did in the pool.

I lead us deeper into the penthouse, where a bowl of raspberry punch is being debauched with vodka, and three guitars on stands now adorn the living room, as does a curved aqua velvet sofa. An array of gold, silver, and platinum albums hangs in frames on the walls.

Win's been redecorating.

I take Adele onto the balcony, which is even busier than the living room. Win's head stands taller than the rest, dark and a little shaggy. Beside him is a natural blonde I'd recognize anywhere, as well as one that's come from a peroxide bottle. Flitter is back!

Luckily Adele is making her way to her father so I can throw my arms around Flitter, who throws her arms around me too.

"The Three Sisters reunited." Calliope grins.

"Look at you, kid." Flitter runs her eyes over my dress. "You scrub up all right. Must be all the lessons we gave you."

Beside her, Calliope looks nothing like the pale woman who emerged from a bungalow not her own this morning. Every eye is drawn her way, to the hair that falls in its natural wave down her spine, to the U-shaped cutout at the back of her dress where skin beckons. Those who've yet to make it in Hollywood gawp from a respectful distance while those who've shared a screen with her trail their fingers over her back.

While Adele is talking to her father, I say to Flitter, "I thought you were out in the desert being an alien."

"And I thought you didn't go to parties," Flitter returns.

"I'm a nanny." I indicate Adele. "But why are you back from the shoot already?"

Flitter looks at Calliope. Calliope looks at Flitter.

"Bronte Bros. dropped me," Flitter elaborates, hand on her hip, head in the air. "So I'm here to audition for the movie Matty's making."

I try not to let my mouth fall open. After Calliope's dream tarnished but her star began to shine, Bronte Bros., Calliope's studio, gave Flitter a contract. But having got the contract she wanted, Flitter stopped going for the big parts, instead trying out for not even the sidekick parts, but the sidekick's younger sister, thus doubling her success at something she never wanted and ceasing to fail at the only thing she hoped for.

But now she's going up against Calliope.

Calliope squeezes her friend's hand. "We always used to go to the same auditions."

"Not all of them," Flitter says under her breath.

My hand is arrested in the act of reaching out for Adele, whose father's been dragged away and who looks like she's about to slink off into the crowd.

Flitter just mentioned the unmentionable.

Calliope doesn't seem to have heard. In order to keep the past shoved deep down beneath our collective heartache, I grab Adele with one hand and with the other, I raise the soda I've chosen in deference to my legal drinking age and the fact that I'm working. "Let's toast. To—"

Calliope grins. "To all the wives who'd be mad at me if I ever wrote a memoir."

Flitter cackles. Adele's eyes pop and I assure her, "She's kidding."

I hope she is.

Flitter points in Win's direction and says, "*Sooooo,* hot voice and cool lips. Or maybe it's the other way around?" She smirks. "Give me the lowdown."

"*Ewwww,*" Adele wrinkles up her entire face.

"This," I tell Flitter, "is Adele Winchester."

"Ah, *you're* the orphan he inherited."

Not for the first time, I wish Flitter wasn't quite so *Flitter.*

With impeccable timing, Win beckons his daughter over and Flitter whispers, "Did you know he's left a trail of dead women in his wake?"

Calliope leans in and, I hate to admit it, so do I. Flitter's always been good at stories.

"Win loves to fall in love." Flitter's arms extend as she delivers the part-scandal, part-truth, good-time-gal soliloquy that she thinks makes everyone like her. "And he loves to get married. In Vegas. His first Vegas wife died of an overdose. His second fell off a balcony. Last year, he cheated on another Vegas wife, who got her revenge by OD'ing in his arms."

Now I feel icky. On the other side of Flitter's story are ruined lives and a girl named Adele.

"But he went to rehab a year ago and now he's sober as a corpse," Flitter continues. "Perhaps the trail of dead wives will end here. I mean, can you imagine being the wife of the owner of the Chateau Marmont? Now *that* would give me power."

"Power that isn't really your own," I say.

I've never thought Flitter was the kind to marry her way into what she wanted. But look at how many tarnished dreams there are in this room. Lacey Magee is just the most obvious—leave anything out in the sun too long and it rusts.

I study my friend, who's as beautiful now as her features always hinted she would be. Not as beautiful as Calliope—that's beyond any mortal—but six months in the desert have made Flitter tan and glowing, brittle too, like she had too much sun and not enough water.

"Power is power, Aria," she says.

We're interrupted by the man who was sleeping in the cabana this morning. He slides his arm around Calliope's waist and she kisses him the way Calliope Burns would, eyes closed, one hand limp at her side from the sheer, overwhelming passion of it all. When she's finished she says to us, "This is Brian. My beau. Brian, this is Aria Jones."

Brian scrutinizes my dimensions like I'm a piece of furniture he isn't sure will fit into a tight space in his apartment. "Never heard of her," he says.

"Thank god," Calliope and I say in unison, laughing, and in my friend's eyes I can still see the girl of seven summers ago.

That should be enough to make me stop. But last I heard, beaux don't wake up in cabana chairs with someone else's naked breasts on them.

"I saw you at the pool this morning," I say to Brian.

"So did I, Aria," Calliope says brusquely. "Don't be boring."

For the first time ever, I think, *Don't become mean, Calliope.*

"Do you think there's any chance they'll go home together tonight?" Flitter says as the couple go off in search of a drink.

"I read about Calliope and Brian in *Seventeen,*" Adele breaks in, having just been deposited back in our midst by her father. "They seemed like the real thing."

I eyeball Flitter, who's probably about to tell Adele that nothing is real, and ask Adele, "Ready for bed?"

She stares at me as if I just asked her to go to Wyoming.

But there are lines of white powder being cut along the edge of the balcony.

Right then, the most spine-chilling scream I've ever heard shatters the revelry. Glasses slip from hands and smash onto the floor. Every other sound is silenced, except for the turntable, which is singing about a purple people eater coming down from out of the sky.

The Santa Anas barrel in and the palm trees bend like whips. White powder flies off the balustrade and into the air.

"Sniff if you're down below!" Flitter shouts.

Everyone laughs hysterically.

It's like the scream never happened.

But then I remember my aunt, who I forgot to check on this afternoon.

"MOVE," I SNAP AT the group in front of me.

They jump aside, startled to see a short green fury bearing down. I take the stairs to the fifth floor, open my aunt's door, and

I'm assaulted by the usual smell: perfume and sweat. Gin. Tarnished dreams.

"Miss Devine?" I call. It's so dark tonight, like the moon is afraid of October and has left the stars to do their pitiful best.

The curtains bulge.

I clutch the back of the sofa, try to make myself believe that it was just the wind.

Suddenly all the lights snap on.

"Jesus Holy Christ!" I shriek, slamming my eyelids shut, grabbing blindly for holy water I can throw at a ghost. When I think I can see again, I open my eyes.

Standing in the doorway is Theo Winchester.

"Would you like to climb up and remove the half of me that's stuck to the ceiling?" I ask coolly, before moving to shield my aunt from view. Having my employer see the ruined woman on the sofa that I've persuaded him to give a room to isn't my idea of a good night.

It occurs to me that the curse I hurled at my aunt seven years ago has just come true. Miss Devine Rey might be clothed, but if she had any idea that someone else could see her in her mucky stupor, she'd feel as if the whole world was laughing at her.

Hot shame crawls over my face.

After a beat, Win says, "I'm checking the rooms." He indicates Miss Devine Rey. "Is she all right?"

My tone turns from cool to icy. "I'm sure you've seen enough addicts to know that she's not all right, but is nevertheless alive."

I shouldn't talk to my boss like this. But I need him to leave. "We're fine, thank you."

Unexpectedly, he walks over to my aunt. He lifts her up as gently as if she were a baby, shifting her position so she's properly on her side and in no danger of tipping onto her back. Then he smooths her hair off her brow.

I remember his dead wives. He's done this numberless times before.

"Thank you," I say. This time I mean it.

He casts his eye around the room and I see it the way he must. The pictures on the walls of Miss Devine, so like the trophy albums that hang on his walls. The scar of red lipstick and saliva across her cheek.

"Adele wanted to say goodnight to you." His voice, prosaic and present in this mausoleum of the past, breaks in.

"She's forgiven me for telling her it was time for bed?" I joke, trying to behave like a governess, rather than the niece of a disaster.

"She has so few people left in her life that I think she'd forgive you just about anything."

God, there are tears in my eyes. I remember fifteen-year-old Aria accepting that the person sleeping on the sofa was who she'd been left with, so she'd have to make the best of it. I want at least one girl who passes through the Marmont to see those around her as the people she chose, rather than the ones she had to accept.

"Did you check the bungalows?" I ask, channeling professionalism rather than pitifulness.

He nods. "Nothing. It was probably just a thing that went bump in the night."

And I swear I hear the Marmont's pipes hiss, *Don't be so sure about that.*

CHAPTER II

...

1957

AFTER THEY SHARE THEIR DREAMS, CALLIOPE AND FLITTER fall asleep. Aria doesn't. What Calliope said about her parents being forgotten—as if there's another death waiting that's worse than what they've already suffered—haunts her. Miss Devine Rey is the only person in California who knew Aria's parents too—Aria's dad was her brother. If Aria frames a conversation with her aunt just right—perhaps over breakfast tomorrow—then maybe she'll get the chance she craves: to bring her parents back to life for just an hour or two.

She decides to go back to her aunt's suite. Isaiah isn't waiting by the elevators, so she has to close the metal grille herself. She thinks she gets out on the right floor, but the corridors are so dimly lit it's hard to tell. The carpet looks redder here, like the snakes are bleeding. There's something with too many arms lurking in the shadows. She backs away, can't find the elevator, must have taken a wrong turn; thinks she's finally found her aunt's room, but when she opens the door, there's no aunt inside.

There's a ghost.

White face, white hand hanging as limply as the silk sheets over the bed. A tube in its mouth and another in its nose. A man wearing a doctor's coat is pulling back the plunger of a syringe connected to the tube as if he's extracting the ghost's soul.

Aria whirls around, knows she has to get out before the man takes her soul too.

She charges into the corridor where a wall opens up and a

woman in a housemaid's uniform steps out. Aria plunges into the opening, finds a stairwell that's so dark she wants to escape. She pushes open a different door only to discover that the ghost is heading straight for her. In the second before she faints, Aria realizes it's just a sheet hiding a woman as if she's a dirty little secret.

ARIA ROUSES, FEAR CRAWLING over her scalp like lice. Even though the sheeted woman appears to be gone, she prays for the Marmont to swallow her up, prays so hard she doesn't see Bob Ashenhurst coming up behind her, carrying a sleeping woman in his arms as if he's Prince Charming doing a bit of maiden-saving at midnight.

Bob doesn't see Aria either, not until he trips over her and drops the woman on the ground. The woman blinks awake.

Aria looks from her to Bob, expects him to ask both the woman and Aria if they're okay. But as the woman comes to properly and she sees Bob, she scrambles away. The look in her eyes—it's like she thinks he's a wolf about to eat her.

She lunges over to Aria, grabs her wrist and Aria is almost certain that she says, in a tiny desperate voice, "Help."

Somehow, Aria leaves her body. She can see herself sitting in the hallway, mouth stretched open, a scream coming out of her louder than any sound she's ever made, so loud that people open their doors and peer out. Her scream stops abruptly when a man wearing an expressionless face and a black suit materializes in front of her.

"Miss Jones," he says. "We haven't been introduced. I'm Mr. Mason, the hotel manager. I'll be sure to have a word to your aunt about your sleepwalking. You should go back to your room immediately."

Aria blinks. "I wasn't . . ." *Wasn't sleepwalking,* she wants to say. But when she looks around, there's nobody in the corridor except her and Mr. Mason. Where did Bob go? Where did the woman go? Is Aria even awake?

She does what characters in books do—pinches herself, and it hurts. She isn't dreaming, not now. Maybe she did sleepwalk. There's no other rational explanation.

When she blinks a second time, the man from the ghost-woman's room is standing in front of her. At least he's real. But was the ghost real?

Of course not. Maybe nothing else was real either.

Aria feels so silly now at four in the morning, standing in a hotel corridor having conjured up ghosts and roused so many people. She remembers her aunt saying to her, *You will be discreet at all times* and she knows she's just been anything but discreet.

Before the sick feeling in her stomach can return, the man says to her, "I'm Doctor Foster. Mr. Mason sent me," and his tone is so much like a warm blanket that every muscle Aria didn't know she'd been holding cramped tight since that awful night in New York releases just a little. "I'll take you back to your aunt's room," he says.

He slips into one of those secret doors in the wall that, moments ago, Aria had wished would open. Now it does, letting her in. It's all so easy and calm and not scary at all. She *must* have sleepwalked and dreamed everything.

The doctor takes out a key and lets them into Room 53.

Inside, Miss Devine Rey is sitting in a chair, weeping. When she sees Aria, she swipes her arm across the table and a glass and a bottle break apart on the floor, glittering like her aunt's tears.

"By god," her aunt roars, "has no one told you not to sneak around at night? There might be no consequences out there"—she waves her arm toward the hallways and another bottle shatters—"but there are more consequences than you could possibly bear in here." She bangs her palms against her head, terrifying, incomprehensible, monstrous.

Fainting, screaming—Aria has done both tonight. Now she

stares mutely while the doctor walks over to Miss Devine Rey and holds her tight, like he is safety and she can drop right into him. Her aunt quiets, her eyes close and she looks far from terrifying—she looks almost as if she's dead.

"Can I go back to Flitter and Calliope's room?" Aria whispers to the doctor.

"That's a good idea. I'll walk you down."

Back in the secret stairway, Doctor Foster says to her, "Would it help if I told you that you saw a woman in a wheelchair earlier, not a ghost? She's in the hospital now and will be fine by morning."

No ghost. But Doctor Foster's words mean she *did* see at least one woman. How can that have been real, but not Bob and the woman he was carrying? Maybe it's just more of that magic Calliope showed her. Maybe everything in Hollywood is an illusion.

And Doctor Foster is the most sensible person she's met so far. His words are soothing, so she fixes on them.

"I'll give your aunt a prescription of things you need. Bus fare so you can get out of here from time to time. Some paper and a pen," he muses. "Then you can give all the things you want to forget to a journal instead of carrying them around with you."

Get out of here. Get out of here. Those words remind Aria of the promise she'd made to herself. And an eerie but practical voice whispers from the cracks in the plaster—pockets full of tissues and candy, both in used condition, will not feed or clothe or house her. If she's to leave, she has to have money.

But what can a beastly not-quite-fourteen-year-old do to earn enough to survive in this world?

ARIA'S SOON FAST ASLEEP. But the night isn't over, not for the chateau. It has work to do.

It makes sure Doctor Foster remembers that on Marian Monti's desk is a stack of white paper. It's monogrammed with her name, but that's no matter.

The Marmont shakes its right arm so the lock to her room unclasps, letting the doctor inside where he can gather up the paper and leave it in Aria's bedroom. The Marmont knows that only when you write things down does anyone believe they really happened. Otherwise, all you have for evidence is your word and your memory—and when you're a girl, they say your word is a lie and your memory a tall story.

In Aria's story, the Marmont knows, she'll either get the world she gives in to or the world she fights for. The Marmont can't see how it will end, just the two paths ahead and the moments that will turn Aria toward one or the other. But if she writes everything down, then maybe at the most critical moment, this record of her history will help her to choose the right path.

Meddling done, the Marmont settles itself into its yellowing foundation stones for the night like an elegant drunk. Or a mischievous drunk perhaps—because it depends on which you think is the right path for Aria Jones.

CHAPTER 12

...

1964

AFTER I'VE SAID GOODNIGHT TO ADELE, I GO BACK TO THE party.

Perhaps the scream frightened the unfrightenable—the crowd's thinned by the time I slip back in. Everyone has distributed themselves into circles. Bob's is large, but Calliope's is the biggest. Bob will have noticed. Calliope will have too.

Flitter is stuck in Bob's circle among the starlets who stare up at him with adoring eyes. "We're holding auditions for extras for *Jane Eyre* next month," he says to them. "Tell the casting director I sent you. That'll get you to the top of the list."

"Thank you," they gush at this extraordinary kindness.

I escape to the balcony with a splash of rum and soda in a glass. The night is eerily still—probably the scream came from farther away and the sound carried here on the wind that had whipped up earlier. I stare up at the sky, but Los Angeles is too bright to let anything shine up there and I wish that it wasn't—until I remember that I no longer wish upon stars.

I sink into an unoccupied couch, sip, feel the rum slide down my throat.

"Are you breaking the law?"

My head snaps to the right. Theo Winchester, twice in one night.

He takes the seat beside me and indicates my drink.

"Yes," I tell him, taking a much larger sip than before.

He lifts one of those melodramatic eyebrows. "Most paid employees would lie."

"Speaking of pay"—perhaps it's the rum talking, or that scream has made me reckless too—"when will I be paid?"

"No chitchat in deference to the party?"

"Only those with substantial bank accounts can afford not to take the opportunity to clarify the most important terms of their employment."

A wry smile settles onto his face. "I was falling asleep inside. But there's no danger of that out here. Is every conversation a boxing match with you, Aria?"

"If boxing doesn't suit, we could try jousting. But I've never learned to ride a horse."

He laughs, and his face relaxes, arranging itself closer to beauty. I can almost see what Calliope and Flitter mean. Tonight he's wearing his signature dark jeans and a dark navy shirt. But his buttons and the buttonholes don't seem to be getting along. And from what I can see of Win's chest, it's—

Irrelevant. I fix my eyes on the city lights.

Win clears his throat. "I need to explain a couple of things about Adele."

He shifts to the edge of the couch, leaning so far forward it's like he's about to run away and says, "It's true what they say—I don't know if I'm Adele's father. I dated her mother back when I was seventeen and just starting out and I thought variety was the thing worth chasing, rather than those rare moments when absolutely nothing changes. I didn't know she'd had a kid." He curses. "Imagine being the kid left with someone you might not even be related to? My single goal is not to screw her up any more than she already is. Given I'm descended from a long line of screwups, that's probably beyond me."

He looks at me over his shoulder, smile mocking his partially spilled guts. "Don't feel too sorry for me, Aria."

"I don't," I tell him. "Anyone who can afford to buy a hotel while I earn fifty dollars a week is beyond my compassion."

He laughs again, then shifts back against the cushions, sinking into the act of sitting as if he might stay here for a minute or two.

"Maybe you've heard some of my history," he says, attention focused on lighting a cigarette for himself and one for me too.

I accept—this is definitely a smoking conversation—then say, "I heard you've left a trail of dead wives in your wake."

He winces. "Thanks for the brutal honesty."

"You would've hated it if I'd lied."

He tosses his hardly smoked cigarette on the floor, grinds it out with his foot. "Well, here's the real version, not the gossip. I married my first wife, Honey, in Vegas to escape the Korean War draft. I'm not blind to the irony of being the man who married to save his own life, but whose wife died instead—of an overdose. What else do the wives of alcoholic rock singers die of? And if you think I learned from that, you'll be disappointed to hear that I married my second wife, Joanie, in Vegas too. Vegas plus an alcoholic equals a very bad decision. She died in a car wreck. Ran off the road while she was drunk."

His voice is flat. But he shrugs like Adele. "I've been sober for six months, so there should be no more Vegas wives."

"How did you end up buying the Marmont?" I ask, sensing he needs a break from talking about dead wives and bad decisions.

Win reaches over to steal the last of my cigarette. I hand it over, then cross to the balustrade and lean my back against it so we don't have to keep turning our heads.

"My father was a studio musician for Millennium Wolf. He had a share in the Chateau Marmont. It was family legend that he won it in a poker game. He died of pancreatic cancer a year ago and the share passed to me. After rehab, I didn't want to rush straight back into making an album and heading out on tour. So I decided it was better to own the whole of something than just a part. The Marmont's reputation for being the place where you go to *not* be seen was what I wanted."

"That is a story that could only be told in Hollywood. Most people buy a Ferrari to fix their midlife crisis, not an entire hotel."

Another surprised bark of laughter. "Jesus, how old do you think I am?"

I grin. "Win, answering that question is bound to cause offense. Twenty-year-olds and movie stars think anyone over twenty-five is old."

"I'm thirty, so by your miserable calculations, I'll soon need a walking stick to carry the weight of my midlife crisis on my hunched back."

I laugh. Across from me, he props his elbows on his knees. He looks like he's in a photo shoot and the photographer has just told him to press all the camera's buttons.

Hot lips indeed.

My stomach clenches for the first time ever.

God, how much rum did I put in my glass?

"Don't call me Win," he says. "Win is a name girls shout at concerts. Win is definitely an alcoholic. Win is also a serial Vegas husband. I'd rather just be Theo."

His words remind me of what I am—not the kind of girl he wants shouting his name in lust. This camaraderie we occasionally fall into is situational—like when I met Flitter and Calliope and we all desperately needed something so we glued ourselves to one another like Band-Aids. Theo's desperate for a solution to his situation with Adele, and I need money. We each know what the other wants and we aren't playing games.

Well, I don't *think* we are.

I turn over what he said. I know how Adele feels—going to sleep every night in the possession of someone who owns you but doesn't love you. Perhaps Theo *will* love her one day though. That's where Adele and I are different.

And that's why I've always wanted to leave—so I won't ever be owned again by someone who doesn't love me.

I want to own myself.

But my goal tonight is to help Theo understand Adele. He's got a lot on his plate—sobriety, a shitty past—but that doesn't excuse him from being a shitty dad.

"Why did Adele get expelled?" I ask, remembering what Calliope told me. Remembering too the girl creeping down the driveway at three in the morning.

Theo joins me at the balustrade, draping his forearms over it and looking out at the glitter. "You know how high schools have mascots like bears and tigers?"

"I didn't go to high school."

"Bullshit."

"It's probably better if you think that. Then you won't fire me."

I'm so good at light and breezy. It's the constant pitch of the Marmont—everyone's so breezy, it's a wonder we don't all just blow away.

Theo rubs his hand over his face and curses.

"If you want to employ someone who graduated from the same school that expelled Adele, that's your choice," I say evenly. "But I don't think it would be a very good one."

He straightens up and faces me. "You're not afraid of giving your opinion, are you? Are you so sure I won't fire you?"

"Are you so sure you'd prefer someone who'd been to high school, but who lied about everything else?"

I turn to face him too. "This is the place where everyone lives lies, not lives. We want everything costumed and scripted and edited, and just one tear falling down a cheek so it's artistic rather than painful. Go ahead, fire me for being real. For being afraid of lots of things except my own opinions. But in my opinion, I should teach Adele to look at this world through her own particular eyes—and then she can decide whether she wants to be a part of it or not. If she goes to Paris instead, she'll know enough to order a coffee and write not-half-bad poetry in a cafe she can find her own way to. She can look for real happiness, rather than think that happiness is pretending to be someone you aren't on a screen."

Theo exhales. Then he says, eyes two pins fixing me to the spot, "Why are you here, Aria Jones?"

I fix my attention on the revelry inside, watching the tight smile Flitter gives Bob, the Hollywood smile Calliope bestows on a man who isn't her beau, the look he gives Calliope, like she really is Lulu Limana, the femme fatale from her latest film.

The man slips his arm around Calliope's waist.

"You were telling me about Adele," I say.

Silence.

Theo takes out another cigarette. Then he says grimly, "The mascot for Hollywood High isn't anything real, like an animal. It's the sheik from the 1920s Rudolph Valentino movie. A year ago I would have thought that was funny. But Adele grew up in Bowling Green, Kentucky. On her first day at Hollywood High, she walked out the door in her Bowling Green clothes and her Bowling Green shoes and her brown hair and I didn't think about the fact that Hollywood High has genetically self-selected to have only blond students who are as entranced with movies as everyone here."

He tosses back water like he wishes it was wine. "Adele turned into an expert petty thief to update her wardrobe. One night, she went to a party, which she left in a car with a boy four years older than her—Christ, he was eighteen, just a couple of years younger than you. He crashed the car and she spent the night in the hospital, just about throwing up the lining of her stomach because she'd drunk too much and taken something else. I still don't know what she did with that boy, but I do know that I never want to sit by her bed in a hospital again."

Holy shit.

I've trusted the word of a thief and a drunk who told me she wasn't doing anything illegal out on the streets of LA after midnight.

I sit back down on the couch.

Theo's going to fire me if I tell him. He'll also fire me if I don't and he finds out.

My only option is to hope the Marmont keeps this secret buried as deep as the rest.

Maybe I'm too trusting, but I don't think Adele's a delinquent—she's a girl who wants her mother. And Theo's a man who *does* love his daughter—but he has no idea how to express it.

I look across at him. *A man who celebrates midnights* is what I thought when I first met him. And yes, out here, he's a pitch-dark slice of night with two black stars for eyes and, oh boy—do I want to wish upon them.

Neither of us speak. Until Theo says in a cadence I haven't heard him use before, "Don't feel too sorry for me, Aria."

"There they are!"

My curse is only slightly less worse than Theo's, and I'm not sure if I'm only cursing because I got a fright, or because the riot of giggling announcing the arrival of Flitter and Calliope has interrupted . . . something. Or nothing, most likely, besides my imagination.

Flitter drapes herself on the couch, pats the space beside her, and coos, "We initiated Aria into the ways of the Marmont seven years ago, now it's time to initiate you, Win."

"I don't know whether that's an invitation or an explanation," Theo says and it's so smooth, that transition, just like Calliope has always been able to do—metamorphose from human to god with just one breath.

In the candlelight, lounging on the couch, cigarette in one hand, charisma in the other, he looks like he could write you a song that'd make your insides burn. And for one second, I imagine how it would feel to step into a fire rather than running to the nearest hose.

Flitter's voice cuts into my wayward thoughts, giving Win a précis of the guests. "That"—she points to a man who has one arm around a man and the other around a woman—"is Duke Graham. He'd thank cocaine in his Oscar's acceptance speech and it wouldn't be ironic. And that"—her sharp finger moves to a weeping woman—"is Pattie Carpenter. Her husband kicked her out, but she bears her crosses on the Chanel-padded shoulders of the gowns her lover gave her. Both her husband and her lover have slipped into the powder room with Nancy Nunn, who writes so-called novels about her life. She's the kind of gal who'd thank both her gynecologist and her priest in her book's dedication, just so you'd wonder . . ." Her hand rests on Win's forearm. She looks good there.

Powerful.

I slip away, take the elevator down to the first floor.

"No stairs tonight?" Isaiah asks me.

"My feet are sore."

"Sore feet, sore heart is what they say."

"Nobody says that," I call, but the elevator is already creaking away.

CHAPTER 13

...

1957

WHEN ARIA CREEPS INTO HER AUNT'S SUITE THE MORNING after her sleepover, she finds the pen and paper Doctor Foster left for her. She runs a fingertip over the supreme elegance of Marian Monti's monogrammed stationery.

One week ago, she could never have imagined she'd be holding in her ordinary hand the personalized stationery of the most famous actress in the country. She feels a thrill—is this how it starts? One piece of star-monogrammed letterhead and soon only immortality will satisfy you.

She picks up the pen. Soon she's written down everything that's happened since she arrived, is so engrossed she hardly hears the knock on the suite door or her aunt's voice.

Then her bedroom door opens.

No *good morning,* from her aunt. Just the pronouncement, "That was Mr. Mason."

The hotel manager from last night.

"I was sleepwalking," Aria tells her aunt.

"You woke an entire floor." Miss Devine Rey's enunciation is filmic, her gestures timed to emphasize *you* and *entire.* "Mr. Mason has had no choice but to give you a warning. Discretion is what I asked for. Screaming is the opposite of discreet."

"I thought I saw a ghost . . ." Aria tries to explain that before last night, stomach-pumping was as alien a concept as women jumping from turrets. But her aunt interrupts.

"Get used to that." Miss Devine wraps her hands around Aria's wrists. "We have no more warnings left. If you put another foot wrong, we'll both be out on the street, where you really will learn how to scream. Today's lesson is to learn to wear an actress's face while you walk on by all the things that scare you."

For the first time since Aria arrived, her aunt has bent down to her eye level. And in Miss Devine's eyes she sees a soul that isn't cruel or terrible, but afraid.

And of everything, *that* is the most terrifying thing she's seen since she arrived.

ARIA'S STILL IN HER library at seven that night because inside the volumes of encyclopedias, she can skip over the things that scare her, can turn the page and the Great Fire of London is replaced by Lady Godiva. The "Naval Observatory to Orleans" volume even has a whole page of optical illusions, and the "Silk, Artificial to Sulphovinic Acid" volume teaches Aria about something called spontaneous human combustion—could she really just catch alight one day?

She jumps when the library door opens. A familiar voice says, "There's a Golden Mare party on the weekend. They're paying a hundred and fifty bucks to every girl who goes. Three week's wages! Beats going to endless auditions and walking away with nothing."

Calliope's voice: "We said we'd never do parties. Not after what Daphne said."

When Aria pops her head over the back of the sofa, Calliope gasps.

"What are you doing here?" Aria asks.

"What are *you* doing here?" Flitter replies. "Nobody knows about this room."

"It's my schoolroom."

"Then we'd better split. I never met a school I couldn't fail," Flitter says.

Aria giggles.

Flitter and Calliope are wearing black skirts, black shirts, and black stockings with a white apron over the top and Aria remembers that they work some nights at the Marmont.

"We sneak in here to take a break from Maisie. We love her, but she is all work and no play." Calliope kicks off her shoes and collapses onto the sofa beside Aria.

"We've been on shift for a half hour, so definitely time for a break." Flitter grins.

Calliope tosses her shoe at her. "I'm hungover. Even my brain hurts."

"I'll cover for you," Flitter says. "You've covered for me. I owe you."

"The first month we arrived," Calliope tells Aria, "Flitter discovered gin. That month must have pickled her liver because she never gets hungover now. Which isn't a goal you should aim for." She eyeballs Aria, who remembers what Flitter said about Calliope's dad being a drunk.

After watching Calliope throw up last night, Aria feels very confident when she says, "I won't ever drink gin or mint juleps."

"The world has a funny way of turning our *won't ever*s into *just once*s and *why not*s," Calliope says quietly. "But I admire your resolve."

"Why do you stay at this hotel?" Aria asks. "Why not someplace else?" *Where there are no ghosts,* she doesn't say.

"The Chateau Marmont is where the people who really *do* matter live," Flitter says.

"And because every actress has a morality clause in her contract. If they do the wrong thing and it ends up in the papers, they get fired," Calliope adds. "But everybody does the wrong thing once in a while. The Marmont is the only place where it stays secret. No cameras permitted. Ever. Staff forbidden to tell."

"Discreet," Aria says, testing out the word.

"The motto of the Marmont." Calliope pulls some sheets of folded paper from her pocket, passes one to Aria, and says, "I need to run lines. Bob's studio is making a movie and my agent's got me an audition for the kind of part that has 'lucky break' written all over it."

Calliope clasps her hands and closes her eyes. "I can feel it. My guardian angel is whispering that if I just get this part, my dreams will come true." She opens her eyes and says to Aria, "You must be my guardian angel because this only happened after you arrived."

"Tell me about the magic in this one," Aria says, tucking her legs up beneath her and closing her eyes too, so she can picture it all.

And Aria can almost hear Calliope's smile dotting all her i's with sequins when she says, "I'd have to kiss Jimmy McLean in the very last scene. Imagine the two of us, smooching like Scarlett and Rhett. Because oh boy, do I ever need kissing badly."

Flitter laughs and Aria's eyes pop open. Calliope might kiss Jimmy McLean!

"You know how they make the kissing noise?" Flitter says. "The Foley sound guy makes out with his arm!"

"*Ewwwwww!*" Aria gags and Calliope laughs. "It's true. One of the least magical of all the illusions."

"Tell you what." Flitter stands. "You two run lines. I'll go back out there so Maisie doesn't hunt us down."

"I can run lines with you too," Aria says, like she has any idea what that means.

"I didn't get an audition, kid. Even more reason to keep my job here."

"If I get the part, I'll get you an audition for something," Calliope says.

Flitter's almost at the door when she replies, "Favors aren't power."

"It's not a favor if you're my friend," Calliope calls.

"That's not how my dream works," are Flitter's last words before she leaves.

"Do anyone's dreams work out the way we dream they will?" Calliope says to nobody in particular.

"Yes" is Aria's firm reply. "They do."

CHAPTER 14

...

1964

AFTER THE PARTY, MY ROOM GREETS ME WITH INTENSE QUIET. I put on my pajamas, slip my feet into a pair of ridiculous white marabou slippers that Judith Crown gave me last year for Christmas, saying, *I'm sure I never paid you enough for sitting,* then take the stairs to the turret. I run a hand over the journals I've kept since I arrived. But I don't feel like writing.

I walk over to the window, throw it open, and climb onto the little Juliet balcony that Bob's sister jumped from.

Over there is Laurel Canyon Boulevard, down there is Santa Monica Boulevard. One would take me north, the other west to the sea or east to the freeways, which lead on to anywhere. And the night throws Theo's question at me like an arrow: *Why are you here?*

Because this is where I was sent.

Once upon a time that was true. But seven years on, has the Chateau Marmont become the place where I've stayed? I told Theo I'd teach Adele enough that she could escape to Paris to search for real happiness. But what do I know about that—besides teaching her to do the opposite of everything I've done? Out there in the world, women have just started to run marathons. A woman has won a Nobel Prize for Physics. Another has flown solo around the world. I, too, could run. Or win. Or fly.

What would that feel like?

Hawaii is all I've ever dared to let myself want: something so small that the Fates won't notice—won't burn that future to ash with the flame from one dropped cigarette.

But what if I dared to want something more?

There's a flash of light in the grounds below. The windows of the bungalow Bob used to live in are illuminated. That's when I realize I haven't seen any builders at the Marmont—and I see everything. If the lights flickered on, someone must be inside. But what kind of builder works in the witching hours?

As suddenly as the lights went on, they're extinguished.

A noise draws my attention to Theo's balcony. Flitter is still beside Theo, her arm draped around his shoulders. *Mrs. Flitter Winchester.* It sounds wrong. But that's unfair. Flitter deserves something after all these years. A part in a movie though. Not my boss.

Now Bob walks out onto the balcony and leans against the balustrade. These days his hair is veneered with Brylcreem, mustache as precisely trimmed as if he uses a stencil, skin barbecued rather than tan. Years of running a studio full of the most beautiful people in the world have made him ruthlessly aware of his shortcomings and he's overcompensating, the effect now less spit and polish and more drool and shellac.

But I'm the only one who sees that.

I step backward—the last thing I want to catch is Bob's eye.

Calliope appears next with a guitar in her hand. She holds it out and says in the voice that's charmed thirty million men all over America, "Will you sing for us, Win?"

His features contract; he's the eagle just before he plunges, ready to tell Calliope to go to hell. But everyone's begging him to sing. He has to comply or be deemed an asshole.

The cheers crescendo as he takes the guitar.

He puts it on his lap, bends his head over it. I lean forward again. I've only ever listened to his music in a background way. Now I want to *hear* it.

What I hear first is gentleness. His hands are holding that guitar the same way he'd held Miss Devine Rey. I recognize the melody but I've never heard it like this, stripped back to candlelight and midnight. The song is about safety, about not having it, never having it and then finding it—but that is dangerous too.

And I wonder—is Theo the opposite of me? Desperate to remain here, which is a kind of running—running into a place where nobody is real and nothing has consequence. Here there's no danger of finding yourself at a Vegas wedding chapel—you screw and move on. Here, stomachs are pumped before you can die.

The song plays on. He's silenced the entire crowd. Only his hands move; I don't know how he can remain so still and yet disturb the entire universe. And for a moment I imagine someone touching me like that—as if they wanted to make music from my bones.

At the very same moment, Theo's head lifts. His eyes meet mine.

I whirl away before he sees the longing. Not for him, but for something more than I knew existed.

A collective gasp rises up from below. Did they see me?

Worse—did Bob see me with my entire soul in my eyes?

"It's just a feather." Flitter's voice.

"A bird, not a ghost," Theo adds.

My damn slippers must have shed one of their feathers. Either that or *I'm* the Marmont's ghost.

AT THE BOTTOM OF the stairs that lead from the turret to the seventh floor, I crash into someone. They don't flinch—they're expecting me.

"I saw you up there," Bob Ashenhurst says. "I didn't know that was where you'd hidden yourself away."

His hair is silvery at the roots, age catching him faster than his crimes ever will, and his cheeks are fleshier—a word that makes me shudder no matter how much I try not to show Bob anything.

He's standing in the middle of the opening to the hall. To squeeze past him would mean my body making contact with his. So I wait. He waits too.

And somehow the snakes that writhe on the Marmont's carpets fill me with their venom. I look right at Bob.

"Yes, I hide in the turret," I say. "Because it's the place your sister jumped from. And even you have enough heart that I know you'll never go up there."

His body sags, just a little, to the right.

I make my escape, glad for my sake and for Calliope's that I can be so cruel.

I'VE ONLY JUST FALLEN asleep when there's a knock on my door, followed by a giggle I'd know anywhere. I scramble out of bed to find Flitter and Calliope, hands squashed over their mouths like five-year-olds trying not to wake their parents.

"Don't you ever sleep?" I groan.

"We haven't been together for ages," Calliope says. "You can't throw your sisters out."

I try not to remember that I have to be at work at eight, which is about four hours away, as I crawl into bed with them.

"Was it always this cozy?" Calliope asks.

"It's Aria," Flitter declares. "She makes everything better."

A snug silence follows. My eyelids have almost closed when Flitter asks, "What do you think of Win? You've seen him the most."

I consider. How to compress into one sentence the singer's voice and the gruff one, the father who doesn't understand so much that's important at the same time as he understands so much that is. The man who's escaped to the Marmont; the man women miss so much that, when he leaves them, they die. The man who didn't want my aunt to fall asleep on her back.

"More real than I'd thought," I conclude.

Calliope laughs. "That's such an Aria answer."

"Those eyelashes of his." Flitter fans herself theatrically. "What I wouldn't give to have those eyelashes tickling my thigh."

"Oh boy." Calliope sighs.

"Don't you have enough men tickling your thighs right now?" I ask her.

She grins. "Probably. Although I hope nobody else thinks that. Thank god for the Marmont."

Yes, the Marmont is the soul of discretion. But I've never seen Calliope so overtly leaving one man's bungalow while pretending to the world that she's in love with someone else. Until now, she's been careful with her Brians and other beaux—*not too many that we think you've been fucked, but just enough that everyone thinks you're fuckable,* is how the studio put it to her. The same studio that filmed her areolas and then pretended to frown about whether to show them to the world.

Of course they will.

Then Calliope props herself on her elbow and says, "I've been meaning to tell you this, Aria, but it's never the right time. I think now it is. What happened all those years ago taught me to be the one who either enjoyed it or who got something out of it. Men have sex for reasons other than love—why shouldn't I?"

Flitter stiffens as, once again, the incident we don't discuss tarnishes our conversation like the bloodstain on the back of your skirt you hope each month to avoid. Calliope doesn't notice. She hugs her knees to her chest, looks Flitter directly in the eye, and says, "You should do what you want too. And you, Aria"—she turns her gaze onto me—"should also."

A WEEK LATER I'M pacing the minuscule lobby with Pilot, terrified that I've done the wrong thing. Every lap I come face-to-face with Phillip, Calliope's admirer. The seams on his white polo shirt are almost breaking as they try to surmount his biceps. His persistence—that he thinks he has the right to stand here waiting for a woman as busy as Calliope—only makes me edgier.

I go out to the pool where the sky is hiding beneath a wash of gray; winter's waiting to pounce. All I can think of are Theo's words, *I never want to sit by her bed in a hospital again* and I hope to god I'm not the reason why that hope is about to be ruined. Will she be back on time? Will she come back at all?

Pilot leaps in the direction of the *Keep Out!* sign and I only just catch him before he barrels through. He barks furiously, either agitated by or interested in whatever he can sense in that bungalow—maybe the builders are eating hot dogs. But I can only worry about one Winchester right now, so I drag a whining Pilot up to the penthouse, settle him with a bowl of food, then return to doing worried laps of the gardens.

The next person I see is Calliope, exiting Matty's bungalow. The orphan drama is gaining momentum and Matty's attracting a crowd of stars, as well as Hollywood High students who want to be Helen, the other orphan who dies tragically in the first half hour from tuberculosis. There's a lot of method acting going on although everyone's clothes cost more than a real orphan could afford.

"Hey," I say to Calliope, who starts.

"Aria. I wish you wouldn't see me every time I'm being my worst self."

"I thought you were doing what you wanted?"

She stares at the ground, presses a hand to her temple—presses it hard, like that would be a better pain than whatever's inside her skull. "It isn't working," she says.

"What isn't?"

Her eyes are unfocused and I wonder what she's taken and how much. I snap my fingers in front of her face. "Calliope?"

Her attention is caught by a girl, in white shorts and a yellow bikini top, who opens the door of Matty's bungalow and goes inside.

"Matty says I'm too old to be an orphan. Melissa"—Calliope

points to the closed door—"is sixteen. She wants the part the way lionesses want baby gazelles." Then she looks at me like the Calliope of a few years before. Ferociously. "But I *need* that role. Think about how few books or movies have just a woman's name as the title."

"*Anna Karenina?*" I offer.

"She dies," Calliope retorts. "Lolita dies. Rebecca dies before the book even starts. Emma is about the only one who lives happily ever after—married, of course. But the men—David Copperfield, Oliver Twist, Huckleberry Finn, Peter Pan—they all live. They have words like *adventures* beside their names. I need this role in a movie that says to everyone that a woman, just a woman, can be a story. I don't want people to remember only the madwoman and the brooding hero. I want them to think of *her.*"

I put my arms around my friend. For the first time, I can almost grasp why Calliope has always chased after her particular and sometimes sordid dream. The screenwriters are men. The directors are men. The producers. The agents. But when Calliope Burns strolls onto that screen, she has real power. For two hours, she is the sun and the moon in a darkened room and people all over the country cheer for her. They want *her* to be the one with the happy ever after.

Or they want that for the person she's pretending to be.

God, what a life.

Into my ear Calliope whispers, "I'm jealous of Flitter." She holds on to me as if this confession can only be given in an underbreath and with absolutely no eye contact. "She's free now. Doesn't have to beg for permission from the studio to be loaned out. To audition for Matty, I had to promise Bronte Bros. that if I got the part, I'd take a role I'd already rejected in their summer blockbuster. You know what it is? A woman who gets made over into something 'better' by a man—and she ends up marrying that man. Malleable and marriageable—what more could anyone want?"

When she pulls back, her casual smile is on her face once

more. "Matty says Melissa is too fresh for the part of Jane Eyre," Calliope goes on. "That he wants to put me and Melissa together, make a blend of our features."

"You sure he's not just angling for a threesome?" I joke because my woodpecker is chattering, alerting us that someone is coming, and this is what we do—put on a show: Hollywood Queen and her Devoted Friend.

"I hope Adele is nowhere within earshot of that conversation."

Win's voice cuts in. I mouth, *Shit,* at Calliope. Theo is *never* here during the day. I turn around with my most innocent expression on my face. "Adele is definitely not here."

"Then where is she?"

He's glaring; he's worried about Adele. I wish Melissa had a grumpy father, wish that I wasn't thinking of ways to go over to that bungalow and knock on the door and stop her from doing whatever she thinks she wants to do with a man who's twenty-seven years older than she is.

"Win." Of all people, Bob appears, clapping Theo on the back and shaking his hand. "I couldn't help overhearing. I hope your daughter hasn't been sneaking out again. I can help search for her if you like." Bob looks right at me, his expression deeply concerned. "Although Aria probably knows better than anyone where she goes at night?"

I want to slap him. He must have seen me and Adele that one time.

It takes every actressy trick I've learned over the past seven years to not hyperventilate. Adele isn't back yet and what kind of idiot trusts a fourteen-year-old with a rebellious past? In approximately five minutes, I'll be sacked, homeless and adrift once again, and Bob will have the revenge he's always wanted.

Theo is glowering. "Sneaking out *again*?"

"Adele's at Schwab's with a friend from Hollywood High," I tell him.

"Adele's at Schwab's with a friend from Hollywood High," he

repeats. "The same Hollywood High where her friends nearly killed her?"

"There is only one Hollywood High," I remind him, trying to calm him, and me too; trying to show Bob that every night when I go to bed I don't remember him saying, *I will never forgive you.*

"Are you out of your mind?" Theo roars. "And what does Bob mean by 'sneaking out *again*'?"

Calliope puts a hand on his arm, but today her magic is definitely fading because when she says, "Win, please be nice to Aria," he tells her to go to hell.

She does.

"You can leave us to it," Theo says to Bob. "Thank you."

Bob once again strolls away from the scene of the crime. At the same time, Melissa exits Matty's bungalow, bikini top awry.

Maybe it's watching Melissa do what I don't want Adele to do, or watching Calliope do what she says she wants but that doesn't seem to make her happy, or because I've never looked after a fourteen-year-old and I'm as scared as Win that I've misjudged the situation—but I don't just tell Win the truth, I throw it at him like a grenade.

"You know what? I can teach Adele math and English, but I can't protect her every hour of every day. I have to teach her to learn who to trust. A girl from Hollywood High called and said she was at Schwab's and she wondered if Adele could join her. Much to Adele's mortification, I spoke to this girl too. Adele said she thinks she's nice. Schwab's is a few doors down, it's broad daylight, and I called ahead and told them to let me know if Adele made any move to leave. Adele has to be allowed to cross the street and catch a bus and explore the city. I give you permission to behead me if it all goes wrong. No, scrap that, I'll behead myself. But you can't lock her up here. You can't—"

Let her be like me. I cut myself off as a voice calls, "I'm back!"

Theo and I whirl around and there she is, back right on time and with chocolate sauce and a smile in the corner of her mouth.

"Why are you yelling at each other?" she asks.

I look at Win. He looks at me.

"Because sometimes I don't listen," he tells her. To me he says, "Although you still have some explaining to do." Then he points at Melissa. "How old is she?"

"Sixteen," I tell him, shocked that he's noticed what everyone else ignores.

He strides off in a blaze of black leather and fury. "You can only come back to the Marmont with your guardian," I hear him tell Melissa.

She turns on the kind of smile Calliope made famous. "*You* could be my guardian," she purrs.

I move in front of Adele, who'd probably prefer an alligator ate her right now rather than watch someone only two years older than she is make moves on her dad.

"I'm certain you wouldn't want that," Theo says darkly.

He turns away, thinking he's solved one problem, and says to Adele, his body rigid with tension like he's trying not to hyperventilate either, "I won't yell if you explain what Bob meant. Over dinner. Or are you too full of ice cream?"

"I only had two scoops because it was almost dinnertime," she says and my throat tightens, which is so very stupid. My mom always used to call out to my dad whenever he took me out for ice cream, *Make sure she only has two scoops or she'll never eat her dinner!*

Maybe Adele's mom once told her the same. Maybe she used her own judgment to figure it out. I don't know. But god, it makes me happy.

I turn, ready to leave Theo and Adele to their dinner, but he says, "Where are you going?"

To my room, to the turret—my list of destinations is predictable and small. I shrug.

"I mean," he amends, "please join us for dinner. I'm serving food and apologies."

"And you want me to serve up explanations?"

"No. I'll take your advice and trust Adele to do that." He smiles at me.

That smile reaches up to the creases around his eyes and into his eyes too, and now he's a rock god and I'm a weak-kneed groupie who ought to know better than to let her stomach clench at the sight of a set of hot lips curving up into a well-practiced smile.

I give myself some fast internal monologue: *Flitter said hot* voice *and cool* lips, *and that is—perhaps only slightly—a more appropriate way for Aria Jones to think of her boss.*

Of course I agree to dinner.

CHAPTER 15

...

1957

IT ISN'T LONG BEFORE ARIA UNDERSTANDS TRULY WHY CALLIOPE and Flitter stay at the Chateau Marmont. On her way to the library each day, she sees Chester Meringue trying to lasso the gothic chandelier—he lassoed Aria instead and made her laugh. Sometimes he even lines her up in the hallway and tosses trick knives at her. In the lobby, there's always someone famous sitting at the baby grand and Aria's feet tap along to the music. Elsewhere, people gather in rooms practicing lines—declaring undying love or readying their pistols, depending on the movie. Writers tap feverishly on typewriters, directors talk about aerial shots and anti-heroes. Through it all parade the starlets like Calliope and Flitter—the ones who want—and the stars like Judith Crown and Marian Monti—the ones who have.

In between reading encyclopedias, Aria applies the inherent creativity of the Chateau Marmont to her own problems: How exactly can a nearly fourteen-year-old orphan earn enough money to get herself to Hawaii and still have enough left over for burgers and ice cream, a house by the sea, a swimsuit, and maybe even some false eyelashes? The lawyer in Manhattan said her aunt was her guardian until she was twenty-one. So that's her deadline. She won't stay here a day beyond her twenty-first birthday, which is seven years away—half the time she's been on earth. But she'll probably need all of that if she wants to gather enough money to never again be owned by someone who doesn't love her; to find that house by the sea where Aria Jones belongs.

Aria hasn't found any answers in her encyclopedias yet. And now her stomach is grumbling. It's ten after five, so she's allowed back to the suite where the first thing that hits her is the smell. Deviled eggs, shrimp cocktail, and a giant fondue she could just about drink.

"Who's it for?" Aria asks, reaching for the bowl of what she assumes are candies, only to have her hand slapped by her aunt.

"Stick to the fondue," Miss Devine says. "I have a soiree on the last Friday each month."

Soon the room is full of people. Aria's aunt sits on her chair by the window, dressed for a party she's ten years too late for in a fox-fur stole and sleek gown, a sculptural iris in a garden of blousy roses. Few people speak to her, Aria observes from her place by the curtains; they incline their heads, then help themselves to her drinks and candies. But when Bob walks in, he makes his way straight to Miss Devine Rey, picks up her hand, kisses it like a gallant knight.

"Oh, he's just too kind," one of the starlets enthuses, and others nod their heads and tell about some other kindness Bob offered to them when they first arrived, like the way he defended Aria from that man who called her a beast.

He moves through the crowd, nodding and saying everyone's name, even Aria's, and she smiles eagerly at this man who greets her despite her being merely ordinary.

She was definitely dreaming the other night. Bob is the least scary thing here.

The next person to enter the room is Judith Crown, carrying a baby dressed in a miniature version of Judith's own gown. Her husband, an actor of almost the same stature, is by their side. The starlets move as one over to Judith, squeezing the baby's cheeks like they're ketchup bottles. It starts to bellow.

Judith says a bewildered, "Oh dear."

That's when Aria has her idea. In Manhattan, she used to run down to Apartment 12 to help Mrs. Goldsworthy with her dear baby, who always settled for Aria.

She dashes forward, almost unable to believe that she, plain Aria Jones, is about to offer assistance to the celebrated Judith Crown. "Let me help."

She takes the baby from Judith, pops her finger in its mouth, letting it suck, and moves away from the excited chatter of hellos by the door.

"You're a treasure!" Judith exclaims, which is almost the best praise Aria has ever received. "Look, Max, isn't she a treasure?"

Her husband, who's eyeing the bowl of candies, says, "I told you that you don't bring babies to the Marmont. It's not like the Roosevelt. No bar. No restaurant. No damn babysitting services."

"I'm the new sitter," Aria says. "I charge one dollar per hour."

Max pulls out his wallet. "Here's a dollar. Now I can get a drink."

"Aria Jones's Sitting Service will take care of everything," Aria says, using a voice like she's heard on radio advertisements, singsong, persuasive. Her eyes lock with her aunt's and she thinks she sees Miss Devine Rey wink at her. Did she just get her aunt's blessing? And is she really holding Judith Crown's money in her own insignificant hand?

When Judith comes to find her later, Aria's ordered formula from Schwab's, wrapped the baby in a blanket, and taken it out onto the terrace where it's quieter. Judith pushes a whole ten-dollar bill Aria's way and Aria walks back into the party with her whole happiness on her face. At the same moment, Calliope enters the suite, not with red-painted lips and hair sprayed stiff, not with her cleavage making its own entrance one foot in front of her. Calliope's hair floats in soft, blond waves. Her lips are pale pink and her pink halter-neck sundress shows off the tanned skin of her back. Aria is witness to the moment when gravity shifts, pulling everyone in the room not down to the earth, but toward Calliope.

But instead of milling around thc studio executives like the other starlets, Calliope heads straight for Aria, taking her hand and leading her into her room.

"How about a story?" Calliope pats the bed. "I always liked it when I was real small and my mama sometimes told me a story at bedtime."

The words *real small* and *sometimes* are heavy with longing, as if Calliope's mama only did this ordinary thing once or twice.

But Aria has questions, of course. "Why does my aunt have these parties?" she asks. "She isn't talking to anyone."

"Well, at most of her parties, a deal is done—a role in a movie won, an idea green-lit, a couple introduced to one another. Every time the story is told of how so-and-so came to star in such-and-such a movie, or how Mr. X met Miss Y, it begins: *It was at one of Miss Devine Rey's Friday soirees.* So Miss Devine lives on, still famous."

"But why doesn't she just act in another movie?"

Calliope shakes her head. "I don't know. But what I do know is that I need to go out there and talk to Bob. Make a good impression before my audition next week." She reaches down, smooths Aria's quilt, tidies the pile of books on the nightstand. "I quit my job this morning. If I'm working, I can never get to these parties. Desperate people do desperate things, is the saying, but maybe desperate people do courageous things. Do you think?"

For the first time ever, Calliope's voice is not filled with certainty. And Aria remembers that while Calliope has a mother still living, she's a long way from home. That she's only four years older than Aria. Yet she's asking Aria, who knows nothing, for advice.

Aria hesitates. One percent of her still clings on to what she thinks she saw, doesn't believe it was an illusion. And that small but insistent part of her makes her whisper, "I thought I saw Bob in the hallway a while back. He was carrying a woman. It looked like . . ." She stops. What did it look like? The only word she can think of is *wrong.*

She searches the air for explanations, catches Bob watching them from his circle in the living room. He does nothing except send another leading man smile their way, but Aria still gets up and closes her bedroom door.

"She was probably drunk," Calliope says. "He was probably helping her."

Which makes more sense than Aria's story.

Calliope stands. "I'm going to have a rent problem in a fortnight unless I get out there and show them what I've got. Tell me to break a leg."

"Break both legs," Aria says.

Soon, she's asleep inside a chateau that's been standing for twenty-eight years, a chateau that knows that seven is just a word and that time is not exact and some years will take mere seconds and others will take all of your youth. That, sooner than it's wanted, a future is coming when Aria will understand all too well how desperate you can be when it comes to getting what you want.

CHAPTER 16

...

1964

I'M BRACED FOR THEO TO INTERROGATE ME AND ADELE AS SOON as we're in the penthouse. But he puts a record on, goes into the kitchen, opens the fridge, tosses Adele an onion and me a carrot, and tells us to start chopping while he throws ground beef into a pan.

Adele stares at me with a question in her eyes.

"Safe for now," I whisper, then turn to Theo and ask, "What are we making?"

"Spaghetti Bolognese."

My stomach, so used to the repetitive menu from Schwab's, groans with delight, which makes Theo and Adele laugh.

I decide to follow Theo's lead and relax. For now.

We chop and fry. I grate a block of Parmigiano Reggiano, which I thought came in a little green canister, and soon it's done and we throw on sweaters and sit outside on the balcony. For the first few minutes we're all very quiet, paying homage to the food and the golden LA night.

"Who's this?" Adele asks as a voice crescendos on the record player.

"Nina Simone," Theo replies.

Her voice is golden too as she sings about running away, leaving behind her wedding band and a warning not to smoke in bed. It's not a sentiment I can see catching on here.

Adele continues to probe, having taken on the role of interrogator that I expected her father to assume. "The way other people have photos everywhere, you have records. Why so many? Do you like singing? I've never seen you do it."

Theo studies his daughter. "You've acquired Aria's habit of three questions per sentence."

"Aria said that's how you learn."

I'm sure Theo really would like to fire me now. But he props his foot on his knee, takes out his cigarette packet, and turns it over in his hands.

"Other people go to church," he says, voice quiet as if he's afraid we might laugh. "I listen to music. In music I find . . ." He considers. "Solace. A sermon about how we live now. A gospel about how we might live if we fixed ourselves. And yes, sometimes I like singing."

"I've never seen you do it," she repeats.

I can hear what she's asking: *Will you sing for me?* But Theo doesn't do subtext.

And Adele, who'd never have taken such a risk a month ago, persists. "Why don't you sing anymore? You're not, like, making a record or anything. You ask me, 'what did you do today,' but I don't know what you do all day."

I push back my chair. I'm going to take the plates to the kitchen and scrub the patterns off the china while the two of them get this over with.

Theo glowers at me. So does Adele.

Two glowering Winchesters are a force not to be reckoned with. I sit back down.

"I'll confess first," Theo says. "Then I'd like to know what Bob meant. Deal?"

Adele nods.

I try not to lean forward too avidly as I wait for the big revelation of what he does all day—and all night too, on construction sites.

"I go out driving," he says, tossing the unopened cigarette pack onto the table. "On the freeways."

My efforts to not look too agape at this massive anticlimax

mustn't succeed, because the Winchester scowl fires at me again. "That's what I do at nights," he says. "During the day I go to AA meetings. And"—he hesitates—"parenting classes."

It takes all of my willpower not to let my dumbfoundedness repeat, *parenting classes*?

Adele is very quiet. I'm almost certain there are tears in her eyes. Because her dad *does* care. How many men in the entire country have ever been to a parenting class? But her rock star dad has.

"I snuck out just once at night." Her words rush out. "Don't blame Aria because she trusted me and that made me feel good."

"Okay," he says slowly, unable to resist sending me one tiny dagger with his eyes.

"I went to Googie's," she says. "Which is basically just across the road."

That makes about as much sense as Theo saying he drives the freeways at night.

"Couldn't you just order what you wanted from Schwab's?" I ask, a little cross now that I find out I've been having a heart attack over what turns out to be a midnight craving.

She shakes her head. Lowers her eyes.

Classic sign of guilt.

Theo must think so too because he says, "Well?" Despite his promise not to yell, his voice is snappy.

Which makes Adele sling a torrent of words at him. "I went there because of Mom, okay? One time when she and I were listening to the radio, one of your songs came on and she laughed and told me how she'd come to LA one summer for vacation and met you and you'd taken her on a couple of dates. One time you took her to Googie's for a burger. And I was missing her that night and it's the only place in the whole state of California where I knew she'd been. So I went there."

She crosses her arms and shoots Theo the glare she inherited from him.

Oh god. This place, so full of beautiful people, all with sad and terrible things inside them. I try again to leave but Adele grabs my hand.

I have no idea what Theo will say. But maybe the parenting classes are working. Or maybe he's a better dad than he thinks. He says only, "Thank you for telling me."

Which is exactly right. It lets Adele know he listened. And it lets Adele blink away the tears she doesn't want to shed right now.

The next couple of minutes are filled only by forks scraping bowls clean. Then Adele looks up. "What do you think about when you're driving?" she asks.

Theo chews, swallows. "About songs I could write. Whether I'll get on a stage again. Whether I'll be able to stay sober. Whether you'll be able to go back to school next year. Why your mom never told me she was pregnant. I think about her having a baby when she was only three years older than you." He clears his throat, trying so hard not to avoid his daughter's eyes while he gives her a piece of his soul. "About why some people die and why some people have to keep living. I think about the mistakes I've made. There are a lot. So I need long roads."

A wry smile. No, a sad smile.

"Wow," Adele says. "That's a lot."

I smile at the teenage understatement. Theo does too. Then he says, "I was thinking I should sell the bike and get a car now that I have a daughter."

"The bike?" Adele and I say in unison.

Theo looks at us like we just shouted *fellatio*. "The bike."

"You have a motorbike?" Adele demands. "Why haven't I been on it?"

"Because we don't go anywhere together," Theo says, obviously having no idea what the fuss is about. "But we should."

Adele jumps up. "Let's go for a ride. I could drive it out of the garage for you. I've been practicing—" she smiles devilishly—"on Lamborghinis."

Theo's eyebrows are not happy. "Where did you get a Lamborghini from?"

"From Jupiter," I supply, and Adele just about kills herself laughing.

"They don't make them on Saturn," she cackles.

Theo stands. "I'm guessing the only way I'll make sense of this conversation is to take you for a ride. How about we drive up to Laurel Canyon?"

"Yes!" she shrieks, and it's the first time I've ever seen her excited about doing anything with her father.

Perhaps Theo's thinking the same because he says gruffly, "Give me a moment," then he disappears into the bedroom with the speed of a greyhound. Maybe he needs to pee—he's so hard to read that either emotion or bladder discomfort could equally be the reason for his vanishment.

Adele is bouncing around, pointing to her bright red Wrangler jeans. "Will these be okay for a motorbike?"

"Perfect," I assure her. "I'll see you in the morning."

She stops the bunny hops. "You have to watch." Before I can remind her that I won't be able to see anything once the bike pulls away, she says, "Please?"

So I agree, because once upon a time I would have given anything for there to have been someone I could have said *please* to—someone who'd have said *yes* in return.

In the garage, Theo and Adele climb onto the bike, her holding the grab rails, not her father. With a burst of thunder, they take off, Adele squealing, and I smile when I think about the state of Theo's ears.

I sit on the curb of Marmont Lane and watch the cars rush past like days. More than two thousand five hundred days have passed since I first stepped out of the taxi right here, but the past forty or so have sped by like motorbikes. It'll be December 1 sooner than I'd imagined and I'll once again stand on this curb with a suitcase in hand.

Above me looms the revolving showgirl, the giantess in silver boots that the guests either shoot at or salute. She's been here as long as I have. The orange tan on her legs is sun faded, as is her lipstick and leotard, but she'll forever entertain anyone who wants to watch.

"Aria. Win hasn't thrown you out, has he?"

There's Bob, standing over me with a smile on his face.

"Nope" is all I say.

He frowns—it's the first time I've ever seen him look perplexed. Then the motorbike comes to a halt in front of me. One of Adele's hands is holding on to her father's back and it makes my mouth smile and my heart hurt when she leaps off and hugs him. Then she says to me, "Your turn!"

Bob looks from Theo and Adele to me. "Well played," he says to me, before he walks away, and for one second I wish Theo *had* thrown me out of the Marmont because then I wouldn't have to keep wondering, month after month, year after year, when Bob will make good on his threat.

He won't, I tell myself. *You have evidence, remember*?

"Your turn," Adele repeats.

"Your dad has better things to do," I say.

"Are you scared?" Theo says, a challenge in his eyes and a grin on his lips and my mouth drops open because right now in his leather jacket astride a motorbike, he is exactly what his songs promise.

And I wonder what the city of angels looks like from higher than the seventh floor of the Chateau Marmont.

I throw my leg over the motorbike.

OFF WE FLY. UP Laurel Canyon Boulevard, then right onto Mulholland Drive. I'm as high as the showgirl, and the city has been painted gold. It's a rare, smog-free night and on the far horizon, the ocean is indigo denim that I want to slide right into.

This is the world.

I'm going to cry on the back of a motorbike.

We slow for a red light. I take the chance to wipe my eyes. At the same time, Theo turns his head, and I don't think I was quick enough because he asks, "Okay?"

I nod.

"That was the first time she's ever hugged me, when she got off the bike," he says gruffly, and do you know how hard it is to keep holding on to the grab rails when you could put your arms around a person and squeeze them the way this bittersweet night is squeezing both your hearts?

When we return, Adele is still jumping up and down. "Wasn't it cool?" she says to me and then, to her father, "I know two guitar chords."

And Theo says, as if he's finally learning to translate his daughter's words into the longing that hides beneath, "There are at least three guitars in the penthouse. Show me?"

She races up the stairs, so eager to tie them together with another thread.

She needs those threads so badly.

If it were me, I'd pick the acoustic guitar. The other two are finned and shark-like—a bit like their owner—but Adele chooses the red one with the word *Fender* scribbled beside the tuning pegs.

She takes a seat on the sofa and says, "I don't think you need to go driving around the freeways anymore. I mean, you can literally do anything. So why, if you could do anything, would you just drive around on the freeways?"

Having delivered that little grenade with the nonchalance of a teenage girl and the wisdom of a sage, she strums, lets her voice dip low as she hums.

Theo sits down beside her. "You can make a song with just two chords. You just hum and play what feels right."

She plays one chord and then another. Theo hums in a different key, and the song is so simple and will go unremarked in all of human history, but it's just too beautiful to watch.

IN THE WITCHING HOURS, nightmares creep beneath my blue cotton quilt. A gas station. A blue Ford Custom. My mother's white pumps melting in the flames.

Then a laugh breaks the night apart like lightning—exultant, wild, cruel.

Then gone.

Footsteps tap, halting outside my room.

All I can see is darkness. All I can hear is breath.

Darkness. Breath. Darkness. Breath.

My door handle rattles like angry bones.

I press my hand over my mouth. I can't scream. The one time I screamed at the Marmont I got my first and only warning.

I stare wildly at the door.

The handle turns.

But while women in movie bedrooms never lock their doors, I do. The key is safe in my hand; I've slept with it beside me since I was thirteen years old, the way other children sleep in the soft embrace of teddy bears.

The footsteps recede.

I'm safe.

Then comes the smell of smoke.

Someone is trying to burn us all down.

CHAPTER 17

...

1957

"WE HAVE A BIRTHDAY PARTY TO ORGANIZE!"

Aria's head jerks up from the flyers she's making to advertise her new babysitting service. "For who?" she says to Flitter, who's just danced through the door.

A fingernail-sized piece of Aria thinks maybe the party is for her. That Flitter and Calliope are planning to celebrate her turning fourteen in six weeks.

But Flitter says, "Calliope," as if that ought to be obvious, and of course it is. Parties and Calliope go together like unicorns and rainbows, whereas plain old Aria is the complement only of uncherished things like the books around her.

"We need cake," she says to hide the sharp stab of understanding—she'll be the only person who knows, on December 1, that it's her birthday. "I'll order one from Schwab's."

"We'll have it here." Flitter casts her eyes over the shelves, pulls the high-heeled shoe lamp closer to the leather chair, drags a table out from a dusty corner, then sets the black cat statue, a gothic candelabra, and a glass diorama depicting a miniaturized nineteenth century ball on top. "Now we have style, magic, drama, and dancing—everything a good party needs."

Aria laughs. If Calliope is the belle of the ball, Flitter is the life of the party. Aria pulls another object off the shelves—a casket holding the skeleton of a bird. "Too weird?" she asks, making Flitter laugh and the sound warms up her insides and makes her see why Flitter is all one-liners and wisecracks.

"Are you getting Calliope a present?" she asks, wondering what she can order from Schwab's that would be good enough for Calliope.

"Come and see."

In the girls' bedroom, Flitter opens the bottom drawer of the dresser and pulls out a book with a red leather cover. Calliope's name is embossed on the front in gold. On the first page is a pencil drawing of a beaming Flitter and Calliope standing in front of a tent at what must be a county fair. Calliope's holding a trophy aloft.

"Did you draw this? It's beautiful."

Flitter shrugs. "We got a photo taken after Calliope won her first beauty pageant. We don't have the photo now because we left home in too much of a hurry. So I drew it, best I could remember. This is gonna be her brag book, where she sticks in all the keepsakes from the movies she's going to star in."

Aria's throat tightens. This book represents Flitter's unshakable belief in her friend, which is one hell of a gift.

"You're a really good friend," she tells Flitter, who stares up at the ceiling rather than let tears shine in her eyes.

"I owe her. Calliope would've finished high school and got good grades no matter how shitty her home life was. But me . . ." She shrugs. "I wasn't as tough. When I had to leave town, Calliope came too because she didn't want me going alone. You don't get many people in your life who become high school dropouts just so you don't have to be alone."

The sound of footsteps means there's no time to ask Flitter why she had to leave town. They hide the book just before Calliope opens the door.

"I've been running lines for my audition for Bob's movie all day and I'm tired of being a dumb blonde," Calliope says as Aria excuses herself to the bathroom.

Aria doesn't hear Flitter's reply because she can't think about anything other than what's happening to her. She's bleeding. The visitor everyone whispers about is here. "Mom?" she whispers, then sags onto the toilet.

Her mom is in a cemetery in New York City and Aria is in the tiny bathroom of two women she's known for only six weeks. Aria has been left to figure out everything herself, but she's so tired of this life where you can be decorating a table for a party with a stiletto shoe lamp one minute and staring at blood in your panties the next.

She pulls up her underwear, tries Flitter's trick of glaring at the ceiling so she won't cry. "Calliope?" she calls out, her voice only a little trembly.

Calliope's head appears around the door, followed by Flitter's. Calliope studies Aria's face and says, "You need some of these."

She pulls out something that resembles a giant padded snow ski and a belt. "She looks just like you did when you came knocking on my window one night and told me you were dying," Calliope says to Flitter. To Aria, she says, "Flitter's mom was very religious and didn't tell Flitter anything about bodies. So when her monthlies arrived, she thought she'd been stabbed. I took her to the bathroom and did what I'm about to do now." Calliope demonstrates what to do with the belt and the snow ski.

Her voice is as soothing as a lullaby as she figures it all out so Aria doesn't have to.

"From that day on she was stuck with getting me supplies each month. At least you have Schwab's," Flitter says, coming back with a clean pair of panties for Aria.

"Your mom didn't buy what you needed?" Aria asks.

"Come out when you're ready." Flitter leaves the bathroom and Calliope follows, calling out, "I have hugs and aspirin waiting for you out here."

After she's cleaned herself up, Aria studies herself in the mirror. She doesn't look any different. But she *feels* different. She got through something big without her mom. There'll be many more things she'll have to get through. While she mightn't want to, now she knows she *can*. She's tougher than she was six weeks ago and maybe that isn't a bad thing. Calliope's tough. Everything Aria's learned so far tells her that, even though when you look at them—Flitter wisecracking and hard-edged, Calliope soft velvet and sunny—you think Flitter is the strongest, it's Calliope who'll survive anything. Aria could learn a thing or two from that.

ONE WEEK LATER, ARIA jumps out of bed. Last night she sat with Flitter and Calliope in the screening room and watched a magical movie about a young orphan girl who found herself a prince. Plus, she has three bookings for babysitting this week, and it's Calliope's audition today and her birthday party tomorrow, so it's going to be a fabulous week. Calliope will get the part and maybe Flitter will get a role too and tomorrow they can stuff themselves with cake. Now Aria needs to set up the RCA Sound Camera to record their party tomorrow. That's going to be her gift to Calliope, the film—a spool of happiness that can be rewound and replayed, joy forever preserved.

She pulls the pieces of the camera off the shelf and lays them out beside the party table, which is set with china plates Maisie borrowed from the penthouse, and pale pink cloth napkins and crystal glasses that Aria found in her aunt's suite. Everything's ready for food and laughter and birthday wishes.

Only half of the camera's instruction booklet remains, so there's a lot of figuring out to do, which takes Aria nearly all day. Finally, as the record player swings into "Great Balls of Fire," she heaves the camera onto its stand, runs her fingers over the buttons, and thinks how magical it is to imprint a person onto a plastic spool, to feed the spool into a projector and meet that person again. To hear their voices, too—because this camera doesn't just record pictures, but sound as well.

When she touches something that makes a noise start up, she

jumps backward, grabbing the instructions and sitting down on the floor, trying to work out what she did.

She doesn't hear the door of the library open, just hears Calliope's ecstatic voice say, "Thank you, Mr. Ashenhurst. I'm so grateful. I know I'll make the movie a success."

CHAPTER 18

...

1964

I RACE OUT OF MY ROOM, THE MEMORY OF MY MOTHER'S WHITE pumps in my dream so real that I think I'll step into a gas station. But I'm in a Marmont corridor where the carpet is red like flames.

I hurtle into the lobby. Phillip is gone. No one at the piano. Nobody at the desk.

I run into the gardens, scan the windows, which are set like wide-open eyes into the facade of the chateau. Behind the windows of the largest penthouse is an orange glow.

Theo's room is on fire.

I race back inside and whack the button for the elevator. The lights show that it's on the seventh floor, exactly where I need to be. It crawls down, not stopping on any other floors, but still taking too long. The doors open and out walks Flitter.

"There's a fire," I shout. "Upstairs. Can't you smell it?"

She sniffs and shakes her head. "I can't smell anything. Are you sure—"

I don't have time to debate. I need water. And I need to wake Theo. I push her aside, leap in, jab the button to close the doors, plead with the elevator to hurry.

Inside Theo's suite, the curtains around the antique wooden bed are ablaze. Curled up, more peaceful in his smoke-infused stupor than I've ever seen him, is Theo.

"Wake up!"

He doesn't move.

"Theo!" I say his name loud enough to wake him, I hope, but not loud enough to rouse the floor and fill the room with people who haven't yet slept off their digestifs. The last thing this room needs is alcohol.

I grab the ice bucket from the dresser and a sculpture of a head, which is thankfully hollow, and run into the bathroom. I fill both with water and toss it on Theo and the fire, rousing the first and dousing the second. Then I grab a vase from the lowboy, throw the flowers onto the floor and hurl more water in Theo's direction.

"What the fuck?" he shouts.

"Get up," I hiss.

He finally jumps out of the bed as fast as if he were, in fact, on fire.

I push the ice bucket into his hands. "Fill it!"

But he doesn't need to. The fire dies all by itself. The only thing left is an ash-colored swamp.

"What the fuck?" he repeats, then comes into full consciousness. "Aria?"

I drop into the nearest chair, the strange white head that I've used as a bucket still on my lap. "I need a drink."

"You've come to the right place for that." Theo's voice is flat.

He disappears and returns with a glass of something brown and potent, undiluted by ice. When I grimace, he says, "This isn't a mint julep occasion. What happened?"

It takes three sips and two grimaces before I can speak. "Why do you have whiskey in your suite?" I ask, like this is our biggest problem.

It's his turn to grimace. "It's like a hair shirt."

I stare, sure that in the light of a day when I hadn't just thrown water all over my boss to stop him from burning alive that would make sense. "What?"

"I have an unhealthy need, according to my counselor, to test myself. To have a bottle in reach, but to not reach for it. It's how I prepare for parties."

"Wow, most people just go buy a new dress," I say, then cringe, hoping he doesn't think I'm mocking him.

He crouches in front of me, giving me a thankfully unscalded face to focus on and asks again, "What happened?"

I tell him about the laugh, the attempt by someone to enter my room, the smell of smoke. Finding fire. "And then it just went out," I conclude.

"Perhaps it was a dream." He sits on the floor, elbows propped on bent knees, head inclined forward.

Suddenly, I'm furious. "You were about to catch on fire." And what if I hadn't locked my door? What then? He's treating this the way everyone here treats everything—as if we've stepped off the set, never to look back at what won't even be there because it was never real.

"Were you smoking?" I demand, advancing on the bed, searching for the ashtray.

But the nightstand's empty.

He pushes himself to his feet. "Stay here," he orders.

I study his face, try to see what he isn't telling me. But his eyes are opaque black, his expression the same as at his party when he looked weary with the flirtations aimed his way as well as bitterly aware that he'd laid his own trap by hosting the soiree in the first place—the expression of a tiger trying to remind itself not to eat you alive.

Tyger Tyger, burning bright, In the forests of the night . . .

"Where are you going?"

"To check on Adele and the hotel." Theo opens the tallboy, pulls out sweatpants and a T-shirt. "You're soaked. The shower's through there. I'll try not to be long."

In an attempt not to imagine that same chilling laugh making threats outside the door while I wait here alone—or perhaps it's because, even though someone just tried to burn Theo alive, he wants me to be dry and warm—I make myself useful in this situation that, even for the Marmont, is preternatural.

"Take this." I pass him a pajama shirt that's draped over a

chair. "A half-dressed Win will be fair game to anyone who forgot to take their 'ludes tonight."

"As practical as ever, Aria," he mocks. He passes me a key. "Lock the door from the inside. Don't open it to anyone."

THE FIRST YEAR AFTER my parents died passed as slowly as the entire thirteen years previous. Then time regained its usual rhythm. But tonight, each minute refuses to give way to the next; the turn of an hour is as distant as the turn of a century.

A sound. I jump so high I just about hit the ceiling. But it's just the executioner's clock announcing 3:00 A.M.—time for the maiden to have her head chopped off.

I smoke five of Theo's cigarettes. Interrogate myself: *What are you so afraid of? It's not as if frightening things haven't happened at the Marmont before.*

Not like this. I know what fires do, who they kill, and how lives are changed forever.

I refill my glass. Where was Theo going? He'd said, *I'll try not to be too long,* almost as if he knew where he was headed. But how could he possibly know who'd set fire to his bed?

Then I remember my aunt.

Shit. Was it her?

I put down the glass. Move toward the door.

It opens by itself.

My scream is cut off by a hand.

Thankfully it's Theo's. As he pulls the door shut behind him and takes his hand away, I almost lose the admittedly tiny degree of professionalism Theo attributes to me by exhaling out my *shit fuckerys* in one long breath.

"Sorry," he says. "I didn't think you'd want everyone finding you in my room at four in the morning." He ushers me into the kitchen. "It was just one of the builders. They're staying in the bungalow they're renovating so they can start work early. They had too much to drink, decided to play a prank and check out the penthouse while I was asleep, must have dropped a lit cigarette somewhere . . ." He stops. "I never thought this was something I'd say about you, but you look like you might pass out."

I shudder. Another fire. Almost another burned body too.

Theo frowns. "Sit down."

I drink the water he passes me, and whisper, "Just like you have dead wives in your wake, I have burned people. My parents . . ." I swallow more water. "They died in a fire at a gas station."

Theo drops onto the stool opposite. "That's a terrible thing to have to live with."

The second hand on the executioner's clock speeds up. No, it's my heart racketing into the room. For a moment I think I can hear Theo's heartbeat too, making music with mine. Then I forget about hearts entirely because Theo's eyes are supernovas, swallowing time and space, compressing the two-foot gap between his chair and mine to inches.

I can almost feel the tips of his beautiful eyelashes brushing against my thigh like flames.

I push myself up. "Goodnight."

"Aria?"

I want to turn around. But Aria Joneses don't sit in rooms and dream about Theo's eyelashes and her thighs. They do not make similes that involve heat—not unless they want to be burned.

Theo steps in front of me. "You saved my life." His voice is quiet. His eyes are not.

His hand stretches out.

And every single part of me wants to go wherever that hand will take me.

But no, stupid Aria. He means for me to shake it, like an employee would upon accepting her boss's gratitude for performing a task in an exemplary manner.

I place my hand inside his. We stand there, hands clasped, eyes

too, and suddenly I want to wish for things I've never even imagined I could have.

I withdraw my hand, recover myself. "You'd better make sure your life was worth saving."

He's laughing as I close the door.

FIND ME A WOMAN in the world who could go to sleep after that.

I haunt the night, perched in the armchair in the turret, unable to stop thinking about Theo's laugh, how it always sounds surprised—as if he'd been worried he'd never laugh again and is delighted to discover that he can.

Or—as if he's delighted that *I'm* the one who makes him laugh.

God. What kind of idiot am I to have a crush on Theo?

But it's worse than that.

I *like* Theo Winchester. As in, I can't stop thinking about what it would be like to kiss him, wondering whether it would be the same as the way he just held my hand—gentle at first, but then not, because neither of us would want it to be gentle anymore.

I'm ridiculous. A stupid, *stupid* girl.

My face is hot, my collarbone damp, and I can't stop thinking about Theo's eyelashes and now, in my mind, his lashes aren't stopping when they reach my thigh.

WHATEVER I'M DREAMING HAS taken hold of me and I can't quite rise up out of it, my body warm, limbs like whiskey, the quilt embracing me. But the sound comes again and I startle awake, unsure where I am. Then I remember—I went up to the turret.

After the fire.

Vroom! Theo's motorbike. That's what roused me. I cross over to the window, see him pull out of the driveway and onto Sunset Boulevard.

It's about 5 A.M. There's a blonde woman on the back of his bike. A woman who has the same haircut as Flitter.

Flitter, who was leaving the seventh floor—Theo's floor—last night, right before the fire.

CHAPTER 19

...

1957

CALLIOPE IS THANKING BOB FOR A PART IN HIS MOVIE!

Aria wants to jump up and congratulate her friend. But Bob is there too and Calliope probably wants to look professional, not have thirteen-year-olds leaping out at her from behind armchairs. So Aria stays where she is, hoping that Bob will leave soon and then they can call Schwab's and have Calliope's party this afternoon instead of tomorrow—a double celebration.

Shoes tap across the floor—Bob's shoes from the sound of it. A cushion sighs as if he just sat down on the sofa in front of the party glasses. The jangle of the song on the record player and the strange whir of the camera muffle Aria's own sigh at Bob settling in rather than leaving.

Then she wonders—maybe that whirring noise means she managed to turn the camera on?

"I'll tell my agent to expect the contract." Calliope's voice, so happy.

"Is your friend Aria planning a party?" is all Bob says and Aria frowns, wondering how he knows that she uses this room, how he knows about this room's existence at all.

Calliope laughs. "It's my birthday tomorrow. So maybe."

Incongruously, the sofa belches and Aria swallows a giggle.

Fabric rustles. There's a metallic clatter, followed by a *ziiiiiiiiip*!

"Happy birthday." Bob's voice.

CHAPTER 20

. . .

1964

IN THE TURRET, WITHOUT A WHISKEY GLASS IN HAND, I REALize I'd been so seduced by Theo—is that what he intended?—that I didn't probe more. About the fire. About the person who'd tried to come into my room. The person who'd laughed that cold, cruel laugh.

I go over everything that happened, stopping when I remember the way Theo spoke before he left the penthouse—almost as if he knew where he was going and who he was about to face.

Did Theo lie? It seems like a big risk for the builders to take, sneaking into the room of the person who's paying them, even if they were drunk.

And it's not the first lie Theo's told. When Adele asked where he went, he didn't mention his witching-hour visits to the bungalow, which I've seen him make at least once. And now that I have occasion to question everything, I remember that on the night of his party he told me about two wives.

Flitter said he'd had three.

Flitter. Who I saw coming down from the seventh floor last night. Who looked like the woman riding off just now with Theo. Who said, *Can you imagine being the wife of the owner of the Chateau Marmont? Now* that *would give me power.*

But what does that have to do with bungalows and builders and fires?

Occam's razor, a horror-movie title for a dull hypothesis, says that the simplest solution is usually the right one. Maybe Theo *was* just shaking my hand last night and my imagination ran away with itself. It wouldn't be the first time. Maybe Flitter went up to the seventh floor because she wanted to experience Theo's eyelashes for herself, but then she'd been scared off by a pack of drunk builders in the corridor.

But why would the builders rattle my doorknob?

The only person I've ever crossed is Bob Ashenhurst and that was so long ago.

Or . . .

Oh no.

I'm running downstairs, this time to the fifth floor. There's Miss Devine Rey on the couch. I pick up her hands, inspect them for burns, look for any evidence that she was wandering the halls.

But there's nothing.

I sit back on my heels, grind my knuckles into my eyes.

"Aria? Is that you?" My aunt's voice. "I told you to keep out of my sight in the afternoons." Her voice is mean, intent on getting rid of the child so she can lie back and enjoy her valium dreams. But the dreams ceased long ago to be the reason for her insensibility. Addiction is the reason. Addiction to pills. To approval. To seeing your name in the magazines. To sex and false eyelashes and a life with no edges so there's nothing to throw yourself off—instead you just dive right in.

She's asleep the next second. And I do something I've never done before. I go into her bedroom and search through her things.

A solidified lipstick from fifteen years ago. A peignoir stained with fluids that even Maisie's determined scrubbing hasn't been able to budge. A pair of sparkling red shoes like Dorothy's. What looks like dried vomit.

I back away. Take a breath. Resume searching.

I find them in the bottom drawer. A stack of notebooks, their pages covered in handwriting. I open one and realize that just as I keep a daily record of my life, so had my aunt, once upon a time. And in those pages, she's a person I don't know.

Toni and I crept down to the garage at two in the morning and persuaded Isaiah to give us the keys to a purple Bugatti. We drove to Malibu, singing along to the radio playing "Swinging on a Star," and "I'm Making Believe." There was nobody at the beach so we took off our clothes, threw ourselves in the water, and swam. Such a small thing, but it felt like I took my whole self off and was the woman I might have been if an agent hadn't seen me walking down Broadway and sent me to Hollywood. I liked that woman splashing in the water, singing out of tune. No, I LOVED her. She felt so free.

But then the wind picked up and we got cold so we drove back and now I can't sleep because I'm wondering if maybe the only reason I loved being that woman for a half hour was because she's the one part I can never play. Tomorrow is the premiere of Tangiers and I'll walk down a red carpet wearing a black Adrian gown with a bright orange horse painted on one side and everyone will want it, but I'm the only one in the world who'll ever have it. Most of those people will still be lining the red carpet when the movie's over, hoping to see me one more time, wanting to take my picture or get my signature on a napkin they'll keep by their bed. Whereas the woman in the water, the only thing she can do is put her swimsuit back on and wait for someone to marry her. Or else, I suppose, she can drown.

The pages turn faster as I'm drawn into the story of a smart and often funny woman who became a star before she even knew if that was what she wanted, but who also had the self-awareness to know that in a world of limited choices, it was perhaps better to be the one with the designer gown.

The movie parts get bigger, the accolades grow, her humor stays intact, until one night, fourteen years ago, when she writes:

I usually write in the morning. But I'll write properly tonight instead. Because this morning I'm just wishing that when I give Bob back his ring, I'll be able to walk away to my lawyer's office and have him break my contract with Bob's studio and get me another contract with Bronte Bros., ACE, or even Millennium Wolf. Whereas tonight, I won't just be wishing, I'll have really broken it off and I'll know for certain how hard I'll have to fight to make the second part come true.

There's only one more entry after that. It's wordless. Doesn't say what happened, whether she went to the lawyer; if Bob fought against her breaking off her engagement and her contract. It's just a photo clipped from a magazine. It shows my aunt and Toni Ashenhurst, Bob's sister. They're smiling, standing between three men, who have their arms draped over the women's shoulders. The caption identifies them as the men who, that same night, signed the contract to sell Golden Mare to Bob Ashenhurst.

The only other thing in the drawer is an enormous diamond engagement ring, the one I've seen on my aunt's hand in *Photoplay,* the one Bob gave her. It's a weighty thing. Why does she still have it? Did she never break off the engagement?

My head starts to ache.

I pick up the phone.

"It's Aria," I tell Doctor Foster. "Can you come to my aunt's room?"

I take the photograph out to the kitchen. And there in the light, I notice something else. Toni Ashenhurst is wearing a ring. It's a gothic-looking thing. The etching on the band and the way the two stones are set into it makes it look like the head of an owl with its two large round eyes upon you. It's one of the objects that's always been in my library.

Doctor Foster lets himself in. "What happened?"

"It's me who needs the doctor."

"You?" He's so incredulous I almost laugh. Because Aria never needs the doctor. Aria is the one who takes care of everything.

"I'm worried she's walking around the hotel at night," I blurt.

I expect the doctor to examine my aunt or examine my head—at least one of us is going mad. Instead, he opens his bag and takes out a box of Tender Leaf tea. There's a teakettle on the stove—there always has been—a once-elegant silver teakettle with a dragon's head for a spout. The outside is tarnished almost to black, but the doctor fills it up, puts it on the stove, then opens a cupboard.

"There's nothing in there besides glasses," I say.

From the back, he pulls out two china cups. "I used to have tea with your aunt every week when you first arrived. I hoped it might . . ." He sighs. "Help."

I blink. The doctor, coming each week to help a woman and a child figure out how to live together. Did we?

He passes me a cup and I tell him, "Someone's roaming the halls at night. They set fire to Theo Winchester's bed. They laughed outside my door. Is it her?" I indicate my aunt.

"Aria!" Miss Devine's voice is shrill. When she tries to sit, it's like she's a marionette saying, "He will *never* forgive you."

As fast as the animation begins, it's over. Miss Devine Rey slumps back into sleep.

"See?" I whisper. "What if she can somehow walk—"

"Up to Win's penthouse?" The doctor covers my trembling hand. "Impossible. Even for Hollywood."

I show him the picture, point to the men. "Who were they?"

The doctor sighs again. "Hollywood's had ties to the mob for decades. Those men were criminals at the least, Mafia at the worst. They owned Golden Mare for years, but maybe they found out that racketeering was more profitable than movies. Whatever, Bob persuaded them to sell to him. Everyone was relieved they were getting out of Hollywood." He pauses. "Can you imagine a scenario where Bob Ashenhurst seemed like a savior?"

My teacup stops halfway to my mouth.

I've always wondered, each time I call Doctor Foster up to the turret to help one of the starlets, what he suspects. I've never asked. Because what do I know really? Only one thing for certain—the rest is just suspicion or, any man in Hollywood would say, my overwrought imaginings.

Everyone believes Bob is a savior.

Maybe I've just found someone else who doesn't.

But it isn't enough. One girl and one doctor and a pile of questions add up to nothing at all.

"Who owns all the things that I moved to the turret?" I ask.

"Toni Ashenhurst."

Bile rises in my throat. That makes it even worse, what Bob did that day in the library with his dead sister's things all around him. But it also makes me more certain than ever that the reason my aunt is like this is because of Bob. He did something. I've misjudged her all these years and now I owe her.

Doctor Foster squeezes my hand. "You know that one day your aunt won't get up at all?"

I close my eyes. The one person in the world who has some ownership of me is going to die, and soon. That's what Maisie said too.

I open my eyes, remember the woman floating in the water at Malibu. The one who hasn't drowned yet. "Can you get her into a rehab facility? I'll pay for it."

"The kind of facility she needs won't be cheap."

"I have money. Just get her a place."

He nods.

Once he's gone, I rest my head in my hand. *What am I doing*? My money will be gone and, with it, my dream. I can't leave here without money.

But nor can I live with myself if I let Miss Devine Rey die.

I'M SO LATE FOR work. I dash back to my room, throw off my pajamas, grab the nearest thing to hand—a psychedelic and very short mini dress that I think is Calliope's or Flitter's—then hurtle up to the seventh floor. My apologies are cut short by Adele saying, "Last night, he"—she points to her father—"dropped his cigarette on the bed and it caught fire! He put it out with this!" She holds up the empty head sculpture and giggles, like it's all just a funny story.

Maybe he did fall asleep with a cigarette. Maybe I should concentrate on doing my job and earning back the money I'm about to spend on my aunt and then walking away from all this, like I've always planned. Because Theo is walking out the door with a gruff, "I have work to do," and it's like one of those big cartoon hammers has banged me on the head until I'm just a flat puddle of Aria.

What was I expecting? Flitter's the one he rides on motorbikes with. I'm the one who douses fires, not the one who ignites passions.

My next thought makes me stand as still as one of the Marmont's antique statues—did I just give all my money to my aunt because I thought there might be something at the Marmont for me?

There's nothing at the Chateau Marmont for me.

I take Adele up to the turret. That's the only way I'll ever make back the money to leave. I give her a set of problems about compound interest and rub my eyes. What I wouldn't give to lie down on the mattress in the corner—the mattress that now has a wrapped present sitting on it.

Hope flares.

But the card says, *Thank you. Love, Nathalie.* The starlet I helped recently. She's gifted me a long, multicolored silk scarf, the kind the heroine in the movie ties over her hair so the lengths of it stream behind her as she sits in a convertible beside a man driving them off into the glorious sunset.

There isn't enough breeze in the garage to make even a hair ribbon stream when I sit inside stationary Lamborghinis.

I put down the scarf, prowl the room, eyes seeing the objects in a new light now that I know it all belonged to Toni Ashenhurst. Did she write journals too? Are they here somewhere, full of evidence, maybe hidden inside the jewelry box her owl ring is kept in? Where even is that?

My fingers itch to pull things off shelves, to search for something that gives me more than the suspicions of one girl plus one doctor and a whole pile of questions. But Adele will think I'm mad if I start doing that now.

I exhale, stare out the window at the gardens. Calliope is making her way to Matty's bungalow. Flitter is lounging by the pool. She waves, shrugging off her caftan, laying her beautiful smile over the dreary fall morning and her beautiful hand on Theo's forearm.

They converse. When Theo walks away, Flitter retakes her seat. From up here, I can just make out Theo continuing along, looking over his shoulder, then ducking under the tape blocking the path to the bungalow that's supposedly being renovated.

I'm about to turn away when Flitter stands up. She too looks over her shoulder, takes the same path. The tape doesn't stop her either. She slips beneath.

I'm not prepared for the force of the punch to my guts.

The bungalow isn't being renovated. It's off limits so it can be used for Theo's trysts.

Which would mean he lied again.

God, I'm such an idiot. So easily seduced by rock stars and whiskey and love songs meant for every girl in America, not me.

There's only one thing I need to focus on: teaching Adele, getting paid, and getting out of here. No more motorbikes or dinners. No more schoolgirl crushes.

I whirl away from the window.

Adele's on the floor, absorbed in reading.

"How's *The Bell Jar*?" I ask, voice thin.

"This is way better than *The Bell Jar*." She holds up one of my journals.

"Adele! Those are scribbles. *Private* scribbles."

"I love this bit." She reads aloud, quoting me to me, and I want to cover my ears. I don't write journals the way everyone else does. I inhabit people who are different from me, but somehow also the same.

" 'When you go home each night to a drunk you can't remember loving,' " Adele reads, " 'and a kid who doesn't understand that laundry and cooking don't just do themselves, and the kid wants something from you but you're empty, so you yell at the kid and regret it two seconds later, knowing the kid will never see the regret, only the anger, just like the drunk sees only the bottle and the backs of his eyelids—that's when you need movies. You need movies so you can believe for just a couple of hours that if you stare at the screen hard enough, the blonde in the convertible with her pink scarf streaming behind her and Cameron Grant right beside her might be you.' "

God, when did I write that? A few years ago, after I'd heard enough about Calliope's life and not enough about Flitter's. When I'd worked out that Hollywood sells the promise that things will get better once the right person comes along—the cowboy who'll drive the bully out of town, the man who'll buy you a wedding ring, the slave who'll rise up and overthrow an empire. Those are the fairies we believe in when we stop believing in Tinkerbell, when we start to believe there's nothing we can do to fix our lives, so we wait for the cowboy, the slave, the prince who'll make everything charming. We let the world batter us until we're too small to even dream, let alone rise up.

I reach out to take the book off her.

But Adele holds on to it and says with the wisdom of someone who's been carefully studying everyone around her so she can figure out how to fit in—God, I remember doing that too, thinking it would save me—"Most people don't think about how we're all connected. But I like stories like that. Everyone has Cinderella inside them and the wicked stepmother too. This book shows you that." She points to my journal. "If you made this into a real book, I'd read it."

I pick up *The Bell Jar.* "*This* is a real book. My journal isn't."

"And Esther has both Cinderella and the stepmother inside her," Adele says, as if she's actually been reading Plath and she understands what it's like to be both lost and hopeful, to have the world see your story through the wrong set of eyes.

Before we can continue our first ever successful English lesson, footsteps sound on the staircase. My eyes run to the door. Nobody comes up here, besides the starlets I lend the mattress to. Of all people, Theo appears, in dark jeans and navy T-shirt, with at least one tattoo slinking down to the end of his deltoid muscle.

I pluck the notebook out of Adele's hands and hide it the same way I close my eyes to keep my soul a secret.

"Calliope Burns is having a party tomorrow night," Theo says, which is a weird hello, but most of my conversations with him aren't exactly normal.

It's Calliope's twenty-fifth birthday. A costume party by the pool—dress as a cliche is the theme.

Theo makes a slow circle of the room, pulling an edition of the *Encyclopedia Americana* off the shelf, running a finger along the bindings of my novels, making me jealous of every single one of those spines.

Then he says, "We should go together. So we don't have to go by ourselves."

Is he talking to Adele?

He's looking at me. Shouldn't he be asking Flitter?

I shake my head, trying to clear out a space for his words to converge into sense.

"You'd prefer to go with a handsome young actor," he says sardonically. "Fine."

He turns to leave. I could let him go. Stick to the vow I made five minutes ago. Think only of the fact that he might have lied.

But the place where his finger stroked the palm of my hand last night is still warm.

Greedy for more.

"I'd prefer to go with you," I call.

He half-turns, enough that I can see the corner of his mouth. Enough that I can see he's smiling.

CHAPTER 21

...

1957

IN THE SILENCE, A CAMERA WHIRS AND THE SOUND OF A ZIPPER unzipping serrates the air.

And Aria can feel something like the Marmont's ceiling pressing down as if the chateau wants her to hide not just behind the chair, but underneath it. She holds herself very still, tries not to breathe, doesn't know why she needs to be invisible, just that she does.

"There's one condition to you getting the part." Bob's voice.

"This isn't a condition," Calliope says very quietly. "This is . . ."

"Power," Bob says.

Aria remembers what Flitter had said the night they lay in bed together and talked about dreams.

Flitter was the only one who'd made the right wish.

Calliope doesn't scream. She doesn't storm out. She doesn't even say no. She does something far worse. She sighs as if she's been tasked with a repetitive chore, like writing out multiplication tables, and she's just looked up to see she still has dozens more to do.

Aria doesn't know what's happening exactly, thankfully can't see, tries to hold the scream in her mouth that she can't let out because nobody screams at the Marmont. Somewhere in this hotel there must be a bonfire of unscreamed screams, and if Aria were brave, she'd crawl out and push Bob right into it.

But she has no warnings left. Nor does her aunt. If Aria screams, they'll be thrown into the street. Miss Devine Rey will storm off down Sunset Boulevard and Aria will be utterly alone. She already has so little—a borrowed room, a camera she doesn't know how to use, a past she can't look at because it burns.

Two friends, one of whom she's betraying.

She shuts her eyes. And her mind gropes its way out of the blindness of childhood. *Is* she betraying Calliope? Does Calliope, who told Aria she's going to do everything she can to affix her star onto the emptiness of time, want Aria to do exactly what she's doing now—nothing?

Aria knows only that the fairies have died, just like Calliope and Flitter said they would.

CHAPTER 22

...

1964

THE DAY OF CALLIOPE'S PARTY, I WAIT UNTIL HALF PAST TEN. THEN I take out my skeleton key and go to the sixth floor, to the suite Bob now occupies. Never a Sunday passes when the man with no soul doesn't go to church.

I want to find something that tells me what happened between Bob and my aunt that night to make her into a woman who'll most likely die unless she goes to rehab soon. This isn't just a story of a washed-up movie star. It's too sudden, the way she went from heroine to villain. My aunt's journals tell me she understood she could only ever swim naked in an ocean perhaps once or twice in a lifetime, and only if it was two in the morning and nobody was around; that there was no freedom, not for a woman in the 1940s. So she might as well wear a Gilbert Adrian gown in the prison that society made for her. But then, in the turn of one page, she locked herself up in her own prison.

Why?

I survey Bob's suite, can feel the tremble in my guts. *Bob isn't here. His room can't hurt you.* But it's the cloying cinnamon of his aftershave that threatens to dump me back into the library where I hid under an armchair, listening to Calliope tarnish her dream.

I take shallow breaths, try to keep the smell outside me as I open a drawer in the credenza. Empty. The kitchen houses only cocktail glasses, vodka, and vermouth. The walls are adorned with movie posters, the mantelpiece with Academy Awards. Pressed shirts hang in the wardrobe; the bathroom cabinet holds a razor, toothbrush, Tylenol, and sleeping pills. It's all so ordinary. Like a set for a movie whose star is a 1960s businessman.

What was I thinking—that Bob would have a box in which he'd keep the evidence of his crimes? I am, once more, being incredibly stupid.

I hurry out of the room, lock the door, jump when I hear someone say my name.

"Aria? What are you doing?"

THANKFULLY IT'S FLITTER, THE one person in this hotel who won't tell Bob she caught me sneaking out of his room.

"I was looking for something that doesn't exist," I say, making myself smile, be breezy, change the subject to Calliope's party. "What cliche are you going as tonight?"

"Hollywood." Flitter grins as we walk to the elevator. "Is there a bigger cliche? Are you babysitting? Somebody needs to tell Win to give you the night off work."

Win. She still calls him Win. Not Theo. It's such a small thing, yet I lavish meaning upon it, let myself be persuaded that being granted the use of a person's true name is more significant than a late-night motorbike ride. Let myself believe that anything Flitter might feel for Theo is trivial, fleeting—ready to be discarded when the next wealthy guest moves into the Marmont.

And then I smile because Theo hasn't just given me the night off work—I'm going with him to the party. Me and Theo Winchester, the man who stood in front of me last night in his pajama pants, chest bare, hair damp.

I wonder what his bottom lip tastes like.

My cheeks are hot. I need a fan. Or a swoon. I definitely need to put a shirt on the Theo in my mind and pretend he doesn't have lips at all because I'm standing in a hallway with Flitter, who's asking me, "Are you okay?"

I tell her the truth. "I'm more than okay. I'm happy."

TO MAKE SURE ADELE is safe and occupied during the party, Theo has the screen from the first floor moved into her room, as well as the projector and a preview copy of a movie called *The Sound of Music* that the studio thinks will most likely bomb and is therefore happy to loan out to anyone influential. It's about a nun who falls in love with a widowed father and they all live happily ever after—the kind of fantasy Hollywood is built on. Adele will watch the movie, and we'll check on her during the night.

But what the hell will I wear? I stand in front of my sparse wardrobe in the land of cliches and I can't think of a single one.

The walls crack like bones, a word drops into the air and suddenly I know.

I'll go to the party as me.

Behold the orphan girl, whose parents have been dispatched in order that she can learn lessons about life—and have a grand adventure too. Heidi, the little princess Sara Crewe, orphan Annie; even the Brontë orphan Jane that everyone's lining up to play.

I decide on black—a sheath dress in honor of orphan Holly Golightly. Mine is cocktail-length and I eschew pearls, because what genuine orphan can afford those?

False lashes—an orphan's eyes should always be soulful—a hint of pale lipstick. I stand in front of the mirror and, for once, I don't think about myself in relation to all the beautiful people at the Marmont. I just see me because, tonight, my pixie cut paired with the false lashes makes my eyes look enormous. My dress skims over my body, my skin is still tan from summer, my smile is huge and nobody would guess that I really am a poor orphan girl.

THEO SAID HE'D CALL past my room at eight. It's three minutes to eight. Two minutes to eight.

One minute.

Stupidly, when someone knocks, I jump. It's probably Flitter needing me to zip her up. It won't be Theo.

Thus with my expectations trampled to beneath even the nadir, I open the door.

It's Theo.

Of course he doesn't smile. He lifts an eyebrow. "Little black dress?"

I laugh. "No. I'm just me. The poor orphan girl."

"I'm just me too," he says, smiling now. "The recovering rock star. Is there a worse cliche?"

This time we both laugh.

There's a crowd waiting for the elevator and another crowd already aboard. When we step in, we're split up, me on one side, him on the other. I can see his face because he's so tall, and can see that he's watching me.

Staring at Theo Winchester in an elevator is the sexiest thing I've ever done.

Which just goes to show how deeply unsexy my life is.

There's a cheer when the doors open. Theo and I wait until everyone has exited, then he comes to stand at my side.

"You two getting out?" Isaiah grins and I nod because I don't think I can speak.

As we cross over the driveway and through the gate to the gardens, Theo says, "Thanks for coming with me."

"Has anyone in the history of the world ever said no to going to a party with you?"

"Is there a moment in the history of Aria where she doesn't turn a serious statement into a joke?" he counters.

"It's a habit I learned from Flitter," I confess. "You'll have to fill me in on all the other bad habits my eclectic collection of Marmont parental figures have left me with."

A man calls out in that drunk, male bird-call way, "Win!" He starts asking questions about when the next album is coming out, so I slip away to find Calliope and wish her a happy birthday, passing Phillip, Calliope's devoted poet, holding a birthday placard.

The gossip flying around the pool sours my mood. "I'll be at the front of the line to see those sweet cherries" is the first comment I hear.

Another man sniggers. "And Calliope refused to reshoot. She *wants* us to cop an eyeful."

I double my speed through the crowd, thankful that Calliope's always easy to find. Tonight she's standing by the edge of the pool wearing a headpiece of stars.

"What's going on?" I ask.

She waves a hand in the air. "Bronte Bros. leaked a story about my peekaboo areola to *Whisper.* Well, they said they didn't leak it, but I'm blonde, not stupid. They want to remind me that they have more power than I do, in case auditioning for *Jane Eyre* gives me any ideas about negotiating for greater independence. They said they want to reshoot the scene so it doesn't violate the Code, but that I'm refusing."

Ah, the Code. That biblical set of commandments that states: *Seduction and rape are difficult subjects and bad material from the viewpoint of the general audience.* Rules the studio bosses hold up with one hand while they fondle a girl with the other.

Calliope keeps her smile on because she's in view of her guests. But I can hear her teeth grinding. This gossip means she needs a serious part in a serious movie more than ever or she and her areolas will never get intimate with an Oscar statuette.

"I'm sorry," I tell her.

"Me too," she says, and it's the only time her smile falters. Then she pops a pill and her smile is back and I take the hint to talk about something else.

"You've come as yourself too?" I point to her crown. "A star?"

"No. I'm Fortune, as in," she simpers, "my face is my fortune."

Flitter shimmies over, no mean feat given she's wearing a foam cutout of the Hollywood sign because yes, the whole of Hollywood is a cliche. She says to me, "I want to know what you were so happy about this afternoon."

Which makes me blush again, and I hope to god it's too dark to see my cheeks. But Calliope says, "Are you blushing? What does the cool-headed Aria have to blush about?"

I search desperately for a distraction, but my eyes stop on the one and only thing they want to look at: Theo Winchester.

He's looking at me too.

Now Flitter and Calliope are looking at me, looking at him.

"Do you have a crush on someone?" Calliope asks.

"On Win?" Flitter shrieks. "I have competition? From you!"

"Stop shrieking," I hiss.

Calliope lowers her voice and fixes her eyes on me. "Aren't you supposed to be in your house at the sea by now?"

"I need more money," I tell her. *I might not even have enough to put Miss Devine through rehab, let alone have anything left for an escape fund,* I don't say.

"But what if Win starts making eyes at you?" Calliope demands.

I remind her, "This is real life, not a movie." And in real life it seems more likely that Theo only invited me to thank me for drowning him last night rather than letting him burn.

The thought lands like a punch.

I hate hurting. I've spent seven years trying to avoid being hurt. I don't have ambitions, don't dream of anything more than escape. So why is it that part of me would happily trade every house by the sea in Hawaii for this night at a party with Theo?

Sixteen-year-old Melissa chooses that moment to arrive—on Bob's arm. Bob approaches Theo with a piece of paper and a fatherly look on his face. "I've been appointed Melissa's guardian. I know you wanted someone to look after her."

He passes the paperwork to Theo, further evidence of how kind and caring Bob is, taking this young, innocent girl under his wing.

Further evidence that Bob always wins.

Melissa sashays through the crowd wearing a white T-shirt about four sizes too small and her bikini bottoms. On the back she's written the word *dumb* in lipstick. On the front, she's written *blonde.*

It's a cliche to say that everyone stares.

"Talk about putting it out there," Flitter says.

The way she's looking at Melissa reminds me of the way Lacey Magee looks at Calliope now. The way Flitter and Calliope used to look at Lacey.

"It's my birthday," Calliope says, turning away. "Let's party like the world's gonna end tomorrow. We'll say hello to Matty." She and Flitter move away, arm in arm.

As for me, everything suddenly feels so endless. There will always be a sixteen-year-old Melissa and a twenty-five-year-old Calliope. There will always be a woman who accepts the double entendres as the price she has to pay for daring to wear a swimsuit to a swimming pool. Or, if she's a different kind of girl, she'll pull her shoulders back and let her basketballs bounce because at some point, she got so damn tired of paying the woman's tax that she told herself to just play along—maybe that way she had a chance of winning.

But she doesn't.

And I'm going back up to my turret because it seems like I'm the only person who's not enjoying the party.

But as I'm walking away, I hear Theo say, "Please don't

leave." His voice is so husky it just about melts the dress off my body.

Now I'm enjoying the party.

"ATTENTION EVERYONE!" CALLIOPE'S VOICE breaks in. She's sitting atop Brian's shoulders, tinkling her champagne glass with a spoon. "Last time I was shooting in Europe, a little number most of you wouldn't have seen"—the crowd laughs; Calliope's last film won an Academy Award—"I found the most extraordinary person. A fortune-teller, descended from fifteen generations of wise women. She's here tonight to predict your futures. Give her a minute to set herself up." Calliope gestures to a black tent covered in moons and stars. "Then you can find out who'll beat you at next year's Oscars."

Everyone starts to chatter excitedly.

"Is it a good thing to know your future?" I ask Theo. "I wouldn't have wanted to know about my parents."

"Some things I'd like to know," he says. "But others . . . I used to drink to not feel the present. If I'd known I was going to suddenly have a fourteen-year-old girl to parent, I'd probably have drunk enough to be dead. Which would have been the worst decision in a lifetime of terrible decisions. Sometimes it's better to have to deal with life as it happens. Because"—he smiles at me—"I'm starting to think life is okay."

Oh, yes it is. Especially now that we're walking deeper into the gardens, where we're hidden by palm trees and jasmine. Music drifts from the speakers—a guitar preparing for a love song by tossing a few gentle chords into the night.

It's one of Theo's songs. He grimaces. "God, couldn't they find some decent music?"

"I love this song," I tell him as we stop in the shadows beside the tree my one-legged bird lives in.

Theo looks at me. "You know what? It's not too bad."

We laugh. Laughter is magnetic; it makes people move closer together. Our bodies obey that primal rule. I try not to think about what's supposed to happen next.

Which is good. Because Theo's attention is diverted by something over my shoulder.

Two people are walking toward the bungalow protected by the *Keep Out!* sign.

Theo calls, "That's off limits."

One of them turns around. It's Flitter. She smiles, and with her Hollywood-white teeth and her red off-the-shoulder cocktail dress, she suddenly makes me feel like a crow. She's so distracting that when I finally take another look at the person she was with—who'd looked for a split second like Bob Ashenhurst—whoever it was has disappeared.

Flitter would never go for a moonlight stroll with Bob.

"Sorry, Win," she says. "I got bored of waiting to hear from the fortune-teller about whether my tits or Melissa's were big enough to get me the part in Matty's film."

How is it possible to do anything other than look at someone's breasts when they say that? Theo is both human and male and his eyes have definitely dropped to Betty Boop level.

"Where's your costume?" I ask because the Hollywood sign is gone. Now she's just a lick of red flame.

"It was hiding all my attractions." She winks at Theo.

I wait for him to move away from me, to reach for Flitter's hand. But a cry goes up from the poolside. The news travels fast: the fortune-teller is ready to begin. And she'll start by telling the fortune of the owner of the Chateau Marmont.

There are so many people looking in our direction that I sidle away from Theo, who's back to the brooding-brows and stormy-thoughts version of himself. "Nobody is telling my future," he mutters, but Flitter slips her arm into his and says, "We can't have ours told until you do. Unless you want this party to turn into a riot, come with me."

She ushers him over to the tent and he disappears inside. I pity the poor fortune-teller who has to face those eyebrows. And I pity myself for having so nearly had the thing that comes after two people step close together in the moonlight.

"Aria Jones."

I jump, then curse at having let my guard down so completely that I was daydreaming about futures rather than blending into the present.

Bob's standing in front of me, wearing a crown. He is himself too: The King of Hollywood.

I turn my back. I have no turret around me, no power out here, and while I hate myself for being the one to flee, I don't have a confrontation with Bob in me tonight.

Before I can leave, he says, playing the game so much better than me, like always, "Did I see you arrive with Win? Things are going well, I take it."

He can't know how I feel.

I plunge away, into the crowds, don't stop until I get to the penthouse.

On the screen, a man is singing a love song to an orphaned woman.

"It's super cheesy," Adele tells me, crunching on popcorn. "But maybe it's like grilled cheese—you really need one every now and again."

I manage a laugh, feel a little better.

"Go back to the party," she orders. "Or I'll start to think you don't trust me."

"You sound like your dad when you're grumpy."

It makes her smile, this further proof that she belongs to Theo.

"Aria?" she calls after me. "You look really pretty."

Pretty isn't beautiful. But it's a damn sight better than beastly or plain.

The smile I'm wearing as I walk back to the party doesn't last. The gossip at the poolside is that the fortune-teller told Flitter she'd marry Win.

"Flitter Reeve, the Queen of the Marmont," someone says.

"What was she in?" is the reply. "That Roman Empire thing from a couple years back?"

"I've never noticed her," the first person muses. "But she is one fine girl."

Yes, Flitter does look exceptionally fine tonight. Her eyes sparkle as everyone takes another look at this woman whose backstory is being rewritten right in front of me.

Has her future just been cast by a fortune-teller? Where does that leave me? Or is it a scheme cooked up by Calliope to get her friend noticed? But Calliope's never been a schemer. Nor has she ever been so medicated. Every time I see her, she's popping pills.

I press through the gossip, looking for Theo, trying to ignore the chatter, trying to remember that I was the one Theo looked at in an elevator full of people.

Judith Crown catches my hand. "The fortune-teller is looking for Aria Jones."

Augusta Hepworth glides over. "It's your turn, Aria."

Between her and Judith, I'm swept over to the tent and pushed inside.

"Aria Jones." A three-pack-a-day-chased-down-with-whiskey voice comes from the darkest corner of the tent. I see her, red scarf pulled over her brow, covering her hair. She has a patch over one eye as if she was once a pirate.

"Sit down," she says.

Like an automaton, I do what I'm told.

"Shuffle the cards. Deal three. One for past, one for present, one for future."

Out comes Death. Then The Lovers, upside down. Finally, The Fool.

The fortune-teller taps the first card. "You know what this means. But Death is your past, Aria, not your future. As for your present, The Lovers reversed means one-sidedness, an imbalance of some kind. Perhaps you're holding on to a dream so tightly you've forgotten that dreams alone aren't enough."

I push back my chair. I can see where this is going. One-sidedness. Theo Winchester has no feelings for Aria Jones. Why would he? I threw a bucket of water on a fire and now I think he likes me? The Fool on the final card looks up at me, laughing.

Yes, I'm a fool.

"Wait!" the fortune-teller says. "You haven't seen your last two cards. Here."

From the deck she pulls out The Tower and then, Judgment.

Yes, Aria Jones who lives in her turret is right now facing her judgment.

I spin away. *Bang!* The chair cracks to the floor.

"I haven't finished," the woman insists.

I freeze. I know that voice. It's almost perfectly disguised, but I know it.

"Calliope?"

"Noooooooooooo!!!!"

A scream comes from outside the tent, so shocking that I scream too.

Both the fortune-teller—is it Calliope?—and I run toward the tent flap. Out by the pool, the crowd has stepped away from something. Something staggering. A flash of red. Red on red.

Flitter is on fire!

She teeters beside the water.

I run toward her. Why am I the only one running? Why is everyone else just staring? She's going to fall, hit her head—burn.

At last someone else runs too. It's Theo. He's closer than me and he hurls himself toward Flitter, but he isn't in time to grab her before she topples into the pool.

I drop to my knees screaming, *"Flitter!"*

CHAPTER 23

...

1957

FINALLY THE NOISES BOB IS MAKING IN THE LIBRARY END. CALLIOPE'S pumps tap across the floor. Before she opens the door, she says, "I have the part." It's not a question.

Bob's voice is relaxed. "You do."

The door shuts.

The *ziiiiiiip* sounds again. Metal clangs, the sofa yawns.

Footsteps. Not walking toward the door, but coming closer to where Aria is hiding.

She scrambles deeper under the chair. *Please make a hole for me to fall into,* she begs the Marmont. *Please.*

But the chateau doesn't do that. Because what happens next won't be what anyone expects.

People see Aria trailing Calliope and Flitter and think she's the kid who isn't too bright—the one who wants to keep up, but who never will. But the Marmont knows that Aria isn't slow or stupid; she's a young lady who will either get the world she gives into or the world she fights for.

Right now in the library, the two paths leading toward those two different futures are waiting.

The Marmont holds its curtains closed and lets out not a breath as Bob reaches down for Aria's wrists and pulls her out from under the chair.

"Lucky for you, I'm not interested in little girls," he says. "Except insofar as I see them creeping around, watching me. I put on that show for you. I'm sure it will keep you quiet."

He lets go of her wrists and walks away.

If the Marmont had a heart it would break over what Aria thinks next: *I'm lucky. Lucky that he only touched my wrists.*

Too many women convince themselves that they're lucky, make themselves believe that what happened to them isn't assault. So the Marmont stops waiting. It wriggles its bedrock so that paintings fall off walls and the piano in the lobby plays an E minor chord and there's a tidal wave in the pool and everyone stops, silent, thinking of the ghost in the turret. In that silence, the camera whirs louder and louder so that it sounds like a voice telling Aria that if her parents had lived and she'd stayed in Manhattan, then what happened to Calliope tonight would have happened anyway. But nobody would have known about it.

Except now, Aria does.

And so . . .

Fight, the camera insists. *Fight.*

CHAPTER 24

...

1964

"FLITTER!"

I lean over the edge of the pool, stretch out a desperate hand toward the red dress. Then there's a splash—Theo's thrown off his leather jacket and his shoes and dove in. He scrapes up Flitter, then wades over to the steps with her.

She's completely limp. Burned up? Dead?

How can she be dead? She's Flitter, the life of every slumber party.

"Call a doctor," Theo barks. Yes, the doctor will fix Flitter. He fixes everyone.

I sprint over to the poolside telephone and once I know Doctor Foster is on his way, I push through the staring, whispering crowd. Nobody is helping Flitter and Theo. He's the only one checking her pulse.

Then a miracle happens. Flitter's head lifts. Her red-lipsticked mouth curves into a smile. Her hand waves.

She winks.

"How's that for a knockout audition, Matty? See, I can be any part a movie needs me to be. It was just special-effects fire. But thank you, my Prince Charming." She kisses Theo full on the mouth.

Everyone applauds. *What an idea for an audition!* they say. *She'll get the part. Look, she's in Win's arms. Maybe the fortune-teller was right.*

I can't breathe. My whole body is shaking. I try to suck in air, try to quell panic and adrenaline. But it won't be calmed, just like the memory of fire can never be stamped out.

"*How could you?*" I scream at my friend. "I thought you were burned and dead like my parents!"

Everyone's eyes turn to me, ranting by the poolside. I advance on Flitter, my hands still visibly trembling, wanting to reach out and shake her, but she stops me dead by saying, "Take it easy. It was a prank."

Take it easy?

I turn and run. Away from the pool. Away from Flitter kissing Theo, who should have thrown her back in the pool and let her drown in her own charade. Away from the recurring vision of my mother's white pumps melting in murderous blue flames.

I run up to the turret and shove my journals into my suitcase along with a photo of my parents. I take the money out of *War and Peace* and put it in an envelope addressed to Doctor Foster, along with a note saying, For Miss Devine Rey's rehab. I keep two hundred dollars for myself.

I'm leaving. What could possibly happen to me out there that's worse than what happens in here? Fires and games and people dying, but not really; starlets and auditions and the relentless ambition to film another made-up story that will stop us from thinking about the real lives we all have to live.

"Aria?"

I gasp, hand flying to my heart, a cliche that fits in so well tonight.

Theo, face inscrutable, is dripping water onto the floor and staring at my suitcase. "Where are you going?"

"Anywhere far from here," I shout at the man who jumped into the pool to save a woman who's beyond saving. "I hate this place. I hate Bob and Matty and Flitter and even Calliope. I hate the screams in the night and the bungalows and that damn wind out there. God, I hate that wind."

The rant that's been sitting inside me since the first night here when I yelled at my aunt pours out. It feels like the whole world is shaking, like the turret is quivering with all the rage I can't let out by screaming through the window and into the night.

Laughter, lawless and wild, rises up from the party that the Queen of Fortune had been ruling over until Hollywood reminded everyone that *it* is king of us all. We're just chessboard pieces—and pawns can become queens and then they can die.

My god, of everyone, Flitter's been the one who's *never* given in to the games. But now, even she has.

The floorboards creak under my feet like a sad little voice saying that maybe seven years of forgettable roles have tarnished her dream too. I step forward, shut the voice out.

But it's taken away my anger. Left me with tears.

I lean my hands on the desk, try to breathe.

Drip, drip, drip. Water falls onto the floor from Theo's clothes.

"You need to change," I tell him. I want him gone. "You'll catch cold."

"If I go downstairs, I'm worried you won't be here when I get back."

"Why?" I'm through with not understanding everything, had enough of plunging from doubt to hope and back again over this man standing in front of me. "Who cares where Aria Jones is? Aria, the name everyone here knows, but no one ever thinks about unless I'm getting in their way or rescuing them. In a world that doesn't care who it burns, I'm just the one waiting around with the water. I don't have a face worth a damn, but I have a heart, and I'd rather have that even if nobody ever looks at it. But right now . . ."

I blink and whisper, "My heart is so damn tired of everything."

The floorboards shift again. Theo takes his chance to get away from the madwoman in the turret. But no—he's walking toward me, rather than away.

He stops just two inches from my body.

"Aria?"

I lift my head up very slowly.

"You're not just the one waiting around with the water," he

says and his voice is whiskey-fire, the kind that makes your insides yearn. "You're the one eating grilled cheese with your eyes closed like it was Beluga caviar. You're the one who would have taken Adele under your wing anyway, even if I'd said you couldn't be her tutor. You're the one who wears your heart in your eyes." He pauses. "In your beautiful green eyes."

His finger reaches out to touch the circle of skin beneath my chin and I jump.

If that's what it feels like to have Theo Winchester touch an ordinary, unerotic part of my body, then I don't think I can ever again think about his eyelashes sweeping over my inner thigh. Because right now, I'm standing on the edge of that world my encyclopedias told me existed—the one where it's possible to feel so much that you could spontaneously combust.

CHAPTER 25

...

1957

ARIA EVENTUALLY PICKS HERSELF UP OFF THE FLOOR, GOES to her aunt's suite, and puts herself to bed. She shoves away the *ziiiiiip* sound and the noises Bob made and thinks about beaches: blue water, soft sand, sun shining down. Nothing bad ever happens at the beach, just sunburn, easily fixed with aloe vera. She falls into an agitated sleep and wakes early on the morning of Calliope's birthday party.

She should put on her black funeral dress, go down to the library, light the candles, and make sure the pink layer cake with the words *Calliope Burns: Star* is in the center of the table. But how will she ever set foot inside that room again? How will she sit there and not tell Flitter, who drew a beautiful picture inside a book meant to celebrate Calliope's future?

All Aria wants now is to be like her aunt and never set foot outside this room again.

There's a knock at the door. Seconds pass. Another knock. Miss Devine must be asleep. Aria will have to see who it is.

She pulls on her robe, trudges to the door. A bellboy hands her a note and she remembers to give him a one-dollar bill from the pile by the door. She's being so outwardly normal while her insides are scrambled.

The note says, *Kid, Calliope got the part! And she got me a part as an extra too. We had to leave early this morning for the studio and we'll be there until late. Eat the cake. Enjoy!*

Aria sees, waiting by the door, the pink layer cake. Whoever delivered it has left a mucky thumbprint marring one of the points of the star.

She steps over the cake, walks into the hall, enters the secret stairwell. She has to yank hard at the door because it's stuck and won't let her in. Down five flights of stairs and out onto the driveway. Along the driveway and onto the street.

She's standing on Sunset Boulevard.

Water touches her face. She looks up. Above her spins a gigantic woman dressed in a leotard, her smile as brilliant as Calliope's, her blue leotard bleached by the sun.

The water is rain, Aria realizes. She doesn't think it's rained the whole time she's been at the chateau. But now it's raining as heavily as one of those Manhattan summer storms that would pour down from a sky that had been bright blue a moment before, magicking up puddles and umbrella hawkers where there'd once been dull concrete and souvenir stands.

Everyone vanishes from the street, jumping into cars and taxis, or entering Schwab's and Googie's. Aria doesn't. A few feet away is a bus stop. She walks toward it—can't wait here for seven more years, no matter that she has even less in her pockets right now than tissues and candy.

A gust of wind, so strong that it almost blows Aria onto the road, whips up. She stumbles forward. Thunder sounds right behind her. No, not thunder—an earthquake. The ground shakes beneath her feet.

She spins around, can't make herself believe what she sees. No earthquake. But the silver dollar the showgirl was holding has fallen down. Its pieces are spread all over the pavement in jagged shards of plastic, like a thousand silver daggers have been thrown right onto the spot where Aria was standing before the wind blew her forward.

But for the sake of two seconds, she'd have been slaughtered by a lucky silver dollar.

Now she's running, faster than she's ever run before. She runs straight back into the Marmont, doesn't stop until she's in her bed, sheets pulled up to her chin.

My god, how naive she is. She isn't even aware of half the dangers in the world, had no idea what men do with the things hiding behind their zippers, could never have comprehended that money, the one thing she wants, could kill you.

If she'd been squashed and taken to a hospital, how would any of the doctors know who to call? Would Flitter or Calliope, busy now with their movie, have realized that Aria was missing or dead? Would her aunt have noticed?

If Aria woke up in a hospital, would she have known what to do—besides calling Schwab's?

Now she understands why her aunt never leaves. The Marmont will tarnish you, but the world can kill. The Marmont is dangerous, but it is safety too.

CHAPTER 26

...

1964

THE DOOR OF THE TURRET BURSTS OPEN. *HOLY SHIT!* WHY AT the most crucial junctures of my life does someone burst into the turret? It's not Flitter this time, it's Doctor Foster. Theo's hand drops to his side and suddenly we're standing a foot apart.

"It's your aunt," Doctor Foster says.

"You're wet. You need to change," I tell Theo so he won't come along and see whatever mess needs to be cleaned up now.

Then I hurry down the stairs with the doctor, who says, "It's good news. A place came up at one of the best rehab facilities in California. But they've got a waiting list longer than Judith Crown's career. If we don't take the place by morning, they'll give it to someone else. I need to leave now to get her there."

"Have you told her?" There's nothing I want less than to be the one to break the news to Miss Devine Rey that there'll be no more reds, no more smack, no more booze.

He nods and it doesn't take any smarts at all to interpret the look on his face: it didn't go well.

Inside the suite, Miss Devine Rey is propped on the couch. Her eyes land on me—two furious little grenades about to explode. But I don't know what it is—perhaps it's the incomprehensible scenes from tonight's party where everyone I thought I knew has behaved in ways I'd never have expected—but I don't shrink back from what I think I'm seeing. Instead I wonder, am I misreading my aunt too?

Maybe she doesn't look angry. Maybe she looks afraid.

Going to rehab means going outside the Marmont. When I left safety and familiarity behind seven years ago, my response had been to hide fear behind fury too.

I sit down and take her hand. "Matty Tamer is directing a movie about an orphan. *Jane Eyre.* There's a character in it, a housekeeper—she tries to warn the orphan. I think you could get the role, once you're better."

"I don't want to go anywhere," she whines.

"If you do, then you can come back to a role made for you—you were the one who warned this orphan." I point to myself.

I have no idea if she'll ever be able to act again, or if Matty would even consider her for a part. But if my aunt goes to rehab with only her past to hold on to, she won't survive. I keep my eyes fixed on hers, trying to make her recall that she's connected to me and to movies, for better or worse, and to a future that hangs in the sky like either a guillotine or a star.

I need to know that people can leave here. That in this room in twenty years' time, it won't be me prostrate on the couch. Or Flitter. Or Calliope.

She stares at me and I let her see it, my soul.

Then she reaches inside her neckline and pulls out a small brass key. She tugs it off the chain and puts it in my hand. "The turret," she whispers. Her eyes close.

I grab her hand. "You can't go to sleep yet. What's the key for?"

"Sorry, Aria," Dr. Foster says. "I gave her a sedative for the journey. You won't be able to wake her."

Dammit. I close my fist around the key. I'll find what it opens if it's the last thing I do.

I pass the doctor my money. "Tell me when you need more. I'll get it somehow."

Then I kiss my aunt's forehead and hope she can hear me when I say, "Legends only exist because people believe in them. Once you're better, make everyone believe in the legend again."

IN THE TURRET, I search for anything with a keyhole, pull clocks and music boxes from the shelves. Examine a writing desk. The jewelry cases. I find the one with the owl ring inside it and hope surges through me.

I empty it of its contents, pull out the lining, shake it until the lid falls off. But there's nothing. The key my aunt gave me doesn't fit any of the locks.

I curse, cast my eyes over the floor, make sure I haven't missed anything. There's stuff everywhere. I need to clean it up before I collect Adele or she'll think I've gone mad.

I move as fast as I can, but it's morning by the time I finish. I end up scooping up the last few items and shoving them onto a shelf before hurrying down to my room to change—no governess turns up for school in the clothes she wore to the party the night before.

I halt in the corridor. The door to my room is wide open.

"Hello?" I whisper.

No reply.

I creep forward, trying to convince myself that Calliope and Flitter will be inside. They'll apologize and we'll hug and everything will be all right.

I reach the doorway. Peer in.

Nothing.

"Hello?" I repeat.

There's no one there.

I no longer care that I'm still wearing my dress from the night before. All I can think of are screams and fires and the laughter that cackled outside my door. Now somebody's broken in.

I run to the front desk, panting by the time I get there. What if I'd been in my room when whoever it was got inside?

"Are you okay?" John the desk clerk asks.

"Someone broke into my room," I huff.

"You sure?" John asks. "I hear you went kind of crazy last night. Maybe you're imagining things?"

"*I* went crazy? What about Flitter?"

"Yeah, I hear she put on a real show. Might get that part everyone wants."

How is this the narrative that's come out of last night? That I'm mad and Flitter's a hero?

John pushes over a box. "Bob was real worried about you. He got you these. Always looking out for everyone. Gave me a proper gold cigarette lighter for my last birthday."

Bob's left me a box of Quaaludes.

To calm the agitated mind of the girl whose aunt relies on the stuff, the girl who screamed at her friend by the pool last night, the girl who's just burst into the lobby like she's a lunatic.

I close my fist around the box. Put on my sensible-Aria face. "Tell Bob I said thank you. And don't worry about the door. It was probably nothing."

I will never forgive you, Bob had said to me six years ago. I have a terrible feeling he's about to prove it—and I'm walking right into his trap.

I ARRIVE AT THE Winchester penthouse more than an hour late, knowing I'm going to be very lucky if I'm not fired on the spot, let alone see the Theo who told me I had beautiful green eyes. Right now, it seems impossible that it really happened.

"I'm sorr—"

Theo and Adele are sitting side by side on the couch, both of them with guitars on their laps.

"I'm having a lesson. I figured he"—Adele grins at her father—"would be a better teacher than you for this."

"Great," I say, daring to glance at Theo, who gives a shrug that has so many possible meanings: *Hey, look at me being a dad.* Or, *Last night we were all a bit overwrought.* Or, *I'd rather it was you on my lap, not my guitar.*

I blink, hoping nobody saw that bit of my overwrought soul in my eyes.

"Take a half hour off," Theo says. "I might as well finish this."

I make myself behave like the Aria they expect. "Well, in a half hour, I'm expecting either a knockout song or that Adele will have knocked you out." I nod at Theo. "Hopefully creative genius will beat out your creative temperaments."

Adele laughs. And Theo smiles at me. "If you see Pilot, send him up," he says. "Adele let him out two hours ago."

I take my mixed-up head to the grove where my little woodpecker lives. If I sit down among the frangipani and jasmine, I'll stop thinking about Calliope and Flitter and my aunt and Bob and Theo. I'll take a deep breath and relax.

Normally my approach is enough for the woodpecker to peep out. But there's no movement. I unwrap the suet I collected on my way here and lean in, searching.

"Oh no." I drop to my knees in the dirt. "No, no, *no.*"

On the ground is a tiny mound of brown feathers ringed with red.

My little bird is dead.

I scrub my face with my hand. How silly to cry. It was just a bird. Maybe it's free now, ghost wings flying away from this place it got trapped in because it had only one leg.

I push back onto my heels, swipe my face again. Something clatters.

Pilot's water bowl. What's that doing out here?

The color of the liquid inside the bowl arrests me. Creamy yellow. I sniff. Coconut and rum.

Someone's put piña colada in Pilot's water bowl.

Bang!

I gasp-scream.

The door of the bungalow behind the *Keep Out!* sign just slammed shut.

But I don't care about that now. Dogs can't metabolize alcohol.

I tear through the garden, climb the Marmont's throat, let myself get spat out on the top floor.

Inside the penthouse, Theo and Adele are on their knees, crouched over something.

No, no, no.

"Is . . . Pilot . . ." I gasp.

Adele turns around, face streaked with tears. Dr. Foster is there too.

He says, very soberly, "Thankfully he'll be all right."

I close my eyes. Bend over. *Thank god.*

"WHAT HAPPENED?" I SINK onto the couch.

"A stupid party trick," Theo says grimly. "It was a pretty wild night."

His eyes brush over my face, then drop back down to Pilot. He runs one hand along Pilot's side, up and back, speaking in a low voice to his dog, his tone the same one I use with the starlets in the turret—a low musical thrum tuned to the key of comfort.

"Why was it wild?" Adele asks, sitting on the ground beside her dad.

She looks frightened and small. I try to lighten the mood. "Well, a fortune-teller said your dad was going to marry Flitter."

"Oh, she's so pretty," Adele says. Then she frowns. "Would she be a good mom?"

Theo manages a laugh. "That's one role she won't be auditioning for."

Relief. He sounds so certain. But I defend my friend. "She was a good mom to me," I say. It's the truth. She was. But now? Since being dropped by her studio, Flitter's become the kind of woman who'd make her friends think she was on fire just to get a part in a movie.

Fire. Screams. A laugh outside my door. Pilot. My bird. "You don't think there's something going on, do you?" I blurt. "With Pilot and the scream—"

"There's nothing going on." Theo cuts me off.

I can see why. Adele looks terrified. She nestles into Theo's side and he puts an arm around her. They look like a family. They *are* a family.

They don't need me. I stand.

"Can you stay?" Adele begs. "Please?"

I retake my seat, determined to say nothing, to frighten nobody. Because it's nice to be invited to stay, to watch Adele stroking Pilot's head, to be included in the sanctuary of the Winchesters' silence.

Until Theo looks up at me and all I can think of is the drop of water that slid down his jaw last night.

I leap up again. "How about I read you a story?" I say to Adele. "I'll go upstairs and get a book."

"Is there one you know by heart?" she asks.

That's how I find myself lying on my back on the couch so I don't have to look at Theo, recounting *We Have Always Lived in the Castle,* a story about a woman who won't leave her castle, who prefers to remain hidden away and unseen. A woman whose life is turned upside down when a handsome stranger arrives. A woman whose castle is eventually burned down around her.

"That's kinda sad," Adele says when I get to the end. "Why would you want to lock yourself away like that?"

It's Theo, with the head of his poisoned dog in his lap and his arm around the teenage daughter he retrieved from a hospital a few months ago, who says, "Sometimes it feels safer not to be in the world."

"I guess." Adele is quiet for a minute, then she says, "But maybe

I should start back at school after New Year? I really like Aria, but I liked going out with my friend too."

Adele is the bravest of us all.

"I'll make dinner," I say, wanting to give them a moment.

I make burgers and we eat them on the couch, talking about nothing in particular while Pilot sleeps in his bed in front of the fire. Adele falls asleep not long after she's eaten and Theo tucks a blanket over her, then comes to sit on the other couch, next to me.

We're both quiet. I'm thinking about Adele going to school after the New Year. I'll have nothing tying me to this castle anymore. Except that I've given all my money to my aunt.

"I can hear you thinking," Theo says.

I smile. "I was trying to do it quietly."

"You never think quietly. You fill entire rooms with the kinetic energy of your musings. What's hurting your brain now?"

You're the one who wears your heart in your eyes, he told me last night, just before he lifted my face up to his. I don't know why he did that. But I know that I can't afford to have my heart in my eyes because I'm leaving the Marmont next month. That's always been my plan.

"Miss Devine Rey's gone to rehab," I tell him.

He whistles. "How did she afford that? I know from paying for my rehab and Marley's too that it isn't cheap."

"Marley?" He told me the names of his wives. Honey and Joanie. Not Marley.

And Flitter said he'd had three wives.

He rubs a hand over his face. "Marley was the wife I didn't marry."

"Well, that makes no sense," I say slowly.

He stares at the couch, scrubs a small stain with his fingernail. "I don't want to tell you this story because . . ." Another attempt to scratch off the stain. "It doesn't make me look that great. And I care about what you think of me."

Oh.

He cares.

Maybe I'm about to embarrass myself. But I've always been honest with him. So I say, "I think a lot of you. I don't know how easy it would be to change that."

A glimmer of a smile. "I might hold you to that." He pauses, seems to steel himself, then says in a voice that's hard to hear, "I met Marley about two years ago. After I'd been to rehab the first time. It was my first sober relationship."

He sighs. "I loved her. But I didn't marry her because the women I married all ended up dead. Not getting married didn't protect her though. I relapsed after six months. Straight back to drinking and partying. And Marley, who'd until then just take a bump of coke at a party, started taking all kinds of things. I was drunk, so she got wasted. We started fighting. We broke up. She moved on to someone worse for her than I was. She almost OD'd a few months back. Someone found her in time. I got her into rehab because if she'd never met me, she'd never have almost died."

"You don't know that," I tell him. "You don't owe her. But it was nice of you all the same."

Then Theo says, voice sharper now, "You paid for your aunt, didn't you? I'm paying you the measly sum of fifty dollars a week—"

"Plus you're covering our rent. Do not," I say, because I will not take charity ever again. "Don't offer to pay me more." Then I ask him, because I need to know what my aunt is facing, "Is it hard? Rehab?"

"The hardest thing I've ever done. Marley too. She almost relapsed her first week out. That's the worst time of all. Thinking you've beaten it, only to find that you live in a world where raindrops remind you of vodka and stop signs make you want a Seconal."

He pauses, starts to say, "Which is why . . ." But at the same time I say, "That sounds like a line from a Theo Winchester song."

He laughs and the firelight dances in his eyes. I'm back to thinking about spontaneous combustion.

I remind myself that his daughter is asleep right here in the room. I start to apologize for interrupting him, but he says, "At the risk of ruining my reputation, I feel like hot cocoa. With marshmallows. Want one?"

Now I'm laughing. "Rock star cocoa. Can't say no to that."

I watch him in the kitchen stirring hot milk on the stove, wearing jeans and a T-shirt because the fire is so hot, a lick of ink curling into his sleeve. When he looks over at me, I don't look away.

He carries the cocoa over, sits on the edge of the coffee table, his back to Adele, one foot propped on the couch, facing me. "I wrote a song last night."

There's an odd expression on his face.

"You look a bit stunned," I say. "I thought writing songs was what a rock star did?"

"I haven't written a song since everything went down with Marley. It's like . . ." He pauses, sips cocoa. "To write a song, you have to love something about life. Every song is about loving and living. But after Marley, after thinking I'd managed to ruin yet another woman's life, life became just this succession of days I had to get through. It was partly why I moved here. Who can't find wonder and awe in a castle? But maybe you don't find that stuff in a place. Maybe you find it in people. Adele's a pretty awesome kid. And"—his eyes meet mine—"there are other awesome people around here too."

I bite my lip so my smile isn't too goofily oversized. "What's the song about?"

"Growing up. Being an adult. About how you can blame your shitty dad for your fuck-ups when you're a kid, but if you're still doing it as an adult, then maybe you haven't grown up yet." His smile is wry. "Not a very sexy subject for a song."

He reaches over and takes one of the guitars off the stand. His fingers move over the strings, a reflex action at first. Then he adjusts his position, plays a different chord and, my god—music. The symphony of lost youth and regrets—that whiskey omelets will curdle your stomach like bad choices, and to not arrive at the Clark County courthouse in Las Vegas for your wedding between eight and nine in the evening because even the justice of the peace has to eat. And that nobody grows up dreaming of waiting for a justice of the peace to finish his pot roast so you can get married wearing a hangover and the fading tinsel of a bad idea. That you can live like all of those things are your life, or you can live in spite of those things being your life.

When he's finished I say, voice a little wobbly, "It's a really good song."

Theo's smile is a bit wobbly too. "Most women would want the song to be about them. And I will write you a song one day, Aria Jones."

For once in my life, I don't know what to say. Because with a backdrop of firelight and music, and with his soul exposed in a C minor chord, we're circling the edges of the two people who'd stood so close together in a turret last night that fire seemed like something I wanted to leap right into.

Theo's eyes are fixed on mine, and for the first time ever, I let him see me, Aria Jones, who is definitely not, in many ways, most women. But in this way—wanting to trace his upper lip with my tongue—I am like every single woman in America.

Theo swallows.

Adele rolls over and we leap away from each other like naughty children.

I smile. Theo does too.

This is the sexiest thing I've ever done.

"We should talk about something," he says. "Staring is too . . ." His eyes meander over my cheekbones, stop when they reach my throat. "Tempting."

Theo Winchester is flirting with me.

I smile even wider. "What shall we talk about?"

"How about I let you do what you like best. Ask questions. Ask me anything."

"There are other things I like better than asking questions."

Now Aria Jones is the one doing the flirting.

Theo leans forward and says very softly, "On some other night very soon I want to find out about all the things you like. Every. Single. One."

Oh, Jesus.

Theo puts his guitar down. His fingers flex.

His daughter exhales an indelicate snore.

We exchange another smile.

"I think I'd better take you up on your offer. I'll ask you . . ." I consider, then recall what he'd said earlier about blaming his father. "Tell me about your dad."

I curse myself. I was doing so well. Why would I ask something so deeply unsexy?

Indeed, Theo rears away. "He was a studio musician for Millennium Wolf. That's all that's worth saying."

I stare at him. "What did he do to you?"

"What makes you think he did anything?" he snaps.

"I recognize a person who carries a lot with them."

He closes his eyes. Doesn't speak. Finally he shakes his head exasperatedly. "This is the part where you're meant to say, 'we can talk about something else if you want to.' "

"Or it's the part where I say that one of the things I like is when people answer my questions," I counter.

He picks up the cigarette packet, lights one, rubs his forehead with his thumb.

"My father." He smokes for a couple of minutes.

"Because of my dad's job, I grew up thinking Hollywood was normal life. My mom was long gone; she caught the gravy train to Nashville with a country singer when I was twelve. My dad started having epic parties. Everyone knew you could go to Roger Winchester's house to let loose. No wife; no rules. People came and went, they'd crash for a few days, never throw their bottles in the trash, never empty the ashtrays—hell, they hardly used ashtrays; that's what the empty bottles were for. It might be Wednesday and someone would ask when the party started and the answer was, it never stopped."

Theo's whole body is rigid, like this story is trying to claw its way out of him and his soul wants to keep it locked up tight.

"I lost my virginity at one of those parties when I was fifteen." He shifts position, comes to sit next to me so I can't see his face when he tells me the rest.

"A woman who was probably in her late thirties found me in the back garden—that's where I'd sit because the parties happened inside or out front. She told me it was every boy's dream to do what she wanted to do. So I figured I should close my eyes and be happy; nothing was wrong because she was a grown-up—although by then I knew that adults weren't reliable guides to good behavior. The next day I wrote a song about it. From then on, writing songs became a thing I did whenever I didn't know how to feel. When I was seventeen, my dad heard me playing the song. He knew Richie King, who'd just started his television show, knew that Richie needed some talent. So I headed down to the Ambassador's Ballroom at Venice Beach, and played my guitar and sang this song that was about being screwed by a much older woman and wishing I could have smiled throughout rather than shut my eyes. Everyone thought it was a sweet song about that moment when you let go of the helium balloon your parents bought you at the county fair. Either I wasn't great at metaphor or folks don't care for subtext. I landed a record deal that night."

Click of the cigarette lighter. Flare of the flame. Glitter of smoke. Ache of truth.

I reach out and take his hand. He holds on, painfully tight.

There's more, and worse, to come.

"The morning after the party, my dad clapped me on the back and called me a lucky son of a bitch. Now I was a man, he said. Which means . . ."

A long, almost endless drag on the cigarette. It makes me shiver, the way he's so intent on that Lucky Strike, like he wants more from it than smoke. Wants to find, in those burning leaves, a way out. I've never seen him drink, never seen him take so much as a Tylenol, but I can see that he's an addict. And he always will be. It's just a question of whether he wins or the booze does.

Theo finally lets go of the smoke. "It means my father knew what was happening. He could have stopped it. Just had to walk out and call my name. But . . ."

The moon lowers, casting Theo's shadow and mine against the wall. We look colossal, big enough to catch hold of the moon and let it take us up into the sky where we could give ourselves the futures that the constellations didn't see fit to grant us in our pasts.

"Instead of the Cheerios, he passed me a whiskey. 'Drink up,' he said. 'Like a man.' That was the day, at age fifteen, when I became an alcoholic just like him."

Dear god. How many people in the rooms at the Chateau Marmont might have been entirely different people but for a story like the one Theo just told? Flitter. Calliope too.

Theo finishes his story by saying, "Pilot was the first thing I bought with the money from my record deal. Something with a heart that was mine. He's been there through it all."

In response I whisper, "Sometimes I think I'm glad my parents are dead. They never had the chance to disappoint me or to make me hate them. Maybe it's easier, what I had."

Theo's thumb strokes the back of my hand very gently. "You're the only person in the world who can hear about someone's miserable childhood and think that becoming an orphan was the better option. You must miss them. Feel nostalgic for them at the very least."

I shake my head. "I don't feel nostalgic. I feel like I could murder someone if it meant getting them back." I pluck the cigarette from his fingers, my exhalation sparkling like the frost of that cold-blooded thought. "What I feel is angrier than nostalgia. Like a wolf standing beside a fawn."

He turns his head toward me. "You know that the girl who isn't an orphan, the one with two parents, is still inside you. She'll always be inside you."

Maybe. Maybe deep down there's not just a girl who wants to wish upon stars, but a girl who still believes that those wishes come true.

CHAPTER 27

. . .

1957

LYING IN HER BED AFTER A SILVER DOLLAR TRIED TO KILL HER, one of the strangest of all the things that have happened at the Marmont ensues. Aria hears, as if it's right outside, the stumble-drag of footsteps belonging to someone who's been fed too many mint juleps spiked with the candies her aunt told her not to eat. The invisible arm of the Marmont pushes Aria up and out of bed, holds her hand as she searches each floor.

On the second floor, she sees actor Karl Douglas propping up a starlet so newly arrived that Aria doesn't even know her name. Karl says to the girl, "I'll give you some audition tips that will land you any part you want."

The not-yet-starlet hovers in front of Karl's door. The only person this not-yet-starlet knows, Aria would bet, is Karl Douglas, who she probably just met at a party, meaning her knowledge extends to his respectable tally of two marriages and his good-guy screen persona where he saves women like the one poised here, deciding.

But is there even a decision for her to make? She needs some tips. She wants a part.

Karl puts his hand on her back, nudges her forward and the thought leaps into Aria's head: Can she make the Marmont world a little safer for those most at risk? If she could do that, maybe she'll survive the next seven years.

"Excuse me!" Aria hurries over. "There's a call for you downstairs."

The starlet blinks.

"She'll call back tomorrow," Karl growls.

"It's your agent," Aria tells the woman, who blinks again, rousing a little from the stupor of whatever Karl filled her glass with.

Aria guides the starlet to the elevator.

"Come back when you've finished," Karl calls.

The elevator doors close. The woman reclines against the wall.

Isaiah studies Aria, who asks him, "Do you have money for a cab?"

He pulls out a couple of bills. Aria passes them to the starlet.

"But the call . . ."

"There's no call."

The woman stumbles. Isaiah catches her.

"No call," she repeats.

Then she walks out through the open doors of the elevator and onto the driveway, turning briefly to say to Aria, "Thank you."

As the elevator ascends, Isaiah says to Aria, "Oh, honey. You let me know whenever you need some help."

She will.

From now on, she'll scoop up fallen starlets and push them in the direction of safety. She'll save them in a way she hadn't saved Calliope.

CHAPTER 28

...

1964

IT'S ALMOST FOUR IN THE MORNING WHEN I SAY TO THEO, "I need to get some sleep. I have a grumpy boss."

He laughs. "I promise he won't be grumpy tomorrow."

My hand slides reluctantly out of his. We're walking to the door when he says, "Can I take you out tomorrow? There's a new band playing at Ciro's. We could check them out."

I take three steps away from him.

Orphan. Rock star.

Poor. Rich.

Nobody. Celebrity.

Never been in the world. Man of the world.

"Aria?" He looks panicked. "Did I misjudge this? I'm sorry . . ."

"It's just . . ." My voice is small like me. "We're so different. And going out . . ." It'd been fine when we were talking about nights that I thought might be spent here. But outside . . .

"We don't have to go to Ciro's. We'll eat at Chasen's. Music's my thing. Food," he teases, "is yours."

I take two more steps away from the man who's lived so much he's had two wives and two Vegas weddings, has played to crowds in London and Paris. The man who can take the elevator down to the garage and drive out of here knowing whether to turn left or right, knowing where he wants the roads to take him.

"Maybe you haven't quite understood this. Besides that night on your bike, I haven't really been past Schwab's all that much." I exhale. Stare at the wall above his head. It sounds crazy. I say it as quietly as I can. "I mean . . . I've never gone farther than Schwab's."

Silence elongates. I imagine what Theo's thinking: *How did I end up in a room with this sequestered child?*

But he asks, "Would you like to go past Schwab's?"

I nod.

"We'll walk along the Strip as far as you want. Buy a hot dog."

I meet his eyes. "That's the kind of thing you'd do with a kid."

"I don't think you're a child."

My fingernails creep up to my mouth, the old habit too hard to resist. "I have no experience with going on a date. In a movie, after the date comes the conflict, the big dramatic moment. Right now I feel like *I'm* the conflict. The human who's never lived."

"Well . . ." Theo comes a little bit nearer. "My expertise is only in drunk Vegas weddings. Maybe we figure this out together."

I GO INTO THE garden, despite it being nighttime. From the gardener's shed I take out a spade, dig a hole, and tuck the body of my little dead bird into the soil.

Then I sit beside its grave and cry.

I was so happy twenty minutes ago. Just like I was happy the day I sat in a library in front of a table set out for a party. Happiness is dangerous.

Suddenly the shadows look like things I've ignored. The builders didn't play the prank on Pilot. If it was one of the wasted actors, why didn't they hang around to laugh over the drunken dog?

Screams. Laughs. Fire. A dead bird too.

All of it is happening to me. As if somebody's trying to drive *me* away.

And in the dirt by my feet there's a red headscarf. Like the one the fortune-teller wore at the party. The fortune-teller who'd sounded just like Calliope.

Who'd said Flitter would marry Theo and that I was a fool with a one-sided dream.

God. What's going on? Calliope's overly medicated and disoriented, but she'd never do any of the other stuff.

But nor did I ever think she'd pretend to be a fortune-teller who made me feel like my future was hopeless.

I bend down to pick up the scarf. And that's where Bob finds me, face tearstained, knees streaked with dirt, shovel in my hand.

Matty, who's with him, says, "Aria?" like he isn't certain it's me.

I wipe my face, brush the dirt off my knees.

"Dear girl," Bob croons, hands in the air the way you talk to a person who's just pointed a gun at you. "Perhaps you should go lie down."

"You don't look so good," Matty agrees.

"Can I help you back up to the turret?" Bob asks, tone solicitous.

Matty frowns. "Turret?"

Oh, Bob is so good at making the woman look like the crazy one.

Until Bob saw me the other night, nobody except the Winchesters, Flitter, and Calliope knew I spent most of my time in the turret. Some people will think that making a home for yourself in a place they believe is haunted is a little mad.

I put the shovel down.

For seven years I've been so invisible that Bob has left me alone. But these last two months I've started to take on form and shape. I'm less ghost, more woman. And tomorrow, I'm going to step outside the Chateau Marmont and go farther than I've ever been. I'll be out in the open. Visible.

And Theo Winchester will be at my side.

I cannot let Bob ruin this too.

Something flutters in the corner of my eye, like the Marmont is beckoning, trying to catch my attention. It's up high, the curtain over the door that leads onto the balcony Toni Ashenhurst jumped from. And that's when I remember.

There's one lock I haven't tried with the key my aunt gave me.

I do something I've never done before. I touch Bob. I pat his arm. Then I say to Matty, "Maybe you should help Bob to go lie down. Seems like even after all these years, he's still haunted by what happened in that turret."

Then I walk away.

I am not going to let Bob win.

CHAPTER 29

...

1958

OCCASIONALLY AT THE MARMONT, THERE ARE SCREENING nights in the small theater at the end of the first-floor corridor. Not-yet-released movies are played to guests like Marian Monti, Judith Crown, and Augusta Hepworth, stars so influential they could convince a rational person to drink diet water.

Tonight's movie is extra special. The supporting actress is someone who's lived at the Marmont for two years: Calliope Burns.

Seated in the front row are the three aforementioned stars, as well as Bob Ashenhurst, Calliope Burns, Flitter Reeve, and Aria Jones. Even Miss Devine Rey has left her room and taken ownership of the last chair in the front row beside Aria, who can't sit still.

This is the night she's been waiting for. Her hand is held tightly in Calliope's. Calliope's other hand clutches Flitter's.

The Three Sisters.

But will they still be sisters when they find out what Aria's done?

Their eyes are fixed to the screen, waiting. But Calliope and Flitter are waiting for something different from Aria.

The lights go down. The projector whirs. Film flickers onto the screen.

Aria turns to look at the boy operating the projector, the one who delivers mint juleps and paracetamol from Schwab's. His name is George. He's an orphan who lives in the dumpster behind Schwab's; he has no aunt to give him a room. He wants to be a Hollywood camera operator and he helped Aria do this—all she had to do in return was ask Isaiah, who usually operates the camera, to pretend to be sick so George could man the camera and meet a few Hollywood directors.

George nods at Aria.

Her heart is going to burst out of her body. Because something is about to happen, something that could either be the right thing or the wrong thing—Aria doesn't know.

Then there it is.

A dim room. It's hard to see much more than a young woman with pale hair. The back of a sofa. The back of a head of brown hair too—hair belonging to a man.

"It's my birthday tomorrow." The woman's voice rings out through the speakers.

The sofa belches as the man shifts. Fabric rustles. A belt buckle clatters.

Ziiiiiiiiip!

The sound crackles, turned right up to its breaking point.

Then the man says, "There's one condition to you getting the part."

His voice is almost recognizable if he just says something more. And look—now he's turning his head to the side. His profile will be visible in one more second. Her face too, because she's stepping forward and the lights are brightening . . .

Music breaks in joyously. The audience gasps. The title, *He's Just a Rebel Without a Girl,* appears on the screen. The lighting illuminates a woman's cheekbones. It's Calliope! She's wearing the half smile, half pout of a girl who's hoping to be found by a rebel in the opening scenes, one who'll teach her, over the next two hours, a bit of bad—but not too much!—to go with her good.

Murmurs move along the rows of seats. *What was that before? He—who was it?—said* a condition? *Do you think . . . ?*

The men whisper, *Wish I could see the rest of that other movie.*

The women search one another's eyes to find out who knows, start to wonder if maybe they aren't the only ones—but what do you do with that knowledge?

The women who don't yet know put their questions aside because they're watching a Hollywood movie, which is all relentless beauty until the credits roll. Then they stand and blink, ready to walk back out into the real world—the one that nobody bothers to make beautiful.

Aria isn't there. She has no desire to face Bob or Calliope after what she just did.

AS SOON AS ARIA makes it out to the hallway, she runs. Within seconds she's disappeared into the Marmont's belly and only lets herself get spat out on the top floor where she makes her way to the one door nobody ever opens.

The doorway to the turret.

Around and around the stairs go, narrow and dark and easy to slip on, to be pushed down, to be broken on. But Aria has been up and down these stairs a thousand times this year, carrying every book and object from her library, even the leather chair with George's help. The only thing left in the library on the ground floor is the red sofa and the Aria who thought she'd lost everything, only to discover that there is always more to lose.

At the top of the stairs she enters her secret room. The books and magazines are stacked in neat piles along the walls, as are her journals. The chair is positioned by the window. There's no heat, just a blanket, a sweater, a coat, and mittens in a box under the chair. There are two lamps: the one with a high-heeled shoe as its base stands by the chair; another taller lamp with a colored glass shade stands sentry by the door, casting rainbows of red, blue, and green onto the ceiling.

Aria stares at those rainbows: the blue is the color of the eyes of the starlet who arrived yesterday; the green like Lacey Magee, who watches every move Calliope makes; the red is like the starlet of two months before whose room hosts parties nobody speaks of but that everyone knows are the wildest in history.

The door opens and Aria jumps. The books could be a weapon, the stairs too. Her vigilance sags when she sees Calliope, remembers that the reason she chose this room is because nobody will come up here and face the ghost who's said to linger, least of all Bob.

Aria stares at Calliope. Calliope stares at Aria.

"I'm sorry," Aria whispers.

A tear breaks from each of Calliope's eyes, leaving thin lines of black on her face. "Don't," she says, shaking her head. "You shouldn't have . . ."

Thunder crashes outside. Three months of rain falls from the sky as Aria cries too.

Aria has looked and looked at the film and she's certain and thankful that it's not absolutely clear that it's Calliope, because what Calliope did will break every morality clause in her studio contract. She's looked and she's looked, and what she believes is that the film issues a threat. It lets Bob know that Aria has a little grenade in her hand—one that she can set off any time she chooses by showing the rest of the film where the identities of the man and the woman become apparent. Bob will know that Aria won't want to show the entire film unless she absolutely has to because doing so will damage Calliope. But Bob will also know that she might, if pushed far enough. And then everyone will see the evidence that he is the Devil of Hollywood, not the king. She has shown enough of the film to keep Flitter, Calliope, Aria, and Miss Devine safe.

She has shown enough to give them a little power.

Only Aria knows that the film cuts out after the section that just aired in the screening room. Only Aria knows that she has less power than she appears to have.

Calliope crouches on the floor, one arm braced against the wall, the other wrapped around her belly. And Aria knows that the grenade did go off and it's blown up the best friendship she's ever had.

"I'm sorry," Aria whispers again. She wipes the back of her hand over her nose. "I dream every night that I stood up and told Bob to go away. Then in the morning I remember I did nothing."

Calliope's sobs are the loudest sound Aria has ever heard and she wonders if they'll travel down through the lungs of the Marmont and people will think it's the ghost. Then in one sudden movement, Calliope is beside her, her head buried in Aria's lap.

"You didn't do anything wrong," Calliope says, and Aria rejects this outright. Her wrongness is irrefutable, and she still isn't sure if what she did tonight is more wrongness or repentance.

Calliope lifts her head. Her eyes are so blue, the same color as the sea Aria dreams of, as if the pain has made her even more beautiful. "Come with me," she urges Calliope. "To Hawaii. There are no Bobs in Hawaii."

She's so sure Calliope will say yes. But Calliope shakes her head. "I wouldn't have called out either if it had been me hiding behind the chair that day. Because it wouldn't have changed anything. Besides . . ." Calliope pushes herself to her feet, crosses to the window, opens it, leans out, and shouts the worst thing of all into the storm. "You eventually forget why you have to give a man like Bob what he wants while still keeping him outside of you. You forget why it hurts less that way."

No, Aria wants to shout too. *No, no, no.*

Calliope pulls her head back into the room. Her face is wet, her makeup a ruin. But now her eyes sparkle, two little jewels in the dark, dark room. "And I just got a standing ovation." Her voice is gentler when she goes on. "It's time to learn the price of things, Aria. It takes real courage to do that. Like Jordan Baker says in a book I know you'll have in one of those piles: 'It takes two to make an accident.' Maybe you think those two things are this town plus ambition. But the way I see it, those two things are what I did with Bob plus a trash can labeled 'things to forget.' And they equal what's going to happen next month when people watch

Rebel Without a Girl and, for two hours, they're not ugly or pimply or stuck with a deadbeat boyfriend. They live in a castle and they sleep beside a king whose one pleasure in life is to make sure they get their happy ending."

More rain, louder now. The stars are trapped behind it, so is the moon. But Aria doesn't need anything more than lamplight to see that one movie won't be enough for someone whose ambitions have no perimeters. Calliope will want bigger dressing rooms, her name in larger font on a billboard.

Mint juleps to speed along the forgetting.

And Aria blinks away the last stupid tears she'll ever shed as a child.

Calliope finishes by saying, "In that film, it's just a man with brown hair and a stupid girl who didn't even say no. The real problem is that Bob knows someone has that film."

"He knows *I* have it," Aria confesses. "He saw me that day in the library."

The door bursts open with a crash. Aria almost leaps from the chair. The ghost!

But it's Flitter.

"I found you!" she cries when she sees Calliope. Then her eyes register Aria's presence and she says, "Don't tell me it's you who's got that film?" She exhales. "Jesus."

CHAPTER 30

...

1964

THE MARMONT URGES ME ON, ITS EXHALATIONS PUSHING ME UP the stairs to the turret. I walk with my aunt's key in my hand to the one door I never lock because nobody goes up here. The door to the balcony where Toni Ashenhurst decided she didn't want to live any longer.

I go out onto the balcony and I search. There's no furniture, nothing besides the balustrade and the walls.

One of the bricks right in the corner is loose. I try to prize it out, but the years have made it stick fast. I hurry back into the turret, find a pair of scissors, use the blade as leverage to wriggle the brick out.

Finally it comes away.

Behind it are folded sheets of paper, a little worse for wear, but not so much that I can't see they're covered in handwriting.

I sit right there on the floor of the balcony and read Toni Ashenhurst's last words.

Dreams and nightmares are the same thing—the difference just depends on your perspective, it begins. It's addressed to my aunt.

> *I should never have persuaded you to give Bob another chance. If I'd developed perspective about him earlier, you'd have broken it off with him months ago and none of this*

would have happened. And "I'm sorry" are the two most pathetic words in the English language. How can they convey all the repentance I feel? They can't. So I'm leaving you this account. My testament. I hope one day you can do something with it so the whole of Hollywood develops perspective too.

There follows a signed statement:

On the night of July 4, 1950, Miss Devine Rey intended to break off her engagement to Bob Ashenhurst, my brother. But she'd promised to do him one favor and she didn't like to go back on her word. She also hoped that if she did him this favor, he'd let her go to another studio without a fight. So her plan was—do the favor, make Bob happy, tell him it was over, and walk away to a studio where there were men in charge, sure, but not quite like Bob.

The favor he'd asked of her was that she go to a party put on by the three men selling Golden Mare to him. Miss Devine Rey, as everyone knows, was a star like no other—to have her at the party where the deal was done would be like having King Midas there. But those men, they were worse than even my brother.

Nobody should forget that as the biggest star of her generation, Miss Devine had to keep herself squeaky clean. She had rules. She never went to Golden Mare studio parties. They were the kind of parties starlets were paid to attend—if they were given a fistful of dollars, they'd be quiet about whatever happened to them there. But this party would be fine, Miss Devine thought—and so did I—because Bob was there. She'd arrive, give Bob back his ring while he was riding high from signing the contract to buy the studio, and smile for the men who were desperate to meet her. I went with her for moral support; we thought my brother wouldn't get too mad at her if I was there.

I waited in the car while Miss Devine told Bob she no longer wanted to marry him. They were over by the pool house, but I could see them from the car. Bob looked furious. I heard him shout at her to keep her ring on her finger while she signed autographs for the men. He didn't want to look like he couldn't keep the eyes of Hollywood's biggest star fixed on him. Because what if that meant the deal didn't get done? Then he marched her inside the pool house.

I want it on the record that Miss Devine would never have gone inside a pool house at a party alone. But Bob was there. The man who said he loved her.

My brother.

When Miss Devine walked in, Bob walked out, saying he'd be back in a moment. But he didn't come back. He chose to pretend that arranging a "meeting" meant those men wanted a kiss on the cheek, maybe an eyeful of cleavage. So I got out of the car and went into the pool house. And those men turned their attention on me too. Yes, we screamed. But nobody came.

I don't know how we got back here to the hotel. Maybe one of us drove. All I remember is Maisie finding us the next day and calling Dr. Foster and that neither of us could get out of bed for a week.

Words from the past batter me. Calliope saying, *You forget why you have to learn that it hurts less that way.* I hadn't ever let myself think about how she'd had to learn that lesson.

I put the paper down, cover the sound of my weeping with my hands. I don't want to read any more of this. But the time is long past for ignoring my aunt and Toni.

I understand now why Miss Devine eats Quaaludes like they're survival.

Miss Devine called Bob a couple of days later. She told him she was going to Photoplay with the story of what happened. He told her to buy a copy of Whisper first. The lead story was about Bob breaking it off with Miss Devine Rey because of her wild behavior. You've all read it. It intimated that she was a drunk seductress with no moral character. He had quotes from the former owners of Golden Mare—the animals in that pool house—to back him up. And the pièce de résistance: a photo of her leaving the pool house, dress awry, staggering.

She telephoned the magazine, hysterical. I could hear what she sounded like, and I knew straightaway they wouldn't believe her. The next article they ran was about her mental state.

The press have history on their side—the stories are always about the women going nuts.

I gave up then. But Miss Devine didn't. She called Photoplay anyway. But now Bob owns a major studio and he can give the press access to his stars or he can deny it. He has a whole team of publicists who don't just bury all his dirty secrets, they cremate them so they can never be dug up later.

Just now, I went to his bungalow. "It was your own fault," he said to me. "You should have stayed in the car."

THE LETTER DROPS TO the ground.

I will never forgive you.

When Bob said those words to me, what I knew of Bob's evil was that he carried women he'd given too many pills to through the Marmont, that he put conditions on movie parts that desperate young starlets paid for with the tarnish staining their dreams. But now I know what he did to my aunt. And that his sister killed herself because of him.

A few nights ago, Bob told me, *well played*. Which means I've been horribly, terribly wrong about him. He doesn't do this for power. He does it for fun.

It's a game.

Which is so much worse.

Power would mean he had something to lose. But some people just like to play; for them it's only important that the game goes on and on. And it has. It isn't just one girl, or two or three. It's a pattern.

It's the way Hollywood works.

His words have kept me small for a very long time.

But right now I have a fury as dark as a murder of crows beating its feathers against my skull.

I push myself back onto my feet.

I STALK OVER TO the bungalows and thump on Matty's door. It's only nine in the morning, so it takes a good five minutes to rouse him.

"Aria, hey," he says, voice still raw, most likely with the misdemeanors from Calliope's party. "Looking for Calliope? She's not here."

I shake my head. "It's my turn to come knocking for favors."

He laughs. "You want a part in the movie?"

"Not on your life. But I want you to audition Miss Devine Rey in about three months' time for the part of the housekeeper."

He stares at me. It's probably too early in the day for sobriety to have emerged out of his nightcap of reds and vodka, so I repeat, "Miss Devine Rey. Hollywood legend."

"But . . ."

The process of deciding which objection to start with is too much for him, so I deal with them all. "She's in rehab. She'll be out in three months. Just think what her name and that kind of publicity will do to your movie. Miss Devine Rey, who hasn't been lured onto the silver screen for nearly fifteen years, has been coaxed out by you. The column inches of press you'll get will fill theaters. You know it will."

He laughs. "Man, that's outta sight! Aria, you're everyone's guardian angel. You know that, right?"

I leave him effusing over how much he digs my idea, then I retrace my steps to the lobby, pass Phillip, still waiting for Calliope to smile at him, walk through the colonnades, out onto the driveway and across Sunset Boulevard. Through the doors of

Schwab's. There, nursing a coffee and waiting for whatever news is happening that day, is Lois, chief gossip columnist for *Photoplay.* Calliope introduced me to her years ago when I first went to Schwab's and I always say hello, refuse to share any gossip.

Today I slide into the booth.

"Aria," she says, like she's always known that one day I'd break and spill Hollywood's guts. "I'll order you a coffee."

"No time," I tell her, even though a coffee would be just the ticket to dislodge the ache in my temples. "Miss Devine Rey is making a comeback. In Matty's movie."

"In *Jane Eyre*?" Her eyes can't stretch wide enough at the scoop. "Noooooooooo."

"Yes," I tell her. "You'll report it?"

Her mind is busy calculating how many copies this will sell, how many advertisers it will bring in, how much money she'll make in bonuses. "I'll do one better—I'll run a Miss Devine Rey feature, remind everyone how good she was." Her face softens. "She was good, wasn't she?"

I'M GOING TO BE late for work again. But I still have one battle to face.

Calliope.

I need to stand in front of her and scan her hair for a cotton thread from a red headscarf, find the indentation left by a black eye patch. I need to know if it was her pretending to be a fortune-teller, and why.

I need to tell her that sisters don't behave like that.

I thought sisters were forevermore.

I guess seven years in Hollywood *is* forevermore.

Up to the sixth floor. Walk over snakes toward the small penthouse. Tap on the door.

No answer.

I turn the handle.

The room is dark, the drapes drawn, the bed hasn't been slept in. On the nightstand is a spilled bottle of pills, like pearls scattered from a broken necklace.

I'm about to call out, *Calliope?* when I hear it. The sound of someone's empty insides. Not even vomiting, not now. But retching, a body trying to get rid of poison and demons and the hangover of dreams.

I close my eyes but the tears leak out.

Seven years ago, Flitter held Calliope's hair off her face while she heaved into a toilet. I brought her a glass of water and made her cry.

Now I'm the one crying.

I want to believe that Brian is in there, holding her hair and telling her to let it all out. I want to not remember Calliope saying to me a couple of weeks ago, *I wish you wouldn't see me every time I'm being my worst self.*

That's the thing that keeps me out here, weeping instead of helping. She won't want me to be the one who helps her.

I run down to my own room, pick up the phone, call Schwab's. "I need paracetamol, Coca Cola, chicken soup, and a packet of hair ties taken to Calliope Burns's room as fast as you can. Leave it outside the bathroom."

I don't know if it's more or less than what a sister would do. But nor did I know that sisters set themselves on fire in front of you, or watched you pull Death and The Fool from a pack of cards. We are no Meg, Jo, and Amy. We chose to be sisters; we made our own blood.

There's no cure for that.

That's how I know this isn't the final battle of the morning.

Along to the lobby now. There's Phillip, the man who writes poetry, which makes everyone think he's a sensitive soul because that's the cliche the movies have made us believe. But this man can't even rhyme *No* and *Go.*

"Phillip."

He blinks, surprised.

"Get out," I tell him. "I can get the hotel owner to come down here and tell you to leave. Or you can slink away now. The Marmont will arrange to have your things sent on."

He tries to be superior; of course he does. "May I ask why?"

"Because you're a creep. I bet that even if I gave you all week, you couldn't come up with a rejoinder better than the one I've been composing in my head just now."

I put on my most bard-like voice and proclaim:

"There once was a girl named Calliope
More famous than you or I'll ever be
She was stalked by a man
About whom she gave not a damn
And who'd better go fuck off quietly."

God, it feels good when Judith Crown, who's sitting at the piano, plays the "Triumphal March" from *Aida*.

Phillip slinks out the door.

If only Bob Ashenhurst could be slayed with a limerick.

CHAPTER 31

...

1958

AS THE CHATEAU MARMONT CONJURES UP GOTHIC STORMS that fill the sky with all the rage the three girls inside don't understand they're allowed to feel, Flitter reaches for Calliope's hand. "They're calling you a goddess. This is your lucky break." Then, very quietly, "Are you okay?"

Calliope's response is a shrug, that little lift of the shoulders that disguises the not-okayness in someone's heart, because to be always not okay is exhausting—and to give into it is deadly.

Flitter's mouth twists into a bitter smile. "Hollywood made our beds and it isn't content to just let us lie in them—we have to sleep in them too." She slings an arm around Calliope's shoulders. "Just don't turn into a pill bottle like Marian Monti or a bitch like Lacey Magee."

"I won't," Calliope promises, and Aria believes her, believes her friend will never succumb to uppers chased with whiskey and downers served with a 3 A.M. espresso.

The thunder cracks once more.

Flitter and Calliope go back downstairs to join the party that Bob's throwing to celebrate the movie. But Calliope's words—*It's time to learn the price of things*—linger in the room as if the Marmont is breathing them out of its lungs. One dollar is how much Aria earns for an hour of babysitting. But one dollar isn't the price of things. No, the price of things becomes clear to her when she's walking back to her aunt's suite and she finds a man waiting outside.

For her.

A man named Bob who says, voice as cordial, as always, "I will never forgive you, my dear."

He walks away, whistling.

The suite door opens behind her. Miss Devine tugs her inside and then, suddenly and peculiarly, Aria is in her aunt's arms for the very first time.

Then Miss Devine pushes her away. "Go to your room. Stay there until Monday when Bob leaves for Europe. Pray that he finds someone there to distract him from you."

Today's my fifteenth birthday, Aria doesn't say to her aunt.

CHAPTER 32

...

1964

I'M GOING ON A DATE WITH THEO WINCHESTER. HAVE ANY OTHER words ever sounded so good?

Theo's sweet-talked Maisie into checking in on Adele while we're out—Adele's been told only that Theo has a meeting and I'm unavailable. Then I'm walking west along Sunset Boulevard, away from the chateau for the first time in my life.

It's cool outside, but not cold. Not like New York where I'd never have stepped outside on a November evening without my coat and scarf. I like the weather in LA, like the way the air doesn't bite you, the way it gentles you unless the Santa Ana winds are having their turn, throwing leaves to the ground like lovers they've grown bored of.

I like walking along beside Theo.

Around us, constellations of neon signs sparkle, earrings glitter. We pass Ciro's and the Sea Witch, satin evening dresses entering the first, drums beating out of the second. Young women parade along the Strip, one wearing a fur coat and shorts; another her bikini; a third a dress made of ribbons. There's so much happiness, nothing scary or frightening at all.

My shoulders relax. I look up at Theo, the castle turret etched into the sky behind him, the clouds aglow with silver linings. I smile and the smile he gives me in return is something private, meant for closed doors and bedsheets and no sleep at all.

"I was worried you were regretting coming," he says, leaning down close to my ear.

I smile at him. "You promised me a hot dog."

"Nothing comes between Aria and her stomach, right?" He touches a hand to my back, guiding me across the street, and I lean right into it.

The hot dog stand is quiet. The guy in charge of mustard beams at Theo and says, "Can I get your autograph, man? 'Hollywood and Vine' is one of my favorite tunes."

Theo takes the proffered pen and scrawls on a napkin. The guy exchanges it for the hot dogs and says, "On the house."

"Thanks, buddy," Theo says, before turning to give me my food.

I stare at him.

"What?"

"Does that happen a lot? People recognizing you like that?"

He shrugs. "It's why I like the Marmont."

For the first time ever, I wonder what it's like to be Calliope, someone more famous than Theo. Could she just walk down here and get a hot dog? Could she just wander among the happy faces like I can?

I haven't checked on her since I sent her the food from Schwab's.

I should have.

A face in the crowd catches my eye. Was that Phillip? The man who never hears *no*?

I stand on tiptoe, crane my neck, but can't see anything. I'm either too short or he was never there. Why would he be lurking here anyway?

I shake my head. Am I seeing things out on Sunset Boulevard, the same way I hear things at the Marmont?

No. I'm in an unfamiliar place. It's normal to be overwhelmed by both that and the fact that I'm on my first ever date.

I take my hot dog and move to the side. Our faces are backlit by neon pink. Past us sashay beautiful legs and beautiful faces—beautiful girls who'd probably have taken Theo by the hand and run with him to Ciro's if he'd asked them to spend an evening there.

He's so very visible. And all I've ever wanted is to be invisible.

"Why me?" I blurt, the craziness forcing its way back into my head.

I gesture to another made-in-LA blonde, a girl shaped from the bones of boulevards and golden dreams. "Why me when you could be eating hot dogs with her. Or her." There goes another one, made of love songs and moonbeams. "Don't you want to write songs about her? I do, and I don't even write songs."

Theo grins at me. "Eat your hot dog."

"I asked you a question."

"Of course you did. But just eat your hot dog. Then I'll answer."

I open my mouth wide and take a bite. Mustard and relish and chili and ketchup drip down my chin. I close my eyes because, as far as hot dogs go, it might be the best one ever.

"Oh god, that's good," I mumble, reaching for the napkins, mopping red sauce off my chin and my hands and then closing my eyes again while I chew. "So good."

The next time I open my eyes, Theo's watching me. There's something strangely shiny about his eyes that makes me pause.

"I could tell you all the *nots*," he says. "All the things you aren't that make me want to go out and get a hot dog with you. That you've never been interested in my autograph or my bank balance or an introduction to my record company or my agent. You don't even know my agent's name, for Christ's sake. You don't want a song or a toke or a line or a trip. You look at me, not Win. But mostly, I want to be here with you because of the way you close your eyes when you eat. Like happiness is just that simple. It isn't ten thousand people screaming your name while you sing a song you used to love before you had to sing it ten thousand times. It's just a really good hot dog on a December night when you're sober enough to know you'll remember every detail—

your ketchup smile, and the way the pink light is making your eyes so green they should name an entire forest after you, and how you still think you don't deserve to be on a date with an idiot like me. I'm pretty sure that even though I've never kissed you, have barely even held your hand, I love you, Aria Jones."

I drop the hot dog. Theo catches it just in time. Then he says, "Can I kiss you?"

I laugh. This is so ridiculous and romantic that I'm expecting the clapper board to fall and for me to realize I've stepped onto a movie set. But when I blink, Theo is still there, wanting me.

"Win! Look, it's Win!" The squeal is at the pitch of toddlers and accidents. A group of beautiful girls forms a circle around Theo.

There are five of them. They hug him and dance around with ease and grace—with hunger too, as if this man has something they want. Is it his autograph? Yes, at first. But once his name is tucked into their purses, the hunger's still there. It's not sated by an effusive chorus sung with heads tipped back and voices so loud that they draw in more girls, the pack answering the call of the wild.

My eyes meet Theo's. His face is grim, and suddenly I know why he needed vodka and why Calliope needs sex and Flitter needs attention. There was a moment, so exquisite, of genuine admiration from the man at the hot dog stand. But these girls have pictures of Win on the walls of their rooms. They've waited in airports and outside hotels; they've lined up in the predawn hours to get tickets to his performance on a CBS variety show. Now they're bored by that—the ordinary beauty of full moons and blue nights isn't enough. They want a hot red Mars pinned to an aching sky.

Their love has teeth.

One girl aims for Theo's lips and he only just manages to turn his head away in time. He grabs my hand and mutters, "Let's go."

We hurry back the way we came.

I've never wanted a drink more in my life. I bet he does too.

When we reach the sidewalk outside the Marmont, the words burst out of him.

"It used to be okay," he says. "People would come to the gigs, maybe throw a few things onto the stage. But now so many of them come because they literally want to fuck your name. Like having Theo Winchester's dick inside them is the meaning of life, the one true orgasm. It messes with your head, knowing that you could point to any one of those girls in the crowd and they'd be at the stage door after the show. My drummer used to joke that it was easier for me to get laid than it was for me to go and buy a pint of milk. But it isn't funny. So I drank because then I didn't have to think about how screwed up it all is."

If there's one thing I do not want to think about ever, it's how many girls have been in Theo Winchester's bed. But this moment isn't about me, so I swallow down the jealousy, reach up a hesitant hand, and stroke his cheek. "It's okay."

We stand—my hand on his cheek, his head bowed toward mine—until the foot traffic starts to gripe at having to go around us. Then we move inside.

I understand why he's run here. Last night, after what he told me about his dad, I thought maybe he'd run into this life of temptation just so he could prove to his dead father that he's a better man—he might want, but he won't ever succumb, not even if he's living in the Garden of Eden. But no. He's run here because the Marmont is a safe haven for those who are so visible they're like the giant forty-foot showgirl.

We don't speak in the elevator. Isaiah takes one look at our faces and concentrates on watching the dial. When we're safe inside the penthouse, I ask Theo the same question I'd once asked Calliope. "Why do you do it?"

"Because once upon a time, standing on a stage and singing a song that you loved and that everyone else loved made you feel like a king. So you keep chasing that feeling forever after. And when you can't find it on a stage anymore, you search for it in a bottle, in a toke, or in the line of a song." He tosses his keys on the counter, braces his forearms against it and says, "Sorry. I shouldn't have said all that stuff out there."

"Well, I'm sure there are plenty of women who'd vote for you as the one true orgasm but . . ." I lose the ability to sustain the joke halfway through.

He covers his face with his hands. "I was hoping I didn't say that out loud."

I want to laugh. This conversation is ludicrous. But I'm also very human and I can't help saying, "Right now I'm feeling a lot like I'm bound to be a disappointment. And I know you'll say I won't be, and I'll have to try to find a way to believe you, but I don't think I can kiss you tonight without feeling like I'm trying to prove something."

Theo manages a wry smile. "That's my first ever rejection. And you know what? I'll take it. And Aria?" He straightens up and comes to stand beside me, leaning against the kitchen counter again, him facing one way, me the other, only our hips touching. "There's one thing I'm glad I said to you. But I don't want you to feel like you have to respond. Because I'm guessing you haven't come across much in the way of love here at the Marmont." He reaches over to cup one hand at the back of my neck, lets his thumb brush oh so lightly over my cheek, and all my resolve about not kissing almost melts away.

"I'm also very aware," he murmurs, "that I'm thirty and you're twenty-one and . . ."

I slide my body between him and the counter. The only space left is between our lips.

Theo inhales sharply.

I stretch up onto my tiptoes. "I've changed my mind about not kissing you," I whisper. "I'll be thinking about it all night anyway, so let's buck the Hollywood trend and go for reality rather than imagination."

He laughs; it tickles my skin, the black leather scent of him teases me too. And now I want his hands to tickle all the parts of my body that Flitter drew onto a sheet of notepaper five years ago.

But he draws away and says very softly, "I want you to be sure. Think about it tonight. Then come and have breakfast with me and Adele tomorrow, if you want to."

"I won't just be thinking tonight, Theo. I'll be dreaming too. So yes." I smile at the hunger lurking in his eyes. "I'll come to breakfast. So long as you promise that tomorrow night we can do everything I dreamed of. And everything you dream of as well."

WHEN I RETURN TO my room, the door is open again. I stop, look behind me, need someone to witness the open door and prove that I'm not seeing things.

Then voices drift out from inside and I shake my head. Maybe I do need Bob's Quaaludes. What with Theo taking me places I never thought I'd go, plus all the strange happenings around here, I'm leaping to overwrought conclusions.

I take the ten steps forward and find my two sisters sitting on my bed, spilling ash over my new quilt from their cigarettes.

Flitter smirks. "We're dying to know where you've been."

"What Flitter means is, we're sorry. About the party," Calliope says.

Flitter waves her cigarette in the air. "Aria forgives everything. But Aria is usually in bed well before now."

Calliope pats the space beside her. Flitter grins like an eager teenager. And my face breaks into a smile too. Everything is changing. But here in this room there's still a bed and three girls—and a place for me.

I climb in between them and reach for a cigarette.

"The orphan auditions are next week," Flitter says. "It's a shortlist of three. Me, Melissa, and Calliope."

I want to care more about this. But in a few hours I'll be having breakfast with Theo. I can't stop smiling at my first ever delicious secret.

Calliope notices. "Something's happened."

"You really are a fortune-teller," I say. Then the words burst out of me, too wonderful to stay hidden. "Theo said he loves me."

Flitter's and Calliope's mouths open so wide they could catch giraffes.

"Love?" Calliope says.

"Win?" Flitter now.

She's still calling him Win. And, despite the motorbike ride, I haven't ever heard Theo mention her. Nor has she ever spoken of him with anything other than casual flirtation. So her reaction can't be jealousy or hurt. It's straightforward disbelief—which hurts even more.

Then Calliope walks over to the record player and taps a fingernail on it.

One of Win's records is cued up and now I feel like those girls on Sunset Strip. Especially when Flitter repeats Win's name with such incredulity it's like I'm dating Jesus Christ.

I shove the quilt aside, spilling ash all over my bed. Jump to my feet. "Why is that so hard to believe? I know I'm not beautiful or famous. But Theo's never made me feel like you're making me feel right now—like I'm beneath him just because I'm ordinary."

Not even ordinary. *Plain. A beast,* the voices from the past hiss.

Calliope strides over to me, stopping just inches from my face. Her eyes aren't the eyes she used to have. They're the eyes of a woman who's taken something—probably many things—to get herself onto her feet and into her smile. I'm about to ask her when she became a person who pretended to be a fortune-teller, who made her friend feel like a fool, and who keeps herself alive with pills rather than dreams, but she says, stealing all of my words, "This isn't *your* dream. What about the ocean, the house by the sea?"

"I was thirteen! Even you told me it was a lonely dream. Why should I be held for the rest of my life to something I said when I was a kid?"

Flitter butts in, tone acid. "Hell, I'd give up a lonely cottage for Win any day."

Calliope whirls around. "Shut up! Shut up for one minute with your stupid unfunny asides." She spins back to me, doesn't see Flitter's face cracking. "If you do this," Calliope says, "you'll be even more invisible than you are right now."

"Not everybody needs the whole world to see them!"

"I'm not saying it right." Calliope turns to Flitter again. "Help me say it right."

But Flitter is on her feet, face pieced back together, only her eyes still broken. "You're on your own, kid," she tells Calliope. "You don't need me."

She walks out the door, and the ground trembles, like the Marmont is as angry as I am—like it's trying to tear down this city made of studio sets and technicolor ghosts.

"Aria." Calliope holds my arms to stop me from going after Flitter. "At least your dream got you out of here. It put you into life. I know life terrifies you, but you need to go out and live it anyway. I keep waiting for you to do that, believing that you will. But if you go straight from here to Win's penthouse and into Win's life, then the life—the lives!—you could have lived will all vanish. Like that."

She snaps her fingers in front of my face.

"It's why I did the fortune-telling thing," she says, shocking me with how easily she admits to it. "I needed to make you think. Like I told you in that tent, death is your past, not your future. Stop just holding on to your dream; go out and chase it to wherever it leads. I need to know that you got away."

Oh, Calliope is so good at making people believe in her. I almost want to tell this Aria person to go chase life, rather than dreams. But I *am* the Aria person—and Theo is my new dream.

And suddenly I'm frozen in place by the thought—the way she's talking, it sounds like *she's* the one who wants me to leave.

Badly enough that she's trying to scare me away?

"If you'd given me and Flitter a set of encyclopedias," Calliope says, trying out a smile to lure me deeper into her spell, "we would have turned straight to the entries for Hollywood and Marian Monti. You're the only person I know who'd read every one from cover to cover. There was nothing Flitter and I could say and you wouldn't ask a question about it. You were curious the way other people dropped acid—evangelically and always searching for something. I believed you'd start on your beach in Hawaii and then you'd see how much world there is out there and you'd tackle it like that set of encyclopedias, not content unless you laid your hands on all of it. But you're *still* here. And you might as well be dead for all the living you've done."

Her voice is raw when she finishes. But I'm done with taking advice from a strung-out actress who can no longer keep her role-playing to the screen—and who doesn't know how to live any more than I do.

"You think because you've pretended to be a princess and an ingenue and a cowgirl and a call girl that you've actually lived those lives? They weren't real, Calliope. Just like you aren't a fortune-teller. Even your name isn't real. There's nothing about you that's real!"

Real. Real. Real.

My cruelty echoes, the Marmont taking her side, not mine—making me the one who's mean. And I don't know why my memory chooses to show me this piece of my life right now, but it does: when I sat in Theo's office and told him that female birds might be quiet, but they were full of birdsong too—and that the woman who'd discovered that fact had been ignored by biology.

I've never sung along to a song, not even when I'm alone in this room. I'm always too scared that Bob might hear me. Flitter, Calliope—have I ever heard them sing? Or is all our birdsong stuck in our throats, glued there by fires and Bobs and hand jobs in libraries and a dream of power that's delivered us only powerlessness?

My face crumples. But Calliope's, hers transforms into an even lovelier smile, the kind you'd sit with in a dark movie theater, popcorn uneaten in your hand, because you're struck by the wonder of it.

"The lives I get to have on-screen, all of them are better than real because they have no consequences," she says. "I can marry, but I never have to be a wife. I can have a child but never have the chance to hurt it. I can die . . ."

Her voice quavers and all my anger collapses and my hand squeezes hers because this might be the saddest thing I've ever heard.

"I can die," she continues, looking at our joined hands, "and then I can stand up and walk away from that dead girl. You have no idea how lovely it is to live a life you can constantly fuck up, but never regret. A life where you can love so often, marry so often—but never have to stay for the divorce."

I interrupt, can't believe I'm saying this to a woman who's not just my friend, but my sister. "Is that what this is all about? You're mad because you wanted the world to love you, but when you see the love that Theo's given me, you want that instead? You liked it better when I was nothing to anyone?"

Calliope sniffs, then wipes her eyes. One set of false lashes comes away—the legs of a wingless creature stuck to the back of her hand. She shocks me by hugging me tight, despite what I just said, and she whispers, "You have so many gifts. You help everyone. You give career advice to actresses and story ideas to writers. Every woman who's passed through the Marmont leaves with a piece of Aria inside them. So go be your own kind of star. If you fall in love with Theo now, you'll be his forevermore. But you'll never be yours."

I draw back from Calliope so she can see my soul in my eyes when I say, trying to put it into a language she understands, "I feel for him the way you feel about your ambitions."

"Then I'm sorry for you," she says.

Then she walks away, and I wonder how this changed from a conversation that was meant to be all mint juleps and giggles to an exchange of all the things the three of us never said over the years but perhaps should have.

CHAPTER 33

...

1958

INSIDE HER ROOM, ARIA STARES AT THE WALL. ALL THE MOMENTS that have led to this one play out and, in each of them, she sees herself make different choices: she pretends to be sick the night her parents go dancing so they stay home with her and are never burned. She throws the stiletto-heeled lamp at Bob's head, and then she and Calliope run out of the library together. She sets fire to the film she took that day so Bob forgets who she is.

That's when she decides. She can't rely on an aunt who might never hug her again, or even on Calliope, who would perhaps not have called out if it had been Aria standing in front of Bob that day. She can only rely on herself.

That means being like the tardigrade, which she read about in the "Sulfur to Tramways, Aerial" volume of her encyclopedias. They're the smallest creatures in the universe, and the most indestructible. They can survive squashing, freezing, even the vacuum of space, which is something Aria hasn't looked up because there are so many frightening things in her life that she can't bear to contemplate anything as terrifying as nothingness. The reason a tardigrade can't be killed or broken or burned is because they shrivel up to one-third of their already tiny size when they're threatened.

Aria will do the same—become invisible. For the next six years, she'll be the ghost, floating silently along the corridors, helping starlets, but too inconspicuous for Bob to notice.

In this place where to be seen is the only thing people want, Aria will be the opposite.

That night she dreams she's setting fire to the hotel, burning all its ghosts and secrets, so there'll be no story left for anyone to tell. What she doesn't see is that one spark jumps out of the fire, higher than all the rest. So high that it lands in the sky, twinkling like a dark and mischievous star, waiting.

CHAPTER 34

...

1964

I REFUSE TO LET CALLIOPE RUIN THIS NIGHT THE SAME WAY SHE ruined the night of the party with her stupid fortune-telling antics. I forget about her, think instead of Theo. Soon I'm drifting in and out of scorching dreams until, at five in the morning it occurs to me that Theo didn't tell me what time to come for breakfast. Five o'clock is too early, but maybe six? I usually collect Adele at eight, so presumably breakfast is sometime before that. Seven?

That's two hours away.

I groan, bury my face in the pillow, and impart a few important facts to my wayward body. One: Adele will be at breakfast. Two: Adele will be with me all day. Nothing can happen until later. So I ought to go to sleep properly or Theo will take one look at the bags under my eyes and ask if I'd like the bellboy to help with my baggage.

But when I close my eyes, I hear Theo saying my name.

My eyes fly open. I *did* go to sleep. The clock on my bedside table says it's half past seven. And the voice isn't a dream. It's coming from the other side of the door!

I leap up and there he is, looking at my sapphire silk pajamas as if he could melt them away with just one of his signature glares.

"Aria," he says, voice very husky. "I rehearsed an entire speech and all of my behavior. You were meant to be dressed and definitely not wearing these." He risks dropping one hand to the silk, then snatches it away like he just touched fire. "Nor were you meant to look quite so much like you just rolled out of bed and wanted to be rolled right back into it. I was supposed to tell you that Adele's made waffles and then we'd walk to the penthouse like two mature adults. But now I can barely remember what a waffle is, let alone the way back to my room."

I open the door wider. "You know, as soon as we get this over with, we'll be much better at concentrating."

"Aria . . ." There it is, my name in his mouth again. "We're not just getting anything over with. Once we start, there'll be no stopping us."

Oh, Jesus. Now *I'm* the one who can't remember what a waffle is.

Theo grins and walks away and I have to get dressed and go upstairs and make small talk with Adele as if I can't feel the hot thumbprint of her father's hand on my cheek.

I put on a pair of white cropped trousers, a navy ribbed T-shirt, brown belt, and ballet flats—professional, but yes, I choose the pants because I like the way my legs look in them and I hope Theo will too.

I don't even have to knock. The door flies open.

"Finally," Adele says, eyeing the waffles the same way Theo's eyeing me. "I'm starving. And Dad's pacing around like a maniac."

Dad. I've never heard Adele call Theo that before. I look over at him and his smile is shaky and his eyes are shiny, like he's been split into heart and ache at the very same time.

"Smells good," I say to Adele, giving him a moment to recover.

When we've finished eating, the phone rings. I can hear Theo talking to someone about bedtimes and supervision.

When he hangs up he says to Adele, "That was your friend Diana's mother."

Adele gapes at him. "You were talking to Diana's mom about bedtimes? You're so embarrassing." Then she grins, drops her faux-whiny voice and says, "Can I please go?"

It transpires that Adele's friend, the one she met at Schwab's, is turning fifteen and her parents want to take both girls out to dinner and then—I almost can't believe the Fates could be so kind—Adele will stay for a sleepover.

Tonight.

I'll have Theo all to myself.

WHILE THEO DRIVES ADELE to her friend's house, I bathe, shave, consider my wardrobe, and settle on my silk pajamas. I'm not planning to wear anything for longer than I have to and they had the desired effect this morning.

I let myself into the penthouse and wait on the balcony. God, it's beautiful out here before all the city lights turn on. Day has melted into night, and the sky is the color of ripe apricots in a white porcelain bowl. The wind has calmed, the gardens are empty, and there's a space in time that's been carved out just for us.

I hear the click of the penthouse door.

I don't turn around. I listen to Theo's footsteps coming closer, but slowly, as if he's drawing out this moment, and I close my eyes and feel all the skin at the back of my neck ache for his lips, or his fingers, or any part of him at all.

Then he's right behind me.

I shiver. "Theo."

"Mmmmm." He slips his arms around me, hands coming to rest on my waist. He isn't breathing.

Nor am I.

Then he turns his face into my hair and whispers my name. I let my head tip back so he can have my throat if he wants to—can have all of me, everything.

"Come inside," he whispers.

But I can't move. His hand has slipped beneath my pajama top and his fingers are circling my navel. When his other hand joins in and starts to climb slowly higher, I have to bite my lip so nobody hears the sound my body wants to make.

"Come inside," he repeats, and this time I do. And once there, I lose myself forever in the look in his eyes that tells me he is all my wishes come true, at last.

HOURS PASS IN WHICH we're nothing but bodies at the whim of one another's touch. Finally, Theo lies on his back, bringing my head down to his shoulder and wrapping his arm around me like he doesn't want me to leave—like he doesn't just want me to help him reach high noon, but to lie quietly with in the predawn hours too.

It's so lovely, just lying here with him.

"I never knew that this time afterwards is a different kind of pleasure," I say sleepily. "I don't know if there's a word for it. Afterplay?"

He smiles. "I like that. But honestly . . . mostly people just get up and leave."

"Well, we should make afterplay compulsory for us. I like it."

"I like it too." He draws my mouth up to his and for a moment he looks so beautiful I want to cry.

"Aria?" he says, sensing the shift in my mood.

"This . . ." I gesture to the bed, try to explain. "Us . . . it all felt too fine for a moment."

"What if it's not *too* anything? What if it's exactly how it's supposed to be?"

What if . . . ?

What if I have a new dream—to keep doing this, with him.

It's two weeks until December the first. The day I'm meant to leave.

I stare at the halo of light around the edge of the curtains, wishing I knew what to do. But there are so many wishes made inside the Marmont that, if wishes were kindling, we'd burn the place down.

I'M LYING ON MY side, wrapped in Theo, his thumb making tiny promises over my skin, when I open one unwilling eye to look at the clock.

"Theo?" I mumble. "What time is Adele coming home?"

"She's being dropped off at ten." He stretches a little too tantalizingly. "I was trying to be a good father and not leave her to run wild all day. But now I hate that good father because something tells me—"

"It's ten minutes to ten." I roll onto my back.

Theo drops his mouth onto my stomach, shifts a little lower.

"Stop." I laugh, pushing him away. "If Adele finds her father and her tutor-governess-whatever in bed together, she won't speak to either of us for at least a week."

"All right. Let's get dressed and arrange ourselves like disinterested adults at the kitchen counter."

Which would be fine, except . . . "I wore my pajamas here. Disinterested adults do not have coffee in their pajamas. Luckily I've seen enough women creatively putting men's wardrobes to use the morning after. I just need one of your T-shirts—"

"You're half my size. There's no way she's going to believe that my T-shirt is yours."

I climb out of bed, smiling at the way his eyes roam my body. "Obviously I'm not going to wear it as a T-shirt. Let's see . . ." I stand in front of the dresser, bend over just enough to show off my derriere.

Theo groans and pulls the pillow over his head.

When he emerges, I'm wearing a mini dress made from a Theo Winchester band T-shirt cinched with a brown belt. He's on his feet the very next minute, determined to find out if I'm wearing anything under the shirt, but I bat him away, laughing, always laughing.

I'd forgotten there was so much laughter inside me.

Five minutes later, Theo's making coffee. I fill a glass with water, then open the freezer to get ice, wanting to settle the flush on my cheeks from the evening's entertainment.

There are two bottles of vodka in there.

I have an unhealthy need to test myself, Theo told me. *To have a bottle in reach but to not reach for it.*

Wouldn't one bottle suffice? And he gave me whiskey, not vodka, the night he nearly burned. Which means there's at least another bottle in the penthouse somewhere.

"Theo . . ."

"Hi!" Adele strolls in, looking happy, like she found her laughter too.

I close the freezer door.

"How was your night?" Theo asks.

"We watched TV until midnight, then told scary stories, like this one . . ." She starts to recount something about a big old house that's haunted by a witch and I wonder—why is it always the women who are said to do the haunting; why are we always the ones locked up alone in the empty houses?

THE NEXT TWO WEEKS pass thusly: breakfast with Theo and Adele; school in the turret; dinner with Theo and Adele, then hours upon hours of Theo. I know it can't go on like this. That soon we'll have to get some proper sleep at the very least. But bliss is its own addiction and, man, those highs. Like Quaaludes, they wipe away my worries about Calliope and Flitter and Bob. About screams in the night and fires. And nothing bad happens. Only good.

Theo and I have two serious conversations. The first is about Adele.

"She knows," he says to me one night as I lie horizontally across the bed, my head on his chest while he smokes.

"Knows what?" I mumble, watching a smoke ring melt into the air.

"Adele told me this morning that we were treating her like a baby and did we really think she was that much of an idiot."

"Oh." I frown. "I thought we were doing a really good job of hiding it."

Theo laughs so hard he's almost crying.

"What's so funny?"

He props himself up on one elbow, strokes a hand through my hair. "When I look at you, what do you see in my eyes?"

Things that make me feel beautiful. Things that make me feel desirable and loved and happy and safe. "Love," I say shyly.

"Do you think nobody else can see that? It was at least three days ago that Jupiter asked when I was going to take you out on a proper date. And Maisie told me I'd better get you something good for your birthday, or else . . ."

"Or else what?"

"She didn't say. But all the people who know you—they know. Why are we hiding?"

Because that's how I live, the ghost of hallways and turrets. Bob's never made good on his threat because I'm so insignificant that I'm not worth hurting.

"It's easier," I tell Theo, rolling away from him.

He lets a beat of silence pass. Then he says, "Lying here now, I feel like I've told you more about me than vice versa. Maybe I haven't asked enough questions."

I brace, but he just asks, "Favorite things?"

"Well . . ." I smile and roll back toward him, knowing I'm supposed to say that he is. "Hot dogs. We never did finish our hot dogs the other night. And you promised me one."

"I can definitely promise you a hot—"

I laugh, head tipped back, then slide my body on top of his.

Turns out I don't mind this game after all. "Theo Winchester, get your filthy mind out of the gutter. Next question?"

"Spoilsport. All right, what do you hate? You like everyone and everyone likes you, but there must be something you don't like."

"Secrets." I don't even have to think. "I hate it when people use a soft word like *secret* to cover up the fact that they're lying."

I don't know what I did but the laughter's gone from the room. Is it because upstairs in my turret is a book with the pages cut out and some money inside it and I haven't told Theo about any of it?

I've always thought other people were the liars, but now it's apparent that I am too.

I press my lips onto Theo's, don't want to answer any more questions except the one that slips from his mouth after he lays me on my back. "Do you like that?"

I nod and whisper, "Yes. Yes I do."

I WAKE A COUPLE of hours later with the scent of smoke in my nostrils. I jump out of bed, run into the living room, fling open the doors to the balcony, sniff. Nothing.

No. Not nothing. It's just not out here. It's in my nostrils, like the fire is inside me.

A bleary-eyed Theo comes yawning out of the bedroom. "What's going on?"

Nothing is burning. Except my nightmares.

Or my sanity.

I take a seat on one of the stools and rub my eyes.

"Tea?" Theo asks.

I nod, then smile at the sight of him, chest bare, filling a teakettle with water. And that's when I hear myself say it, say something I haven't said since I was thirteen years old and lived on the other side of the country and had never heard of the Chateau Marmont. "I love you."

Oh, the look on his face. I hadn't known that telling someone you loved them only made you love them even more.

He drops the teakettle and his mouth curves into the most beautiful smile. "Aria Jones," he says. "Will you marry me? Next week preferably, because I don't want to wait any longer to know that we are each other's for the rest of our lives."

"Mar . . . Wha . . . ?"

Did I hear that right? But when will he go back to recording an album and being out with the wolf pack of girls who want Win inside them? Where will we live and what will I be if I'm not Aria Jones, ghost of the Chateau Marmont? Who would Aria Winchester be? Someone happy to sit in a house in the hills while her husband is in some other city singing a song that used to be about her, but that has become about some other girl?

Theo waits. Doesn't get mad at me for not replying. He just waits for me, Aria Jones.

I walk over to him. Lift up a hand. Trace my fingertip over his brow. Once upon a time, I couldn't decide if his face was handsome or unlovely. But look at his eyes, the way they soften to gunmetal whenever he's in a room with me, as if there was always a flash of blue hiding in the dark and he just needed to find his tenderness.

He really wants this.

I'd been so sure that the only thing I wanted was to not be hurt. But what if my wish wasn't about a *not*? Wasn't about pain, but about love?

I grin. "I, Aria Jones, take you Theo—" I don't get to finish. He's kissing my neck so hard that I can't stop laughing, my joy the only sound that echoes in the Marmont tonight.

Well, it echoes for about two minutes. Then I hear myself say, "Can we not tell anyone about it until afterwards?"

Theo's whole face creases into a frown. "Are you ashamed of me?"

"Ashamed?" I gape at him. "Theo, you are literally a man most women would kill to have standing half-naked across from them. Why would I be ashamed of you?"

"Because all I do is stand on a stage and sing. Whereas you're the smartest woman—no, the smartest person—I know."

"Well, you do play the guitar as well as sing." I smile, trying to get back to what we had a few hours ago—the two of us wound together like music, point and counterpoint.

He doesn't smile.

"Theo," I say. "I could never be ashamed of you. I'm just . . ." My voice cracks.

He cups my chin. "Tell me."

"I'm scared," I whisper, slipping my arms around his waist. "Every time I think I'm exquisitely, ridiculously happy, something terrible happens. I know it's stupid, but I feel like until we're actually married, I'll keep waiting for us to be burned up in a fire."

CHAPTER 35

...

1959

ARIA JONES IS SIXTEEN YEARS OLD TODAY. SHE'S STANDING outside the Chateau Marmont, Flitter on one side, Calliope the other. Their present is to take her across the road to Schwab's.

"Baby steps," Calliope says.

"I can't believe you haven't left this place," Flitter adds.

Aria looks up at the showgirl. She spins happily. Her silver dollar doesn't topple. So Aria steps onto Sunset Boulevard with her friends and hurries across to the other side. There. She made it!

It's the best birthday present ever.

"Calliope Burns!" Jim, the man who works the soda stand calls, and Calliope squeezes her way over and clears three occupied seats with her smile. Then Jim makes Aria a Schwab's Special, which is so full of chocolate and ice cream she won't be able to eat for a week.

It's early evening and all the seats along the soda fountain are full. It's standing room only, the room buzzy with chatter, cigarette smoke, and laughter. Jim makes the special for Calliope and Flitter too, and Flitter holds up her spoon and says, "Happy birthday, Aria."

They chink spoons and take a bite, and it's like that first sleepover. The three sisters close their eyes and savor the gooey, delectable glory that is an ice cream sundae made just for you on your birthday.

"Let me take a picture." Jim pulls out a Polaroid camera and captures the three of them, smiling and chocolate-smeared, arms around one another.

He passes it to Aria and she knows that this, *this* is the best birthday present of all.

"Calliope Burns?" Someone thrusts out a napkin for Calliope to sign, then a dozen people want her autograph and her sundae melts into liquid gloop while she signs and smiles and Flitter and Aria scrape every last mouthful from their glasses.

Then Marian Monti walks in and the crowd moves over to her.

"Sometimes it's nice not to be the most famous person in the room," Calliope says.

Flitter tips up her glass and drinks the last bit of ice cream. "Lucky for me, being the least famous is my natural state."

"It won't take much longer," Calliope reassures her.

It's been three years. After less time than that, the starlets usually become stars—or else they vanish.

"I get one birthday wish," Aria says to Flitter. "Since I don't believe in wishes anymore, you can have it."

Many people would mock a secondhand wish. But Flitter closes her eyes and scrunches up her face like she's putting everything she has into making her wish.

Someone squeezes into their group. Marian Monti, looking like a blonder, plumper, slightly more frayed version of Calliope. She kisses Aria's cheek. "Happy birthday."

She passes Aria a gift—a beautiful, autographed, first edition of *Bonjour Tristesse* by Françoise Sagan.

"People think it's a vulgar little book," Marian says. "But it's really about a powerful woman. That's why they don't like it." She winks and sashays off, the most famous woman in Hollywood, who sleeps on the mattress in the turret on the nights when her husband's had too much to drink and his fists are looking for trouble.

"You want to go back and curl up with your new book, don't

you?" Calliope smiles at the way Aria's hand is trying hard not to open the covers and dive right in.

"Not yet." Flitter hoists a bag onto the counter. "Our gift is education." She takes out a notepad and pen.

"Education?" Aria wrinkles her nose.

"Of the best kind," Calliope reassures her.

Flitter sketches a very detailed picture of a naked man and a naked woman although, based on Aria's frequent sightings by the poolside, she's being extremely generous to the man. "This," Flitter announces, "is the Three Sisters School of Sex Education."

Aria starts laughing because the face she's drawn on the man is an excellent likeness of Peter Oldham, the sexiest man in Hollywood, who'll be Calliope's leading man in her next film. "How true to life is this?" she asks, indicating his nether regions.

"Very," Calliope reassures her, and now they're all laughing.

The next half hour is filled with much hilarity as Flitter and Calliope give Aria comprehensive diagrams about the things she could do with a man. The only time she stops laughing is when Flitter describes the act that got Calliope her breakthrough role in a movie.

"Here are some supplies to get you started," Calliope interrupts, opening the bag and giving Aria a pack of condoms and a box of Enovid, the new drug that almost every starlet at the Marmont takes: a highly effective contraceptive that doctors won't let you have other than for menstrual disorders—unless you're buddies with Dr. Foster and the pharmacists at Schwab's. "Have fun, but stay safe."

"Thus concludes your formal education," Flitter says. "You've read everything in the library, you've finally left the castle, and now you know how to do the no-pants dance. I officially proclaim you an adult."

But there's one more thing Aria needs to do before she's really an adult.

Back at the Marmont, she goes down to the garage to find

Jupiter. He's sitting behind the wheel of Peter Oldham's red Ferrari Superamerica, eyes closed, a dream of freedom behind his lids. When Aria slips into the passenger seat, his eyes fly open and the dreams fly away, guilt and fear replacing them. He relaxes when he sees that it's just her.

"You near on gave me a heart attack." He pops open the glove box, takes out Peter Oldham's Marlboros. "Smoke?"

Aria accepts the cigarette. Jupiter lights it for her with the actor's gold lighter, which costs more than Jupiter will earn in his lifetime.

She inhales for courage. "I need you to kiss me."

He chokes on smoke. "What?"

"I've seen plenty of scenes that wouldn't pass the Hollywood Code on cabanas by the pool. But I've hardly ever seen anyone kiss. People only kiss in the movies. And Flitter and Calliope forgot to explain kissing." She pulls Flitter's drawings out of her bag.

Jupiter takes one look and groans. "Jesus, Aria. You need better friends."

"I have exactly the right friends. Ones who'll show me what I need to know so I understand what I'm saying yes to. And so I don't find myself in a room saying no to a man who pretends not to hear."

Jupiter repeats, "Jesus, Aria." He stubs his cigarette out in the ashtray. "All right. I'll kiss you. But given what you just said, maybe it's better if you kiss me first."

Before she loses her courage, Aria leans forward and touches her lips to Jupiter's. It's soft. Warm. Nice. She draws back. "How did I do?"

He grins. "Not sure. You better do it again."

She laughs. Then she does do it again, a little harder, a little longer, and over the course of about twenty minutes, in a bright red Ferrari, she learns how to kiss.

CHAPTER 36

...

1964

WHEN I STEP OUT OF MY ROOM THREE DAYS BEFORE THE wedding, a crowd is gathered in the corridor. The elevator is broken and nobody knows where the stairs are. When I pass through the lobby, the piano is all sharps. A cabana floats in the pool and the starlets stare, not knowing how to save it.

But at the penthouse, Theo greets me with a kiss. "My agent organized someone to bring up a rack of wedding dresses. I'm taking Adele out so you can spend the day choosing one. You don't even need to leave the Marmont to do it."

He and Adele look so pleased with themselves. But all I can think is, *you told your agent?*

Of course he did. Theo's agent has to send out the press release informing everyone of our marriage after we're away on our honeymoon, which will be one whole month on the French Riviera. We'll hire a car and I'll finally wear the scarf Nathalie gave me and it will ripple behind me like freedom.

"Aria," Adele says, clearly exasperated by my distinct lack of enthusiasm. "Choose a dress. We're going out to buy me a dress and do you see me pretending I don't want one?" She aims her Winchester brows at me, then drags Theo out the door.

"I love you!" he calls over his shoulder.

Pilot bounds over, all tail wags and comfort. So I rub him behind the ears and decide to enjoy the very first time in my life when I get to choose a dress of my own.

I hear the rack rattling down the hall long before it arrives. Followed by Bob's voice.

I throw the door open, wanting to get the dresses inside as fast as I can. Out there waiting for me is the woman from the store.

And Bob.

"Aria, dear," he says with a smile that's like barbed wire in a forest of tulle. "This charming young lady wasn't sure where to find Theo Winchester's penthouse with her delivery of wedding gowns. I didn't even have to ask who they were for because I heard this morning that you're the lucky woman."

Heard? How?

"Come in," I tell the saleslady, reminding myself, *I'm marrying Theo. Bob's no longer a threat.*

Surely?

But it takes at least another minute to wrangle the stupid, attention-seeking rack inside.

Before I can shut the door, Bob proffers an envelope. "This was waiting for you in the lobby. I told them I'd bring it up."

I grab the envelope, shove the door closed on Bob saying, "I hope nothing ruins your special day!"

I tear open the envelope. Inside is a card. The tarot Fool from Calliope's party. He's carrying his bundle on his back, face upturned to the sky. Were he to look down, he'd see the edge of the cliff he's about to walk right over.

I crumple it up in my hand. Did Calliope send it?

Even though I've told myself not to bite my fingernails until after the wedding, they're between my teeth.

I'm getting married in three days' time on December 1, which was always meant to be my last day at the Marmont. Then I'll be in France. Calliope can predict futures and Flitter can set herself alight and Bob can make threats and none of it will matter.

Except it will. Because I know what Bob is truly capable of.

My breath is loud. In front of me, the wedding gowns look like the specters of women who expected happiness and got served life instead.

I have to get this over with.

I point to the first dress on the rack: a pale pink mini dress with cap sleeves.

"Oooh," the sales assistant enthuses, glad I'm behaving somewhat normally at last. "That will look darling with your short hair."

"I'll take it."

"You're not going to try it on?"

"Isn't it bad luck?"

"Only if the groom sees you. You need a veil too. Something like this."

She pulls out a tiny hat with a short, chin-length veil and places it on my head and now I can see the world through rose-colored tulle.

The door clicks and Theo hurries in, calling, "I forgot my wallet!" One hand is faux-shading his eyes. But he's human, and humans always want to look.

He peeks.

He sees me in the veil.

I hurl it off my head. "It's bad luck!"

"Only if he sees the dress," the woman consoles me.

But nobody knows where the bad luck really lives. In gas stations and libraries. In vodka bottles and Vegas chapels. In stars that should have had the decency to fall before you wished upon them.

WHAT I DO NEXT is madness. I go up to the turret, Pilot glued to my heels—I try to leave him in the penthouse, but he won't stop whining. I take out my suitcase and pack. Not with things I need for my honeymoon. But with things I'd need if I ran.

Where I think I might be running to, or why, I can't say. All I know is that into my life came fire, then other people's ambitions, and my god, what an inferno they made.

Pilot picks up my shoes in his mouth and drags them out of the case. I put them back in. He removes them again.

I squat down, wrap my arms around him. "Are you trying to tell me I'm being paranoid?"

He wags his tail.

I'm talking to a dog. Packing suitcases. Thinking bridal veils are augurs of doom. Not speaking to my friends. I really am the madwoman in the castle.

But even that doesn't stop me.

"Sorry, boy," I tell Pilot.

I gather up my journals and add them to the suitcase. On top I place *War and Peace,* which only holds the money from the past couple of weeks.

Then I creep downstairs to my aunt's suite, go into her bedroom, take out the diamond engagement ring, and hide that in my suitcase too.

That night, when Jupiter and Isaiah are on their break, I drag the suitcase down to the garage. There's a secret in that garage—a tunnel that runs underneath the spinning showgirl and into what used to be the Players Club. The club is abandoned now, but the tunnel still stands with all of its secrets. Tonight, it's a witness to my affairs.

I leave the suitcase hidden behind a pillar near the exit, in case instead of a wedding in three days' time, there's another fire where my future burns.

CHAPTER 37

1960

THE MORNING OF ARIA'S SEVENTEENTH BIRTHDAY IS GRAY WITH storms. It has to be this way, the Marmont knows, because in almost four years' time there needs to be a collision on a staircase. Erecting a prison of rain around Aria is one way to make sure that happens. Luckily the chateau can shut all its doors and close all its windows so it doesn't have to look at the smile on Aria's face, a smile it knows she won't be wearing by evening.

When she wakes, Aria goes into the living room. Her aunt made it to her bed rather than passing out on the couch, which means it was one of her better nights. She might be up soon and they can have a birthday breakfast together.

Aria calls Schwab's and orders French toast with extra syrup just the way Miss Devine likes it. Half an hour later, the food is set out on the table with coffee and her aunt's daily supply of gin and 'ludes.

Another half hour ticks past. Aria goes into the kitchen and stares at the oven, wondering if she should put all the food inside to keep it warm. She turns a couple of knobs but nothing happens. It doesn't even work.

She tiptoes over to her aunt's bedroom and pushes open the door. "Miss Devine?"

No response. Miss Devine might have made it to her room last night, but she won't be leaving it for hours.

Aria tosses the food in the trash. Calliope is away filming another movie with Peter Oldham. Flitter is on set in a nonspeaking role in a low budget film, playing a maid. "I've cleaned enough rooms at the Marmont that I don't even have to act," she told Aria with a grin that looked more like a grimace.

Maybe she can spend the day with Jupiter, riding cars that don't go anywhere. But when she gets to the garage, George is there. "Jupiter's sick," he tells her. "Got that flu everyone's been passing around. Isaiah and Maisie too."

Marian Monti's in Europe. Judith Crown and the babies are in Hawaii. Augusta Hepworth is in New York.

That's okay, Aria tells herself. She'll visit her bird.

But a year's worth of rain is falling down. Her little bird tries its best to come out, but the raindrops are the same size as the bird and they almost knock it out of the tree.

So Aria and her umbrella cross the road to Schwab's. It's almost empty. She doesn't need Calliope's smile to secure a seat at the soda fountain. Jim is sick too and Aria doesn't know the man making sundaes.

She orders a Schwab's Special.

"We got vanilla, strawberry, or chocolate," he says.

"Chocolate, please."

Five minutes later he pushes a glass across the counter. It's three-quarters full rather than overflowing. The ice cream is too cold for such a wintry day. Nobody comes into or out of Schwab's. Nobody kisses her cheek or gives her a present.

She puts down her spoon. Hops off the stool. Goes back outside. Crosses the road. There's a bus stop a bit farther down. She walks toward it before she can change her mind.

But it's a bad day for buses. She waits for a half hour, getting wetter and wetter. When a bus does come, the driver doesn't see her in her black dress; the day is so gray that Aria blends into it, truly invisible. As it passes, it throws up a cascade of water, soaking her from head to toe.

That's okay, Aria tells herself again.

She goes back to her suite, has a shower, puts on a different dress, then takes the elevator to the lobby and crosses through the gardens to Matty Tamer's bungalow. He's one of the few people who hasn't left town and his party from the night before is still going. Bob's out of town, so she's in no danger of running into him.

Aria walks into the bungalow, picks up a bottle of who knows what, and pours herself a shot. She swallows it down, swallows again to keep it from coming back up. Then she talks to a man a couple of years older than her who arrived last week with two parts dreams and one part innocence still in his eyes. She gives herself a stage name, tells him she's Edwina Elliott—the best she can come up with after no breakfast and no presents and a drenching from a bus.

It doesn't take long before she's making out with him in the corner of the room.

She lets him go a little further than Jupiter did. It's a fair exchange—she needs someone's arms around her on her birthday.

CHAPTER 38

...

1964

IT'S MY WEDDING DAY. AND I FEEL A JOY SO STRONG I KNOW IT'S enough to ward off the careless future. Today, only the sun will burn.

And tonight, desire will.

Soon, people start knocking on my door. Somehow, word has gotten out.

Judith Crown arrives first. She gives me a tiara. "For Princess Aria," she says.

"Tell me those are rhinestones," I say, gawping at myself in the mirror.

"Aria." She straightens the glove over which she's wearing sapphire and diamond knuckle-dusters. "Since when have you known me to consort with rhinestones?"

Augusta Hepworth is next, bringing with her three houseboys carrying a dinner set for twelve. "There's nothing better than having a few friends around for a meal," she says.

Nathalie arrives with a cocktail set, Maisie with napkins she's embroidered with my initials and Theo's. Paul Rydell, the writer with a penchant for aiming his rifle at the showgirl, turns up with a replica of his muse-nemesis. Isaiah and Jupiter appear with a beautiful leather-covered notebook and fountain pen that makes me cry so hard I can't even say thank you. Even Chester Meringue pays me a visit, making me a gift of his juggling balls.

"Life's a juggle, Aria," he says. "You should always keep a few tricks up your sleeve." He plucks a red rose out from behind my ear. "Thanks for always stopping to talk to a fellow who was on his way down rather than up."

I'm blubbering when Calliope arrives.

"You came," I sob.

"Of course," she says.

She orders me to lie down while she calls Schwab's for tea bags and Coke.

"What kind of cocktail are you going to make with that?"

She laughs. "One that will restore you to your natural beauty."

Five minutes later, I'm on the bed alternating between applying cold Coke cans and wet tea bags to my eyes. We don't mention the argument we had. Like true sisters, we fight and forget.

I know it wasn't Calliope who sent me the tarot Fool.

When she's satisfied that my eyes look less puffy, she produces a divine set of pale pink lingerie. I put it on without bothering to turn around because we're well past the point of hiding anything from each other. Then we start to transform Aria Jones into a bride.

As Calliope wields her tools I ask, "Do you think she'll come?"

"Flitter won't miss your wedding. Not for anything."

I haven't seen Flitter since she stormed out. I don't know how her audition went. Nor Calliope's. "How did it go?" I ask.

"Matty said I was the best. The part's mine." Her voice is flat.

She retrieves her purse, takes out a yellow bottle, and swallows two pills. Then she sits on the bed, elbows on knees, chin propped on her hands. I can see us both in the mirror, my reflection larger because I'm closer to the glass. My face is glowing with anticipation and expertly applied rouge. Calliope's isn't that of a woman who just got what she wanted.

"Should we celebrate?" I ask her.

"Should we?" she returns.

"I'm happy," I tell her. "Theo makes me so happy."

"Acting makes me happy," she says. "I never used to think

about the acting, just the immortality. But I quite like the process too." She swallows another pill. "You know you can just be in love with Win. You don't have to marry him."

"But why shouldn't I?"

There we are in the mirror, one woman in pink lingerie, one in a blue dress. One with brown hair, one with blonde. One known by only a handful of people, one known by many. Our faces look like question marks.

Calliope turns her back to the mirror. "I think I'd prefer to be the madwoman, not the orphan."

"But she's the one who burns it all down."

"Does she though? The orphan never leaps. Whereas the madwoman—she leaps. Besides, shouldn't we be more scared of the man who made the woman mad than of the woman herself?"

A knock interrupts before I can tell Calliope that *she's* being the madwoman.

Theo's voice calls, "Can I come in?"

"Sure," I say because I'm not wearing my dress, so it isn't bad luck if he sees me. And just look at my face in the mirror, look at my smile. Look at the way my hands slide into his hair, look at the way we kiss.

Oh, look at the way we kiss.

"I love you," we both say at the very same time and then we laugh.

Theo and I together—we are a night and a star, a match and a flame, a sea and the deep water within.

And we are getting married.

CHAPTER 39

...

1961

ON ARIA'S EIGHTEENTH BIRTHDAY, SHE ORDERS FRENCH toast and an ice cream sundae from Schwab's. She puts out the Limoges china she stole from the penthouse, lace napkins too. A crystal glass.

When the food arrives, she eats it washed down with half a bottle of French champagne. Then she stands up, smooths down her dress, goes downstairs, and steps outside. With French champagne courage, she'll do it. She really will.

But there's rain *and* wind today. Water so thick she can't see the showgirl's face, can only see the silver dollar teetering as a gust of wind slams into it.

She hurries back inside.

The hotel is so quiet. So she knocks on the doors of the few guests who have children staying with them in house, offers to take the children off their hands, ends up entertaining six children in the lobby with the baby grand piano. By the time evening's come around, she's earned one hundred dollars.

That was okay, Aria tells herself later when she's tucked up in the turret, writing in her journal. When she's at the beach, in the place where Aria finally belongs, she'll be all by herself. So she might as well get used to it.

Won't you be lonely? The echo of Calliope's voice.

"If I'm by myself, no one can ever hurt me." Aria says it aloud to the empty room. The walls of the Marmont toss one word back at her: *Hurt. Hurt. Hurt.*

She puts her hands over her ears.

If only there was a hand she could put over her heart. Because that's where the pain is, the pain she can't look at because she's afraid it might be the color and shape of loneliness.

CHAPTER 40

...

1964

ONCE I'M IN MY PINK WEDDING DRESS AND CALLIOPE'S gone to get ready, I leave my room. I'll go up to the turret, pull a book off the shelf and read, let the young Aria Jones whose pleasures were only to be found in that high tower above the world have one final moment before the new Aria Winchester takes her place.

Night has fallen. There's a promise of full moon, but the clouds are coming in. The Chateau Marmont is lit only by the city and the showgirl, everything tinged with green and red as if this is an intersection and the traffic lights can't agree whether I should stop or go.

I'm about to climb up the stairs from the seventh floor when I hear Flitter call, "Aria!"

I turn to my friend. She's here!

Her dress is the same color as the showgirl's and Flitter has the same coruscating brightness. "I have a wedding gift for you," she says.

I take her hand. Smile. We descend the spine of the Marmont like we've done a thousand times before, then cross through the lobby and into the garden.

"Did you get me a statue of you and Calliope? What kind of present means we have to go outside?" I try to joke, but the vomity feeling I had when I first arrived here is back.

From the penthouse balcony I can hear Pilot barking so loud it's like thunder. The showgirl's lights flash: green red, green red. *Go. Stop. Go.*

Stop.

"Over here." Flitter points to the path barricaded by the sign that reads: *Keep Out!*

I TUG MY HAND but she's holding on too tightly. "Flitter!" I dig my pink heels into the ground. "We can't go down there."

Flashes of memory: Theo slipping under the barrier; Flitter too. A woman who looked like Flitter on the back of Theo's motorbike. Flitter saying, *Can you imagine being the wife of the owner of the Chateau Marmont?*

No. No, no, no.

But I know this story. The orphan Jane Eyre finds out on her wedding day that the rich and powerful man she's about to marry is already married to someone else.

I try so hard to pull away.

"Flitter?" Calliope's voice is behind us now.

Oh God. Is she in on it too? The fire and the laughter and the screams and the fortune-telling and the little dead bird weren't enough to chase me away from having someone who really loved me? Now this?

"You got my message," Flitter says grimly to Calliope. "Come on."

The pills Calliope's taken shine like cracked glass in her eyes. "You'll get your shoes dirty," she says to me.

"I'm not going down there," I tell Flitter, panic in my voice.

"She can't go down there," Calliope reiterates.

But, somehow, we're on the wrong side of the barrier, Flitter pressing us on.

The palm trees hiss. The showgirl's lights are bright red now. Pilot barks louder. My eyes meet Calliope's. Her soul is in hers and it's as frightened as mine.

It's not Calliope who's in on this. It's all Flitter.

CHAPTER 41

...

1964

I CAN SEE THE BUNGALOW NOW. A LIGHT IS ON INSIDE. THIS WINdow isn't visible from the pool; you can only see it if you ignore the *Keep Out!* sign and walk down the forbidden path.

The light falls on the heads of two people. One is a tall man, the other a woman. He has dark hair; hers is fair. They're embracing. They aren't construction workers. There's no evidence of construction anywhere: no tools, no cement mixers, no rubble or sand or mortar. Just a bungalow with two people embracing inside it.

One of them has dark hair. I've touched that hair. I've kissed that hair.

That hair belongs to a man who's embracing another woman.

Tenderly.

It wasn't Flitter on the back of a motorbike. It was this woman.

I was wrong again.

I've seen a photograph of her in an album in Theo's penthouse. Marley, the wife he loved so much that he didn't marry her, lest she end up dead.

She's so very alive.

And I am dead.

This, here, is the fire.

CHAPTER 42

...

1964

CALLIOPE GROPES FOR MY HAND. FOOTSTEPS SOUND BEhind us.

Bob Ashenhurst.

He smiles at Flitter. "The part is yours. I'll tell Matty I've overridden his decision."

"The part?" Calliope repeats.

"Jane Eyre, the orphan girl," Bob says, smiling at her now.

Then at me.

It isn't the breeze that whispers; it isn't the palm trees either. It's the castle itself, letting out a memory the same way you find a piece of the puzzle hiding beneath the rug on the floor. The memory is Flitter saying to Calliope long ago: *So long as it doesn't turn you into a pill bottle like Marian Monti or a bitch like Lacey Magee.* And of something Bob said to me that same night: *I will never forgive you.*

For seven years he's been thinking: *Why hurt the orphan when she's small and low?* There's so much more to hurt when you're happy.

He's been waiting to cut the points off Calliope's star too. Waiting until we both had farther to fall.

All this time, Flitter and I were afraid Calliope would be the one to turn. But Flitter—what have the past seven years turned her into?

And me—what did it turn me into?

A woman who's holding her friend's hand while she watches her lover and her sister betray her in two different ways.

"Y-you . . ." Calliope stutters at Flitter, trying to piece it together.

"She found out somehow that Win's a liar," I say dully. "Then she told Bob. In exchange for what she's always wanted. Power. And—"

"The part," Calliope finishes, both of us staring, not at Bob who we thought was the worst thing at the Marmont, but at Flitter. Who'll most likely become the new Calliope. After her will come another girl, then another, right up until the world ends.

Once upon a time, Calliope tarnished Flitter's dream. Bob tarnished Calliope's and the world tarnished mine, but really it was ambition that tarnished everything.

Flitter's ambition was always for herself. Calliope's is to hold everyone's hearts in her hands. Bob's is to keep getting away with the game he plays. Mine was for a place of my own.

None of us wanted consequence.

But something always comes after.

I take a step away from Flitter. Away from Bob, who probably, as a boy, caught birds in nets just so he could watch the glitter of life die in their eyes when he slit their throats. Away from Theo, whose father watched the glitter of life die in his son's eyes one morning over breakfast and who then became a man who drank and sang and married his way through life—a man I was supposed to marry today but who, at the very least, is a colossal liar.

I told him how much I hated secrets and lies.

But there is no renovation. No construction workers.

There's just a woman he's embracing the way you hold someone you care deeply for.

On the table behind them are needles, glistening like the diamonds in the wedding tiara I will never wear.

Finally, I run. Down the path, toward the pool. I'm almost there when I hear Win's voice roaring, "Aria?"

"What the fuck did you do?" he spits at someone: Flitter, Calliope, Bob—I don't know. Know only that I need to get away from here with the suitcase I packed because part of me always knew that marriage shouldn't be the dream of a poor orphan girl if she ever wanted to rise up out of her story.

ARIA'S FRIENDS LOOK IN her room, in the turret, in Calliope's suite, because those are the places where Aria can always be found. Not tonight. The Chateau Marmont is the only one who knows where she is and of course it won't tell.

When Jupiter, the only other person who knows about the tunnel, approaches the entrance to search for Aria, the handbrake on one of the Lamborghinis releases and it rolls forward, hitting a Corvette. Jupiter hurries to rein in the Lambo and forgets all about the tunnel until much later, when it's empty.

The Marmont waits for two hours before it pushes the young woman in the short pink dress out onto the Strip. She's carrying the blue suitcase that will give her purple bruises on her shins before the night is over. Just as she did seven years ago when she stood in the very same spot, she looks at the edifice of the Chateau Marmont. This time she doesn't glare.

The fire inside her has been blown out.

But the Chateau Marmont crosses its curtains and hopes that something in her future will rekindle it, because this—this is the path the castle wanted her to take all along.

PART II

.....

ARIA JONES

The puppet master, open-mouthed, wide-eyed, impotent at the last, saw his dolls break free of their strings, abandon the rituals he had ordained for them since time began and start to live for themselves; the king, aghast, witnesses the revolt of his pawns.

—ANGELA CARTER

CHAPTER 43

...

1964

I STOP INSIDE THE AIRPORT TERMINAL WITH MY CHILD'S SUITCASE in my hand, terrified that there are no flights leaving so late at night—terrified that the Chateau Marmont's grasp reaches this far. Then I see a lady in a blue suit and hat, her white gloves bright in the lights.

"I need to buy a ticket," I say.

"Where to?" she asks tiredly, as if she's seen it all before in dreamtown LA: the girl with a suitcase and no ticket, running from something.

"Anywhere."

"There's a flight to Rome via New York and Paris at 21:00."

I hand over some of the money I got from pawning Miss Devine Rey's engagement ring on the way here, as well as the green booklet I got last year when Calliope was renewing her passport. She'd given one set of forms to Flitter and one to me, telling us that we all needed to know we were unsnared birds, free to cross oceans.

Perhaps she really can see the future.

Not long after, I'm sitting on an airplane beside a tanned and rather beautiful man and only then do I let myself burst into tears.

I SEARCH DESPAIRINGLY IN my purse, but it holds only money and my passport. My arms are bare—I don't even have a sleeve to mop up my tears. I rifle through the seat pocket, searching for Kleenex. I don't notice the plane take off, don't realize we're flying, don't comprehend anything until the beautiful man leans across and says, "Here." He's holding out a folded white handkerchief.

"Thank you," I sob, curling into the window with the handkerchief and letting it all out. Too much for one square of cotton.

The man summons the stewardess and asks for Kleenex, sends her away when she brings just one and begs her to fetch the whole box.

From LA to New York, I make my way through that box. I cry for Nathalie, for Judith Crown, for my aunt, for seven years' worth of starlets. I cry for them because, if I started crying for me, no amount of Kleenex would be enough.

After we refuel in New York, the desperate stewardess gives me a blanket, suggests I sleep, tells the man beside me that unfortunately there are no spare seats and she cannot move him. She thinks I'm like the Marmont—something to run from. Maybe I am. Maybe that's why Theo—

I shut my eyes tight against all thoughts of him. Him and Marley.

Flitter and Bob.

Calliope. What will she do now that she can't be the orphan in a movie that carries just a woman's name? Become the madwoman instead?

And me. What will I do?

"Signorina." The man beside me offers his folded jacket to rest my head on. "Sleep."

I do. I'm so exhausted that I don't even dream. Perhaps dreams only exist on land; perhaps in the sky, where castles in the air live, dreams don't bother you.

I WAKE AS THE airplane touches down in Paris. A place entirely new. There's no story in Paris about Aria Jones. Nor in Rome, where the flight will terminate. I could do absolutely anything once I get there.

Except be with Theo.

My stomach cramps with memory. Theo. Marley. The embrace. The syringes. Bob. Flitter. Me, running.

For the first time tonight, the rational part of my mind breaks through: *Why didn't I ask Theo what was going on*?

Because Bob was there. Because Flitter, who was meant to be my sister, didn't care that the thing she was selling to Bob was me. Her soul too. And Calliope's.

But what if the Theo who told me I had beautiful green eyes, the Theo who loved me because of the way I ate hot dogs—what if he could have explained it to me somehow?

I can almost hear the Marmont's water pipes hissing from across the sea, insisting on this simple truth: How could Theo possibly explain that the bungalow he said was being renovated was actually inhabited by his ex-lover? A woman with embraces in her arms and needles on her table? How could anyone ever say that a recovering alcoholic found in that situation a half hour before their wedding was innocent of wrongdoing?

The warning signs I ignored flash red like the dawn sky as we take off from Paris: bottles of vodka in the freezer, impulsive and regretted weddings, a man who can find sex faster than he can buy a pint of milk.

As if to make sure I've really learned my lesson, a movie begins on the screen at the front of the airplane: *He's Just a Rebel Without a Girl*. There are Calliope's cheekbones and her half smile in the first film she made for Bob's studio after she tarnished her dream.

Later, the stewardess's voice comes over the loudspeaker. We'll soon be landing in Rome.

But Rome isn't the beach. I need the water; it's all I've ever wanted.

I need to not think of Theo.

The handkerchief twists in my hands.

"Signorina, can I get you anything more?" the beautiful man asks.

"Water," I say.

He summons the stewardess and asks for a glass of water.

"No." I shake my head. "I mean where is the water in Italy?"

I know the answer. I've read encyclopedias and atlases and the works of di Lampedusa and Manzoni. But I can't recall details, just water, and the way it can drown you.

"Venice?" the man says and my brain seizes on that.

Venice. *La Serenissima.* City of masks.

A place that lives on top of everything that has ever been drowned.

I'VE NEVER WANTED TO believe in fate. To do that means I accept that my parents were meant to die and I was always supposed to be stupid enough to fall in love with a man who told lies the same way he smoked cigarettes—with charm and ease, one foot grinding out the ash at the end. But something has put me on a plane beside a man who lives in Rome, and who also has a house in Venice where his two sisters live. They have a spare room that they rent out.

"The house is on the Rio dei Santi Apostoli," he tells me. "A canal."

"Water," I repeat.

On any other night I'd tell myself that this is the kind of story only the guileless movie heroine wearing a white cotton dress would believe. But my life has gone so far astray that I write down the address. "Thank you. And I'm sorry about your handkerchief."

"If one of my sisters was sitting on an airplane crying her heart right out of her body, I'd want someone to give her a handkerchief too," he says.

I start weeping all over again.

ON THE TRAIN FROM Rome to Venice, I stare out the window, can't take my eyes off the crammed-together houses set among antique palaces, the church spires that rise up like swords, the fig trees waiting patiently to fruit. Perhaps I'm still in shock, but the woman who couldn't make herself take a bus downtown has no fear about being in a foreign country so far from home because . . . I don't have a home. Maybe I'll find one here. Maybe I'll find a place so magical that I'll never think about Theo again, never remember the way his fingertips would land on my skin with such friction and heat that they birthed new stars all over my body.

Everything leads back to Theo.

Then to Flitter and Bob.

And Calliope. Who learned to jerk men off so she could keep them outside her body.

There are worse things to be than Aria Jones, jilted fiancée.

We pull into the Stazione di Venezia Santa Lucia. I step down onto the platform, my suitcase banging against my shins, and study the map that the beautiful man drew for me before he disembarked in Rome. I follow the directions to the Grand Canal.

There I find the water. So much water. Water that's alive in a way I never knew water could be. Water taxis dart like swallows through the blue. Houses in shades of pink, ocher, and cream, ornamented with red awnings, pillars, mosaics, and gold, dip their feet into the canal. Words I can't understand sing through the air, as does laughter, gulls' cries, the plucked string of a violin, and a voice answering with a barcarolle. I see one gondola, then another.

I had no idea there was so much world in one small city.

In Venice I could be like Calliope, could give myself a new name, could leave Aria behind. But . . .

There, and there, and over there too, palaces edge the canal, palaces so ancient I'm certain that if I prized out a brick, the building would bleed history all over my hands. How many people over how many hundreds of years have stood in this exact place and felt not just their mouths drop open, but their spirit fall open too?

Calliope once told me how insignificant we would all be unless we were famous. But with the Grand Canal undulating beneath my feet in a city where my insignificance in the whole spool of time could easily overwhelm me, I tilt my head up toward the sky. I don't want a new name. I like Aria Jones. I mightn't like what's happened to her, but Aria is more a part of me than Theo Winchester could ever be, even if we *had* married. And Aria Jones is standing on a Venetian bridge watching a gondolier flick his boat to and fro like a fish. This is a dream that Aria Jones never even thought to dream.

So I keep walking along roads that have no cars, no giant glittering showgirls. There are fruit stands lit up with oranges and apples. There are no studios or backlots, but bell towers and churches. Reverence and worship of a different kind.

I take a wrong turn twice, going left too early and then too late, before I arrive at the Sotoportego del Magazen, a strange little colonnaded corridor that runs alongside the Santi Apostoli canal and beneath a building. It takes me to the doorstep of the house where two sisters will have received a telephone call from their brother, letting them know to expect me.

I haven't eaten since I left Los Angeles two days ago. I haven't slept, except for the hours between New York and Paris. I've just walked for twenty-five minutes, carrying everything I have left in the world. All of me is sore, especially the pain in my shins, and I concentrate on letting it hurt more than my heart.

I knock on the door.

Two women stare at me. One says, "Aria?" The other says, "You need to sit down."

And I do, right there on the doorstep, too tired to go any farther.

I WAKE UP IN a small, plain room with blue-painted walls, a white quilt on the bed. Through the window, I hear Italian voices calling out *"Òe!"* and the response *"Òe pope."*

Fabric rustles in the doorway. Two faces peek at me.

"Buongiorno," I say and the women giggle.

"Marzia," the first one—the younger one—says.

"Alessia," the other chimes in. Her hair is shining black and pulled into a bun whereas Marzia wears hers loose, breaking in waves over her shoulders.

"Soup," Alessia tells me, bringing over a bowl of something that makes my stomach roar.

Marzia giggles again at the sound. She reminds me of Flitter.

I squeeze my eyes shut.

"You don't like?" Marzia asks, her eyes huge and brown.

"I do." I shovel it into my mouth like a storybook orphan fed just one bowl of gruel each day.

When I'm done, Alessia disappears and brings back another bowl.

"Oh no," I tell her. "I can't eat all your food."

"You pay for room and board," Alessia says. "And this is the soup that heals broken hearts."

I choke, push the soup away, close my eyes, fall asleep. When I wake, I think at least another day has passed. I lie there listening for the sounds of Venice. But what I hear in the swish of the blue curtains in the breeze, as if I'm destined to always be in communication with the souls of old houses, is Calliope's voice telling me that I might as well be dead for all the living I've done.

As much as everything hurts, I don't want to be dead. So my only choice is to get out of bed and make a start on living.

CHAPTER 44

...

1964–1965

MARZIA TAKES ME THROUGH CANNAREGIO, WHERE THEIR townhouse is located. She speaks good English, tells me that her brother insisted that she and her sister learn the language after school each day, that they've practiced on English and American guests over the years.

"For an American, you are quiet," she observes.

I'm quiet because on the tip of my tongue sits one word: *Theo.* And the memory of my wedding day—when I didn't get married.

I follow her into and out of churches—so many of them—and listen when she shows me where to catch the vaporetto that will take me up and down the canal streets if I am, like most Americans, afraid to walk.

"I like to walk," I tell her.

We finish in the Campo Santa Maria Nova at a cafe that spills onto the square. Marzia orders coffee that sits as thick on my tongue as lies.

Eventually she sighs. "You don't say where you are from or why you are here. Okay, keep your secrets. But now you are here, what will you do?"

"Walk," I tell her. "I'll just walk."

She gives a little shrug, impatient with me for being such a disappointing American. She wouldn't be disappointed with Calliope or Flitter. They'd make her smile.

"Off you go then." She points to the square.

Over the coming days I explore the old ghetto in Cannaregio, squeeze myself into Calle Varisco, the narrowest street in the city, startled by the silence. It was never silent in Los Angeles—and that's something I only know now because I've heard the way a different city exhales. With only people and boats, you can find sudden swathes where nothing makes a sound at all.

I walk over to the markets near the Rialto Bridge where slippery fish are lined up in rows on ice. Women shake their heads at the vendors and raise their voices until suddenly they smile and the fish is wrapped in newspaper and put in a basket on the woman's arm. There are so many things I've never seen before: milky-gray oysters, tiny crabs called moeche and enormous ones that look like rocks. I'm staring at those when the man who runs the stall picks one up and waggles it in front of me in a way that's possibly supposed to look tantalizing. I jump back because those legs are fearsome. His belly laugh rings out in the square, not unkindly, and it makes me laugh too.

Suddenly I'm surrounded by women telling me, in louder and louder Italian when I fail to understand, something about the crab. Cooking instructions? Me, Aria Jones, who's only ever made burgers and grilled cheese, is being told in a language she doesn't speak how to prepare a terrifying crab for dinner. There's so much lip-smacking and smiling encouragement for the *piccola ragazza americana* that I succumb, leaving the market with a pungent newspaper-wrapped bundle under my arm, smiling when I think of how Bob just paid for a Venetian crab for my dinner—I used some money from his engagement ring to pay for it.

Back at the townhouse, I present Alessia with my bounty and she nods as if I finally did something right.

"You will help," she tells me.

I spend the afternoon in a lemon-yellow kitchen with a blue-canal view, piano notes exploding from the record player like fireworks.

"Scarlatti. A genius." Alessia indicates the record player as she cracks open the cooked crab and instructs me to dress it with olive oil, parsley, pepper, salt, and lemon juice.

I scoop the meat into each half of the empty crab shells, which no longer look like rocks, but exotic porcelain bowls. I call for Marzia.

The two sisters share one shell and I eat the other, all of us silent at the wooden table in the kitchen because a Scarlatti sonata is the only sound you need when you eat a Venetian spider crab for the very first time in a life where you never expected Venice or sisters or Scarlatti or crabs that can be tamed into deliciousness.

I would never have lived this moment if I'd married Theo is all I can think once the crab is eaten and the kitchen tidied and Scarlatti silenced and nighttime has enveloped the world.

I PLUNGE BACK INTO the streets the next day and the next, the gutsy smell of fish from the markets still caught in my nose. Everything here is stronger: voices, coffee, religion, liquor. The memory of Theo's face. It lurches up when I brush against a leather jacket in a street.

I take a vaporetto to the Lido where there are beaches rather than leather jackets. But the beach is sallow, waveless; nothing like the beach I had in my mind when I was almost fourteen and thought I'd spend my life alone by the water.

Won't you get lonely? I spin around. But no one's there except memory.

Suddenly I'm fourteen years old and a silver dollar is about to squash me flat and it might be days before anyone finds me and then all I'll be is Jane Doe in a Venetian morgue. I'll die alone and is there anything worse than to think, at the end of a life, that you meant absolutely nothing to anyone?

A gull shrieks, pulling me out of the past. There are no silver dollars here. Not even a wave could sweep me off this beach. Perhaps there were more people at the Chateau Marmont who knew who I was than there are here, but the person they knew was half dead.

Here, I'm half alive.

The next week I wind my way through Castello, Dorsoduro, dodge tourists and pigeons in San Marco. I need to walk far enough that every dark-haired man on the street doesn't remind me of Theo, until music drifting from a window doesn't make me stop to listen in case it's one of Theo's songs, until he isn't the first thing I think of when I wake—even before I wake; until he doesn't live inside every dream that disturbs my sleep.

Along the Calle de la Bande, I look at the window of every shop. There are painted masks—how Calliope would love those—and leather-bound notebooks in whose pages I can see Theo writing a song.

Keep walking, Aria.

I pass stores selling colored glass, white lace, blue velvet brocade, iron door knockers shaped like lions.

In another window, there's a typewriter in a creamy shade of celadon green.

Hermes 3000, it says on the front panel of this box-sized little beauty. The sign propped up beside it reads: *Compagno di viaggio portatile.*

Viaggio means travel. After a month as a tourist, that's one word I recognize. Portable travel companion? Is that really what it means, or is the flicker of loneliness from the Lido still traveling alongside me?

What would I do with a typewriter anyway? Pen and paper have always been good enough for my journals before now.

I continue on into the next street. Now it's a store with brightly colored dresses in the window that arrests me. The dresses look so happy, as if you could put them on and nothing sad or terrible could ever penetrate all of that joy.

I push open the door, go inside.

"*Buongiorno!*" A woman made out of sunbeams and smiles welcomes me.

"*Guardo, solo,*" I say haltingly, hoping to tell her I'm just taking a look, but possibly telling her I have a million dollars to spend.

"Try," she tells me. She scoops up an armful of things, not even asking my size, and shoos me into a fitting room.

For the very first time in my life, I shop for clothes.

I try everything on slowly, half-expecting her to tell me to hurry up, but instead she flings open the curtain whenever she wants to, no matter if I'm in my underwear, and offers her opinions freely. "No," and "*Mamma mia*"—which I'm not sure is approval or disapproval.

Finally, when I'm the one who flings open the curtain because I've found the one that makes me smile—an adorable mustard-gold coatdress with long sleeves and a short skirt—she claps her hands with delight.

"Perfect," she pronounces. "Made for you."

I sit on a stool at the counter while she wraps the dress in bright pink paper. In a jumble of English and Italian words, we talk and she tells me—I think—that she's twenty-two years old and opened her shop last year.

"You come back," she says as she passes me the shopping bag and I promise I will.

I walk away, taking with me not just my dress but some of the happiness she radiated—so much that it drew me in from the street. She's just one year older than me and already has her own shop. If I sat on a bed beside her and wondered what jobs women could have, like Calliope and I once did, she probably wouldn't ever run out of ideas.

What could I do, what talent do I have that would make me smile the same way?

I walk on, making discoveries, but finding no answers.

I discover a cafe where the coffee is milkier and thinner than most Venetians drink, coffee that tastes more like truth than lies. I discover another that makes the best *cicchetti* for lunch. I look at my money and discover that walking won't pay my rent, just like it doesn't cure broken hearts.

I discover that no matter how far I walk, how many dresses I buy, how many coffees I drink and crabs I crack, I will always think of Theo.

But as I stand in my room in my new mustard coatdress, I understand that I have to think of Aria Jones too.

If Aria Jones hadn't seen Theo embrace another woman, if Flitter hadn't put ambition ahead of friendship, if Bob hadn't been so intent on revenge, then I wouldn't know how lovely a Venetian canal can be when touched by the sun.

I thought love was beautiful, but the world is beautiful too. The real world. The world that you have to live in.

I've never lived on solid ground. My domain has been proscribed by my name, which is Italian for *air,* Isaiah once told me. Air: the place of dreams. Dreams of water and running. Dreams of a wedding to Theo, dreams that never considered the everydayness of how marriage would work—as if we were just going to remain as we were, him riding freeways, me teaching Adele and scooping up starlets. The pain of my parents' deaths hit my body like a wrecking ball and I've tried to live out of my body ever since. Like Calliope, who wants to pin herself to the sky.

But human beings aren't meant to live in the air.

The next day I go into every cafe in Cannaregio and ask for a job. They refuse; I'm *troppa americana* and my Italian is *orribile.* I try the ones close to San Marco where the tourists gather. I ask at three cafes, then four. Five. I try an osteria, a trattoria, until I finally get offered a position as a waitress at one of the most touristy, right on the piazza.

I walk home satisfied. I have the means to live. Now I need to figure out *how* to live.

CHAPTER 45

...

1965

One morning when I wake, I hear a man's voice. I tiptoe downstairs, peer over the banister and there, sitting at the table with his sisters, is the beautiful Italian I met on the plane.

He rises to his feet when he sees me. "You look different," he says.

"It probably helps that I'm not crying." I slip into my chair.

"I'm Arturo," he says as I reach for the biscotti, dunk it in my coffee, and bite into it, letting its sweetness mix with the sharpness of the coffee to make something quite perfect.

I only realize I've closed my eyes when I open them again.

"Aria likes biscotti," Marzia tells her brother.

"But not proper coffee," Alessia adds chidingly.

"Give her time," Arturo says, like I'll still be here months from now.

I don't know what it is—time, ease, biscotti—but I behave a little more like myself. The questions I haven't asked come tumbling out. "Have you always lived here?"

Arturo nods. "Our family has been here for one hundred years."

"Wow." I try to imagine having a home that's part of your blood. Is the Chateau Marmont in my blood? Or am I in its blood?

"Are those your parents?" I nod at a framed photo of a man and a woman dressed in their best clothes, holding hands, a smiling crowd around them.

Marzia nods soberly.

Her brother elaborates, "They died five years ago. Our mother had cancer. One month later, our father died of a broken heart. Marzia was sixteen, Alessia twenty."

"We started letting out two rooms so we had money to stay," Marzia says.

"And Arturo sends money from Rome," Alessia adds, lest I think her brother has abandoned his sisters to poverty and service.

My mind is circling the one dreadful thing we have in common. "You think your parents are a permanent part of your world," I say. "It's one of the most shocking things when you find out you were only given them for a very short time."

Three sets of eyes stare at me. It's the first clue I've given them about Aria Jones.

"What do you do in Rome?" I ask Arturo to turn the conversation away.

"I own two cinemas there. And one each in Florence, Genoa, and Venice. Movies are big business in Italy."

"In America too," I say grimly.

Oh yes, the Fates who put me on the same airplane as Arturo are definitely chuckling behind their hands. I escaped one city of made-up lives only to land in the home of someone else who deals in imaginary lives.

I search for a conversational segue that isn't about movies and make-believe, nor about dead parents. "How do guests find you?" I ask Marzia and Alessia. "You don't have a sign out front."

"We have a friend at the tourist bureau," Alessia replies. "When all the hotels are full, they send people here. Arturo knows people from America. They sometimes stay."

"Would you like more guests?" I ask and I immediately hear Calliope's voice whispering in my ear, *You help everyone.*

I hadn't thought much about what she said that day, but now that I'm sitting at a table with nice people who cared enough to bring me bowls of soup, I find that I *do* want to help.

"Where to find them?" Alessia says with a bewildered shrug, as if she doesn't know why tourists don't just fall out of the sky.

"You need to advertise," I tell her. "If I was a tourist, I'd much rather stay here and look out the window at that gorgeous view than stay at a hotel."

Marzia beams while her brother asks, "Are you a tourist, Aria?"

I nod. "I'm on my grand tour. Hopefully I'll come to a better end than Daisy Miller."

It's a stupid joke to make with Italians who are unlikely to have read Henry James. But Arturo nods as if he understands, then they all try not to stare at my eyes, which are damp, because now I'm remembering Calliope and her assertion that there were so few stories named after a woman who didn't die at the end. Of course Daisy dies. And I feel a pang of affection for my dearest friend, who wanted me to go out and find my happily ever after, rather than just taking the only one offered to me.

"What else will you tell us about yourself, Aria?" Arturo asks now.

I copy Alessia's shrug.

"Do you think your story isn't worth telling?" Arturo prods. "Or that we aren't worthy of having it told to us?"

I stand up. "I'm late for work."

Behind me, Marzia scolds her brother, who replies, "When someone is silent, they need to know the listeners hear that too."

I DO TWO THINGS after that conversation—two peculiar, spontaneous things that feel, on reflection, a bit like living.

I go to the shop on Calle de la Bande where I saw the pretty green typewriter. It's like the Marmont, that typewriter, whispering things to me that so far I've not understood. Now I think I do.

I hand over the *lira* I've made from waitressing. I have only enough money left to pay my board this week, so I'll have to take some extra shifts at the restaurant. But that's okay. Once upon a time I thought that I couldn't step into the world unless I had enough money to pay for every unforeseen circumstance for years to come. I wanted so much safety around me that I couldn't live. Now I have just enough safety, and perhaps that's all you really need.

I take the typewriter into work and, in the break between lunch service and dinner, I type the address of Marzia and Alessia's home, giving it a name—Castello Fantasticare—that the tourists will love. I cut up the paper into small rectangles and stack them on the counter. When I leave that night, the pile is smaller and that makes me smile.

I slip back into the townhouse after eleven o'clock. Marzia and Alessia aren't usually awake at this time, so I almost drop the typewriter when a voice says, "What is that?"

Arturo's in a chair in the living room, right by the window. Only one of the lamps is lit—and I notice how I don't brace. Three months ago, if I'd walked into a room at the Marmont with one man I hardly knew and just one lamp lit, I'd have been searching my pockets for pistols I'd have wished I owned. Here, I don't think about pistols or bracing, just about how tired my body is from working, but how eager I am to go upstairs and wind a sheet of paper into the typewriter and rest my hands on the keys.

I want to play the music of stories. That could be the thing that will make me smile.

"Drink?" Arturo offers, indicating the bottle of Amaro beside him.

I nod because he and his sisters have been good to me and I want to be respectful in return. I place the typewriter down, sip, and screw up my face. "It tastes like something you'd give to someone you hate."

He laughs. "Amaretto then? It's sweeter." He pours my new drink. "My sisters had three telephone calls this afternoon. The newly baptized Castello Fantasticare is likely to be booked out by summer." He nods at my typewriter. "I'm guessing your friend had something to do with it."

"It's the least I could do to say thank you."

"You're paying us. You don't have to thank us," he replies drily.

"You took a big chance on a weeping woman on a plane. So I do."

I sip the Amaretto. It's not a mint julep, and Arturo isn't Calliope. Venice is not LA. And I like that, even as I miss the hot breath of the Santa Anas bursting through doorways like a forty-foot showgirl ready to shake a few hairs loose from their lacquer.

Maybe that's what I want to do too.

"Is that why you bought the typewriter?" Arturo asks. "To help my sisters?"

"Not just that. I'm going to use it to tell one story. And find another."

"No more silence?"

I smile. "Probably still some of that."

He laughs. "Would you like to go out for a drink tomorrow night, Aria?"

"I . . . I don't know," I splutter.

He laughs again, but with less humor. "Americans should learn not to be so honest."

"I'm not sure that Americans are honest. At least not in Hollywood." I bite my lip. I've as good as told him where I came from. "I'll let you know in the morning."

I DON'T THINK ABOUT Arturo or his question as I stand at the open window in my room. I think about stories. How the word can mean two entirely different things—an account of events, or else a lie. A true story, or a tall story. How we believe some stories simply because of the way they're told or because of who tells them. If it's told on the silver screen by a beautiful woman, then we all *want* to believe. If it's told by a charming male studio executive with a killer publicity team, then boy do we ever believe it.

It's cold outside, probably only forty-five degrees, but tonight I want the water scent and the water sound, want to breathe in history and wonder, want to listen to the hum of the two gondoliers who've stopped to chat, holding their poles against the wall so their gondolas don't float away. There are so many stories out there. Just look at all the stories that glitter above me, woven into constellations: Cassiopeia, who boasted of her beauty and was hung in the sky as punishment; Ursa Major, a casualty of Zeus's wandering eye; Pegasus, the winged horse shaped from the blood of the beheaded Medusa. Beauty, cruelty, and stories—all of life spangled above me in the night.

I take one last inhale, then I pull the quilt off the bed, wrap myself in it, stack my journals on the table, and place the typewriter beside them.

I remember Judith Crown, how she'd sit with her hands on the keys of the piano in the lobby of the Chateau Marmont before she began to play, as if in that thirty seconds she was feeling the thrum of all the music stored inside the piano, waiting impatiently for somebody to sit down and let it all out.

That's how I feel.

Flitter, Calliope, and I—we were three intelligent women who lived in a city built on fantasy and we still didn't have the imagination to believe that anything would change. But my imagination has since been fed by this city and now it is astronomical.

I open the journal on top of the pile, roll a blank piece of paper into the typewriter.

Flitter once said that Hollywood made our beds and then

forced us to not just lie in them, but to sleep in them too. But that's not true. Hollywood didn't do that.

The men did that.

Men are just flesh and blood. We can fight flesh and blood.

And we don't even need pistols to do it.

Calliope Burns: A Novel, I type.

CHAPTER 46

...

1965

TO FIGURE OUT HOW TO LIVE, YOU HAVE TO *LIVE.* I'VE NEVER driven a car, never swum in the ocean, never really been on a date besides walking to a hot dog stand. I think part of what Calliope was telling me the night we fought was to make sure I truly understood what love is.

I do understand. I could lie down right now like Arturo's father and die of a broken heart. I honestly could.

But Theo is a liar. He doesn't deserve my dead heart.

And I'm in Venice giving Aria Jones a life.

So, "Yes," I tell Arturo in the morning. "I'll go out with you."

ARTURO ARRIVES AT THE restaurant at five o'clock—Monday is my only half day and I'm usually finished by now. Through the curtain separating the kitchen from the dining room, I observe him. He's classically good-looking, a man who shines at midday when the sun is bright and you can see how clear blue his eyes are. A man who'd be asleep at midnight, who'd miss the full moons and the stars. But he's a kind man too—he saved this damsel in distress.

I put down the dishrag, ready to say, *Buongiorno, Arturo,* when the radio changes to a new song and my hands wrap around the edge of the countertop.

It's the symphony of lost youth and regrets that I once heard played in a Chateau Marmont penthouse.

One of the waiters sings along. A waitress hums. I try very hard to breathe.

At the end, the announcer says that Theo Winchester's new number one hit in America is taking Italy, taking the world, by storm. He's touring Europe next month.

He's coming to Rome.

The waiter looks at the waitress. "Want to go with me?" he asks and she beams. *"Sì."*

I look up at the ceiling. Theo's song is number one. I'm so happy for him.

But I don't think I can listen to that song again without dying from grief.

And waiting out front for me is another man. One I'm going on a date with because life is always about the next step forward, the one you have to take even when you have sorrow ensnared inside you like a bird, beating its wings against your chest.

I tug off my apron, smooth a hand over my striped knit dress from a new Italian fashion brand called Missoni—so new that they need customers and charge prices I can afford. I pull my trench coat on, tie a scarf over my hair.

When I step outside, Arturo says, "You look more Italian than the Italian women do."

"I'm going to take that as a compliment."

"You should," he replies, and I'm not sure that I want him to look at me that way.

"I'm not . . ." I start.

"Not in search of *amore,*" he finishes. "Sometimes the things you aren't looking for find you anyway."

Like Theo found me.

I follow him into Castello, to the Campo Santi Giovanni e Paolo. Beside the square stands the basilica, an aged but colossal beauty that reminds me of Miss Devine Rey.

My heart squeezes. I've hardly thought of my aunt since I fled. Is she better now? I should write to her, let her know that I'm okay. Maybe she might care about that, the same way I care about her.

The basilica adjoins a building with a white marble facade and shimmering trompe l'oeil decorations. How people stare. One woman makes the sign of the cross, another wipes a tear from her eye. Yet another goes right up close to the pictures and studies the skill, the artistry, the miracle of how many centuries those pictures have lasted for.

It isn't always a bad thing to be looked at.

Now I wish it was Calliope standing next to me in the square so I could say, *I'm sorry.* I thought that because I'd read my way through a library, I knew everything. But there's still so much to learn.

Which is why I'm sitting down on the terrace of an osteria with a view of the Rio dei Mendicanti, opposite Arturo.

The waiter passes me a blanket, which I tuck around my legs to keep out the chill. Arturo orders a bottle of Montepulciano. I've never had that before. When I sip, I discover it's like drinking a soft leather jacket.

Like drinking Theo.

The waiter's voice pushes through that aching thought. When Arturo finishes, I open my mouth to ask for the *sarde in saor,* the vinegary sardines I've developed a taste for, but the waiter is walking away and I realize Arturo has ordered for the two of us. Which is what the men in movies always do.

I remember Theo whispering *Do you like that?*—his heart asking my body how else it could love me.

A man who cares what a woman wants is no small thing, I want to tell Calliope. Perhaps she's never known a man like that. Perhaps she hadn't even known a man could be like that.

God, I want to hug her.

God, I want to kiss Theo.

"Are you all right?" Arturo asks as the *polenta e schie* and risotto are placed on the table.

"Yes," I tell him. The lie falls off my tongue as easily as Theo's lies about builders and renovations and weddings had fallen off his.

I push the risotto around the edges of my plate. Because I lied too. I never told Theo that my dream was of escaping, never told him what my heart really wanted.

Even with Theo I was hiding.

"YOU DON'T LIKE RISOTTO," Arturo asks once his plate is clean and mine still full.

"I ate too many leftovers at work," I lie again.

"You like the food there?"

He wants me to say no, wants me to like Montepulciano and risotto, Italian cinema and Amari.

"I like hot dogs especially," I tell him.

He laughs, disbelieving.

We stand up and Arturo offers me his arm. We walk along in silence, let Venice be the fluent conversation we cannot make flow between us.

Then he says, "Thank you for helping my sisters," and he's genuine in his gratitude.

He loves his sisters, is happy to let them stay in Venice and run a business rather than making them move with him to Rome where he can orchestrate their lives, even as he thinks it's his role to order food for me.

Humans are so full of contradictions. It's something you don't see on the screen. The gangster is always a gangster. The gun moll always his slave. And the orphan is always ready to subsume herself for others because she's perennially afraid of the moment when someone doesn't want her anymore.

"Will you tell me about Hollywood, Aria?" he asks.

Instead I point to a building and ask, even though I already know it's the Chiesa Maria di Santa Maria dei Miracoli, "Which church is that?"

He pauses for a second before he tells me, then we talk about church and religion, unfamiliar things to me, as we walk.

When we arrive back at the house, Marzia is singing along to the radio, to a song written in heartbreak, a language we each learn by accident.

Theo's song.

I thank Arturo for dinner, go up to my room, sit down at the typewriter. The story that pours out of me is about a woman who everyone believes has everything she wants, but who has nothing at all when the spotlight is off and the theaters are empty. Because, as the buildings outside will attest, you cannot enjoy immortality. You're either six feet under or ash. Your legend is for others to weep over, or to smile at. Not you.

But everyone needs something for themselves. And this story is for Calliope.

AS THE WEATHER WARMS, the tourists return. A guest takes up residence in the second room—an American woman about my age who's on her way to Rome to rendezvous with a man. Her limbs are thin, her torso curved, and she's tall enough to look Theo in the eye.

When will I stop comparing everyone to Theo?

"Is your friend American too?" I ask her over breakfast.

"No, he's a real Parisian." She crunches biscotti without dunking it first, leaving crumbs all over the table. "He told me to come to Rome when I'd finished my obligations in Paris—I was a fit model at the house of Christian Dior for a season. I don't know why he went to Rome," she finishes with a puzzled frown. "A vacation? He said he'd be there through the spring."

"What part of America are you from?" Arturo asks.

"San Francisco."

"San Francisco!" he cries and then he asks her about the Golden Gate Bridge and fog and diners and all the things he knows about from movies. She answers all his questions, doesn't deflect with a question of her own about a church whose name she already knows.

I have more work to do before I can declare that I'm truly living.

As I'm leaving, Arturo slips into the foyer. It's a week since our date. I've worked every night following and have only seen him at breakfast. He says with a wry smile, "Do you think anyone will be waiting for her in Rome?"

"Yes," I tell him, because I don't want him to be another man who thinks that a woman traipsing across Europe is following an already-broken dream. I want to believe there's a story where girls who do wild and improbable things really do find what they're looking for.

His face lights up. "There might be a movie in that! We follow the girl across Europe, bracing ourselves for her disappointment on the Spanish Steps. We track her as she walks up each stair, tensed for heartbreak at the top. And instead—"

"She finds hope," I finish.

"Not necessarily in the form of a Parisian though," Arturo says, studying my face.

"Not necessarily."

Then he asks, "Aria, don't you want to be found?"

"Only by me." I slip out the door.

ARTURO IS GONE WHEN I return. So is the girl. "They went to Rome together," Marzia says, incredulous. "My brother and that girl."

I can't help laughing. Yes, the world is incurably romantic.

CHAPTER 47

...

1965

In early summer, the water outside my window catches the golden clouds from the sky each sunrise and lets them float in the canal for a half hour like lazy tourists. After sunset, the water invites the moon for a dip and she accepts, a pond of milk in an indigo sea. During the daytime in between, the market at Campo San Leonardo is lined with thick stalks of white asparagus and lustrous artichokes that float in bowls of water. I buy some of each, even though I have no idea what to do with them. Marzia will show me.

On my way home, every wall I pass is dressed in purple wisteria. The air is redolent with brioche and sunshine and I start humming aloud, uncaring who hears.

Until I realize the song I'm humming is Theo's.

I stop on the Ponte Chiodo, which is a stupid thing to do. There are no handrails and it's too precarious for anyone to go around me. Curses sound from behind and in front and I apologize, move on, Theo's words still on my tongue.

He's playing in Rome this week. Marzia and Alessia are going to see him. They'll visit their brother too, who they tell me has taken leave of his senses and been seduced by the woman who was meant to go to Rome for a Parisian.

"A little passion is good for everyone," I tell them, smiling.

Lives move forward. Passions start and die. I came to Venice because of the water. Because of Theo and Calliope and Flitter and Bob.

But mostly, I now think, I came because of me.

As I cross through the Sotoportego del Magazen, I'm thinking that I need to leave soon. Marzia and Alessia are now charging twice as much for the other room, and could do the same with mine if I left. I'm holding them back the same way I once held myself back. There's more I need to find out about myself, like what else can I do besides survive in an unfamiliar city? What does the water look like farther south? And—am I only thinking about the water farther south because that's where Theo is?

I don't see the person sitting on the doorstep until I almost stand on them.

"*Buongiorno,* Aria," a voice says, more forlorn than I've ever heard it.

For the second time that day, I stop still. There, waiting for me, is Calliope Burns.

I leap on her, scattering asparagus and artichokes all around us. We hold on to one another for long enough for me to feel that she's lost her famous curves, is as thin as the child-Aria who first met this woman almost eight years ago.

"You're dislodging my eyelashes." She pushes me away and we both cry-laugh because who cares about eyelashes when the day brings you the gift of a person you'd worried you'd left in your past?

I gather up the vegetables as well as her suitcase and take her up to my room. She crosses immediately to the window, stares down at the Rio dei Santi Apostoli, then exhales as if she's never been so relieved in all her life.

"I can see why you haven't come back." She takes in the gondoliers, the light, the way it's all so different from the Chateau Marmont.

"How did you find me?" I sit on the bed, the shock catching me now.

"Theo and Flitter thought you'd taken a train, but I always knew you'd fly away. I went to the airport and discovered that the only plane leaving that night stopped in New York, where you'd never go, not after what happened there, then Paris, where there's no water besides a filthy river. That left Rome. You might recall that I know some movie people and you're living in the home of a man who owns a few cinemas. It's taken months of calls."

I remember Arturo asking me if I wanted to be found. Now I know why.

She turns around and I gasp aloud because Calliope Burns is no longer shining. She looks empty, a paper bag crumpled, flattened and thrown away. She's cut her hair so it's shorter than mine.

"Yes, I look dreadful," she agrees. "Can I sleep here tonight? Like old times?"

"Of course," I say. "I have to go to work soon, but I'll bring burgers back with me."

It's exactly like old times. Calliope is sound asleep when I return and I eat her burger as well as my own and wonder how long it will be before she breaks.

IT TAKES A FULL week before Calliope gets out of bed. I find her sitting in a chair by the window late one night when I come home from work with more burgers.

"You're feeling better?" I ask, but stop when I see what's in her lap. My book. Typed in black across the front are the words: *Calliope Burns: A Novel.*

She stands up, holding the stack of typed papers to her chest, scooches across the bed, and pats the space next to her. "Aria, come and sit by me."

I can't look at her. Is she angry?

But she slings an arm around me, brings my head down to rest on her shoulder and leans hers atop my own. The mirror shows two young women, one who's twenty-one, the other soon to be twenty-six. We each have cropped heads: one blonde, the other brown. The blonde's skin is so pale I can almost see the blood circulating beneath, except her blood doesn't seem to be circulating, not really. The brunette's skin is tanned from all the walking she's done; her cheeks glow. As for the blonde, her eyes are the only things that glow, not with health, but with a frightening, chemical glitter.

I watch the blonde's mouth open and she says something I refuse to hear. I keep staring at our reflections, trying to make Calliope turn back into a past version of herself as tears run like frightened children down my face.

Calliope wraps her other arm around me and hugs me even though that's what I ought to be doing for her.

I have a brain tumor.

I have a brain tumor.

That's what she said.

I pull away. "They can do something, right? You're Calliope Burns. They'll be able to do something for Calliope Burns."

She rubs her thumbs over my cheeks, mopping up my tears like my mother used to. "I've had some radiation. It shrank the tumor a little. But it's just buying me time, Aria. In reality, the woman who wanted to be immortal won't even live to be thirty."

I shake my head, refuse to believe this story. "No."

"Unfortunately, yes. The headaches I was having—that was the start. And the fatigue. And the strange things I was doing, like the fortune-teller. I know everyone thought I was taking something. But something was taking on me." She smiles a little. "I told my doctor that the only good thing about having a brain tumor is that it proves I have a brain."

"That's a terrible joke!"

"Shall I tell you about Theo instead? That story has a much better ending."

Do I want to hear about Theo?

"He found his voice again," I say. "I'm glad."

She waves a hand dismissively. "That's not what I mean. I mean—do you really think he'd *ever* cheat on you? Every man

I've been with has cheated on me, so I have a great deal of experience in assessing whether a man is a cheater or not. The woman you saw was his ex-lover, Marley."

My mouth twists. "I know. He was keeping the one woman from his past who he actually loved in a bungalow that he said was being renovated. Nothing suspicious there."

"But what you don't know is that she'd been in rehab to kick—"

"I do know that. He told me, and that he paid for her. Further proof of—"

Now she cuts me off. "Of your overactive imagination. I blame the Marmont. Nobody can grow up in a Gothic castle and not become inventive. But the truth is that, after rehab, she needed somewhere to stay where she'd be safe from dealers and friends and parties. Theo felt guilty about what happened when he broke up with her, so, when she called him one night—soon after she left rehab—with a baggie of heroin in her hand, he went to get her. He told her he'd give her a bungalow at the Marmont to stay in for six months while she found her sober feet."

She almost relapsed her first week out. That's the worst time of all.

Theo said that to me the night I discovered how much I enjoyed flirting with him. Which would have been the perfect moment to bring up the fact that he'd stashed her in a bungalow. But he didn't.

To Calliope I say, "Putting a recovering addict into the Marmont is a bit like sending a dieter into a candy shop."

"Not if you have a full-time nurse, paid for by Theo, and are living in a bungalow nobody can enter because it's meant to be a construction hazard. He visited her every day to check in with her. He took her out one time on his bike to tell her about you, to ask her if she thought he could really have a sober relationship. She told him yes. There's nothing between them. He was hugging her that night because she'd been clean six months and was leaving the Marmont the next day. The needles you saw were for her methadone therapy. It's coming up for a year now and she's still clean. So I'd say that maybe what Theo did for her saved her. But obviously he should have told you."

Maybe what Theo did for her saved her. But it didn't save us. We loved, but we didn't trust. We were both too lost to know how. When we were together we felt found—but we needed to feel found alone too.

"It doesn't matter," I tell her. "I still can't go back. What happened that night made me run. But . . ." I say it aloud for the first time. "But it's not why I'm staying away. I needed to learn how to live. And lately I've been wondering if I need to do something even more than that. Something like . . ." I struggle with how to describe it. "Like I need to unearth my own self from my soul. I need to build those parts of me that don't yet exist, but could."

Calliope's beam is almost to full power when she says, "I think you're right."

I don't say, *I think Theo needs to do the same.* But I believe it. He needs to discover the truth I've learned in Venice: that it doesn't matter if you're running from or running to—you'll never catch up to yourself unless you stop.

That's why we have to remain apart for now. He might find someone else while I figure myself out; in fact, he most likely will. Maybe then I'll wish I *had* run to him now instead of staying here. But I'm almost certain that if I do, it will end all over again in much the same way—and I don't think I can survive that heartbreak a second time.

"Aria?"

Calliope's voice returns me to the room. And I remember the other things that happened at the Chateau Marmont, things that aren't explained by Marley living in one of the bungalows—things I once thought, even if only briefly, that Calliope might have had a hand in. "What about the screams? The fire? What about Pilot being fed vodka?"

Calliope frowns. "I don't know. Maybe it was Marley, having some kind of withdrawal night terrors?"

"Why would she set fire to Theo's bed?"

"I have no idea." Calliope shrugs. "We may have discovered that I have a brain, but that doesn't mean it's any good at solving puzzles."

I don't laugh. "I used to feel like the Marmont was alive. Like the building itself was the one screaming and laughing and lighting fires."

"I used to think it was the ghost," Calliope says with a grim smile. "I believed in her, you know. Thought she was the one who spiked my drink at my birthday party so I was sick for three days afterward."

I remember the retching. That I didn't go into the bathroom.

She shakes her head, divining my thoughts. "I would have yelled at you to leave. I'm glad you didn't come in."

We're quiet a moment, then I ask, "How's Miss Devine Rey?"

Calliope finally laughs. "She's back from rehab in fine form, ruling over everyone from her new court by the pool. She lies on a cabana swathed in jeweled caftans and dispenses advice to all the starlets."

Calliope mimics my aunt's sonorous tones. " 'Have meetings with anyone from a studio at Schwab's, never in an office with a closed door.' Or, 'Everyone has a good side. Know yours. If you don't know it, ask me.' And, 'Cooking is for ordinary people. Extraordinary people call Schwab's.' "

I laugh hysterically. "Did I create a monster?"

"Bob thinks so," Calliope says, eyes shining with amusement. "He's lost his poolside throne. She's taken your old room because it's within her means, had a fire sale of all her pictures and memorabilia, and then she gave Theo an envelope full of money for the past year's rent, telling him to pay you back for everything you spent on her behalf. And she's declaiming her lines from *Jane Eyre*—she got the part of the housekeeper, thanks to you."

"Shouldn't they be close to wrapping that up by now?"

It's the only time Calliope looks sad. "They've barely started filming. Matty broke his leg, then the house they were going to use was crushed by a falling tree. The movie's cursed. The only reason I want it to go ahead is for Miss Devine's sake."

"And Flitter?" I make myself ask.

"Has moved to the Beverly Wilshire. With Brian." Calliope giggles. "God help her. He'll spend all the money she has, then work his way through all the money she doesn't have before the year is out." She sighs. "I miss her. I'm lost without my sisters."

That's when I feel it. An extraordinary sweetness, like honey scooped from a hive, followed by an emptiness inside me where something used to live. Nostalgia. Which means—I did have a home.

"I miss . . ." I don't know how to say it.

"'Remembrance of things past is not necessarily the remembrance of things as they were,'" Calliope quotes.

I stare at her. "That's Proust."

"One of my characters said it in a movie. I didn't understand it then, but I do now—when I think of the past, in the bed we all shared is the Flitter who made a deal with Bob."

"Also in that bed is a girl called Calliope who loved me when she didn't have to."

That's when Calliope starts to cry. Only for a minute or two. Then she sits up straight, one hand on my breastbone, holding me at arm's length so she can say something right to my face. "Publish this." She holds up my manuscript.

"It didn't feel right, sending it out without telling you." My voice is low, ashamed. I wrote her into a story and I can't imagine how it would feel to have your life taken from you and retold into what? Truth? Or more lies?

She shakes her head. "This is your story. Not mine. See?" She points to the cover. "It says: *A Novel.* Your version of this person is yours. And it's very good. Better than any book I've read."

I roll my eyes. "When did you last read a book?"

"All right. Better than any story I've come across. And I've come across quite a few."

And I feel that hideous but exquisite pain in my chest, the one you feel when you're with someone you love and something they say makes you love yourself, just a little. It *is* a good book.

If I hadn't come to Venice, if I hadn't left Theo behind, I wouldn't have written it.

I'm crying again and she is too, and this time she pulls off her false lashes and says, "They probably just make me look sicker."

She unfurls from the bed, walks to the window, and inhales. If only all that life out there could find its way inside her, then, one day, there'd be a fifty, a sixty, a seventy-year-old woman who'd still equal lightning plus auroras to the power of heaven.

"You're the only person I've told," she says. "The only one I'm going to tell. I have to work out how to . . . I don't know, disappear. If the studio finds out . . ." She grimaces. "I'm a valuable asset to them. They might force me to have more treatment, or do something crazy like appoint a guardian, say that nobody should trust decisions made by a twenty-five-year-old woman with a hell of a lot of cash in the bank and who probably isn't of sound mind. I'm scared they'll try and take away what time I have left. So . . ."

I want to tell her that the studio wouldn't do that, but from what I've seen, the studios will do almost anything to control the women who make money for them. I also want to ask her how long she has, but I'm afraid. What if she says just a few weeks?

She answers my unspoken question. "About a year. Maybe eighteen months if I have more radiotherapy."

I don't know if she's lying. If she's giving me the Hollywood version of her ending. In my book, Calliope Burns goes back to the Chateau Marmont and burns it to the ground. The final scene is her, phoenix-like in the turret, while everything except her is consumed by the pyre she lit.

With her back to me, she whispers, "Do you know what makes me cry at night? I never fell in love. Like you once said to me, I'll die without ever knowing what it's like to be loved the way Theo loved you, or to love another person the way you loved Theo. Imagine dying without that . . ."

Her voice cracks and I jump up and tuck her head against my chest and my voice is fierce when I tell her, "You *did* fall in love. Remember in *A Rebel Without a Girl*, the way Jimmy McLean kisses you at the end? That was love. And what about you and Peter Oldham? Three movies that made the whole world feel like we were the ones who'd never been in love because what you two had . . ." I sigh, remembering the tug of longing when I watched Calliope on the screen each of those times.

"That *was* special, wasn't it?" she concedes.

"Magical." I tighten my arms around her. "Once in a lifetime. But you got to have it more than once."

Before I can offer her any more lies that are also truths, she runs her fingertips over the title of my book. "This is a novel. You can't call it *Calliope Burns* because I'm real." The smile she gives me is the Calliope Burns special, the one people line up to see the same way they crowd the piazza outside the Palazzo Ducale to watch the golden orb of an April moon scatter its light over the water.

"My name is Helen," she says. "Helen Burns."

I walk over to the typewriter, insert a sheet of paper and type: *Helen Burns: A Novel.* Then I tear up the original title page and replace it with the true one.

"Do you know what I just learned, Aria?" Calliope's voice is wistful. "That to be truly seen by one person is better than being seen on a screen by millions. I wanted to be loved by the world. But the world can't love. Only people can."

My tears come in a deluge. Because my friend is dying and life sends us our lessons too late sometimes. What if Calliope had been able to burn, truly, for one person—and he'd burned for her too?

What a star that would have made.

"I'm going to New York next week," she tells me. "I'm going

to deliver your manuscript to the best publishing house in the country. How long will you be here for? I'll need to tell them where to send your check."

I laugh. "In the event that there's a check to send, I'll be in Capri. I like being surrounded by water. So that seems like a good place to go. I'll leave the same day you do."

"Are you prepared?" she asks me then. "For what this might unleash?"

Is it the tumor making her say things that are a little crazy? All my book will unleash are rejection letters from publishers. I'm prepared for those.

Outside, the sun plummets, setting fire to the hem of the sky. The light transforms Calliope's face so her eyes are suddenly ferocious, her jaw a sharp line of bone. "When this is published, you'll have given me my revenge. That's a gift I never thought I'd have."

Back in the library, I'd hated myself for not calling out. In this book I am, at last, calling out—no, I'm screaming, strident and bloody, on behalf of Nathalie and every other woman who's bled, wept, and retched on the mattress in my turret. But maybe it's more than that. Maybe it *is* revenge.

For me. For Calliope. For my aunt.

"I'm scared that everyone will think it's made up," I tell her. "That he'll get away with it until the end of time. But . . ." I pause, make myself whisper the improbable. "Even if somehow a miracle happens and people believe it, will it be enough?"

She stares at the bundle of paper in her arms. There's something terrifying in her eyes when she says, "I don't know." A beat. "I spoke to your aunt."

I don't need to ask about what. It's there in her eyes. Calliope knows too.

"Do you think it will be enough for her?" Calliope asks, almost like she's daring me.

I shake my head. What vengeance could ever be enough for her?

The sun is gone now. The sick and failing Calliope returns and says to me, "Promise me that every time you move, you'll tell me where you're going so I can always reach you via the poste restante."

"So long as you promise to tell me when . . ."

"When I'm about to die?" Calliope smiles. "I'll never die. This"—she taps the manuscript—"will make me immortal. And thanks to you, it'll be me who's immortal, not just my face."

WHEN CALLIOPE FALLS ASLEEP, I stand at my window, unable to not think of Theo, who'll have just finished his show in Rome. He's maybe back in his hotel room or out at a party with beautiful Italian women. I close my eyes against that idea and from the mist outside, which is the color of ghosts and dreams, I hear a whisper, "Aria?"

Theo's voice, as if he's standing at a window too and, just like at the Chateau Marmont, magic makes sounds travel beyond their limits. And for the first time I let myself remember.

The stairwell, the way we collided and my whole world exploded. The way he always made coffee for me, that I only had to tell him once how I liked it and then he made it exactly right every time. He wanted to know how I liked everything: coffee, steak, pillows, sex. I remember the sound of the sheets crackling like the fires he lit on my skin.

I remember the leathery nicotine freshness of him, a scent I'd pay a million dollars for, just so I could spray it on my sheets and roll myself in them—a little cave of him.

CHAPTER 48

...

1965

CAPRI IS ENDLESS WATER. IT'S BIKINIS AND SUNSHINE; IT'S a blue I never saw in any of the artworks that hung in the Gallerie dell'Accadamia in Venice. It's another restaurant job at night, serving cocktails to tourists who are so stunned by all the beauty that they tip too much and I can save a little bit of money for my future, whatever that turns out to be.

It feels even more like fantasy when I receive a telegram from Calliope.

You're officially Aria Jones, author, it says. *See, your mom knew you needed a knockout name.*

It takes an hour of letting that sink in before I can read the rest of the message. She says that *Helen Burns* will be published by one of the biggest publishing houses in New York. A contract will be waiting for me by week's end at the post office in Sorrento—along with a check. Apparently the publishing house is so eager to sign me that they've already sent the check as an incentive. I can cash it pending my signature.

Maybe it'll be enough that I won't have to work for a month or two and I can travel around before I settle somewhere else and find another waitressing job.

That's as much as I let myself think. Where I come from, conditions are always attached to offers. I don't want to let myself get excited, only to discover that I'll need to sell myself as well as my book.

I've only just started to become myself—I can't sell those tiny, just-discovered pieces of Aria to anyone.

A few days later I trade my bikini for the tiniest miniskirt in the world and a crop top—tanned stomachs are the only accessory, besides turbans and sunglasses, that people in Capri wear. Needless to say, I've become a devoted Caprian over the past month.

I catch the boat to the mainland, take my time winding my way from the port to the city center. I stop at the Basilica di Sant'Antonino, sit on a pew, and soak in both the quiet and the quiver in the air, like in Hollywood, where people stared reverently at billboards and a sidewalk paved with stars. We all need idols, it seems. We all want something more than what we have in our skins.

Why aren't we enough for ourselves?

Am I enough for myself yet?

It's early afternoon when I arrive at the post office. I collect the envelope and take it over to an uncrowded corner near a trash can so that, if I slit it open and find that the sacrifice required to be an author is Aria Jones, I can throw it all away.

Out slides a check for twenty-five thousand dollars.

Holy cow!

I stuff the check into my string bag so fast that anyone watching would think it was a gun, then I hurry back to the port and onto the boat. I stand near the front, see nothing of the blue water, feel nothing of the wind, can only imagine that my time serving food to strangers in exotic locales has caused me to lose my ability to read.

After I disembark, I run back to my room, ignoring the shouted, "*Buongiorno,* Aria," from one of the waiters I work with, lock the door behind me, snap on the lights, pull out the check, and read it again.

It still says twenty-five thousand dollars.

Holy, holy, holy cow!

I starfish on the bed and scream because it's impossible to be quiet when you've got a check for that much money in your hands.

Five minutes later, my bed's a ruin and three people have knocked on the door to make sure I'm not being murdered. I make myself sit up, make myself believe that, despite there being two more envelopes enclosed with the first, none of them will ruin my Hollywood ending.

The handwriting on one is Calliope's. *Celebrate* is all it says.

Dare I?

I pick up the other envelope, run my finger over the seal. The most dream-crushing thing could be inside. I could set it down, put on my bikini, go to the beach, swim until sunset, and not think about how much you have to give to get twenty-five thousand dollars.

But haven't I already survived the most heart-bruising thing I can imagine?

I open the envelope.

It's from my publisher.

It says that I'll receive an editorial letter and the marked-up manuscript by special delivery to the post office in Sorrento in about a fortnight. They want to publish as soon as possible, and ask that I please attend to the edits promptly.

That's it. No other conditions.

"Well," I say to the empty room. "I don't have much to do besides working on my tan and that"—I check my reflection in the mirror—"is perfect. So, yes, I can be very prompt."

Should I move to Sorrento to do the work? Should I check into the Gatto Bianco here on Capri like all the famous people, and enjoy a little luxury?

No. I spent seven years in a hotel and my time in hotels is done.

I drop the check into the drawer of the desk in the tiny apartment I've been renting, which has whitewashed floors, a wooden chair and table, a blue jug stuffed with hydrangeas from the market, a cascade of bright pink bougainvillea flowers tumbling over the outside walls, and a view of the Punto Carena lighthouse and all the sea stretching west. Then I go to work at the restaurant like usual.

Two weeks later, I quit my waitressing job, catch the ferry to Sorrento, and deposit the check into a new bank account that Calliope's opened for me using one hundred telegrams and her name to get it done because single women aren't allowed to have their own bank account—unless your best friend is a Hollywood movie star. I withdraw enough to cover rent and food for three months. I have no real idea how long it takes to edit a manuscript, but I can come back and get more if I need longer.

Then I go to the post office and collect my manuscript. It's bound tightly with string and is scribbled all over with comments like: *I'm not quite sure what her motivations are here? Please elucidate.* Or, *Dig deeper. We need to feel this happening, not just be told that it happened. Always the scenes that you're most scared of writing are the scenes you most need to write.*

It's time to be brave.

I return to my room, roll paper into my little green Hermes 3000 and start from the beginning, not letting it pour out in a rush of words from my journals mingled with words from my nightmares and dreams like I did in Venice. I make myself type no more than five to ten pages every day. I buy a record player so that every time I want to squirm away from what I'm writing by going to the beach, diving into the water, and washing memory away, I have something to ground me. A Scarlatti sonata. A Theo Winchester anthem.

My god, that man can write music.

I remember that Adele liked to have music playing when she worked in my turret and the memory makes me smile. Adele. I haven't let myself think about her because yes, that bruises my heart too.

Is she back at school? Has she made friends? Has she learned to love her father?

And what about Flitter? Will I see her again? Or my aunt? I'd like to see her holding court by the pool.

I let the questions with no answers come at me, one after the other, don't close my eyes or push them away. I feel them. Then I unleash all of my bruises and all of my smiles into the story I'm writing.

No, Calliope, I write to her. *I wasn't prepared for what it would unleash in me. But I'm letting it out anyway.*

That wasn't what I meant, she writes back. *I meant—are you prepared for what it might unleash upon the world?*

I shake my head. That's definitely the tumor talking.

For three months, I type and swim and type some more, because what Calliope said to me is the last thing I think about each night: *This will make me immortal.*

I need to make that wish come true for her before she dies. But also—I let myself think it at last—I want what I talked about with Calliope.

I want a reckoning. One that locks Bob up in a turret room, bleeding what's left of his soul onto a dirty mattress while the starlets dance, unashamed and unfettered, around the pool below.

THE BOOK IS DONE. Three hundred pages of my soul and Calliope's and my aunt's and one hundred more women, so many forgotten, who were seen to have nothing more than two stars for eyes, a hundred-dollar bill for a body, and enough entrances for a man to walk right through. But also so many women who kept going. Women I'm so proud to have known.

I hug the stack of pages to my chest and remember leaving a store in Venice with the very first dress I'd ever bought for myself tucked into a bag, thinking: *What talent do I have that would make me smile?* It makes me smile to take the ferry to Sorrento with my book tucked into my basket, makes me smile to wrap the typed pages in brown paper, makes me smile to hand the parcel over to the desk clerk, a parcel addressed to the biggest publishing house in New York City. It makes me smile, yes, but it also makes me wonder: *What now? What can I do next that will make me smile like this?*

There's more that I want to do. One book isn't enough to keep future Nathalies and Calliopes safe. They'll still arrive in Hollywood, still be prey to the Bobs, even if by some miracle, enough people read my book to understand what the Bobs are capable of. Writing the book has made me see that one part of the vow I made so many years ago was a vow worth making: to try to keep the starlets safe. What I no longer believe is that I have to be invisible to do it.

I want the book to be the mattress in the turret now that I'm no longer there. No—I hope the book is *better* than the mattress in the turret. That it saves more, faster.

But can an inanimate object save anyone?

The question sits in my head as I check the poste restante for mail. There's a letter waiting for me and I open it, expecting it to be from Calliope. But it reads: *Aria. You saved my life. Thank you. Miss Devine Rey.*

Oh! As I reread my aunt's words, the smile on my face is so enormous that a stranger says to me with a knowing smile, "Ah, a love letter."

Yes, I suppose it is. My aunt will most likely never say that she loves me. And yet, her letter tells me that she does.

I pay for some paper and write a reply, telling Miss Devine about my book. At the bottom of the letter, I say, *This morning I was wondering if reading my book might save some future starlet. But after reading your letter, I'm wondering—what if there was something that could be done before the saving had to happen? Something I could do that stopped a starlet from ever starting to drown?*

Then I add: *Please write back.* Of everyone alive, it's Miss Devine who's seen enough of Hollywood to help me find the answers to my questions.

When I return to Capri, I walk down to the beach for the first time in days. The late afternoon sun is warm and strong and I tip my head back so the rays fall on my face, melting away the tight muscles in my neck and shoulders from sitting too long at the typewriter. And only now does it hit me, right there on the sand when I realize I have nothing to rush back to my room to do. I've written a book and it's going to be published and I still have the best part of twenty-five thousand dollars sitting in a bank account.

I should dance on the sand. I should throw myself into the water.

The sand is crowded with vacationers. As is the sea. So many people and me, alone.

I sit down, try to recover my smile, as well as the pride that I have in myself at last. Over there is a group of people I know, Americans and Italians, all working the restaurants and hotels just as I was doing before I quit like every other fly-by-night American who comes here to get a tan and live cheaply and swim all day. With them is a man I went out with a few times. I could join them, swim with them, sit beside the man at dinner and we might kiss again. I could tell them about my book.

But I don't want that. I want my people.

Who are my people? The ones who'd dance with me on the sand, then leap into the water, holding my hand?

What if—*please God, no*—what if I've found myself, only to lose everyone that I love?

The sea crashes and retreats, crashes and retreats. It offers no advice.

It's up to me to figure out what to do.

It always has been.

I return to my room. Pack my suitcase. Catch the ferry out of Italy.

CHAPTER 49

...

1965

HYDRA, GREECE. WATER IN A DIFFERENT SHADE OF BLUE. MORE bikinis and sunshine. Then Saint-Tropez. The same. Another place where I learn enough words of a new language that I can ask people what they want to eat and can order my own coffee too.

She'll know enough to order a coffee and write not-half-bad poetry in a cafe she can find her own way to.

Words I said to Theo a year ago about Adele. Words that apply to me now. I finally know how to live. But that isn't enough for the Aria Jones I've become.

I spend my time alternating between lying on a beach, serving platters of *fruits de mer,* and puzzling over the question—what can I do to make sure that starlets no longer need to be saved? My aunt has written back more than once and she says that what's needed is someone who can get to the girls before they get to Bob. Which is true, but I can't block all roads leading to Hollywood and stand at each barricade delivering tutorials.

My aunt keeps saying, *You'll think of something. You always do.* She believes in me. I never knew what a lovely gift that was—to be given someone's faith. But my own faith in myself keeps getting snagged on the same thought: only people with power can stop things from happening.

I might no longer be invisible, but I still have no power.

Oh yes, Flitter really had been the only one of us to make the right wish.

As the year gives way to December, the tourists vanish from the South of France and so do opportunities for waitresses. It's time to move on. I could just stay here now that I have money. But what if I need that money for whatever answers I come up with? And while Saint-Tropez is lovely, it isn't my place. I still haven't found that. Will I ever?

I fold up my apron and stare out at the abandoned sea, waiting for Joaquin, the Spanish bartender, to finish. As soon as he bounds down the steps and sees my face, he knows. He shrugs. "Our time is up?"

We haven't exactly been dating; dating is something you leave your apartment to do. Most of our interactions have taken place in my bed or his. I had to find out if I was just the kind of person who mistook sex for love. But while Joaquin is kind and considerate and I enjoy his company, he doesn't make me burn the way Theo did.

"Yes." I kiss his cheek. "*Bon chance, Joaquin.*"

He smiles and wishes me good luck too, untroubled by my leaving because I didn't make him burn either.

I take the train to Paris, where there are restaurants on every corner. Art too—it's like Venice in that way; every building is ancient and gargoyled and roofed with gold. Here it's the Eiffel Tower rather than the Grand Canal that makes me stop and stare. Just look at it, black lace overlaid on a wintry sky. And suddenly snow starts falling in huge sparkling flakes, like the stars have decided to come down and say hello.

I haven't seen snow since I lived in New York with my parents.

What a long, long way I've come.

I close my eyes and make a wish upon a snowflake that my parents can see me now from heaven, and that they're smiling.

Soon, the snow turns from delightful flurry to freezing rain. I escape into the English-language bookstore where I meander up and down the aisles, see a beautiful early edition of *We Have Always Lived in the Castle,* wish I could send it to Adele. But I don't know how Theo would feel about that, don't know if he'd prefer me to leave Adele alone. Don't know if he hates me, has gotten married again, or if he even thinks about me at all.

I leave the "Special Editions" section, progress to "New Fiction," run my eyes over the covers and then I make a noise so loud that everyone turns to see. I reach out my hand. Pick up *Helen Burns: A Novel.*

I knew it was being published in the winter. But I didn't realize it would be available across the Atlantic. My own copies from my publisher have been lost twice by the French postal service, packages proving to be far more problematic to deliver via the poste restante service than letters.

Look at how beautiful it is! The cover is bright red with a stylized strip of film running diagonally across it, almost like gift wrap, until you look closer and see that trapped in the film is a woman. My name, Aria Jones, is just below the title.

Me, Aria Jones, the orphan who was meant to have a small and unremarkable life, has written a book that's being sold in a Paris bookshop.

This is another moment I'd never have lived if I'd married Theo.

It's both the saddest thing I've ever thought and also the most necessary.

Two girls walk past and one of them reaches out to take one of my books from the stack. "Jolie told me this was good," she says to her friend. She presents it to the cashier. Hands over her money. Leaves with my book in a paper bag.

My book!

Pride, joy, shock, I don't know what—everything magnificent and incredible—is swirling inside me. Once again I want to dance, not on the sand this time, but around the entire store. But once again I'm alone.

And Fate isn't done with me today.

A song starts to play on the radio. When the singer's voice kicks in, I know it's Theo.

It's a song about love. A love that came at the wrong time for two people. A love that had to happen, a love that had to hurt. A love they had to leave behind because it would have hurt them all the more if they'd stayed together, stuck in the life they'd given into, instead of walking outside and finding the life that let each of them become who they really were.

A love that still makes the singer wake at night, crying out his lover's name.

And I know—it's the song Theo once said he'd write for me.

THE LONELINESS THAT SETTLES inside me afterward is so acute that I can't do anything except return to the Île Saint-Louis, an island in the middle of the Seine where I've rented an apartment, buy an ice cream from Berthillon, eat it with my eyes closed, pretend Theo is watching me, then fall asleep, exhausted.

The next day, I haul myself up. Despite the song, why would Theo Winchester—Win, rock star, heartthrob, the one true orgasm—ever wait around for me? And if I really think that song is about me, then why aren't I jumping on a plane back to LA?

Because I can't go back until I know how I'm going to save those girls from drowning. If I go back now—and by some miracle Theo still wants me—then I'd lose myself in him all over again. I can't lose Aria until she's a whole, complete, and entire person.

I pull on my white cropped trousers and a black short-sleeved shirt that I tie at the front just beneath my breasts—my Italian island habits are hard to shake. I make the concession of pulling on a coat in deference to the weather. Then I walk over to the Île de la Cité, stroll across the Pont Neuf, see in the facade of the Louvre a little of the inspiration for the Chateau Marmont, pretend I'm just being a *flâneuse,* but my dreams are tugging me toward the post office. I can't shake the feeling that there's a message waiting for me.

But what if I go in and there's nothing and then I have to face the fact that my loneliness has made me believe that songs are portents, when all they really mean is that I miss Theo. A year of roaming has taught me there's no cure for that.

It's five minutes before closing time when I finally slip inside, braced for disappointment. But there are several letters waiting for me, including a much-redirected package.

Only when I'm back in my apartment standing in front of the flower-boxed windows that overlook the domes of the Left Bank do I let myself examine the envelopes. The package is from my publisher. There's a letter from them too. The next has been addressed in Calliope's wildly scrawling script.

And the third.

The third has been written by a hand that has touched me, everywhere.

I shove it inside the drawer, lock it in, like I'm scared it will vaporize in the air.

Then I sit down at my desk and open the package. Finally I have my very own copy of my book! I hug it to my chest like it's the most precious thing I've ever owned. Can't stop smiling. Can't stop turning the pages and looking at all those words that I wrote in a house beside a Venetian canal.

Eventually, I open the envelope from my publisher.

Congratulations, Aria, the letter says. *You're a bestseller.*

Enclosed is another check, pages from magazines, and a newspaper clipping.

I open the check first. Another twenty-five thousand. What can I possibly do with fifty thousand dollars, when I once would have been happy with so much less?

I shove the check into a drawer too.

Then I unfold the magazine pages. And with those in my hand and my book in my lap, I start to sob. I still don't own a handkerchief. Of course I forgot to buy Kleenex. I use my sleeve to wipe my face. The whole, complete, and entire Aria is made up of pieces of the old, broken one too.

The first is a clipping from *Cosmopolitan*, headlined, "Aria

Jones: The Star Who Never Wanted to Shine." Underneath, there's a photo of Judith Crown, Nathalie Green, Augusta Hepworth, and Miss Devine. They're sitting by the pool at the Marmont, holding my book.

"She used to babysit my children," reads a quote from Judith. "They loved her. Perhaps more than me."

"Of course we know Aria," says Nathalie, whose latest movie from Bob's studio has been a huge hit. "Every woman in Hollywood knows Aria."

I remember Calliope telling me that every woman who walked into the Chateau Marmont left with a bit of Aria inside them. I hadn't believed her. Now, maybe, I do.

An entire page is taken up with a photograph of Calliope from a couple of years ago. She looks like a super-giant star, the biggest and brightest in any universe, the kind that burns so brightly it dies young, its life blown apart in one earth-shaking supernova.

I read the words beneath the picture:

> The book is widely believed to be about movie star Calliope Burns, whose ascent to fame is all the more remarkable if this origin story is true. When contacted for comment, Miss Burns issued a statement: "Aria Jones has written a wonderful novel about a town that's like Manderley—so beautiful it could make you cry. Because behind all that careless beauty are terrible people who ought to be damned, but who are crowned king instead. Her book demonstrates that the true hero in life isn't the one we see, but the one who's too busy saving lives to be seen." When questioned further about the identity of a male executive in the book named Ben, Miss Burns said, "You could substitute any of their names and the story would still be true."
>
> Despite being panned by the critics, the book has

> found its way into the hands of plenty of readers, hitting *The New York Times* bestseller list this week.

"What?"

There's nobody to answer my question. I rummage through the pages in the envelope, find the newspaper, and unfold it. And there it is: *The New York Times* bestseller list. *Helen Burns* by Aria Jones is listed in eighth place.

Holy, holy, holy shit.

I drop onto the bed, so shocked I can't starfish or scream.

Somehow, out of a book about Calliope, my name has become not just known, but featured on a list of bestselling books.

I glance over my shoulder. See the ghosts of three girls who used to sit in a bed together and share their souls and their joys. I wish there was someone here beside me who'd scream and starfish too, so then I'd know it was real. When you smile and there's no one to return it, it doesn't feel quite so much like pleasure.

Next envelope, Aria. The one from Calliope. That will make me smile, I bet.

Inside the envelope are more clippings. *Look at what you unleashed,* she's written.

It's an assortment of newspaper reviews. The first says that my book is the depraved imaginings of a woman not pretty enough to be a Hollywood star. The next: A sordid affair about silly young starlets who ought to have known better. And the next: A tale about women who romped around in their bikinis for studio execs and then complained when those execs wanted to take their bikinis off.

They *hate* my book. I've unleashed only vitriol.

I almost don't read the final piece of folded paper—I'm not sure my ego will survive. I'm ready to become a pile of dust in a city with so much history it doesn't need mine.

But I make myself peep. It's a letter from my aunt.

I set it free, Aria, she writes. Attached is a page from *Harper's Bazaar.*

Set what free?

I start to read.

> Helen Burns wipes away the makeup, tears away the costumes, pulls down the sets that keep secrets hidden behind low-cut dresses and a Wild West panorama. But the secret's out; the West is a barbarous place that feeds on the bodies of women who are so young they don't even know what rape is. We interviewed one of Hollywood's most famous stars of yesteryear, who shared her own story of how she was sold by a man she thought she loved.

And there's my aunt's story about the pool house. And the woman who jumped.

"Holy shit." I say it aloud this time.

This is the fire.

I'm finally burning everything down.

By the time I realize there's one more piece of paper, night has fallen. I cross over to the window, needing the beauty of Paris to brace me because, *What now?*

Outside, the Eiffel Tower is the largest constellation of all. Celestial, but forged from steel. And staring at that beautiful iron lady, I remember sitting on a beach in Capri, wanting my people. Since I was thirteen-and-three-quarters, I've been desperate to find a place where Aria Jones belongs. But places can't love you. Only people can. And I have so many people. More than I ever realized. All of them are forged from steel too.

I belong in the world with all of them.

I unfurl the final page: another note from my publisher. *Mr. Bob Ashenhurst would like to purchase the film rights for your book.*

Oh, I'll bet he does.

He wants those rights so he can bury my book beneath one hundred feet of lies.

And finally, after so much ocean and travel and months spent out in the world, I know—it's no longer time for me to run.

This is a moment. Moments pass, like fires burn out. But add a few letters to that word *moment* and you have a movement.

Suddenly, unbelievably, I have power. My name is on a bestseller list. My book is in the hands of many. My aunt has told her story. And there's something Bob wants from me.

And now I know exactly what I can do to make sure that, from now on, there will never be another Calliope who'll walk into a room to find a studio boss with an unzipped fly. There will only be dreams untarnished.

You get the future you give in to, or the one you fight for.

It's time for me to be the star of my own goddamn life.

CHAPTER 50

...

1965–1966

I CAN NOW AFFORD TO MAKE STRINGS OF LONG DISTANCE CALLS, SO I telephone the Marmont and ask to be put through to my aunt.

"It's Aria," I tell her.

"At last," she cries.

She sounds so happy. So alive. So exactly like her name—a brilliant ray of light. "You . . . you . . ." I don't know what exactly to say besides something so sentimental she'll probably hang up on me.

In the background there's the splash and shriek of people poolside, no matter that it's winter. And above that, what could be the sniff of someone trying not to cry.

Then her voice comes back on the line saying, "Enough of that. Tell me how I can help."

So I do. When I've finished, I hear her say in a voice designed to carry, "Girls, you wouldn't believe what Aria's up to now. You'll love it."

Through the phone line, just like I could always sense the Marmont's vibrations, I can feel the eager attention of the women, the furious hackles of the men.

But I remember Flitter. I will wield my power with honor, not as a weapon.

I end the call by asking my aunt for the number of her lawyer. Then I say to her, words a rush of disbelief, still tinged with the fear of thirteen-year-old Aria, "You beat him. You won against Bob."

But Miss Devine says, "Not yet, Aria. Not yet."

She hangs up before I can ask her what she means.

I want to convince myself it's nothing. But when I asked Calliope, *Will it be enough?* she said, *I don't know.*

That was before the book came out, before we knew that people would not only read it, but believe it. Well—my eyes fall on the critiques written by every male book reviewer in America—I guess not everyone believes it.

Which means my aunt and Calliope are right. It isn't enough.

I dial Mr. Henry Larousse, my aunt's lawyer. He remembers me from my younger years when Miss Devine Rey still had visitors.

"You've set Hollywood ablaze," he says.

"I want to control that blaze," I tell him. "Just a little."

"Withdraw the book, you mean? That might prove rather difficult."

I take a deep breath. "No. I want you to draw up the papers for a new business. Aria Jones, Talent Management Agency. I'm going to give all of those young girls—and the older ones too—an agent who'll look after them, rather than one who'll let a man take whatever he wants from them. And—" I inhale another, deeper breath and remind myself that Calliope once told me I had gifts. Even so, what I'm about to do is preposterous. Isn't it?

No. Bob Ashenhurst is preposterous.

"I want you to draw up papers to establish a production company: Aria International Pictures. The first movie I'm making is *Helen Burns.*"

Because I want everyone to know that a woman, just a woman, can be a story. And she can be an entire remembered person too.

Mr. Larousse chortles. "Well done, Miss Jones. Well done."

OVER THE NEXT FORTNIGHT, I send telegrams to every star and starlet who's ever stayed at the Marmont. I tell them about my new agency and ask them to leave their details with Mr. Larousse if they're interested in having me represent them. I telegram Calliope and ask her to spread the word; Miss Devine is already having meetings for me at the Marmont poolside.

It'll soon be out in the open, what I'm doing. Maybe that's why I wake up each night with the memory of the words *I will never forgive you* echoing in my head. But perhaps I'm finally a whole, complete, and entire person because, despite the dreams, I don't call Mr. Larousse and ask him to rescind all of my actions.

Once everything is in motion, I stop at a brasserie and order the prix fixe menu for dinner, still not used to the idea that I could order caviar if I wanted to. My table is out on the sidewalk with a view over the Seine, which turns all the lights into water stars.

After I have a glass of wine and a plate of steak frites in front of me, I put my hand into my purse and pull out the letter that I haven't read yet.

I won't be complete until I've faced the most painful piece of my past.

Dear Aria, the letter from Theo begins.

See? It'll be fine. A *Dear Aria* letter is an ordinary, unremarkable letter. Nobody would ever cry over a *Dear Aria* letter.

A mouthful of wine. A handful of *frites.*

Onto the next line.

I'm sorry. I thought that if I told you I'd let Marley stay in the bungalow, you wouldn't understand. I mean, what woman in the world could possibly understand that the man she's about to marry has his ex-lover hidden in a bungalow a few yards away? But I should have given you the chance to understand. Instead, I lied. And when you found out that I was just another man who told lies to make his own life easier and didn't care who got hurt, you decided you didn't want to see me again. I get it.

But I wanted to tell you that I read your book. Adele read it too. She said to tell you it was outta sight. I know it doesn't *mean anything to you, not anymore, but I'm so proud of you. And I also know that I shouldn't have asked you to marry me. I should have seen that I'd had the chance to live—a fucked-up life maybe, but a life nonetheless. You hadn't had that chance. Asking you to marry me was like saying I wanted you to mother Adele while I went off and partied around the world. It was trapping you into a different cage than the Marmont. And I needed to figure out for myself that I don't need to keep my freezer stashed with vodka just to prove that I can stay sober. Anyway, my life isn't so fucked-up now. Adele's at school. She said to tell you that she misses you. And I'm finally playing songs that I like.*

I love you. Always.
Theo

I cry. Of course I cry.

I cry until I know that I won't die from this grief.

I'll do something about it instead.

THANKS TO MR. LAROUSSE, I'm now the proprietor of two businesses. More than thirty women have made appointments to speak to me when I'm back.

Which means—it's time to return to Hollywood.

I pack my suitcase—two suitcases now that I've bought so many clothes. In Italy, it was the Missoni siblings' rainbow-striped knits. In Paris, it's been Pierre Cardin and Courrèges and their orange and green mini dresses, colors I wouldn't be able to wear if I was blond, colors that work because I have brown hair and green eyes.

Once the suitcases are packed, I write one final telegram. To Flitter. I tell her to come to my office the first week I'm back.

When I'm done, I can't put the pen down. Instead, I pick up a blank piece of paper.

Before I met Theo, I'd lived in two cities and kissed three men. I've now lived in three countries and twice as many cities, have kissed perhaps eight men. And I still love Theo.

But I know now that I don't *need* him. I really am a whole, complete, and entire person with her own future ahead of her, even without him.

But I want him.

God, I want him.

Dear Theo, I write.

CHAPTER 51

...

1966

AS I WALK THROUGH THE AIRPORT THE NEXT MORNING, I STOP when I see a woman walking beside me. She's dressed in a pair of leopard-print velvet trousers and a black knit T-shirt. Her hair isn't short anymore, but pulled back into a low ponytail and tied with a scarf. She has a pair of black sunglasses on her face. She looks chic and determined and more than one young man's head turns to follow her. I smile at her in the glass and she smiles back.

She's no longer invisible.

ON MY WAY PAST the newsstand, a headline on the international edition of *The New York Times* jumps out at me like a monster: "Infamous Hollywood Hotel Burns Down."

Not the Marmont.

I fumble in my purse. Push a few francs over to the proprietor, take a copy. I don't even move aside before I start to read that the Chateau Marmont has gone up in flames.

No, no, no.

Apparently a fire started at around midnight in the turret of the hotel. Several people saw two ghostly figures on the roof outside the turret.

Sources linked to the hotel tell us that at least one body may have been found in the ashes, the article says. And many high-profile guests are reported to be missing.

An impatient passerby jostles me. I trip and almost fall.

What if I'm too late?

But also: *What have I done*?

At the end of *Helen Burns,* the Chateau Marmont goes up in flames. The fire is lit by Helen, aka Calliope.

CHAPTER 52

...

1966

When I get off the plane in LA, I race over to the newsstand. It's on the front page of the *Los Angeles Times:* "Hollywood Legend Dead."

Oh god.

My aunt? Calliope?

Theo?

Who?

The subheading reads: "Male Corpse Identified."

I sink into a chair, newspaper clutched in my hands.

Two ghostly figures dressed in silver were seen on the roof, the paper reiterates.

> Guests have long believed the turret of the Chateau Marmont to be haunted by Toni Ashenhurst, the sister of Hollywood studio boss Bob Ashenhurst. Miss Ashenhurst was wearing a silver dress when she jumped to her death from the roof of the Chateau Marmont fifteen years ago.

I stop reading. I didn't know what she was wearing when she died. But ghosts don't light fires. Ghosts don't exist.

Then how to explain the screams at the Chateau Marmont, the fire in Theo's room?

I drop my eyes to the next paragraph. You're listening to people who make stuff up for a living, the police sergeant in charge of the investigation has told the newspaper. The smoke from the fire is most likely what people saw on the roof.

Yes. There's no such thing as ghosts.

But the next paragraph says that a source close to the investigation has revealed exclusively to the *Los Angeles Times* that the bones of a woman have also been discovered in the ashes.

And Calliope Burns is missing.

I drop the newspaper onto my lap. Stare at a plane taking off into the sky. Going up higher and higher, past the clouds, up to where all the brightest lights are strung. Did she plan this? Was this her way of, quite literally, going out in a blaze?

But Calliope wouldn't choose fire. She knows how I feel about fire.

I try to breathe more slowly. To be rational. The article says only that Calliope is missing. It doesn't say that the bones—if there really are any—are hers.

I start to feel a little better. Except that the next sentence begins with the words, A male victim has officially been identified.

I don't breathe at all as I read on.

> During the fire, Bob Ashenhurst, owner of Golden Mare, reportedly jumped from the roof to his death, which some are saying is an admission of guilt—that he is indeed the studio executive named Ben Coles in the bestselling novel, *Helen Burns*—and that he's also guilty of the allegations made against him by the legendary Miss Devine Rey. Some speculate that he lured Miss Calliope Burns up onto the roof in the hopes of making her fall to her death, but that the plan backfired.

Bob is dead.

He's the one who's been burned up by fire. The Fates have finally given the right person the terrible future he deserved.

Oh, the relief! The beautiful, glorious relief.

I push myself onto my feet, stride out of the airport and hail a taxi.

"Take me to the Chateau Marmont."

SMOKE IS STILL RISING from the ruins of the castle where I spent seven years of my life. The turret stands, as do the bungalows, but a large part of the main building is gone—the part that housed Theo's penthouse. Above me, the sky is almost white, the charred chateau stark against it like black bones.

I think I can hear it weeping.

God, this place. I swipe my hands across my cheeks, fight back an almost uncontrollable urge to wrap my arms around the nearest pillar.

I know this feeling. It's why I wrapped my arms around Theo when he told me about his childhood; why I wrapped my arms around Calliope when she told me she was dying; why my aunt hugged me the night I showed a film of Bob Ashenhurst on a sofa in a library with Calliope.

Love. I love this place.

I don't want it to be dead too.

Then a figure appears from out of the smoke.

It looks so much like the romantic hero striding through the mist toward his beloved that everything freezes—my body, my tears, time itself.

Theo! I'm about to cry out.

Then fantasy dissolves. The figure becomes a policeman.

One hour back in Hollywood and I'm already deluded.

Or perhaps I'm just human. Hopeful. Because to not hope means you don't believe in the future. And how do you make yourself get out of bed in the morning if the present you haven't yet changed into something better is all you have?

The policeman takes his cap off and rubs his forehead.

I recognize him. A friend of Jupiter; the cop who always responded to calls from Marmont guests who thought a party had gotten a bit out of hand—guests who didn't understand the rule that you always call reception first.

"James!" I call from the sidewalk.

He makes his way over. "What a mess."

"What happened?"

"We're still figuring that out. All I know is that the fire started in the penthouse."

The penthouse. Theo. Adele. She'll be sixteen now. I bet she's smart and beautiful. I bet she goes out at night for a ride around the city with her dad and then they sit down and play songs together. I bet she even has her own guitar now.

Please God, let her have her own guitar. Please don't let her be just white sky and black bones too.

And Theo. Please let him still be Theo Winchester of the cool voice and hot lips.

"What about . . ." My voice wobbles. "What about the people in the penthouse?"

"Dead," James says.

He catches me before I drop to the ground.

"Jeez," he says. "Come and sit down."

He helps me through the colonnaded entry, which still stands, and into the lobby and onto the velvet sofa. It isn't damaged at all, just carries the faint smell of smoke. The piano sits there waiting for Judith Crown to stun us all into silence.

"I didn't know you were friends with Bob Ashenhurst," James says.

"I hate Bob Ashenhurst."

James frowns. "But he lived in the penthouse."

A whisper. Not my own. It's coming from the turret, the Marmont breathing the words, *It will all be okay, Aria. You'll see . . .*

I stare at James, hope flickering. "Theo Winchester lived in the penthouse."

"Nah. He and his kid moved out a while back. Bought some fancy place in Topanga Canyon. So you can stop fretting." James winks. "My missus digs him too. Sings along to his records while she's cooking dinner. I can't see the attraction—he looks more like a car thief than a heartthrob."

I giggle. Stupidly, wildly, unrestrainedly. "He does look a bit like a car thief. But he has the heart of a prince."

James grins. "Sound like you have yourself a crush."

Oh, yes I do. Theo's alive! He's in Topanga Canyon with Adele.

And hope, that most Hollywood and also human thing, silvers my soul.

But James is saying something else now. I force myself to pay attention.

"Calliope Burns. You wrote that book about her."

"The bones," I say, remembering the newspaper.

"Damn newspapers," James grouches. "The only bones we found were from a bird."

He barely gives me a beat to enjoy more sweet relief.

"You're her friend, right?" he says. "My wife sings along to Win, but I'm the one dragging her to see every Calliope Burns movie. Man, she was something."

"She *is* something," I insist, fear catching up to me again.

"Yeah, but she's missing. Vanished. Poof." His fingers open into stars. "Every guest has been accounted for. 'Cept her. Some people say they saw her go up to the turret with your aunt. That it was the two of them on the roof. Which is kind of unreal, isn't it? I mean, didn't your book say she set this place on fire? And then there *is* a fire and she vanishes."

"A story isn't real," I tell James. But my voice is quiet. Because so much of my book *was* real. It was only the ending that I invented. But stories can't *become* real.

Except they do. Just look at the story everyone used to believe about Bob.

And James said that people saw my aunt and Calliope going up into the turret. Two people who wanted more revenge than my book offered.

"I found something kind of weird," James says.

I lean forward, don't need the Marmont to hiss at me to pay attention.

"Because I have this huge crush on her, I don't want her to get into trouble, you know?" James continues.

I stand up. "Show me."

CHAPTER 53

...

1966

JAMES TAKES ME INSIDE THE CRUMBLING WALLS, POINTING OUT where not to walk. We take the staff staircase, the one where I first bumped into Theo, up to the seventh floor. Somehow, it's still intact. Then we walk through the part of the building that remains, stopping at the suite—just half a room now—next to the penthouse. The kitchen is incinerated. The dressing table not even scorched. Two of the walls are missing.

"Fire's a funny thing," James says. "Devours some things, doesn't even lick another."

On the dressing table is the photo of me, Calliope, and Flitter that was taken at Schwab's on my sixteenth birthday. "Was this Calliope's room?"

James nods.

"What about her usual suite?"

"Maisie told me she asked for this one when she got back from Europe." Then he points. "That's the weird thing."

Untouched by the fire is a projector. It's a very specific type of projector: one that can play film that's had sound printed magnetically onto it by something like an RCA Sound Camera.

Once upon a time when I was fourteen years old, I used that projector to show a crowd of people a film that I'd recorded on an RCA Sound Camera.

Why is it in Calliope's room?

"Not that. This."

James directs my eyes lower, to the cavity that the Murphy

bed folds into. Inside is a length of piping that's been fitted into a hole in the wall adjoining the penthouse. The pipe runs across to the sound speaker of the projector.

"Someone carved a hole through the wall," James says. "It's thinner there because it's the bed cavity. It's right behind Bob Ashenhurst's bed too. That's why he didn't notice the hole on his side."

Whatever was playing on the projector was being piped straight into the penthouse. Bob would never have known where the sound was coming from.

It would have seemed like it was in his dreams—or in his nightmares.

I walk over to the projector. The reel of film loaded into it is labeled: *Toni Ashenhurst. Audition Tape For Frightened Victim in* The Spiral Staircase.

I remember Maisie telling me about Bob's sister, Toni. She'd gone to auditions, but it had never come to anything.

I turn the projector on.

There's no footage, because there's no wall left to project onto. But the sound plays, turned up to full volume.

"No!" a young woman screams, giving her all to get a part that had no name besides "Frightened Victim." "You devil! You belong in hell! *Nooooooooooo!*"

I switch the projector off.

You devil. You belong in hell.

No.

The words echo, the Marmont magnifying the sound so it's all the more terrifying.

Calliope was playing, directly into Bob's room, a soundtrack of Bob's dead sister screaming out that he was a devil.

Which he was. And she knew it better than anyone.

Now he's dead.

What's in this room isn't weird. It's revenge.

"Shall we put everything back in the storeroom?" I ask James.

He nods, relieved to have had the decision made for him. "I

wouldn't want Miss Calliope to get into trouble. Even if she is dead." His face crumples. A tough policeman who's seen death and terror is about to cry for Calliope Burns.

I think I am too.

MY NEXT STOP IS the Beverly Wilshire, where my aunt has decamped while she waits for her Chateau Marmont home to be rebuilt. She greets me with an extravagant hug and I cling to her for so long that she eventually pushes me away.

"It's very good to see you," I say when I draw back. She's alive and well and, my god, look at her—as radiant as any spotlight.

"You too. But that's quite enough emotion for one morning."

I smile as she ushers me inside. Not everything can change, I guess.

"I went to the Chateau Marmont," I tell her once she's arranged herself and her magnificent pink batwing sleeves in the seat opposite me.

"A tragedy." Tears sparkle artfully in her eyes. Then she picks up a seltzer water and waves a hand, signaling that it's time to move on.

"I went up to Calliope's room."

She chokes on her seltzer water, then continues to cough long past the point when she ought to have recovered. I interrupt her performance. "I saw the projector."

Now Miss Devine Rey stops all pretense. She looks at me properly and says, "Calliope told me about the screams, the fire in Win's room, the other things that happened at the Marmont. It sounded like somebody was trying—"

She cuts herself off, pulls out her compact, and re-powders her nose.

Hanging on a hook by the door is a silver cape. It looks gauzy and light. Ghostlike. The kind of thing that, if you were to wear it at night in the dimly lit halls of the Marmont and then out onto a roof with a man who's heard his dead sister screaming in the night, might make somebody go mad.

But all I really know for sure is that Bob is dead and nobody will weep over that.

"Throw away the cape," I say.

"Oops." She smiles, her soul unbothered by her part in whatever happened a few nights ago. Nor should it be.

But some things are still too ambiguous. "There's something we need to do for Calliope," I say.

ARIA JONES AND THE legendary Miss Devine Rey walk through the doors of Schwab's. Lois, the reporter from *Photoplay,* notices us—she always has her eyes on the door. I wave to Jim, who calls out, "A Schwab's Special, Miss Aria?"

"Yes, please."

While we wait for my sundae, Miss Devine signs napkins for all the customers. Then we let ourselves be collared by Lois.

"Aria Jones, you dark horse," she says. "What a book. And Miss Devine Rey," she breathes, staring at my aunt as if she's Joan of Arc and Cleopatra rolled into one saintly and enchanting bundle.

"We can't talk right now," my aunt says with a palpable sense of drama. "My niece has just heard the news about Calliope Burns and is so distressed to lose her best friend that she needs something for her headache."

"Lost?" Lois gasps, her fingers itching to pick up her pen and write down the quote, word for word. "You mean they've confirmed that she died in the fire?"

"Hush now, dear." My aunt pats my back and I dutifully pretend to sob.

Miss Devine leans in close to Lois, tears brimming in her eyes. "You know the police. Always needing quadruple verification. They won't confirm anything officially. But you heard it from me—my niece found a ring in the grounds of the Chateau Marmont near where those bones were unearthed. Calliope Burns will shine her light from our screens no more."

"My deepest condolences." Lois manages another thirty seconds of small talk before she dashes off, not wanting to waste any time in writing her scoop.

I smile at my aunt. "Are you sure you don't want to go back to acting?"

She straightens into the queenly posture I remember from my earliest days at the Marmont. "My business cards are waiting for me on my desk in the offices of Aria Jones: Talent Management Agency. But first," she says, raising her hand into the air, fingers curved around an imaginary glass, "To Calliope Burns. Who's just been given the end she wanted."

The tears I had to pretend I was weeping moments ago soak my eyes now. I thought I'd have the chance to say goodbye. But all I can do is raise my sundae in the air too.

"To Calliope," I say.

The world will believe she went out in a blaze of glory. But I know she's out there somewhere, dying.

CHAPTER 54

...

1966

IN THE TAXI AFTERWARD, MY AUNT FILLS ME IN ON THE arrangements she's made. "You wanted a room with a view of the sea, so your new assistant, Peggy, has booked you a suite at the Casa del Mar in Santa Monica until you find someplace to live. Peggy is Jupiter's sister. She's excellent. She could manage a sobriety party in a bar."

I laugh. "You must be well on your way to recovery if you're making jokes like that."

"I have an association in my mind now with Bob and alcohol. And Bob and Quaaludes. Reaching for those is like reaching for him." She shudders, like rehab has cracked the hard shell she hid her heart inside and now she's starting to feel things properly.

I want to kiss her cheeks, I'm so proud of her. To endure what she went through in that pool house and to now be embarking on her second and maybe better life. I must be wearing my soul in my eyes because she knows what I'm thinking and says, "Absolutely not. You'll crush my sleeves."

It reminds me of Calliope and the eyelashes we'd always unglue with our teary hugs. My soul must look sad now because my aunt makes an exasperated sound and squeezes my hand, holding on tight, palm full of love.

"We're here," she says, withdrawing her hand and reassuming her regal air. "I'll see you in the morning."

"Maybe we'll progress to a good-morning peck on the cheek

by then," I say with a grin. I slip out of the car before she can throw something at me.

In my hotel room, I do one thing before I fall into the bed—I call Theo's agent; it's the only number I have for anyone connected to Theo.

His agent's assistant tells me in a sing-song voice—as if she thinks I'm just another groupie—that she has my letter to Theo on her desk. "He's not in LA right now, Miss Jones. We'll pass it on when he returns."

"Do you know when that will be?"

"I can't give that information out."

He's not dead, I remind myself as I hang up. *That's what really matters.*

Luckily the jet lag means I sleep soundly, rather than worrying about Theo, waking to find it's seven in the morning.

Time to check out my new office.

I dress in a black scoop neck T-shirt and a black silk A-line skirt with white polka dots. It falls to just below my knee, but its demure length is absolutely negated by the slit up the front to almost the top of my thigh. I cinch a wide belt around my waist, then go down to the front desk and ask for my car to be brought around. As I wait, I marvel again at what money can do. Money can hire you an assistant who can buy a car for you and then have that car delivered to the nice hotel she's booked you into, the one that, as you requested, must have a view over the water.

The valet pulls up in a bright red Alfa Romeo Spider.

Oh yes, Peggy knows her stuff.

I tie the scarf that Nathalie gave me over my hair. It will stream behind me as I speed around the curves, just like I always pictured. But the thing that's different is that I won't be sitting beside a handsome man who has one hand on the wheel and one hand on my leg. I'll be the one driving, and I quite like that.

I settle into the driver's seat and put into practice the lessons a young Italian gave me in Naples. If you can drive in Naples, you can drive anywhere.

My office is in Malibu. View of the water, again.

Water puts out fire.

When I pull into the parking lot, I see a sign that reads: *Aria Jones Productions and Talent Management.*

I don't think I've ever smiled so hard in all my life. Because this is my company, and with it I'm going to do my best to stop starlets from drowning.

PEGGY IS INSIDE, RUNNING her hands over her brand-new typewriter the same way I just ran my hands over the rump of my car. "Miss Jones!"

"Call me Aria," I tell her. "Thanks for the car. I love it. How's Jupiter?"

"He said to tell you that nobody does pretend driving better than you did."

I laugh. "Did you tell him you'd bought an Alfa Romeo so I could do real driving?"

"He helped me choose it."

Oh yes, I can just see Jupiter, the man who taught me to kiss, going with the sister who looks just like him—right down to the dimple in her left cheek—to pick the ballsiest car in the lot.

I beckon Peggy into my office.

She opens a notebook and begins to read out my messages while I take off my scarf and sunglasses and admire the view of the Pacific Ocean.

"Your publishing house called. They're reprinting again because of the news about . . ." She puts her notepad down. "The news about Calliope Burns. They say . . ." Another pause, thus proving she has a heart rather than a Hollywood publicist's soul. "They say even more people will buy the book now that she's . . . dead."

"It doesn't surprise me," I say flatly. "What else?" I need to move on from Calliope because I'm no longer wearing sunglasses.

"You have back-to-back appointments all day. Your first is with Flitter Reeve." She checks her watch. "In about twenty minutes."

So Flitter agreed to come.

I sit down in my chair, pretending I'd intended to do that, not that I needed to do it for the sake of my legs. Even though I invited her, I don't know how it will feel to be in the same room again. And without Calliope beside us. I don't even know if Flitter knows that Calliope's sick—that she's waiting for death somewhere out there.

Then Peggy claps her hand to her forehead. "I forgot the most important thing!" She pulls out an envelope from the front of her notebook. "This arrived a couple of days ago."

Peggy watches while I pull out a check for one million dollars.

I throw it onto the desk like it's a hot potato.

I stare at Peggy. She stares at me.

"Where . . . ? Who . . . ?"

"There was a note with it." Peggy passes me a typewritten piece of paper. It's unsigned, impossible to tell who sent it except . . .

It's scented. I know that scent as well as my own.

Calliope Burns.

The note reads, *To help fund Helen Burns. She deserves a spectacular movie. xx*

"Holy shit. Sorry," I apologize to Peggy. "It's just—"

Peggy smiles. "I'd be cursing if someone sent me a million bucks. But it looks like there's something else in there."

I reach back into the envelope, pull out a folded sheaf of paper and discover that in my hand is the last will and testament of Helen Burns. Miss Devine Rey is named as the executor of the estate.

Miss Aria Jones, my sister, the will reads, *is my sole beneficiary.*

There's no time to reach for my sunglasses before my eyes fill up. Especially when I see the penciled note in the corner, *Don't worry, I'll make sure there's a proper death certificate when the time comes. xx*

Once upon a time I'd wondered who'd be the one to dance with me on the sand and leap with me into the water when the most momentous thing in my life happened. But I've always known it would be Calliope.

I squeeze my eyes shut and concentrate on sending the words *thank you* out into the air. Then I clear my throat. Exhale.

"It looks like we're in business," I say. "With this check, plus what I can contribute from my royalties, I should be able to raise enough from other sources—"

Peggy interrupts. "Are you ready for more?" She hands me another check.

Half a million this time. Clipped to the check is a note: *Love, Theo.*

"Shit," I curse again, because now tears are running down my cheeks. "My damn eyelashes."

Peggy stands. "I'll get some tissues."

I stop her. "Can you find out where Theo Winchester is?"

Her eyes bulge. "Is that from Win?" She points to the check.

I nod.

"Man, I'm going to like it here. Yes, I'll find out where he is. Give me a few days."

"ARIA."

My head whips up from my zealous inspection of Theo's note and my mind leaps out of his daydreamed bed.

Flitter.

She's come.

"Holy cow." She whistles. "You look good, Aria Jones." Her voice is as sassy as ever and only a little bit broken.

She looks good too. Blackmail and dealing with the devil

haven't harmed her looks, but I suppose if they did, then half the people in Hollywood would be as ugly as the things they do to stay here. She's let the platinum in her hair soften to honey—perhaps the hair and makeup team on her latest movie told her it would suit her better. Except she doesn't have a latest movie. *Jane Eyre* was never made and won't be now that Bob's dead.

When I don't reply, she subsides into the chair opposite, eyes fixed to the desk. "I know you asked me here because you want to tell me to go to hell. Believe me, I'm already there. But I want to explain so that you only hate me half as much as you do now."

I tell her the truth, wonder if she'll still recognize the concept. "I don't hate you. In a weird way, you helped me. Although it might have been nice if it had hurt a little less."

"Jesus Holy Christ, between you and Calliope, I'll soon be so forgiven that I might accidentally start going to church."

I actually laugh. "With a mouth like yours, I don't think there's any danger of God letting you in."

She grins. "It's good to see you."

Yes it is. She did something bad. But Flitter isn't bad.

Not yet.

"You saw Calliope?" I ask, because for Calliope to have forgiven Flitter, there must have been a meeting.

"Yes." Flitter's eyes lock with mine and there it is—her soul. The soul of a woman who's never spoken about her family. All I know is that her mother wouldn't even buy her period supplies. That Calliope did it for her. *Religious* was the adjective Calliope used. But religion doesn't leave those kinds of scars in a pair of otherwise beautiful eyes. Fear does. Suffering too. Only a person who's been scared throughout their entire childhood would look like Flitter does now.

What did he do to you? I'd once asked Theo about his dad. I could ask the same of Flitter about her mom, but I don't think she'll tell me.

Then Flitter blinks, hiding her pain beneath the wit and the smile.

"All that screaming, and Pilot and the fire in Win's room, and the other stuff . . ." She pauses. "I need a shot of whatever's in that decanter." She nods at the sideboard.

I stand, take the lid off the crystal decanter, and sniff. Tequila.

I pour two glasses. Swallow the contents of one, top it up, pass the other to Flitter.

"Bottoms up," she says, and we both swallow and grimace.

Flitter puts down her glass. "First of all, Bob hated that Win kicked him out of his bungalow. He hated that, at the Marmont, Win had more power than him. So he started using a special-effects machine to let screams and voices out into the Marmont at night. He hoped people would leave the hotel—or that Win would. And then Bob could be king again. Then that night when you went for a ride on Win's bike—the night Bob thought Win would throw *you* out for not telling him about Adele sneaking out—that's when Bob realized you might have more power than he wanted. He figured out that Win must have feelings for you, could see that you were starting to be properly happy. So he pounced. He lit the fire in Win's room with special-effects fire—the same stuff I used at Calliope's party. He poisoned Pilot, killed your bird, made sure the door of your room was unlocked—he wanted you to feel haunted. And you did."

Yes, I did. Theo might have been worried the night of the fire that Marley was regressing, but all I could think about were ghosts.

Flitter crosses to the decanter and pours herself one more shot before continuing. "Bob was planning to light another fire in Win's room and plant some evidence to show that you, the madwoman in the turret, had done that and all the other things too. He wanted everyone to think you'd gone crazy and then when the police investigated the fire, you'd be thrown into the loony bin. What policeman in his right mind would take the word of a mad, friendless orphan over that of the King of Hollywood? And you didn't really help matters by living in a turret and getting around the Marmont with a shovel in your hand."

I remember Bob catching me in the dirt with a shovel. The

Quaaludes he made sure people knew he'd left for me at reception. How easily he could have made out that the orphan girl with a mad addict for an aunt was a lunatic.

Flitter swallows her second shot before she goes on. "I saw Bob coming out of Win's room the night of the first penthouse fire. I'd gone up there because . . ." She shrugs. "Because I was stupid. Anyway, the next day when I heard about the fire, I went to see Bob. Told him I was going to tell you that he did it. He laughed at me."

Of course he did. Who'd believe Flitter, the woman who'd been dumped by her studio and who hadn't ever had a part in a movie where she spoke more than a line?

"I knew he hated that you had that film of him and Calliope, had that little bit of power over him—proof that he wasn't who everyone believed he was—and that you could unleash it at any time. But I didn't know what he was planning to do about it. He told me that day. He said he could make it so it was just you who was the madwoman, or he could make it so I was too. Turned out all I'd done by confronting him was to make everything worse for the two of us, but better for him. Now he could get off on the idea of me knowing he was trying to ruin you. So his ultimatum was that I could either help him and be complicit, or be deemed a lunatic. Which is every woman's dream set of choices."

Flitter reaches into her bag, pulls out a cigarette, lights it, and takes a long, angry drag.

"So I told him I'd help. But"—she raises a hand to ward off my glare—"I was buying myself a little time. Wanted to see if I could come up with something that would hurt you enough to satisfy Bob, sure, but not get you locked away in a madhouse."

"Every woman's dream set of choices," I repeat sarcastically. "To either be hurt or be lacerated."

"You're neither hurt nor lacerated," Flitter says. "You have the moral high ground, there's no need to be a drama queen too."

I can't help but laugh. Being told by an actress not to be a drama queen is like being told by Bob that murder is immoral.

She smiles a little. "Besides, I was a bitch back then. There was too much shit I hadn't dealt with. I needed to get out of that place as much as you and Calliope did. I needed to see who Flitter Reeve was without Calliope Burns beside her. It took seeing Calliope this past winter to understand that it doesn't matter how famous you are, you can still get cancer and die. That somehow, *I'm* the lucky one and Calliope isn't."

So Flitter knows everything. And she's kept Calliope's secret. That means something. Besides, her words resonate. She *did* need to find out who she was without Calliope, just like I needed to find out who I was without Theo.

"All right," I tell her. "I'm back to being Aria Jones, the least dramatic of the Three Sisters. Finish your story."

Another smile. Bigger this time. "I snooped around. I was a little obsessed with Win back then, so I followed him one time to the bungalow. That's how I found out Marley was there. So I gave Bob his own set of choices. Choice number one: he'd give me the part in *Jane Eyre.* I'd make sure you found out about Marley, and then you'd leave. Bob laughed. In his eyes, that plan didn't ruin you quite enough. You'd be getting away with your reputation intact. He'd prefer you had nothing. But I told him to hear me out. Listen to option two and then he could decide. So he indulged me. Option two, I said, would be me screening the entire film of him and Calliope. I told him I knew where you'd hidden it."

I inhale sharply. "That would have ruined Calliope too."

"You're right." She jabs her cigarette into the ashtray. "But I was betting on the fact that he wouldn't want anyone seeing the whole film—that he'd choose anything over that. And I gave him option one because I got a starring role. I had one moment of power in my whole life and I used it badly. I'm sorry."

I tell her the truth. "If you hadn't done what you did that night, then I might not be sitting in this office with an appointment book full of women who want me to represent them. You did a terrible thing. Luckily it worked out all right. And now . . ."

I pause as dramatically as Miss Devine Rey would. Surely I get to be a drama queen just once in my life? "I'm making a movie. *Helen Burns.* You're going to star as Calliope. Because everything we do in the real world has consequences. This is your consequence."

Flitter's jaw just about hits the desk. I've never seen her speechless, and believe me, it isn't her best look.

"Me?" she whispers.

"You," I tell her. "Otherwise the Three Sisters end in betrayal outside a bungalow with Bob watching on. We deserve more than that. So you're going to play Calliope and . . ." I lean across my desk, palms pressed onto the wood and look her straight in the eye. "You are damn well going to make her immortal."

CHAPTER 55

...

1966

IT'S NINE O'CLOCK IN THE EVENING AT THE END OF MY FIRST week at work before the last starlet in our appointment book leaves and I can finally sit down with a glass of tequila—my first since my meeting with Flitter—and toast myself.

I've just finished my drink and I'm about to pack up when my aunt steps into my office.

"We've done a good week's work," she says, voice as showy as her outfit—a bright red caftan with elaborate silver embroidery, like she's ready to plunge into a pool or take to the stage.

After my meetings, each actress sits down with Miss Devine, who's in charge of the soft side of the business—pastoral care, if you like—which is no less important than finding the work for them, which is my domain. Drifting through my door all week has come the sound of chatter and laughter and occasional tears, and it's made me smile because my aunt is *good* at this. She knows when to pet them and when to tell them to get it together. From all the effusive goodbyes, it sounds like they love her.

And it sounds like she loves her second chance at life too.

Now she's eyeing my tequila glass. "Is that a good idea?"

I laugh. Miss Devine Rey giving out temperance advice. Who'd have thought?

"I needed it this week. But the hardest things are done."

My aunt shakes her head. "You have another appointment."

I look at my diary. "No, I'm going home."

She walks away, calling over her shoulder, "I'm going to be late for my date with Dr. Foster."

"What?" I shriek, while my heart does a little dance. My aunt and Dr. Foster!

She makes a noise that sounds a lot like a giggle, tells whoever's waiting, "It's through there," then I hear the front door open and shut as my aunt leaves for her date.

I stand up, ready to try to save one more starlet.

But the person who enters my office isn't a starlet. He's tall, dark-haired. He hovers uncertainly in the doorway like every single starlet this week who couldn't quite believe that there was a female agent named Aria Jones who'd been recommended by every famous actress in Hollywood, one who wouldn't make them give goodnight kisses to get a part.

What do you say to the man you love when you haven't seen him for over a year and you want to run into his arms like this is your very own Hollywood finale?

I say nothing. I just stand there and smile while my insides spontaneously combust.

Theo curses profanely. Of course he does. "You look very . . ." He exhales. "Good."

My smile widens. "I thought you were a songwriter? Is 'very good' the best you can come up with?"

He's smiling too when he says, "I wrote you a whole song. Won't that do?"

"I heard it," I tell him. "In Paris. It made me cry."

"I'm sorry," he says. "For everything. But I promise not to hide any more exes in bungalows—"

"And I promise not to make lifelong plans to run off without you."

"That," he says, walking over to me at last, "sounds like a good deal to me."

When there's no gap between us anymore, when the cotton

of his shirt grazes mine every time he inhales, he says, "You still wear your heart in your eyes. In your beautiful green eyes."

I smile. "What's it saying?"

"Something indecent. But also very, very hot."

I laugh like I haven't laughed in a year. Theo does too.

He draws me in until there are no more spaces between us, and now he's staring at my lips as indecently as if what we're about to do is beyond all my wildest imaginings—and my imaginings are pretty damn wild.

So, Reader, I kiss him. Wouldn't you?

EPILOGUE

…

VENICE, 1967

I CROSS OVER THE CANAL AT THE PONTE DEI SANTI APOSTOLI, THEN walk through the Sotoportego del Magazen, that strange corridor that runs beneath the building above. The water beside me sparkles with a thousand tiny spotlights. A guitar strums and a gondolier sings a barcarolle, like the world knows that nothing less will do for this particular scene.

I push open the door. In the living room, Marzia, Alessia, and Arturo greet me with somber faces, then point to the stairs. My hand reaches for Flitter. There are no wisecracks from her today, just fissures in her eyes where the pain leaks out like tears. It's what makes her such a good actress.

Up we climb.

In the bed in my old room is a woman. Her hair is almost gone, her face pale, her hands thin. She blinks when she sees us. "You weren't supposed to figure out where I was," she croaks.

I ignore that and point to her left ring finger, which is adorned with an enormous diamond. "You're engaged?"

"Arturo asked me. He thinks it's romantic to have a wife who dies young. And you know I've never been opposed to romance."

Maybe we should cry—dying young is a tragedy. But Calliope, Flitter, and I, we all start laughing.

Now the room feels full—full of color and sound and love. Full of Calliope's smile. She's still lightning plus auroras to the power of heaven. Always will be.

She sits up slowly, propping herself on her pillows, then reaches over to her nightstand. Her hand struggles to pick up the magazine lying there. *Time* magazine.

The cover photo is of three young women at Schwab's with chocolate and smiles all over their faces, taken from a dusty old Polaroid that I salvaged from Calliope's burned-out room at the Chateau Marmont. "The Three Queens," the headline reads.

Calliope opens the magazine to the article inside. There are two photographs inset on the pages. The first is of Miss Devine and Adele Winchester, who's now a junior assistant at my agency and who is, everyone says, a terrifyingly good blend of me and my aunt. Somehow, Adele gets away with calling my aunt *Auntie D,* whereas I still have to call her Miss Devine. Adele mostly manages the screenwriters—she's always had a nose for a good story.

The second photograph is of me and Theo kissing in the lobby of the Chateau Marmont, which we're rebuilding. It's the one photo we released to the press of our wedding day. I'm wearing a silver beaded and sequined mini dress—not a pink tulle veil in sight. Theo looks so good I could swoon—in fifty years' time, I bet he still makes me swoon.

"You look so happy," Calliope says, fingertip resting on the photograph.

"Where did you get that?" I ask.

"Marzia and Alessia bought all the copies in Venice," she says. "They give them to everyone, tell them about the famous guest who used to live with them."

"Do they tell everyone about the famous guest who lives here now?" I ask softly, sitting beside her on the bed.

Flitter lets out a huge sob. Then she rearranges her face and there it is—the Flitter grin. "Well, they'll have to tell everyone about the *three* famous guests now."

Calliope laughs, runs her finger along the paragraph that talks about Flitter, who just won an Oscar for *Helen Burns.* " 'Flitter Reeve is the greatest actress of her generation,' " Calliope reads aloud and Flitter strikes her most actressy pose.

Then she takes the magazine from Calliope and finds the part that describes the insatiable appetite that everyone has for anything even tangentially related to Calliope Burns, the beautiful actress who died in her prime, whose films are being rediscovered, whose face is on T-shirts and mugs and calendars. Calliope is the number one name for babies born this year.

"'She's immortal,'" Flitter announces, quoting *Time* magazine.

"Pfft," Calliope says, not able to hide the tears brimming in her eyes as she tugs the magazine away from Flitter. This time she doesn't just read aloud a sentence, but a whole paragraph that somehow says that Aria Jones has forever changed the culture of Hollywood. That no woman in the future will ever have to get on her knees for a part; that Aria Jones (who has been utterly modern and refused to take the Winchester surname) is making movies for women and they're spectacularly profitable. *Helen Burns,* the movie with just a woman's name as the title, is the highest grossing movie this year. That Aria Jones declined to be interviewed for the article, but it was no matter. All the actresses she agents have spoken to *Time* about her.

"You always wanted to be surrounded by the sea," Calliope says, putting down the magazine, which means I can finally stop blushing. "And you are—by a sea of women."

I burst into tears, despite my vow not to cry today. Luckily Flitter is prepared and she produces a fistful of handkerchiefs from her bag.

"Enough of that," Calliope scolds. "Tell me why you're here."

I find my smile again. So does Flitter. We climb into the bed beside Calliope.

On cue, Arturo wheels in a screen; his sisters carry a projector. Calliope watches in wonderment as they set everything up. Then they bring up trays of burgers, fries, and mint juleps and leave us be.

Helen Burns flickers to life on the screen.

Flitter and I put our arms around our friend. "We're having a sleepover," I tell Calliope.

"Shh," Flitter grouses. "You're meant to be watching me act my heart out."

"You're not going to eat those, are you?" I say, relieving Calliope of her fries.

We pull up the covers. I rest my head against Calliope's, Flitter does too. Three women snuggled together in a single bed—three women whose every wish came true.

AUTHOR'S NOTE

...

When I was ten years old, I borrowed *Jane Eyre* from the library. The book had one of those old-fashioned illustrated covers where Rochester looms large on his white horse and Jane is relegated to a small corner. I was a serious and bookish child and I thought it was important to read classic literature if I ever wanted to be a grown-up. And the deeper I got into this novel, the more grown-up I felt. A madwoman! An excitingly steely man! A gothic mansion! Passion, a concept I hadn't understood until I read this book. Oh, and a woman called Jane.

That same year, the BBC adapted *Jane Eyre,* screened in Australia on the ABC. Eleven episodes over eleven weeks. Never have I ever been more engrossed in the TV. Never have I ever been more terrified by what was hiding in the attic. Never have I ever been more obsessed with a brooding, dark-haired hero. Yes, *Jane Eyre* left a deep impression on me. I've watched every movie adaptation since and reread the book many times.

Over the years, I realized that the characters who most stayed with me were Rochester and his wife. And I began to wonder how Jane felt after her happy ending. She was a woman who "gasped" for liberty, who was fascinated by Lapland, Siberia, and "the vast sweep of the Arctic Zone," who looked at the horizon beyond Lowood School and said of the blue peaks she saw in the distance, "it was those I longed to surmount." Somehow, the woman whose name was on the cover of the book had not only been outshone by a man and madness, she never really got what she'd most yearned for. Which didn't seem fair.

So, for all those readers who picked up on the *Jane Eyre* undertones—yes, I thought it was time that Jane got a story where she was the real star.

A QUICK NOTE ABOUT the Chateau Marmont: I stayed at the hotel on two occasions while writing this book and, suffice to say, I love it as much as Aria does. You can truly feel the history bleeding from the walls. In my opinion, it's as close to sentient as a building can get!

I have altered the layout of the hotel and grounds ever so slightly. And I have adapted certain events from its past, as I explain below. Very occasionally, I've referenced songs or movies that may have been released a few months later than the timeline in my book.

IN 1913, THERE WAS the Woman Suffrage Procession, the first civil rights protest ever staged in Washington D.C. One hundred women were hospitalized after being violently attacked by spectators who didn't believe women should have the right to vote. In 1970, the Women's Strike For Equality saw tens of thousands of women bring Manhattan to a standstill. In 2017, the global Women's March had women walking the streets in every continent to protest the threats being made to our reproductive, civil, and human rights. It seemed like a real moment of unity. Of strength. Of hope.

And yet . . .

Hollywood is a microcosm of the world. The Chateau Marmont certainly was a microcosm of Hollywood.

Almost everything in the book is based on something that

happened. Similarly, almost everything in the book is invented. But interested readers might like to know that Natalie Wood was only sixteen years old when she became forty-four-year-old Nicholas Ray's lover. He was the director of *Rebel Without a Cause,* and their affair was conducted in a bungalow at the Chateau Marmont. Natalie was seventeen years old when Kirk Douglas allegedly raped her at the Chateau Marmont and everyone agreed that she shouldn't breathe a word of it because it would ruin her career forever.

In 1937, starlet Patrica Douglas, just twenty years old, responded to an advertisement from MGM studios for what she thought was a casting call. She was dressed in a cowgirl costume and bused out to Culver City with one hundred other women to entertain a party of men who'd been promised—unknown to the women—"a stag affair, out in the wild and woolly west where men are men" (*The Guardian*). Patricia was one of many women assaulted and raped that night. She was the only one who tried to take her attackers to court. But the studio used its contacts to make sure that the case went nowhere and that Patrica Douglas was never heard of again. As MGM's hired thug Eddie Mannix said, "We had her killed."

Fast forward to 2017. We all cheered Jodi Kantor's and Megan Twohey's exposé of Harvey Weinstein in *The New York Times,* and Ronan Farrow's reporting in *The New Yorker* of similar allegations around the treatment of women in Hollywood. So much ground seemed to have been gained and so many terrible, systemic practices appeared to have been exposed, never to happen again.

And yet, here we are in 2026.

Perhaps a fairytale ending where one woman changes a system that is emblematic of the world we live in is ridiculous. But writing this book made me remember each and every day to hope. And that's not nothing. We all have a bit of Aria inside us after having read this book. What will she make us believe in? How will she help us change the world?

ACKNOWLEDGMENTS

…

MY MOST HEARTFELT THANKS GO TO MY READERS ALL around the world. You have no idea how much it means to me that you read, enjoy, and champion my books. Since I was a little girl, I'd always dreamed of being a writer, and you've made it possible for me to live my dream.

To my publishers, Hachette Australia and Ballantine Books in the US, my deepest gratitude for your ongoing faith in me and for urging me on when I wanted to try something a little different with this book. Rebecca Saunders, this is book number ten for us, a milestone well worth acknowledging. Thank you for always pushing me and for making me a better writer. Hilary Teeman and Elsa Richardson-Bach in the US, your editorial support has once again been outstanding. Special thanks to Georgie Harrison and Kate Taperell for working so incredibly hard on the publicity; to Melissa Wilson for sheer marketing brilliance; to Lil Kovats, Chris Sims, Gemma Shaw, Tonile Wortley, and the entire sales team for being the most phenomenal ambassadors for my books; to Vanessa Radnidge for stepping in and superbly managing a slightly stressful fortnight; to Joel Naoum, Louise Stark, and Alysha Farry for always being there when needed. Enormous gratitude to my translation publishers, too.

Kevan Lyon, the best agent on the planet, thank you multiplied by infinity.

Alice Wood—what can I say? I'm a writer lost for the right

words to express how much your hard work, moral support, and creative genius have contributed to my success.

Kathleen Carter, this has been our first book together and I've loved every minute of working with you. Another excellent creative brain to have on the team.

Sara Foster, Dervla McTiernan, Rachael Johns, and Anthea Hodgson, you guys are the only writerly WhatsApp group that an author needs. Thanks for always being ready to respond to anything and everything, and for setting the high bar when it comes to writing retreats! And to the Lyonesses for being my support system on the other side of the world.

Booksellers and bookshops, I would be nothing without you. Thank you for every order, review, recommendation, in-store display, and piece of shelf space you've given my books.

The Chateau Marmont, I loved every minute of my two stays in your rooms. I'll definitely be back—and we'll have a mint julep together by the pool.

My family. Love always.

Finally, to Charlotte Brontë for writing *Jane Eyre*. I have loved that book since I was ten. Spending the past couple of years thinking about it almost nonstop has been an excellent way to pass the time.

The CHATEAU ON SUNSET

...

NATASHA LESTER

Random House Book Club

Because Stories Are Better Shared™

A BOOK CLUB GUIDE

STEP INTO THE CHATEAU MARMONT, WHERE MOVIES, MUSIC, AND MORE AWAIT . . .

. . .

AND REMEMBER: IF YOU MUST GET INTO TROUBLE, DO IT AT the Chateau Marmont.

NOW SHOWING IN THE CHATEAU SCREENING ROOM

Bonnie and Clyde (1967) dir. Arthur Penn

How to Marry a Millionaire (1953) dir. Jean Negulesco

The Sound of Music (1965) dir. Robert Wise

Rebel Without a Cause (1955) dir. Nicholas Ray

Myra Breckinridge (1970) dir. Mike Sarne (filmed inside the Chateau Marmont in 1969)

A Star Is Born (with Judy Garland) (1954) dir. George Cukor

Casablanca (1942) dir. Michael Curtiz

The Long Hot Summer (1958) dir. Martin Ritt

Gone with the Wind (1939) dir. Victor Fleming

Breakfast at Tiffany's (1961) dir. Blake Edwards

THE RECORD PLAYING AT THE POOL

Side A

"California Girls" by The Beach Boys

"Don't Smoke in Bed" by Nina Simone

"Light My Fire" by The Doors

"Swinging on a Star" by Bing Crosby

"Cry to Me" by The Rolling Stones

Side B

"Great Balls of Fire" by Jerry Lee Lewis

"Heartbreak Hotel" by Elvis Presley

"I'm Making Believe" by The Ink Spots, Ella Fitzgerald

Sonata in D Minor K. 1 by Scarlatti

IN ARIA'S LIBRARY

Jane Eyre by Charlotte Brontë

The Bell Jar by Sylvia Plath

We Have Always Lived in the Castle by Shirley Jackson

Bonjour Tristesse by Françoise Sagan

The Borrowers by Mary Norton

Daisy Miller by Henry James

War and Peace by Leo Tolstoy

The Secret Garden by Frances Hodgson Burnett

Rebecca by Daphne du Maurier

Breakfast at Tiffany's by Truman Capote

Heidi by Johanna Spyri

Anna Karenina by Leo Tolstoy

Myra Breckinridge by Gore Vidal

A Little Princess by Frances Hodgson Burnett

In Search of Lost Time by Marcel Proust

"The Tyger" by William Blake

Little Women by Louisa May Alcott

SCHWAB'S MINT JULEP

MAKES 1
COCKTAIL

Ingredients

8–10 mint leaves
2 oz bourbon
1 oz simple syrup
Mint sprigs
Crushed ice

Directions

1. Place mint in a tall glass or julep tin and press the leaves to release their oils.
2. Add bourbon, sugar syrup, and crushed ice.
3. Stir together until combined.
4. Top with crushed ice.
5. Garnish with mint sprigs.
6. Enjoy!

DISCUSSION QUESTIONS

. . .

1. *The Chateau on Sunset* is based on Charlotte Brontë's *Jane Eyre.* In what ways is *Chateau* similar, and where does it deviate from *Jane Eyre*?

2. The Chateau Marmont is a real place with a real reputation that informs the novel. Do you think its mystique and discretion are beneficial to the guests there, or more harmful?

3. Consider each of the Three Sisters' dreams. How did Aria, Calliope, and Flitter compromise or stand by their ideals in order to achieve these dreams? How far would you go to achieve your own dreams?

4. The Chateau Marmont is a strong character in the story. Discuss how the Marmont's actions change the paths the other characters are on. Do you think they would have found their way without the Marmont's help?

5. Discuss how the dual timelines in the story reveal information and inform the present for both the reader and for the characters. What does it mean that the past timeline stops once Aria leaves the Marmont?

6. Identify and discuss the use of symbolism and imagery in the novel. How do these literary devices enhance the themes and emotional impact of the story? Consider specific examples, such as the figurative and literal use of stars.

7. Fire plays a huge part in Aria's life. Discuss the instances of fire in the story and how its effect changes for Aria.

8. How do different settings in the novel, such as the Marmont, Hollywood, and Venice, contribute to the overall themes of the story? Analyze how these settings influence Aria's interactions and emotional states.

ABOUT THE AUTHOR

...

Natasha Lester is *The New York Times* bestselling author of *The Paris Seamstress, The Paris Orphan,* and *The Paris Secret,* and a former marketing executive for L'Oréal. Her novels have been international bestsellers and are translated into twenty-one different languages and published all around the world. When she's not writing, she loves collecting vintage fashion, practicing the art of fashion illustration, and traveling the world. Natasha lives with her husband and three children in Perth, Western Australia.

ABOUT THE TYPE

...

This book was set in Dante, a typeface designed by Giovanni Mardersteig (1892–1977). Conceived as a private type for the Officina Bodoni in Verona, Italy, Dante was originally cut only for hand composition by Charles Malin, the famous Parisian punch cutter, between 1946 and 1952. Its first use was in an edition of Boccaccio's *Trattatello in laude di Dante* that appeared in 1954. The Monotype Corporation's version of Dante followed in 1957. Though modeled on the Aldine type used for Pietro Cardinal Bembo's treatise *De Aetna* in 1495, Dante is a thoroughly modern interpretation of that venerable face.